The Shaft

Angus Silvie

Published in Great Britain July 2023

Copyright Angus Silvie 2023

This book is sold subject to the condition that it shall not, by way of trade or otherwise, be lent, re-sold, hired out or otherwise circulated without the author's prior consent in any form of binding or cover other than that in which it is published and without a similar condition including this condition being imposed upon the subsequent purchaser.

Acknowledgements

Special thanks to Bryan Wilson

Preliminary Note

Some of the methods in this book used by tradesmen and experts in their fields may, to experts in real life, stretch credulity just a fraction. I am aware of this, but my hope is that to the rest of us who are less knowledgeable in those fields, this will not be too noticeable and so will not affect the enjoyment of the story. After all, it is fiction, and people often do things you might not expect in real life too!

Chapter 1 - 1894..7
Chapter 2 - 2019 11
Chapter 3 - 1894 14
Chapter 4 - Tuesday 17
Chapter 5 - 1895 20
Chapter 6 - Saturday 24
Chapter 7 - 1895 30
Chapter 8 33
Chapter 9 - Sunday 38
Chapter 10 43
Chapter 11 47
Chapter 12 - 1895 54
Chapter 13 58
Chapter 14 60
Chapter 15 - Monday..64
Chapter 16 68
Chapter 17 70
Chapter 18 78
Chapter 19 81
Chapter 20 - Tuesday 86
Chapter 21 91
Chapter 22 - Wednesday 99
Chapter 23..105
Chapter 24..109
Chapter 25..115
Chapter 26..119
Chapter 27..124
Chapter 28..129
Chapter 29 - Friday 137
Chapter 30 - Saturday 139
Chapter 31..148
Chapter 32..160
Chapter 33..164
Chapter 34..169
Chapter 35..176
Chapter 36..183
Chapter 37..189
Chapter 38..195

Chapter 39 200
Chapter 40 207
Chapter 41 216
Chapter 42 - Sunday 223
Chapter 43 232
Chapter 44 241
Chapter 45 - Monday 244
Chapter 46 255
Chapter 47 259
Chapter 48 271
Chapter 49 282
Chapter 50 290
Chapter 51 - Tuesday 296
Chapter 52 301
Chapter 53 311
Chapter 54 318
Chapter 55 323
Chapter 56 330
Chapter 57 335
Chapter 58 337
Chapter 59 - Wednesday 340
Chapter 60 344
Chapter 61 353
Chapter 62 355
Chapter 63 360
Chapter 64 362
Chapter 65 369
Chapter 66 - Thursday 374
Chapter 67 377
Chapter 68 382
Author's Note 384
Other Books By Angus Silvie 385

CHAPTER 1 - 1894

"I'd get that capped properly, sir, soon as you can," suggested Smeek, his attempts to see into the hole hampered by an understandable reticence to get too close to it. "You should thank your lucky stars you weren't standing there when it caved in."

Herbert Ridley had wisely positioned himself a few steps behind Smeek, about fifteen feet from where the hole had appeared in his lawn. He decided not to berate the builder for his witless observation despite the fact that the likelihood that he should be aimlessly standing there in the middle of the lawn, in the precise spot where the hole appeared, at the exact time of the collapse, was statistically incalculably small.

"How deep do you think it is?" he asked, instead.

Smeek rubbed the bristles on his chin and scrunched up his scraggy face as though this would help an answer to emerge. He turned to face his inquisitor and shrugged.

"Hard to say with these old mine shafts. Assuming that's what it is – might be a well, but this is mining country, ain't it?"

Ridley's right eyebrow remained raised, telling Smeek that a more comprehensive answer was expected. Smeek huffed and hitched up his ancient trousers before getting down on his hands and knees and crawling forward with all the confidence of a man traversing a lightly frozen lake with bricks tied to his shoes.

He reached the hole, dropped to his stomach and inched his head forward until his eyes were level with the edge. Remembering just in time to remove his hat, he peered slowly over into the abyss.

There was a long pause as he surveyed the blackness below, his eyes adjusting.

"Can you see anything?" asked Ridley eventually, losing patience.

Smeek inclined his head upwards to squint back at his employer.

"Can't see the bottom, sir, no. Have you perchance tried dropping a stone in?"

Ridley was amused at Smeek's attempt to use a word that would probably have earned him a slap if used in conversation with his friends.

"Yes," he admitted, "a couple of knocks as it bounced off the walls, then nothing. Not a sound. Couldn't even hear a splash. But I will confess

I threw it in from a distance of some yards so perhaps that is not surprising."

Smeek reversed backwards and, once at a safe distance, got to his feet. He sucked his teeth and raised himself onto his toes as though he was about to say something important.

"Must be a long way down then."

Ridley was beginning to wonder if Smeek could contribute anything to the situation other than stating the obvious. He had used him for odd jobs around the house before and assumed that his experience as a passably competent builder would have given him some insight into how best to deal with an unwanted hole in his lawn, even one that was about five feet across and of unfathomable depth. So far, though, the man had not dazzled him with insight.

Ridley was well aware, though, that he was in a bit of a hole of his own; his options as to what he should do now were limited. If he brought in a specialist firm, they would notify the authorities, as they would be obliged to do. Old abandoned mine shafts needed to be recorded, mapped, and documented. His insurance firm would need to be notified. Someone would probably tell the newspapers. Everyone would know about it. None of this was good news.

His magnificent new house, named after himself, was only two years old, for goodness sake, and had cost him a fortune to build. All the latest innovations of the Victorian age and designed to impress. The entrance porch even had a stained glass window above the doors imprinted with his family motto – "LITIGARE, VELIT, SUCCEDERE" – just above the year in which the house was completed: 1892. He had always made sure that the English translation of those words – strive, achieve, succeed - were etched into his psyche. They had motivated him, guided him, and taken him to a level of wealth and status that he was sure none of his ancestors had managed.

At the time, 1892 had felt like one of the best years of his life, yet so many things had gone wrong since then. Now, to top it all, it appeared that Ridley Manor had been precariously built over the top of an old lead mine, and all his accomplishments could be for nothing; the motto above his door an ironic signal of arrogance preceding a terrible downfall. The house could prove uninsurable, and its value would plummet, possibly becoming unsaleable and therefore almost valueless. It might even have to be knocked down! His mind had raced with worst case scenarios, however unlikely.

No, he had to keep this quiet. Smeek might be a simpleton and perhaps not the most highly trained artisan in the area, but he'd been reliable and adequately trustworthy with every little job he had been called in to help with during the building of the house. With suitable encouragement he may be persuaded to fashion a cover for the hole and say no more about it. That was the plan when Ridley called him over, at any rate; now he wasn't so sure. But it was too late now - Smeek knew about the hole.

"So......." Ridley hesitated, then took the plunge. "Is this a job you could handle yourself, then? On your own?"

Smeek took a deep breath, looked at the ground, and shook his head slowly, with all the gravitas and consideration of a man weighing up whether or not to tell his wife that he was having an affair. Ridley recalled that this was not the first time he had seen this performance.

Having finished shaking his head, Smeek pursed his lips then smacked them open for effect. "Not something I've tackled before, sir. It's a big job. I'd have to have a think about it. Do some costings, you know?"

Ridley grunted an acknowledgement. He never liked it when a tradesman couldn't give him a rough price on the spot, as this usually, in his view, meant that they needed time to invent some faintly plausible additional tasks and unused materials that could be hidden within the invoice. Also, from his perspective it didn't look like a big job at all when compared to, say, building a house, but so many tradesmen seemed to employ this transparent strategy, hoping to fool the holder of the purse strings into loosening them further than was justified. All it loosened, in Ridley's opinion, were the bonds of trust between the two parties.

But money wasn't the main issue here. He'd take the hit just to get this seen to in good time and without fuss. At least Smeek hadn't said that the job was beyond him. Perhaps this whole thing could be kept under wraps after all.

"Very well. How long do you need? I want this dealt with quickly, you understand?"

"Of course, sir, yes. Course you do. Like you said before, the less people as who knows about it, the better. I understand. Just give me an hour or so to measure up and work out materials and labour and timings and so forth, and I'll 'ave the figures."

It seemed Smeek had realised that coaxing more money out of Mr Ridley was only a good plan if Mr Ridley didn't lose patience and hire someone else.

"Good." Ridley clicked his heels together and turned smartly, talking over his shoulder as he headed towards the house. "I'll be in my study."

Smeek nodded for no real reason, then re-addressed himself to the hole. It wasn't so much the mechanics of capping the hole that concerned him; after all, some sturdy timbers across the top with a solid infill of rubble and earth above should do the job.

No, his worry was falling in. He would have to lay the timbers across at the level where the stone started, which looked to be about three feet down, and he wasn't going to be leaning in with someone holding his legs, no sir. Instant death would be but a sneeze away. He would need some kind of harness, perhaps even a winch.

He looked carefully at the point at which the stone stopped and the earth began. The original cap must have been laid there, then covered with soil, but the timbers had presumably rotted, collapsed, and taken the earth above down with them. There was no sign of them now other than a few stumps of wood, and some holes at the sides where the beams had been inserted. He shook his head. No matter, he would just have to start from scratch. He rummaged in his coat pocket and brought out a grubby notebook, then a pencil. He licked his finger and turned the pages until he found a blank one, and, frowning with concentration, began making notes.

CHAPTER 2 - 2019

"I see what you mean. Impressive."

Trey craned his neck upwards, admiring the huge, ornate mahogany-framed skylight that crowned the heavily-wallpapered central entrance area of the house and flooded it with a dusty light.

Miriam Welsby, smartly suited and clutching a plastic orange folder accessory, gave a practised smile.

"Double-height as you can see, and round the edges above you have the banisters for the upper floor passageways."

Lauren had been given the same spiel when she had arranged a viewing for herself a few days earlier. Trey had been busy with work so they agreed that she should check it out first, just to get their foot in the door. She suspected that Miriam always enjoyed showing clients around Ridley Manor just to see their reactions when they first walked through the porch and into that magnificent communal space. Trey's response to it was exactly what she, and, no doubt, Miriam had hoped for - with luck he would feel the same way about the apartment.

Out of force of habit Trey whipped out his phone and took an artless photo of the skylight.

Lauren nudged him. "You won't need pictures if you are living here, you know."

He looked at her and smiled. "Good point."

"This way," said Miriam in the style of a tour guide, leading them across the slightly worn red and black patterned Axminster, to a door in the corner.

"Here we are!" she announced, as though they had travelled rather further than twelve feet.

Inside, the apartment was pretty much as Lauren had described to him. Unless a piece of the ceiling fell on their heads as they walked round, Trey knew he wasn't going to be objecting to their having this as their first home together. Lauren had her heart set on the place, and he would have to come up with some pretty good reasons why he didn't want to live there in order to avoid never hearing the end of it. Ok, he was like a fish out of water – he'd been brought up in a crummy council flat in Derby – but he was on a journey of self-improvement, and this was a great start. There probably weren't that many mixed race guys who lived in stately homes, but that was part of the attraction.

"Recently fitted kitchen," Miriam was saying, "and the furniture is included, which is a real benefit if it is your first home." She knew they were first time buyers.

Trey looked at the tired sofa and peeling sideboard and understood why the previous owner had decided not to take the furniture – he didn't blame them. But beggars can't be choosers, and it would save time and expense just to be able to move straight in and worry about replacing stuff later when they could afford to. In fact, as Lauren had pointed out during her preparatory persuasion offensive, they had been so focused on saving a deposit that they hadn't really budgeted for furniture anyway, so this was a plus point.

All of the rooms looked fine, good sizes, and being on the ground floor they had nice views into the gardens from almost every aspect.

"Lauren said it had a cellar?"

Miriam had been saving this as her pièce de résistance. "It certainly has. Very unusual for an apartment so it's a real bonus. You have to access it from the garden though."

The French doors took them out into the grounds at the back – mostly lawn but with some organised borders interspersed with a few small stone statues of once-naked warriors and nymphs clothed now mostly in moss and despondency. Behind the lawn, some sixty feet or so from the house, was a large, well-tended ornamental garden with red-brick corridors between the beds.

The group of three walked along the well-weathered stone slabs adjacent to the house, until they reached a low wall that guarded some steps leading down to a door underneath the apartment's lounge.

Miriam pulled the bunch of keys out of her bag and it was obvious which one was for the cellar; it was twice the size of all the others.

"I expect this is still the original lock," she explained, as though this was a prized feature as opposed to a security issue.

She had some trouble poking the key in and getting it to turn, but after some light wrestling with that and the door handle, the solid old door creaked open.

"There's a switch in here somewhere," she said, feeling around. Suddenly there was light, and walking in, Trey was amazed at how large it was.

"Just under twenty feet by seventeen." Miriam pre-empted the question. "It's a great size. Good ceiling height too. You won't bump your head."

As a six footer the clearance above his head had not escaped Trey's notice. Nor had a dilapidated home-made work bench, the size of a small dresser, which occupied the far wall in the corner. It offered a selection of old rusted metal tools on nails and hooks which a succession of previous owners had presumably left there in case they ever proved useful, which they doubtless never did. A small metal vice was screwed to the front of it.

On the right hand wall was a coal bunker, about four feet square, and half full.

"Don't need that, do we?" asked Trey.

Miriam shook her head. "Not really. It is all central heating now, gas boiler. I expect that coal has been there a long time. More trouble than it was worth to remove it."

They emerged back into the garden and had a walk round. Lauren grabbed Trey's arm. "Well?" she asked, "what do you think?"

He knew what he was expected to think, which fortunately on this occasion coincided neatly with his own view. He liked it.

"Looks good to me," he whispered. "You reckon this is better than the one on the second floor, then?"

"Yes, I saw that last time and this one is bigger and has the cellar, and there's not much difference in the price. Also you can just walk straight into the garden. Much better."

Trey didn't need much convincing. Although he had no immediate use for a huge cellar, the mere fact that it existed was enough to swing it for him. "Ok. I'm happy. Let's make an offer, then."

CHAPTER 3 - 1894

Smeek did manage to cap the mine shaft, and although the bill that he presented to Ridley was of substantial proportions, it was fair. The man had had to construct a sturdy wooden frame that braced the shaft, then a pulley system that could lower a seat up and down through a system of ropes. It had taken him three and a half days just to design and build it; he was particularly careful to ensure that any rope slippage would not result in the seat suddenly beginning a rapid and unplanned descent, especially if he was on it at the time. He had no helpers, as this all had to be covertly, so any winching up and down would have to be done by himself. This was no easy task.

There wasn't a minute of every day when Smeek did not wish that he had never taken the job on. The thought of that hole, and him hovering above it, gave him the shivers. He didn't have a great head for heights to begin with, and this was not helping. To those who say that you should confront your fears in order to overcome them, well, he would like to see them say that while dangling over a dark, stygian gateway to the earth's core.

But he managed it. At times, while he sat in his suspended chair and worked at making a platform to rest the beams on, he almost forgot what was beneath him, but those were just fleeting moments.

It took him just two days to cover the shaft, and never before had he got through so many heartbeats in such a short time, or worked so quickly to complete a job. When he re-laid that final slab of turf it felt as though he had just stepped off a hot air balloon that he had steered across the Atlantic. The relief was immeasurable.

Herbert Ridley was relieved too. Looking, a few weeks later, at the freshly re-turfed patch of lawn that had now blended nicely into the rest of the grass, a visitor strolling innocently across the lawn would never know what lay beneath. Ridley could begin to forget that the hole ever existed.

Yet something nagged at him. Even when he was at his factory, overseeing production and involved in discussions and meetings, his mind regularly flitted back to something Smeek had told him.

"There's a tunnel down there, sir," the builder had reported breathlessly, having heard Ridley's carriage in the drive and run round to the front to catch him, on the day that he had first lowered himself into the hole. "About twenty, maybe twenty-five feet down from where the stone starts, leading off from the shaft. The lamp can just make it out."

Ridley had followed him back round to the garden, although it was soon clear that unless you lowered yourself down to where Smeek was working, you wouldn't be able to see the tunnel, and Ridley wasn't about to risk Smeek's seat contraption himself and endanger his life hanging over the seemingly bottomless hole. He would take Smeek's word for it – after all, the man had no reason to lie.

"Which direction does it head?" he asked, almost not wanting to hear the answer.

"Directly towards the house, sir," replied Smeek, rather too enthusiastically.

"Damn. That's not good."

"No sir, it's not, but it's quite a way down, isn't it? Even if it does go under the house, the foundations wouldn't reach it."

"That's true enough. After all, we saw nothing untoward when we excavated for the cellars, so we......" he trailed off, thinking. "How deep below ground are the floors of the cellars, do you think?"

Ridley knew that Smeek had used the cellars previously: when one of the outhouses was being extended, Ridley had instructed him to take all his tools and materials to the garden cellar at the end of each day. He abhorred any kind of mess, and of course it kept the tools safe, so Smeek had been happy to oblige.

"Well, sir, I'd say the floors of the cellars are no more than seven or eight feet below ground level. Although those main floor timbers are substantial, so that's another foot or so before you get to the floorboards. So that could give you.... let me see... ten to fifteen feet of clearance from the tunnel?"

"Suppose the tunnel slopes upwards?"

Smeek scratched at his cheek and scrunched up his nose, pleased to be asked his opinion on a subject for which no answer that he gave could at this stage be disproved, and therefore keen to give the impression that deep thought was at play.

"It's entirely possible, sir," he replied eventually, hoping that he would not have to elaborate.

Ridley knew that such speculation was inconsequential, but he needed to think out loud and bounce his thoughts off a stooge. He glanced again at the hole. The tunnel could always slope downwards of course – wasn't that more logical? Or was it designed so any rainwater would drain into the shaft?

"Could you lower yourself down to the tunnel, perhaps? Shine a lamp into it?"

Smeek shuddered. "Not for all the tea in China, sir. It's bad enough dangling a few feet down, I don't mind telling you, but at least I can rest my feet on the top of the stone edges. Further down and you've no purchase – look, there's no steps or hand holds built in, like some of them have. How they got down there and did all that so long ago and with basic tools, it fair blows the mind....." He paused, shaking his head in puzzlement to the extent that Ridley began to wonder whether the poor fellow's mind had indeed actually been blown. But then Smeek snapped back and resumed.

"And if the rope broke, there's nothing to grab onto, is there? Then boom! Dead."

Ridley doubted whether any explosions would occur when you hit the bottom but he knew what was meant. He glanced at the house, standing large and solid, imperiously daring the ground to crumble beneath it. "We're about, what, twenty five feet or so from the house. So I suppose that even if it did slope up, it shouldn't do so at a steep angle."

"That's true enough, sir. My advice," and Smeek looked conspiratorially around him to emphasise his own role in the suggestion, "is to tell no one, then once it is capped, forget all about it. Your secret is safe with me. There is nothing you can do about it so why worry yourself? Eh?"

Ridley remained impassive. Smeek was saying nothing they had not already agreed, but he'd realised what Smeek was insinuating, even if inadvertently. Your secret is safe with me, he had said, and that held a hidden implication. Something would be expected in return, in the guise of a steady stream of work, no doubt, at the very least. A continued favoured status as builder and handyman of choice. Otherwise.... He sighed.

"You're right. Let's finish this job, forget about the tunnel, and move on with our lives. I'll leave you to it."

He nodded curtly and headed back round to the front of the house.

And now, a month later, with the hole safely plugged, he really ought to be following Smeek's advice and forgetting about it. But he couldn't. He kept thinking about that tunnel.

CHAPTER 4 - TUESDAY

"How many flats did you say there were?"

Trey was kneeling over an open cardboard packing box, playing a solitary game of pass the parcel as he unwrapped the layers and layers of newspaper in which Lauren had painstakingly smothered every implement and ornament.

"Seven. I've told you that at least twice already. And be careful with that paperweight."

Trey looked at the solid glass lump in his hand, now finally freed from its newspaper straitjacket, and wondered how clumsy he would have to be to damage it in any way. Even if he dropped it on the carpet, it would be unlikely to shatter into a thousand pieces. Not that he would care. What was the point of paperweights anyway? No one used them for holding bits of paper down. They just sat uselessly around, cluttering up mantelpieces. Lauren liked them though, so he would bite his tongue. No point raking over a dead argument.

"We'll need to get to know all our new neighbours, then," he said, "find out about the community management meetings, or whatever they are called. I did bump into one of them earlier when the removal guys were still here. John, his name was. Came out to say hello."

Lauren pushed some stray blonde hairs back behind her ears and sighed. Trey's man-sense felt the frost from twenty paces and he glanced over. He knew what she would be thinking: married eighteen months and still no clue about the difference between what information was worth sharing and what wasn't. She would be thinking back to last Sunday when he told her that a racing driver she had never heard of had just won a grand prix, and comparing it to how Trey had filed news of their new neighbour at the back of his brain.

She stopped washing up the unwrapped cutlery and stared at him expectantly.

"Ah, right, you want to know what he said. Sorry, I forgot, what with all the unpacking and......." He trailed off.

"Yes, I do want to know please. Which flat is he from?"

"The other ground floor one, next to us. He looks about sixty. Big stocky guy, wavy grey hair. Seemed nice enough. Said he retired early.

He's married to, er, someone. Bethany. No, Melody. Was that it? No. Oh, I can't remember."

"I would have remembered."

"I know. You always remember names."

"Yeah, why wouldn't you? After all, that's the first thing you are going to say if you meet them, aren't you? 'Hello there' is just... lazy. And obvious, that you've forgotten."

"Melanie! That was it! Ha, I knew it would come to me. You can take your riding cap off now."

"What do you mean?"

"After you've climbed down from your high horse."

He grinned.

Lauren shook her head with a sad smile, and resumed her washing up. "Did he say anything about the other neighbours? I'm guessing you didn't ask him?"

"No, he didn't mention them. He could see I was pre-occupied so he just introduced himself, we exchanged pleasantries, then he went back inside. We'll meet them all soon enough. Why don't we put a note through all their doors introducing ourselves?"

Lauren raised an eyebrow. She obviously hadn't expected that.

"That's a good idea actually. Better still, we could have a flat-warming party and invite them all round for a natter!"

Trey's heart sunk. He thought he had escaped from his self-dug hole with a brilliant suggestion but now it had backfired. The last thing he wanted was a menagerie of odd people of indeterminate ages poking their noses around his new flat and attempting strained small talk for hours on end.

He just wanted to get everything straight in the three days he had given himself away from his work: some time to set up his little office in the corner of the lounge, then he could plough straight back into work. He had three pieces of computer art he was working on, and you have to earn those commissions. People won't come back if you can't deliver on time, and it was a cut throat market. It was alright for Lauren – nursing is a tough job, granted, but at least you knew you were going to get paid every week. Being self-employed afforded no such reassurances.

"Trey?"

"What?"

"You haven't answered me. About having a housewarming party?"

Trey scratched his ear. "I'm not sure."

"Why?"

"For a start they won't all be able to come."

"How do you know?"

"Well, it's unlikely they'll all be free at the same time. Also, some of them might not like each other, so that could be awkward. And you'll be too busy. You have to go back to work soon, and you won't have had time to arrange anything before that. Then by the time we are ready to host anything we will probably have met most of them. Also, we'll see them all anyway when they have the next community meeting, whenever that is."

"That could be months away."

"It might be next week."

Lauren spent half a second considering the comprehensive counter position that Trey had tendered.

"No, I want to meet them all. It will be nice. And if they come round now it will be much better as we'll have a good excuse for the place being a mess. All we need is some drinks and a few nibbles. Let's plan it for Saturday afternoon, around 3:00pm. I'll do some notes."

She grabbed a tea towel and started drying up; the conversation was over. A darkish cloud had started to settle on Trey's immediate horizon.

CHAPTER 5 - 1895

It was March 1895 and four cold months had passed since the mine shaft had enjoyed its brief dalliance with daylight. On the surface, nothing had changed. The ground had not subsided and the house had not fallen down. All was well.

Herbert Ridley continued to think about the shaft, though. Was he a bit hasty in covering it up? How deep was it? He should at least have found that out before commissioning Smeek to seal it up. It would not have been too hard to attach a rock to the end of an extremely long rope and lower it down as far as it would go before the rope lost its tautness. And what about that tunnel? That was what was really bugging him. Where did it lead and how long was it? Were there more tunnels further down?

He had spent some time at the local library but found no record of the exact location of any historical mines in the area, even on the crude maps that dated back to the last century. Derbyshire was once a hive of mining activity, yet for some reason, there was no record of any workings around the village of Hixton. The nearest he could find was a good seven miles away. He wondered why that was.

Perhaps it was because lead mining in this area of the country went back centuries, even back to the Romans. This shaft might have been part of a system of excavated tunnels built and abandoned hundreds of years ago.

He did not want to start asking questions in other institutions like the Public Records Office in case this drew attention to his reasons for investigating, so he came to a bit of a dead end.

There was one thing he could do though. And this explained why he was now standing with Edward Smeek, known to his friends as Ted but to Mr Ridley as Smeek, in the somewhat unnecessarily spacious cellar that led off the garden and was used for storage. There were the main cellars, of course, a suite of bricked rooms accessed from a door under the main stairs, but this external one was closest to the position of the hidden mineshaft, and Smeek had calculated that if the tunnel leading off the shaft remained straight and true, then it should pass directly beneath where they were standing. It was a temptation Ridley had been unable to resist.

The work would be out of sight, even to the occasional servant, and certainly to the world at large. Only he and Smeek would know.

"So you think here, then?" said Ridley, pointing to the floor about three feet from the wall on one side of the room.

Smeek toyed with his straggly beard, keen once again to appear wiser than would be expected. "Aye, well, that's where it should be, yes. Down there."

Of course he had no idea if the tunnel was down there or not, but this was paid work so he wasn't standing there to shed doubt on the venture.

For his part Ridley was well aware that this could be a fool's errand and he could be about to pay Smeek to dig a big useless hole in his cellar. But he also knew from his business world that people who venture nothing gain nothing. Reward follows from risk but rarely from inaction. This was also a bit of an adventure; it gave him something outside work to take his mind off Eleanor.

It had been almost a year now, but it felt more. A year since she lay in their bed upstairs, so weakened by the illness that she could barely open her eyes, and, feeling the end coming, had mustered the strength for one last squeeze of his hand before softly passing away and becoming still for ever.

Even now his eyes welled up whenever that memory strayed into his head, as it often did. With Eleanor gone, and with it the promise of children, he found himself on his own in the house that they had designed between them. In his grief he released all the staff, except for one cook who came in from six until eight, a cleaner one day a week, and a gardener who he called upon as and when needed. He wanted to be alone with his thoughts of Eleanor, to walk the rooms with her spirit, to talk to her without worrying if servants were listening.

Smeek didn't really count, he was just brought for odd jobs. And today he was needed for what really was an odd job: to dig a hole rather than covering one up. Opening up the shaft under the lawn again was not really an option; any one of his occasional servants would notice it at some point and start asking questions or gossiping with their friends.

In one corner of the cellar stood a pile of bricks that would line the new hole when dug, with some thick timbers for support. This was to be done properly and safely.

Ridley frowned. "You'll be careful, won't you? I don't want this hole destabilising the foundations or anything. It's rather too close to that wall for my liking. Now, tell me again what we agreed about explosives. I want to hear you repeat it, so I can be sure it has sunk in. It is very important you have understood what we agreed and do not under any circumstance deviate from that."

Smeek ignored the blatant besmirching of his character, so used was he by now to having his abilities questioned by those of a higher social status.

"No charges until I'm four feet deep, sir. Hand drill a minimum of twelve inch holes. Small cubes of gelignite, just enough to crack and loosen the rock. Like firecrackers."

"Exactly. And only when necessary. No risks, no short cuts. Is that clear?"

Smeek nodded.

"You do know what you are doing, don't you?"

Smeek began to bristle, then remembered his position and also the fact that it would be steady work for a number of weeks, not something he wanted to jeopardise.

"Mr Ridley, sir, I've been in the trade now for nigh on thirty years, man and boy. I've dug more holes in the ground than you've had hot dinners, I'd wager." He nodded firmly to emphasise this obvious untruth, and wiped his nose with his sleeve.

"Granted, this one is unusual, and it won't be quick with that kind of depth, but the principle's the same. And I'll shore it up as I go. It'll be safe enough."

"Alright. Good. How long will it take you then?"

Smeek sucked in his teeth. "That's a question now, sir, isn't it? Hard to say, see - it depends on the ground and what it's made of."

"Presumably the same material as we encountered when digging out the foundations of the house – limestone."

Smeek cleared his throat. "Well, aye, yessir, probably it will be, yes."

"So that will probably be what you will be digging through. That being the case, how long will it take?"

Smeek found himself outwitted, something that often happened without him having noticed, but that on this occasion was as plain as the wart on his neck.

"Haa-eurgh!"

He coughed forcibly and cleared his throat again, giving himself more time to come up with a plausible answer. He knew that to flourish an ambitious estimate would put him under intense pressure, but anything too tardy and Ridley might tell him to sling his 'ook.

Unfortunately the manufactured cough had brought up into his mouth a large deposit of fresh yellowy phlegm, which ordinarily he would have gobbed onto the floor without a second's hesitation. In the master's cellar, however, and with the master standing there, this would not be warmly received, so he manoeuvred it to the side of his mouth and cursed the need for good manners.

"Well?"

Smeek made some faces to indicate that a calculated estimate was occupying his thoughts, despite the phlegm situation being equally high on his agenda. He was already regretting telling Ridley how extensive his hole digging career had been, given that of the very few holes he had actually dug, none were anything like as deep or as awkward as this one.

"I'd say……er……. depending on various things, and such, probably a couple of months or so. Maybe three?"

Ridley noted the upward inflexion that betrayed a lack of certainty. But then he supposed that Smeek would not have dug a hole quite like this one before, so he couldn't be too harsh on the man. A ballpark figure would do for now.

He nodded and moved on.

"The young lad who's helping you, doing most of the donkey work I'd wager - he knows nothing?"

"All I've told him is that it's going to be an ice store, like we agreed, sir. Nice and deep to keep the ice frozen. He won't know ice stores should be outside – he's not paid to think, so he'll know no different. He's a strong lad but his brain ain't too lively. He's not going to be writing any books, if you catch my meaning."

Ridley smiled, but only because he doubted that Smeek could claim any superiority on that front.

"And if we do start to break through into any tunnels," Smeek continued, "I'll tell him his job's done and send him packing before he starts asking questions."

Ridley nodded. "Good luck," he said, as he walked away. Smeek waited until he had gone, then walked over to a dark corner and emptied his mouth onto the floor.

CHAPTER 6 - SATURDAY

"Lauren! Very nice to meet you!" boomed John Firwell, bottle of wine in an outstretched hand.

"Oh! Thank you, that's very kind of you. You didn't need to, really. I'm assuming you are John? Hello!"

She laughed self-consciously, took the wine, and opened the door wider, beckoning him in. She was about to ask if Melanie was with him, but as he moved forward he revealed behind him a lady of a similar age, smiling broadly in a brightly patterned dress, all greens and blues fighting each other.

"I'm Melanie. How nice of you to invite us all," she beamed, although it was hard to tell how much she meant it, as Lauren noticed that the smile dropped from her face as soon as she was through the door. But then isn't that to be expected? She realised that she was reading too much into her first impressions.

Trey was designated to be part two of the welcoming committee. Once the guests had traversed along the small hallway and through the only open door available to them, they would find him strategically placed on one side of the room, poised and waiting with an unnatural smile. Next to him, a table offered white bowls optimistically filled to the brim with crisps, cakes, and confectionary concoctions - none of which, it had to be said, were of sufficient status to grace an ambassador's reception – and some soft drinks and fruit juices.

"Hello, welcome!" he said slightly too enthusiastically, as John and Melanie, eyes darting around the room, hesitantly appeared.

"Can I get you a drink? There's snacks too."

It was a routine he was to perform another four times, because, somewhat surprisingly, almost everyone turned up. It is not often you get to see the inside of a neighbour's apartment unless you go to all the trouble of sufficiently befriending them and engineering a reason to be invited round, so this may have been a factor.

Lauren circulated the room, getting to know everyone as much as she could. She had a gift for gaining people's confidences, Trey had noticed, and could always find something to say that would kick-start any stalled conversation. People liked talking to her, as she did most of the work. As a nurse, he supposed you needed to be a people person. It was why he wasn't a nurse.

In fact, Trey found it almost impossible to steer a discussion on any subject, being more comfortable in commenting on what others said and leaving it at that. He did have to explain three times that Trey was short for Treyvon, but he was used to doing that.

He found himself talking, but mostly listening, to Tony and Suzanne, from Flat 4 on the first floor, as they explained what it was like to live in Ridley Manor. They were a couple of advancing years, which was a polite way of saying that to him they looked very old. Probably around seventy-ish.

"Have you been married long?" Suzanne was asking, turning the conversation to him. Trey noticed she had rather startling pale green eyes.

"About eighteen months. You?" he felt obliged to ask.

Suzanne laughed. "Oh, far too long!" She glanced at Tony. "I'll bet you can't even remember, can you?"

Tony, looking crisp in a blue jacket and beige trousers, was momentarily startled at being invited to put his foot in this man-trap. He recovered quickly though. "Of course I can. Forty-seven. No, wait a minute. We were married in nineteen seventy…. er… what year are we in now? Ah right, forty-eight, that's what I meant. Yes, forty-eight."

Suzanne glanced knowingly at Trey before addressing her husband. "You were right the first time - it's forty-seven. You should have the courage of your convictions."

Tony appeared unsure as to whether this shed him in good light or bad. He cricked his neck and coughed. "Well, there you go, like I said then."

"That's a long time to be married," observed Trey.

Suzanne put her hand on his arm and smiled. "You'd be amazed at how quickly those anniversaries come round. You'll find yourselves celebrating ten years before you know it."

Trey forced out a little laugh but could think of nothing clever to say. He usually relied on Lauren for that, but she was over with everyone else on the other side of the room, taking centre stage already. As is often the case in social situations, Trey wondered what they were talking about and imagined it was more interesting than the conversation he was in now. He started to wish he was in the other group, but then one of them broke away and wandered over.

"Hello all," she said, "alright if I grab a few more crisps?"

"Help yourself," replied Trey, as convention dictates.

"They're talking about America over there," said Anita, shaking her head. "Not my favourite subject."

"Why's that then?" asked Trey, feeling that someone had to.

"As a place it just doesn't interest me. It's too big, too loud, too in-your-face, you know? I'm not good with it. Puts me off."

"Have you been there?"

"Yes, once. Hated it. My agent organised it. We were going to crack America, you know? She got me a spot in a book fair in Chicago, the whole meet-the-author, sign the books shebang. So I flew all the way out there, stayed in some crummy motel, then it turned out that the book fair was in a deadbeat conference centre on the edge of town and hardly anyone turned up. I sat there like a lemon. Complete disaster and waste of money. Sacked my agent after that."

Trey had to ask. "What do you write?"

Anita threw her head back and laughed. "Trashy romance. Churn 'em out, three or four a year. It's a living, just. Do you know the big irony though?"

Tony and Suzanne looked at each other. They knew what was coming, and Trey had a good idea too.

"Can't find a man myself! How about that, eh? Four years now since the divorce, and since then, nothing. Doesn't help that my job involves me sitting on my own all day. Do you know any good single men, Trey?"

Her eyes bored into him. Trey shuffled his feet. He wasn't about to drop any of his friends in it.

"No, sorry."

"All the married men say that. Funny that, isn't it? Can't blame them though. I'm not good with men, although I shouldn't say that, should I?"

She wasn't unattractive, thought Trey. Late thirties, maybe, glossy black hair that spread over her shoulders. Impressive eyebrows that weren't painted on. A mouth that curved up nicely at the edges even when frowning. A propulsive personality too, by the looks of things, which might help to attract some men but conversely could just as easily deter even more. He would position himself firmly in the second of those categories.

"You'll find someone when you least expect," suggested Suzanne with a kind smile, possibly basing these words of wisdom on a poster she saw once in a souvenir shop.

Anita gave a wry snort. "I've not been expecting anything for ages now and it's not helped. Still, life's not all about men, is it?"

The two women laughed. The men guessed it could be unwise to stridently disagree with that statement and so forced out a vacant grin in a show of passive yet insincere solidarity.

After another ten minutes of small talk they all merged themselves back into the larger group, who had moved on from the subject of America. The conversation slung back and forth like a mouse in a maze trying to escape, with much retracing of paths and sudden turns into dead end tangents. It is how many group conversations operate. They conclude when the mouse has covered enough ground and emerges gratefully into freedom, at which point the participants decide they have done talking now and would like to leave.

It was only once everyone had gone, and some initial clearing up had been completed, that the two hosts could begin their post mortem, and critically review the characters they had just met, in much the same way that their guests would be simultaneously discussing them in the neighbouring apartments.

"Thank God that's over," said Trey as he dropped onto the sofa. "So stressful."

"Nonsense," said Lauren, joining him. "It was fun meeting everyone. Right, I'll run through what I learned about everybody, then you can chip in if you want."

"With what?"

"What you thought about them. Any gossip, that kind of thing. Let's start with Tony and Suzanne, seeing as you were with them for much of the time. They're in Flat 4, right above us I think. From what I gathered. He's a retired town planner, and she was a teacher."

Trey reflected that this was news to him. How did she know that?

"He was very dapper, wasn't he, with his little white goatee all neatly trimmed. I thought maybe he was ex-army, the way he spoke, like an old sergeant major or something."

"He certainly wasn't short of an opinion. I saw Suzanne roll her eyes a few times too, which was funny. Anyway, they've been here about fifteen years, I think she said."

"What about John and Melanie? Hard to read her."

"I didn't warm to John. After the initial greeting he seemed a bit gruff and impatient, especially when Melanie spoke. Looked at her like she was telling everyone about the holes in his underpants. Really disapproving, you know?"

"Yeah, I know what you mean. Melanie herself seemed alright though."

Lauren stretched her legs out in front of her and leant back. "Nice enough on the surface, yes. It just felt like she was hiding something. Mind you, I got the feeling that she ran that travel company they sold, and John was just the figurehead. I reckon she was the brains behind it. So maybe she kept things from him and is used to only saying what she needs to say while he's around. I don't know. That's just me reading between the lines. I could be wrong, of course."

Trey judged it best not to agree too enthusiastically with her last sentence - he was married now, and not a fool.

"And Anita?"

He guessed Lauren would either love her or hate her, and his money wasn't on the mutual admiration betting slip. If Anita liked to distribute her thoughts as much as Lauren did, and from what he had seen, she did, the conversation would never be big enough for the both of them.

Lauren pursed her lips. That was enough to tell him he was right.

"She's quite, er, how shall I put it, opinionated, isn't she? Well I thought so, anyway. Seemed to engage mouth before brain. Quite annoying actually."

"Don't sit on the fence."

"Well, you know me, I say it as it is. I didn't really like her, that's all. What did you think?"

Trey was experienced enough to know that the wrong answer here would be to say 'I really liked her'. No, that would be a very bad move, even if he did. He engaged his diplomacy setting.

"Yeah, not my cup of tea either. I didn't actively dislike her, but then you were with her for much longer."

"Too long."

Wow, thought Trey, Anita really did make an impression. Lauren wasn't normally quite so quick to make up her mind about somebody. He changed the subject.

"The chap in the top flat didn't turn up, did he?"

"Norman? No. But Melanie was telling me a bit about him. Have you seen him yet?"

"No."

"Me neither. But that's no surprise as he keeps to himself. Bit of a strange character, she said. All wild shaggy hair and a big brown beard. Doesn't say much, just grunts at you, and occasionally gives you a disconcerting grin when you are not expecting him to. He's a gardener, which is quite handy as he looks after the grounds here in his spare time and only charges a nominal rate."

"So that's his white van in the parking area?"

"I guess so. Bit of an eyesore isn't it?"

"Yeah, surprised it's passed its MOT by the look of it. Unless he's driving it illegally. That's a shame if it's going to be parked there all the time. Baston Landscaping Ltd, it said on it. I remember wondering if that was a visiting tradesman."

Lauren shook her head. "No, Baston is his surname, I think. Sounds like we should just keep him at arm's length, like everyone else does."

"Especially if he prefers it that way. Then there was Jean....."

Lauren relaxed, and grinned. "Oh yes, Jean. Poor old dear, she must be pushing eighty."

"At least."

"You could see there were signs of early-onset dementia there in terms of her memory – she repeated herself a few times. And it doesn't help that she can't hear very well."

"Some of the things she said were kind of weird."

Lauren put her arm around Trey's shoulders. "I'm used to that, babe."

"Ha ha. But they were, though, weren't they?"

"Yes, but you could see from the way everyone didn't pick up on it that they know what she's like. You just nod, don't you, and carry on the conversation. The strangest thing, though, was when she was leaving. I think you were still back in the lounge. Do you know what she said?"

"Goodbye?"

Lauren grabbed a cushion and playfully walloped him in the stomach with it.

"Yes, obviously that, but also, she said 'I have to wash the monkeys tonight'. She has monkeys!"

Trey swivelled round to face his wife. "Shut the front door! How can she... no, of course she doesn't. You can't keep monkeys in an apartment, especially not at her age. There must be a law against it."

"You'd think, wouldn't you? So anyway, I asked what she meant, and she said Bobby and Neville, I think it was, one was a lemur and the other a marmoset, and she'd had them for about thirty years."

"Do monkeys live that long?"

"I suppose so. They're related to us aren't they?"

"Not really, no."

"Well, the point being she gives them a bath every four weeks, she said, and tonight was their bath night."

"That is just so bizarre. An eighty year old woman with dementia giving baths to monkeys? Is she allowed to keep them? We'll have to ask the others about that when we next see them."

Lauren spotted a piece of crisp on the floor and got up to retrieve it.

"She's on the first floor, isn't she, Flat 3? So she's got John and Melanie below her. If the monkeys are chattering away all day some of the sound must travel through the floor and ceiling, that must be so annoying."

Trey rose to his feet too, now conscious that by staying seated he was looking lazy.

"Well, at least they are not howler monkeys are they? Maybe they don't make much noise. We've not heard anything here."

Lauren came back from the kitchen where she had disposed of the errant crisp fragment.

"I think that is enough monkey talk for now. It's all conjecture anyway."

"I thought you enjoyed conjecture? Isn't that what women spend much of their time doing?"

Trey was ready this time. He knew he had poked a hornet's nest so he flung himself back on the sofa and curled up into a ball and waited for the cushion attack, which duly commenced.

"At least women are occupying their brains while the men stand there thinking of nothing," said Lauren, firmly emphasising each word with a strategically placed blow.

Trey took his punishment then grabbed the cushion, pulling Lauren towards him so that she collapsed on top of him. Their faces were inches apart, and seeing the expectant look he was giving her, she leaned in and kissed him.

"I think I've seen enough of this lounge so far today," she said, "how about we spend some time in the bedroom?"

Trey gave her a squeeze. "I like the sound of that. We can create some monkey business of our own."

CHAPTER 7 - 1895

Ridley would remember the date. April the seventeenth, 1895, a Wednesday. Three and a half months, no less, since Smeek had started digging in the cellar, and nearing the point where Ridley would have cut his losses and declared time on the venture.

He had arrived home shortly after seven to find Smeek still on site, sitting on the wide granite steps that led to the front door, barely visible in the chill dusk of the early evening.

He alighted from his carriage and wished the driver good night, then walked towards Smeek, who was now awkwardly rising to his feet on unsteady legs.

"Eh-up!" he exclaimed. "Been sittin' down too long. I was just about to give up and head home, if truth be told."

"You've news for me then, I take it?" said Ridley as he approached, getting straight to the point.

"I have indeed, sir!" said the builder. "Thought I should stay to tell you."

There was an awkward moment as they looked at each other, Smeek offering Ridley the chance to cast him a morsel of appreciation, but realising quickly, from the look of impatient curiosity that greeted him, that this would not be forthcoming.

"Well?" said Ridley.

Smeek hitched up his trousers, a manoeuvre forced upon him more frequently in later years by an obstinately expanding belly. "I'll show you, sir," he said, before adding rather unnecessarily, "it's in the cellar."

He set off before waiting for a reply, and Ridley, deciding that there was no point asking further questions, had trouble keeping up with him as he scurried around the house to the back and headed straight down into the dark, underground space, lit only by two flickering oil lamps.

Once they were both inside, Smeek turned to face his employer, the unsteady light from the lamps painting dancing shadows on his glistening face, which then proceeded to break into a gap-toothed grin; a prelude to the big reveal.

"I've found it, sir! I felt the air rush up as soon as my pick went though. I've found the tunnel!"

It was clear that he was as surprised as anyone that his back-of-an-envelope calculation had proved correct, particularly as his analysis, if you could call it that, had not even involved an envelope, or indeed any kind of written computation. He'd just started with the direction of the tunnel leading off the shaft, and then walked in a straight line across the grass until he got to the house and found himself by the cellar door. And by jingo he had only gone and guessed right. So most of his pleasure at the news he had just announced was derived purely from an indulgent appreciation of his own imagined cleverness.

Ridley found himself experiencing a curious mix of excitement and disappointment. He was delighted that he had not being paying Smeek for nothing, and that his venture had borne fruit, but at the same time worried that his magnificent house had indeed been built over a mine and consequently risked collapse.

"Good lord!" was his measured response. "That's astonishing." He peered into the hole. "Bring one of those lamps over, will you?"

Smeek scampered over to the nearest oil lamp and held it over the hole. A golden light spread its reach into the bricked vent below them, mainly illuminating the wooden ladder that was strapped to one side.

"How far down did you have to go?" asked Ridley, still not sure that he could see anything.

Smeek looked pleased with himself once more. "I measured it, sir. Eighteen and a half feet to the top of the tunnel. I was starting to think my ladder wasn't going to be long enough."

"That's a little less than we thought. So the tunnel must head slightly upwards from the shaft, not down."

"If my calculations are correct, sir, yes."

"I have no reason to doubt them. Unless the height of the tunnel ceiling varies, of course, or the tunnel rises and falls to adjust to the path of least resistance."

Smeek said nothing; he hadn't thought of any of that.

"A good job it maintained a straight trajectory too. Have you dropped down into the tunnel?"

"Oh no, sir, not got that far yet. I've just made a small opening, but I wanted to tell you straight away, and anyway it was getting late. Hard to tell, but looks like I might have come in just to one side of the top of the passage, so tomorrow I'll open it all out, finish off the brickwork and the cross beams down there, and get a lamp into it."

"The boy helping you – did he....?"

"He saw nothing, sir. As chance would 'ave it, I'd given the lad a turn on the rope and bucket and taken over the digging. Soon as I felt that first breath of air from the floor through the hole I'd made, I came up and told him his work was done and off he went. He did wonder how much ice you were putting down there as I went deeper but I told him that was your business and not ours. At least he swallowed the ice story as we reckoned he would."

"So no one else knows. Good."

Ridley straightened his jaw and looked up suddenly.

"I'll be home early tomorrow. I have two meetings I can't avoid in the morning, but then I can leave Winterton in charge for the rest of the day. I'll be home by one. That will give you time to finish off. I would suggest that you wait until I return before venturing into the tunnel. Safer, don't you think?"

Smeek looked slightly disappointed but wasn't going to argue. "Of course, sir." He knew Ridley would be none the wiser whether he had already explored the tunnel or not.

"Good. Excellent, in fact." He headed for the door, then after two steps stopped and turned round. "Well done, Smeek, well done."

And as Smeek basked in the rare praise that had unexpectedly come his way, Ridley exited the door and climbed back up the steps into the garden, a strange excitement in his heart that he hadn't felt for well over a year.

CHAPTER 8

"Sir?"

"What?"

Winterton looked up from his paperwork, peering over his half moon spectacles. "The order, sir? From Waveneys? Are we happy with thirty two pounds?"

Ridley's mind re-focused. "And they want it by next Wednesday? That should be achievable, shouldn't it? Have you spoken to Copely and checked he can handle it?"

"Yes sir. In preparation for the meeting." He pushed his glasses up his nose and coughed slightly. "As I mentioned. Just now."

Ridley rubbed his left eye and sat up straight. "Did you? Sorry. I missed that."

He looked round at the four besuited gentleman at the table, each looking slightly uncomfortable at this unusual turn of events, but obliged to nod in confirmation that Winterton had indeed said what he said that he had said.

They glanced at each other. Mr Ridley was normally on top of every detail. You don't get to build and run a manufacturing company with this kind of turnover, by the age of thirty six, if you can't follow a conversation.

Ridley shook his head a little, annoyed at his own lack of professionalism. "You must forgive me. I have some things on my mind currently."

The four men nodded gravely and muttered some platitudes. They knew on which side their bread was buttered.

"I presume that is why you are leaving early today, Herbert?" ventured Wilkins, rather bravely prodding for more detail.

Ridley looked at him impassively. "Yes," he said.

They would get no more than that from him; the brevity of his reply made this clear.

The review of weekly orders resumed and was completed with no further lapses in concentration. Soon after, Ridley was on his way home, able now to rekindle his imagination with thoughts of tunnels and explorations.

As the carriage jolted over the potholes and pebbles of his daily commute, he pictured an underground warren of rooms and secret bunkers all lit by electricity. If he could ensure that any tunnels were indeed at least twelve feet below his house, and shore them up where required, surely that would be enough to ensure that it would not affect the structural integrity of the building, in which case a surveyor's report confirming this would then enable him to go public about their existence. That would be a weight off his mind.

After that, why not organise tours of the ancient mines. His own home could be an additional business! Perhaps there were other minerals down there too that could be mined. He'd need to engage a geologist.

He was conscious that his mind was flitting through ideas like a butterfly seeking the best flower, but without ideas mankind would still be in loincloths. All it takes is one spark of a thought to light a fire.

Who would have thought, when he was that young adolescent poring through adventure books and reading all about explorers fighting their way through jungles to explore hidden cave systems, that he might have his very own underground kingdom right beneath his house! And instead of fighting off tigers and snakes, all he would need to do would be to walk downstairs.

And so it was in this state of heightened expectation and anticipation that Ridley, having arrived back home, clomped down the stone steps, burst through the door of the cellar, and looked around. Smeek was nowhere to be seen, but there were noises down below.

Ridley peered into the hole in the floor and could see bobs of light moving to and fro some way below, accompanied by some occasional banging and grunting. A voice uttered a choice expletive, clearly discernible even at this distance. Ridley smiled.

"Smeek!" he called down.

The noises below abruptly stopped. A short silence followed, then "I'm coming up, sir!"

Ridley could see the top of Smeek's head, looking like a freshly dusted inedible cake, emerging out of the gloom. He had attached the lamp to his belt so that he could use two hands on the ladder and the light swung about wildly as he climbed.

Ridley considered briefly whether to help to pull him up, but was instantly dissuaded of this by the nauseating odour that Smeek was sending up ahead of him.

The builder emerged from the shaft, clambering off the ladder with a grunt and onto the cellar floor. Breathing heavily, he ruffled his hair to loosen and dislodge the materials that had been roosting there.

Ridley stood smartly back as a plume of grey dust rose and subsided around Smeek's head; much of it coming to rest on clothes seemingly already comprised more of filth than cloth. It occurred to Ridley that he himself was still in his business attire, and very few people who ventured into dirty tunnels did so wearing smart suits and shiny shoes. He would have to change. But first, some questions.

"What's it like down there? How big is the tunnel?"

Smeek ran his sleeve across his glistening brow, painting horizontal black smudges across his forehead.

"It's about the same as the shaft, I'd say, sir. Five feet or so wide and tall, so as you 'ave to stoop. Circular, too, so not easy to stand in. Can't see why they couldn't have made the floor flat. Also there's no timbers as that I could see, which is odd."

"Maybe the rock is hard enough not to need them?"

"Maybe. It's mostly limestone 'ere though, and that's quite soft. There's some wood there now though. I've made holes either side of the tunnel at the top, wedged in some beams, and built the brickwork up from there to meet what I'd already done further up. So the vent should be secure now."

"Good, good."

Ridley paused. He felt he had to ask. "Have you gone further along the tunnel? Just to look?"

Smeek had been tempted, and indeed before descending he had certainly intended to have a quick look around, but planned bravery can easily be quashed by the realities of experience. He'd only had to hold up the lamp and see the pipes of hewn stone leading on each side to ominous black discs of nothingness where the light ran out, and where his imagination started painting blinking red eyes, and that was enough for him. He wasn't going any further. Far better to keep himself right next to his escape route.

"No, I didn't," he replied. "To be truthful, sir, I was quite happy when you called me up. I don't like it down there, especially bein' on my own and all. I'm not enjoying this job at all. Not at all."

Ridley gave a brusque nod. Smeek's state of mind was not really his concern, as long as the job was done. He wasn't going to start offering danger money or anything, especially as Smeek hadn't asked for it. His business empire wasn't built on philanthropy. But he wasn't averse to occasional encouragement, if earned, and so he tossed a meagre scrap of it.

"You've done well, Smeek. Now, wait there, will you, while I get changed. I won't be long."

Five minutes later he was back wearing clothes that, whilst more comfortable, were still smarter than anything Smeek went to church in.

"So!" said Ridley, in the same manner in which he might bring a table of executives to order, "shall we begin?"

"Begin what, sir?"

"To explore of course. Have a look at what we have down there. We'll take a lamp each. I thought initially, we could head along back to the shaft. Then we can peer down, see if it is easier to see how far down it goes."

Smeek looked apprehensive. This wasn't what he had signed up for.

"What if the tunnel has collapsed along the way, sir? The roof might have caved in."

"Then we come back! Come along Smeek, don't tell me you've no backbone. I'd thought better of you."

Ridley's bravado was fuelled by the advantage he had over Smeek in not yet having stepped into the tunnel. He had not felt the dank oppressiveness of the gloomy, hemmed in space, or experienced the still, stale, noiseless air. Smeek knew this, but he also knew who was paying his wages. He sighed.

"Alright then. If you go first, sir, I'll be right behind you."

This seemed to be the best compromise. If Ridley suddenly fell down a hole or was attacked by a mutant spider or something, Smeek would be safe. He watched as Ridley grabbed a lamp and manoeuvred himself onto the ladder, then started descending one rung at a time, his lamp clanking against the wood as he went.

"You should have left your lamp down there," Ridley called up once he was half way down. "Easier to have both hands free." He grunted. "And you could see where you are aiming for."

Smeek decided not to answer back, but instead wearily took hold of the lamp that Ridley would rather he had not brought up, and attached the hook to his belt. He wondered why the man below him, being of such sharp intellect, had not thought to do the same, but there was no point saying anything now.

He stepped onto the rungs in order to follow his employer down. His feet were becoming far too well acquainted with this ladder.

There was a short drop at the bottom as the ladder did not quite extend to the base of the tunnel, and in any case the circular nature of the walls would always have required a final slither to the floor. Ridley landed on his backside and shuffled to one side to allow space for Smeek to follow him. The last thing he needed was an overweight and decidedly pungent builder falling on his head.

He held the lamp up, looking around. Smeek was right, there were no supporting timbers, and the stone walls of the tunnel were smoother than you might expect given the primitive tools that were presumably available to the men who created it.

He touched the sides and could feel grooves and scratches with small ridges in between, as though someone had raked butter with a fork.

The air down here was cool but not cold. The fact that they had effectively created a ventilation shaft above them meant that there was at least a bit of air movement, which brought with it the smell of something slightly bitter – he couldn't put his finger on it. Smeek's clothes, yes, but something else too.

Smeek landed with a thump and a cloud of dust beside him, and the extra light from his lamp gave them a modicum of additional mental comfort. He looked askance at his employer.

"See what I mean? Doesn't look like no lead mining tunnel I've seen before."

"Have you seen many?"

Smeek sniffed. "Well, no, but it's a figure of speech, ain't it? What I'm sayin' is that mine tunnels shouldn't be round and with walls this smooth. Not in my opinion anyway."

Ridley didn't know one way or the other – this was not his area of expertise. He could see why Smeek had not relished the atmosphere down here though. It was claustrophobic and a little spooky and, when they weren't talking, oppressively quiet.

"Just think," he said, just to break the silence if nothing else, "we could be the first human beings to set foot here for hundreds of years."

"And I 'ope we're the last," replied Smeek rather ungraciously.

"We'll see. Right, come on, let's find that shaft."

Ridley got to his feet, but couldn't stand upright as the ceiling was too low, so hunched over and bent his knees.

"Bit awkward. Just mind your head. Here we go, then."

CHAPTER 9 - SUNDAY

"I see the PM's going to make a statement in the House this afternoon."

Tony, in Flat 4, lowered his Daily Telegraph and peered at Suzanne, who was across the table, eating her toast with one hand and holding a pen in the other. He wanted to make sure she had actually heard what he had said and wasn't just going to say "oh yes?" in that automatic way that she did when he relayed any interesting information to her and she wasn't really listening, which seemed to be a lot of the time these days.

Suzanne's eyes were concentrating on today's sudoko challenge. He wished he'd never bought her that puzzle book, but it was the sort of cheap and easy impulse buy that can provide a desperate husband with a Christmas solution for bulking up the volume of gifts with minimum expense or effort, so after approximately one second of careful thought, Tony had bought the book.

It was added to his collection of Christmas Trifles, as he called them, to supplement the main present and make it look as though he had put considerably more effort into delighting his wife than was actually the case.

The feeling of relief from the husband at having found something to give his partner does unfortunately often far outweigh the feelings of pleasure experienced by the recipient, but on this occasion he had struck gold and Suzanne had become addicted to 'waking up the old brainbox' every morning. The book was three hundred and sixty five pages long, one for each day, and so still had well over a hundred to go.

The long pause before she answered was a strong clue as to what was coming.

"Oh yes?" she said, directing the response at her pen.

He persevered.

"Do you know why?"

"No....."

He could tell that she was using ninety nine per cent of her brain to work out which number belonged in the box, and the other one per cent to fend him off.

"He's going to announce a ban on carrots."

He watched her, intrigued.

There was a pause as her brain caught up with what had come through her ears. She looked up.

"Why would he want to do that?"

He sighed inwardly. That was the end of his little game and he'd barely started it.

"He doesn't. I was……."

"……. trying to catch me out?" Suzanne finished his sentence.

Tony cleared his throat self-consciously and lowered his gaze to the tablecloth.

"Well, perhaps."

"I think you mean yes. So what is he giving a speech about then, if it's so important?"

Tony debated whether it was worth telling her – it didn't seem so momentous now. But he knew that it would turn into a full blown argument if he didn't.

"It won't be a speech so much as an apology, I expect. He has to explain why his brother has an offshore account that doesn't pay tax, and why he had one too until recently. Should be a squirmfest."

Suzanne shook her head sadly, but for the wrong reasons. "It's very kind of you to keep me updated but you know that politics doesn't interest me unless it affects me. Does it affect me?"

Tony quickly found a way in which it could.

"If the PM is forced to resign then that could trigger a general election."

"Is that likely?"

"It's possible."

"I'll be interested when it becomes probable or definite."

She took a mouthful of toast, fired a sweet-as-pie smile at him, and turned her attention back to her sudoko.

Tony harrumphed and made a show of carefully folding up the newspaper, as though it was hardly worth him reading the rest of it if he could not bring to his wife's attention matters of such great significance.

He stood up and pushed his chair back.

"I'm going for my morning constitutional," he announced grandly, heading for the hallway wreathed in a sulk.

Suzanne, wholly unaffected by his performance, barely looked up. "Have fun."

He had put his walking boots on and was just reaching for his coat when he heard "oh, lambchop!" coming from the other room.

He hated being called that, but it was a term of endearment from their courting days that Suzanne had stuck with despite becoming a vegan.

He poked his head back into the lounge.

"Yes?"

"If you run into that new couple downstairs, Trey and Lauren, can you thank them for inviting us round yesterday?"

"I shouldn't think I will. Run into them, that is."

"But if you do....."

"Yes, yes, of course, I would have done anyway. You don't have to tell me how to be sociable."

Tony winced internally. He'd just given his wife an open goal to aim at, but thankfully she resisted the temptation.

"Just reminding you, love, that's all."

Tony withdrew his head from the doorframe; no sense prolonging this mundane conversation.

"I'll be off then," he said, grabbing his coat and making good his escape.

The fresh sharp blast of clean morning air that assailed him as he heaved open the huge fortified slab of a front door was as refreshing as a bucket of iced water over your head in a heatwave. Just what he needed.

It was why he almost always took a stroll at this time of day, especially in the summer. It enlivens your senses, keeps you active, and keeps you on top of your game – something that Tony felt he almost always was. Now that it was September, he needed his slightly thicker jacket, but that was ok; he liked the cold. Sweating was not something that Tony did, as a rule, if he could help it. Apart from anything else it made your clothes smell, and this was not something to be encouraged.

He glanced at his watch. Eight thirty five. Perfect. He might avoid Norman.

For some reason the guy always seemed to be lurking around somewhere on his route. Tony could be happily trolling along the path around the edge of the garden, seemingly alone with his thoughts, when suddenly Norman would appear from behind a bush, secateurs in hand, grinning.

"Alright?" he would say. Tony often felt he should reply "no, you scared the living daylights out of me - can you not do that please?", but being a civilised member of the human race his automatic response was always a polite "oh! Good morning, Norman."

He knew there was no point in further small talk as thankfully Norman had no need for it. Almost before Tony had finished speaking Norman would be turning back to the bush he had been pruning, seemingly more interested in the company of his foliage than that of a human.

This suited Tony and so he would continue on his way, his heart rate raised but now safe in the knowledge that he knew where Norman was.

Better, of course, was that he did not encounter him at all, and today, this early, there was a good chance that he would not. It brought him an additional level of contentment as he strode around the pitted stone slabs that edged the garden.

As he walked he breathed deeply: two breaths out, then one breath in. His father had once taught him that if you wanted clean air in your lungs – and why wouldn't you – then when you have breathed out, breathe out again before breathing in. Expel all that air, every last drop, as though you are blowing into a breathalyser tube. That wasn't the analogy used by his father, primarily because they hadn't been invented back then, but the principle was the same.

Tony had never scientifically checked this advice but it seemed logical, so on one section of the path – for Tony was a creature of habit – he always made a point of emptying his lungs with a series of two big sighs out and a large one in.

It was another reason for trying to avoid Norman because if, as he breathed in dramatically, Norman emerged suddenly from behind a bush, Tony's nostrils would be instantly introduced to the pungent aroma of the man, and that was a scent he didn't want filling up his lungs, as it defeated the whole point of the exercise. Norman really needed to wash his gardening clothes, and one of these years one of the other residents needed to summon up the courage to tell him.

Thankfully, and as he anticipated, his circuit of the garden revealed no lurking Normans today.

There was some woodland adjacent to the grounds, easily accessed from the garden by stepping over a long-crumbled wall. The residents had plans to repair the wall and put a gate in, but it was well down the priority list and there always seemed to be something more pressing that rose up and sucked their budgeted funds away.

A well-worn path through the trees was kept fresh by the regular passage of Tony's feet, and, on occasions, any of the other residents who felt like taking a short cut onto the main road in the direction of the nearest shops. It was a nicer walk than the main road, and it cut the corner where the road took a longer route via a roundabout and a right angle turn.

This was ancient woodland, a remnant from when vast swathes of the country were carpeted in thick, verdant forest. Squirrels scampered amongst the remaining hazels, sycamores, alders, rowans, and hoary old oak trees, and although they were not far from the road, the trees filtered out the noise so effectively that at times Tony could imagine himself to be transported back eight hundred years, surrounded by thousands of square miles of humanless nature.

But over the centuries man had torn through the forests and thrown down vast nets of concrete highways that bisected them into smaller and smaller chunks, and now Huntston Wood was just a token reminder of what used to be.

Tony navigated his way through the trees, following the soft mulched path. Being a creature of habit, he always strode purposefully along the same route, arms swinging slightly too much, pumping that air into his system and impressing anyone who saw him, he assumed, with the vigour with which he carried himself.

A colour caught his eye. Something red in the distance to his right. The path took him a little closer but there were brambles and ferns in the way. It looked like an old jacket. He had not noticed it before so it must be newly abandoned. How could people just dump unwanted clothes in the forest like that? He shook his head in disgust.

He would come back on tomorrow's morning walk with a black sack and a pick-up stick, well-used from the community litter-picking sessions he liked to organise. At least there were still *some* people who had pride in their community.

He continued on his way until he emerged through a gap into the undergrowth onto the main road. He could have headed on towards the shops, but instead turned back up to the roundabout, then back along the road skirting the forest, towards Ridley Manor. A quick diversion across the road, up a sparsely populated side street, and back down again, and ten minutes later he was back at the gates of the manor.

Not a huge circuit, just enough to keep himself active and functioning to his full potential which, he convinced himself, was undimmed even at seventy three.

CHAPTER 10

"Keep your voice down, will you?"

Melanie, in Flat 1, put her hands on her hips and assumed a sing-song voice.

"Why, because people will hear?? Well let them, I don't care. People should know what an idiot you are. How could you be so stupid, John? What on earth possessed you?"

John snapped shut the book that had been open on his lap and heaved himself up from his comfortably upholstered chair in order to prepare for a battle he had known was coming.

"Look, I made a mistake, ok? It was one slip-up, that's all."

"A pretty damned expensive slip-up. Why do you think he's known as Shady Steve? Isn't there a clue in the name?"

Despite being determined to fight his corner, as he always did, John felt on this occasion like a gladiator sent to fight a lion with his shoelaces tied together. In this case though, he had tied the laces himself. Perhaps he shouldn't put up a furious defence, given that he didn't really have one. He decided to reverse his usual combative strategy, a move which he hoped would catch the lion off guard, and offered an admittedly flaccid promise in lieu of a fight.

"I'll make it up to you, ok? Just tell me what you...."

Mel wasn't listening, though. She never did these days.

"*Shady* Steve?" she interrupted. "And thanks to him, and you, we've now got twenty five cases of Chateau Dishwater piled up in the study and zero chance of any of the profits he promised you. Don't you think if it was that good a business opportunity he wouldn't have just kept it all for himself to sell on?"

John exhaled a sigh of frustration and strode over to the window. He stared into the garden, seeing nothing but buying himself time. Well, conciliation hadn't worked - she was still determined to rub his face in it, just like she always did. Ok, he made a mistake. Who doesn't? She wasn't exactly Mrs Perfect either sometimes. This whole manufactured argument, only just begun, was pointless, but it had to be had, otherwise she'd never stop with it. He would just have to plough on with the excuses.

"He's got a warehouse full of the stuff. Too much to sell on himself, he said."

"Any other of your pub buddies make an investment?"

"None of them could afford to."

Mel snorted. "Well of course they said that, they had some sense. No, just Money-bags Magoo here who fell into his trap, was it?"

"It's wasn't a trap and I didn't fall into it. He showed me a web page with some really good reviews."

"Written by him?"

"No, but….."

"But what?"

"Turns out it was for a different vintage. The previous year was a great wine, but the following one, the one we've got, was not so good. Pretty terrible, as it turns out."

"You can say that again. The sink still reeks from that bottle we had to pour down it from lunch; it was so foul. If you sold that to any of your friends they'd want their money back."

"Well I know that now, obviously. Good job you've got the gift of hindsight."

"It hardly needed hindsight, did it, to see he was conning you? You'll just have to tell Shady Steve to come and collect it all, and give you your £1,000 back. A *thousand* pounds." She shook her head despairingly. "That's more than £3 a bottle he stung you for, John."

John turned round to face her again. He could see from her face that this discussion wasn't going to get any easier.

"Yes, but…. ok. Right. Look, on that website it was selling for £12 a bottle, alright?"

"Really?"

He paused, then held his hand up. "Ok, it turned out that was the previous year's."

Melanie groaned, then brightened. "You can get him on that, though, can't you? Misleading sales tactics, showing you the wrong year?"

"He'll just maintain that he didn't say it was the same year as those reviews, and maybe he didn't – I can't remember. Also, it was sold as seen. I can't get him to take it back."

"What, you have a contract that says sold as seen, do you? Were lawyers at the pub table?"

John fumbled in his pocket and pulled out a folded up piece of notepaper, uneven half circles at the top edge where it had been ripped from the binder.

"Look, this is the receipt Steve gave me." He stepped forward and thrust it at his wife.

"See, it says 'received, the sum of one thousand pounds in exchange for 25 cases of Minervois 75cl, Chateau Vondeau, 2014, sold as seen.' Signed by both of us."

Mel stood staring at it, mouth open.

"This scrap of paper is good enough, is it John? As a receipt for a thousand pounds? If you bought a roll of toilet paper in a pound shop you'd expect a better receipt than this. Look, it even has the year on it. Did you not spot it was a different year? Let me guess: no you didn't." She paused. "And I'll bet I know why, too."

Spotting her arched eyebrow, John weighed up whether to confess to being drunk or dumb, or both. The lion was on top of him now, pinning his arms down. He knew this would happen.

"One thing I have learned over the years," he sighed, "is that even when I am right, I am always wrong, but yes, I might have had a few sherries."

"Beers, you mean. And I'll bet Steve was happy to top you up with some whiskies before he mentioned his get-rich-quick scheme. Yes?"

"Possibly."

"He saw you coming, didn't he?"

"Possibly."

Mel gave out a sigh that was not new to John's ears, but this was immediately superseded by a sudden look of horror that John correctly deduced could not have been related to his last answer.

"You know what we've done?" she said.

John waited for what was bound to be even more bad news.

"We've only gone and given one of those damn bottles to Trey and Lauren. Oh Lord, what will they think of us?"

John recalled that the bottle had stood unopened on the table, possibly because the white wine that Tony and Suzanne had brought looked more appealing. Trey and Lauren would probably keep the red for a special occasion now, which would rapidly become less special when they opened it.

"Ah," he said, gravely. "That's not good, is it?"

"No, John, it's not. We can hardly go and demand the bottle back, can we?"

"That would appear un-neighbourly."

"What on earth will they think of us? Welcoming them to the manor with a bottle of drinking vinegar. You'll just have to go and tell them the truth."

"Me?"

"Who else? You got us into this mess. You'd better go round tonight before they've had a chance to drink it. Take them a replacement."

Before John could attempt any form of further objection, Mel thrust the crumpled receipt back into his hand, as a sign that the immediate post mortem was over. She had milked this as much as she could – now it was time to sort the problem.

"Right, well, those cases can't stay in the study. You'll have to stick them down in the cellars, there's more than enough room down there. Then I'll speak to Lydia."

"Who's Lydia?"

"Lydia Browning. I used to use her for corporate events, to do the catering. She might take them at a pound or two a bottle, as spares. If they've run out of booze at a cheap wedding, they can break this stuff out and everyone will be too far gone to notice how awful it is. That's how I'll sell it to her anyway. Maybe less focus on the 'awful' bit, though."

"But, that will lose us money."

"Yes, John, it will. But it's better than it all turning into horse piss in the cellar over the next thirty years and losing us a thousand pounds, isn't it? My God, this is like something out of a TV sitcom."

John grimaced. "Only trying to make us money, for crying out loud. Anyone would think I'd killed someone."

Melanie stared at him as though he had just told her that trees were animals, then shook her head sadly as she headed off to get her mobile out of her handbag. "It's no less stupid, is it? Aaagh!" The cry of frustration as she left the room was one with which John was all too familiar.

CHAPTER 11

In Flat 6, Anita reflected on whether you could have an artist's block, in the same way that you have a writer's block.

But then artists are quite often told what to do – they get commissions. So that young man downstairs, Trey, he probably doesn't have to think as much as she does. He just draws what he is asked to. Not that thinking was helping her much at the moment.

Most of her stories had a pretty standard formula involving a strong, handsome stud and a beautiful but misunderstood woman who after a few unlikely hurdles manages to secure her man, but she still had to differentiate each book somehow.

She had used up all her own experiences, limited though they were, and also covered off rich people, poor people, and middle-class people. She had achieved better sales writing about the rich people, perhaps because readers from the other two classes can aspire to be rich, but wealthier readers can't really empathise so easily with those below them. Yep, she would do rich again. But where to set it? How would the protagonists be different from all the others?

Her writing desk faced the window, and was set into a little alcove with a low ceiling. To rest her eyes she could look up from the laptop and stare at the distant trees, or down into the garden. She would watch the magpies cack-cack-ing as they chased each other from statue to fence and back again. Less easy to see were the smaller birds, but sometimes a few collared doves fluttered down onto the lawn, pecked around for a while, then exploded upwards in a rush of clattering wings.

Anita tried to force some inspirational thoughts to the open laptop in front of her but the more she stared out of the window, the more she kept finding herself thinking about Trey. She had been really quite taken with him. It was such a shame he was already spoken for. He was a good decade younger than her too, but that wasn't illegal, was it?

He could easily be a hero in one of her books. Tall, dark, enigmatic, slightly shy. Yes, maybe she could write about him, and use her imagination in that way; set a story around him. He could be a viscount, heir to a fortune but happiest with a paintbrush – although of course in her tale it would not be a digital brush. Physical is always far more stimulating.

Now she just needed to understand his character, and that might be a good reason for getting to know him a bit better. After all, they were kindred spirits, weren't they? Masters of the arts, in their own way.

He had said he worked from home too, so he would be on his own right now, assuming Lauren had gone to work. Down there, alone, just like her. She felt a nice shudder. Perhaps she could go down and see him, ask for some milk or something. No, that was old hat. She would have to come up with a better idea than that. As she considered this, a plot for a book began to form.

***

Back in Flat 2, Trey pressed send. Job done. Well, until he got a reply telling him that the image needed a bit more contrast, or the girl in the picture had hands that were slightly too big. There was always something.

This one was only a small job though, just an image for a book cover. Two hundred pounds, but it was enough for two big weekly food shops, so not to be sniffed at.

He checked his Facebook page. Aha! Result! Someone had bought the coal. That was handy – he thought no one would want to be bothered coming round to collect it, but on these local marketplace groups you could chuck anything on there at a tempting price and someone usually ends up taking the bait.

He didn't know how much coal was down there, so he'd just taken a photo and done some measurements. Buyers had to make their own calculations.

He'd agreed with Lauren that they would keep a bag for themselves just in case, but they would certainly never need all of it. He'd asked all the neighbours at the housewarming party but they'd all politely declined. Roaring fires in your lounge were more trouble than they were worth these days.

Ned, his name was, and he'd asked if he could collect tomorrow. Trey messaged back: eleven o'clock fine by me.

He sat back and glanced at his watch. Half past three. Lauren's shift finished at six. He had better wander down to the cellar and make sure everything was ready for Ned.

As he tightened the laces on his outdoor shoes, the doorbell went. It is not normal to jump out of your skin at the sound of a doorbell, but when the bell is right above the shoe rack, and you are kneeling next to the shoe rack, it is a forgivable reaction, especially if you are not expecting anyone.

The unfortunate consequence for the person with their finger on the buzzer is that when the near-heart attack victim answers the door, they can give the impression of being not best pleased to see you, hence Trey's unexpectedly grim expression when he opened the door and found Anita standing before him.

Quickly realising who it was, Trey replaced grim with grin and tried to appear delighted that she had called by.

"Anita!" he cried with forced bonhomie. At least he had remembered her name, assuming that this was indeed her name and he hadn't mixed her up with someone. It seemed he was on safe ground, though, as his guest smiled back.

"Hello, Trey!"

There was an awkward pause as Trey waited for her to say why she was there, and Anita reminded herself of what Trey looked like.

Trey spoke first. "Is there something I can help you with?"

Anita pulled herself together. "There might be, yes. I'm not disturbing you, am I?"

Trey briefly wondered if he should make up a way in which Anita could be disturbing him. "By your very presence before me" would be exceptionally rude so he wouldn't say that. In any case you only have a split second to come up with something convincing; beyond that and it is clear to the caller that you are manufacturing a response.

"No, not at all. I was only just about to go down to the cellar."

Anita gave a nervous laugh. "Oh that's good. You never know what a young man might be doing on his own, do you?"

Trey could tell by the flicker of a pained expression in her smile that Anita wished she hadn't just said that. What was it Lauren had said? Engage mouth before brain or something. Well, that was a good example. To save them both from an awkward moment, he ignored what she had just said.

"Come in, please."

He noticed how quickly she accepted his invitation, starting to move forward before the 'please' was out of his mouth.

He closed the door and led her through to the lounge, now cleared of the pile of cardboard packing boxes that had been a feature of one corner of the room when she was last here.

"Have a seat." He extended an arm at the sofa.

"Oh, no, I'm fine thanks, I won't be long." That should put him at his ease, thought Anita correctly. She clasped her hands together and tried to appear businesslike.

"You're an illustrator, aren't you?"

Trey nodded.

"And I am an author, as you know. I was thinking, for my next book, I'll need a cover image. Normally my agent arranges all that, but to be honest the last couple of covers haven't been that impressive and I was thinking of suggesting that we try something different. Would you be interested?"

If Trey had never done a book cover before he could have felt comfortable in saying that he didn't normally take on commissions like that, but seeing as literally that same afternoon he had been working on what could only be described as a book cover, he felt that this would be morally questionable.

So with no ready-made excuse, what else could he say. "Thank you, yes. Depending on what you were asking for, of course."

Keeping distance from your clients, he had found, was often a good thing, in that they didn't pester you every five minutes. Once they think you're their friend they treat you like every change is a favour rather than costing you time and money, and become quite aggrieved if you charge them extra. Having a client upstairs could be more trouble than it is worth.

Anita, though, appeared more delighted than he was expecting.

"Excellent!" she announced, as though the deal was done. Her wide grin masked the fact that she had not discussed this with her agent, and indeed there was nothing particularly the matter with her last two book covers either – in fact she had been quite pleased with them.

But a little subterfuge wouldn't hurt anyone. It is not as though she would ask him to do any unpaid work, other than discussing her ideas with him and seeing what images might work.

Trey smiled politely. "What's the subject matter likely to be?"

"Oh, the usual. Romance, you know. So there'll be a couple in there somewhere on the cover, or maybe just one of them – I haven't decided yet."

"Don't you want to see any samples of my work first? My approach might not fit with what you are after."

Anita felt a fool for not thinking of this but tried to style it out. "Yes, yes, of course. I just wanted to check you were amenable first. You know. Have you got any examples, then, to hand?"

"Yes, of course. Wait there a minute."

He hurried out of the room and returned a few minutes later clutching a very large laptop, which he placed carefully on the dining table, then opened up.

He sat down at one of the chairs and motioned Anita to the other. "Come and have a look."

"That's a monster screen," noted Anita as she sat down. "Way bigger than mine. But I suppose you need that."

Trey grunted as he moved the cursor around. "Yep, you need to see every detail when you're creating something visual. I used to have a PC and a huge monitor but this is much easier."

An image of a small rowing boat being tossed about on some white-crested waves appeared, with dark looming skies above.

"You did that?" Anita was more impressed than she had anticipated.

"Yes, it was for a poster for a lifeboat charity. Charged half-rates for that one. Then there's this......"

A train was snaking across some lush countryside, all in a golden evening light.

"For a train company?"

"How did you guess. This next one was for a city corporate. They sponsored a rugby team, hence the theme."

Two men in suits were shaking hands, but the way they were standing, their outline had been made to look like a giant rugby goalpost, and down below a rugby player was kicking a goal over their outstretched arms.

"Now that is really clever," said Anita, genuinely impressed. "You thought that up?"

"Yep."

"They're really varied too. You've got range. Well done!"

"Thanks."

Although more than happy to receive praise, Trey was a little uncomfortable in responding to it, especially when administered in the manner of a secondary school teacher assessing the work of a 14 year old pupil. He moved on, skipping through a few more examples before judging that she had seen enough and closing down the image viewer.

"Well, that gives you an idea, anyway," he said, getting up.

"It does, it does," agreed Anita, following suit. She began to think that maybe she should use him after all. He was good, very good. "Thank you so much. You are very talented."

"I don't know about that. Anyway, hopefully that has given you something to think about."

"Oh definitely."

"Good."

"Yes."

The conversation had dribbled to a close. At this point social norms dictate that the onus is on the guest to announce that they had better be leaving – it is less acceptable for the host to point this out.

Both Trey and Anita realised that this moment had arrived, so Trey said nothing, assuming that an awkward silence would act as the heavy hand on Anita's back.

But Anita's mind, being more focused on her own desires than that of her host, had just flitted back to an earlier comment.

"Did you say you had a cellar?"

She knew they had a cellar, as Sidney, the strange old fellow who used to own the apartment, had mentioned it to her once when she had asked him what was behind the door under his flat. He didn't really use it, though, so she hadn't engineered an opportunity to have a look inside. This could be about to change. So what if she was a bit of a nosy parker? It wasn't harming anyone. Anyway, nosy was just another name for curious, and no one thinks the worse of you for being curious, do they?

Trey looked a little uncertain. Where was this heading?

"Yes, we do," he said.

"And you said you're going there now?"

"Yes."

Anita put on her best smile and stuck out one hip. "I know this is a bit cheeky, but could I come too? I've always wondered what was down there, behind that door. I only want to have a quick look, then I'll be out of your hair!"

Trey was starting to see why Lauren hadn't taken to this woman. Most people would wait until they were a friend before asking to poke around their neighbour's property, and even then they probably wouldn't. But

Anita had just dived straight in. Not that it mattered really. After all, it was only a cellar. It would be easier to say yes than refuse.

"Alright," he said. "Follow me."

He headed for the French windows and opened one side. They descended the marble step, and walked along the moss stained slabs, down the time-blackened stone steps to the cellar door.

As he inserted the large key he glanced at Anita and could see a strange excitement in her eyes, as though she had never seen a cellar before.

The door swung open with a creak and Trey reached for the light.

"Oooooh," exclaimed Anita behind him, "look how big it is. That sounded a bit rude, didn't it. Sorry. I meant the cellar. But of course you knew that." She giggled like a girl. "Don't mind me, I'm always like this. It is much bigger than I expected, though. You're so lucky having this big space."

She eased past him and floated round it, examining each wall as though it was a different, wondrous material and repeatedly glancing up at the beams. She wandered over to the wooden structure on the floor.

"Look at all this coal! I know you said you had some but I didn't think there would be this much. No wonder you want rid of it. Oh look! There's a key up there on a hook. I'm sure you'll find all kinds of treasures in here."

Trey walked over. "A key? Where?"

Anita pointed above her head.

"On that beam, to the left. Can you see it?"

She took hold of Trey's arm and pulled him closer to her so that she could direct his gaze.

Feeling extremely uncomfortable now, Trey peered up and saw an old key with a hooped end, about the size of a large match in length, hanging rather obviously now that he was looking at it, above the coal pen.

"Oh yes. I hadn't seen that. I wonder what that's for."

He manoeuvred himself out of her hold and stepped back towards the door. He was quickly deciding that there wasn't really anything urgent that needed doing after all.

"Right! Everything's fine," he announced. "Let's head back."

Anita's surprised expression implied she might have been expecting Trey to lay on some cream tea and scones while they were down there, or at least do something useful.

She blinked twice. "Oh! Ok!"

Trey waited by the door as she brushed past, and followed her out, locking the door behind him. He turned to find her standing rather closer to him than he had expected, rummaging in her clothes. He stepped back slightly, back against the door, and was relieved to see her pull out some keys which she jangled at him.

"Don't worry about me getting back, I've got the front door key, so I'll go round the front rather than......"

She left the words hanging. Ordinarily Trey might have jumped in with an insistence that she take the easier route back through his apartment, but for some reason he didn't.

Anita didn't seem to notice though. She gave him a bright smile. "Well, thank you for showing me the cellar. Oh, and your artwork, of course. I'll be in touch, as they say!"

"Ok, thank you," replied Trey, polite yet with enthusiasm filtered out. "I'll see you around."

Anita couldn't help herself. "I'm always up there," she said, pointing at the sky but meaning her apartment, a hint of a smirk on her lips.

Then she quickly turned, avoiding the need to explain herself, and climbed the steps up to ground level before clipping off round the corner.

Thank the Lord for that, thought Trey. I'd only work with her if she paid me triple rates. She would be such hard work, and he sensed she might be after more than his artwork. Lauren had been right not to like her, possibly for more reasons that she could have imagined.

Trey was a good looking guy, he knew that. Before he met and married Lauren he'd had his fair share of female attention, and who wouldn't welcome that. The only down side was gently breaking it to some of his admirers that he wasn't interested; he hoped he wasn't going to have to be in that position with Anita.

She knew he was married though. Surely she wouldn't be so daft as to...... no, he must be imagining things. Perhaps making little suggestive comments was just how she was with every man who she did not actively dislike, although it would be unfortunate for them if she was. No wonder she was struggling to attract men if she was as forward as that.

He headed back to his apartment, thankful to be doing so on his own. Fifty yards away, quietly dead-heading roses that were spread between two dark green cone-shaped conifers, Norman kept his head down. What Anita was doing was no concern of his, but it was duly noted.

CHAPTER 12 - 1895

They had gone only ten yards or so before Ridley suddenly stopped, causing Smeek, following close behind, to almost bang his forehead on his employer's backside.

"What is it?" cried Smeek, becoming more fearful with every step.

"The shaft!" said Ridley, "I think I can see it up ahead. About another ten feet. Be careful."

Smeek realised, as they got closer, that one swift shove could seal the fate of the man in front of him, but it was a thought he wished he hadn't had. With it came the concept of falling down that very deep hole, a hole he had hoped never to reacquaint himself with when he finally laid that last sod of turf over the top of the damned thing. Already he felt a bit giddy.

Perhaps aware of potential misadventure, Ridley twisted his head and hissed at Smeek "you stay here. I'll inch forward and take a look."

"Right you are, sir" said Smeek, putting up little resistance.

Ridley dropped to his knees and began to shuffle forward. In front of him he could see, with gathering brightness, the far wall of the shaft, and in front of that the opening into it, and of course the dark maw of its entrance to the depths below.

With just a few feet of solid ground to go, he laid down on his stomach, not caring about the dampness, and inched forward, holding the lamp out in front of him. Gradually his head got closer, until he was able to peer over the edge.

He hung the lamp in the void and strained his eyes to see as far down as he could. Again, the walls were almost symmetrically smooth and round. The workmanship these men had displayed was really impressive.

Unsurprisingly, he still couldn't see the bottom, but then they were only about twenty feet from the surface so it wasn't as though he could see a lot further down than Smeek was able to look before. One thing caught his eye, though. Right at the extremities of the reach of the light, a black blob on the far side. Another tunnel.

So there were more, a whole network of them no doubt. Assuming this shaft went down hundreds of feet, there would be tunnels everywhere down there. There would have been no point in sinking the shaft otherwise.

He eased himself back a little and sat up, looking back at the expectant Smeek, whose open-mouthed expression was that of someone watching their Granny walking a tightrope above a canyon with no safety harness.

Ridley smiled. "Close your mouth, Smeek, you'll catch a fly. Well, actually, you won't will you, not down here."

Smeek joined his lips together then opened them again to speak. "What did you see, sir?"

"There's another tunnel down there, on the other side, probably about twenty feet further down."

They both considered this, realising that as things stood, there was nothing much they could do about that.

"What now, then?" asked Smeek. "Go back?"

For him this was a rhetorical question; after all, there was no obvious alternative. He began to shuffle himself round to face the other way.

"Wait!" said Ridley suddenly, then "ssshh!"

He held up his hand and inclined his head towards the shaft.

"I can hear something."

Smeek said nothing but he could feel his heart beating faster. He didn't like this. He quietly and subtly began to edge himself back the way they had come.

Ridley strained to listen. There it was again. A sort of a scrabbling noise, very faint, from way down below. Scratching, perhaps.

Then nothing. Silence again. Were his ears playing tricks on him? He glanced round to confer with Smeek, but Smeek was not where Smeek should have been, right behind him. Instead he was ten feet away, silhouetted by his lamp, inching back to the vent.

"Smeek!" hissed Ridley. Smeek froze but before Ridley could say anything else, he heard the noise again, louder this time, accompanied this time by a different sound – a sort of low staccato hum.

Ridley wasn't going to start dangling his lamp, and his head, back over the shaft now. The noise might be nothing, but self-preservation instincts had kicked in, and pushed curiosity firmly to one side.

He hurriedly got to his feet. "Go!" he whispered to Smeek in front of him, "back to the vent, quickly!"

Smeek, now vindicated, did not need a second invitation. He set off at a gallop, head bent down, arms outstretched to help propel him off the sides of the walls for extra forward momentum. Ridley followed close behind, legs stumbling, conscious that their footsteps were echoing noisily behind them.

It was only when they stopped beneath the vent that he became aware of just how much louder the noise behind them was now. He had not heard anything like it before; a deep hum, overlaid with a kind of ticking coming in bursts like a machine gun. He was sure he could hear some slithering and scrabbling too, or maybe he was imagining that. Whatever it was, it was coming up the shaft.

Smeek could hear it too and it gave him the energy of a man half his age. He pulled himself up onto the ladder and began to ascend it like an Olympian competitor.

Ridley took one last glance back down the tunnel. He saw nothing but he wasn't waiting around. He dropped the lamp and grabbed the bottom rung of the ladder, hauling himself up. His hands lacked no urgency in taking the place of Smeek's feet as they departed each rung.

The noise was coming, louder and louder. He was half way up the vent now, and glanced down as he climbed. The lamp was flickering violently on the ground and he could feel the air being pushed up past him.

Smeek reached the top and threw himself off the ladder and onto the cellar floor, closely followed by Ridley, both of them panting loudly.

"Extinguish your lamp, man!" commanded Ridley, as he rolled himself over to peer cautiously back down into the vent.

Smeek hurriedly snuffed the flame and came to join Ridley at the side of the hole. Surely they were safe up here? He tensed himself to rush for the cellar door though.

Below, they could see the little square of light dancing madly as the noise grew louder. Then suddenly there was a flash of movement. A scream of noise up the vent. Something dark, something large, rushing through. And then the light from the lamp was gone, extinguished with a grinding crash, and the noise started to subside.

Gradually the rat-a-tat hum and the scratching faded, until at last silence returned.

The two men, one lying on his front, the other crouching on his hands and knees, looked at each other in bewildered shock.

"What, in the name of blazes, was that, sir?" exclaimed Smeek, beads of sweat running down his temples and into the top of his beard.

Ridley shook his head. "I don't think I want to know. My Lord, that was terrifying."

"It was some kind of animal, wasn't it? It must have been. I mean, that noise it made. What else could it have been? That was no machine."

Ridley pushed himself up and sat down on the floor, arms around his knees, breathing heavily.

"No," he agreed, "there'd be no machine down there in any event, would there, not working like that, pushing itself up vertical shafts and into tunnels, all on its own. It had to be an animal, although how it can get up that shaft like that, heaven only knows."

He shook his head in disbelief then glanced across at Smeek. "Hard to tell how big it was, too. Soon as that lamp was pushed over, it just went dark. It went through so quickly."

Smeek wiped his brow with his sleeve. "Oh, it was big, sir, real big. It had to be. You could feel the air, couldn't you, as it got nearer. And to make that kind of a racket, that was no mouse."

Despite his emotions Ridley had to smile at the thought of the two of them fleeing for their lives from a terrifying mouse. He turned his attention to a more pressing matter.

"Have we got a door for this vent, Smeek? Something we can seal it with?"

Smeek raised himself up with all the grace of a newly born baby giraffe, then, his eyes adjusting to the gloom, slowly looked around, as though hoping to see an old trapdoor leaning against a wall.

"No sir," he confessed. "I hadn't got round to that yet."

Ridley looked up at him. "I think it is something you had better get round to now, don't you? Rather quickly, too."

CHAPTER 13

The trapdoor that Smeek constructed was about as heavy as he could make it, whilst still ensuring that, in the unlikely event that anyone should want to access the vent again, it did not require a ship's chain and an elephant to open it, just the limbs of two very strong men.

Although the hole itself was only about three feet square, he chiselled around its edges to create a large enough indent for a four foot square slab, consisting of four inch deep hardwood beams tightly battened and screwed together with thick metal struts. The door was secured to the floor with two enormous hinges that he had sourced from a scrap yard and looked as though they could have serviced a drawbridge. He reckoned the whole thing would stop even the mightiest of humans from escaping, but as this was no human that they were dealing with, only time would tell.

A very chunky metal padlock – the largest he could find - secured the hasp holding it down, and the key was left out of sight on a nail up on one of the rafters that supported the floor above.

As he hung the key in its resting place, Smeek's relief at finishing this particular job was palpable. Never had he taken so few tea breaks during a job or worked so quickly to complete it. Once he had collected the materials, the vent was covered within a day, during which time no further noises were heard from below, and no creatures leapt up out of the darkness to devour him. Mr Ridley was perhaps deliberately conspicuous by his absence but, to be fair, returned from work early, if only to satisfy himself that Smeek was still alive and, equally importantly, that the trapdoor was in place.

The two men then took additional precautions by building a coal bunker right over the top of it. Well, Smeek built it; Ridley had the slightly less strenuous but no less onerous task of ordering the coal and then paying for it all.

The house already had a coal bunker, of course, on the west side, so this one would serve only one purpose – to ensure that whatever creature it was that was down there, it would be faced not only with a very weighty and well secured trapdoor, but also a few hundredweight of coal on top of it, should it ever decide to squeeze up the vent and try to break out (assuming it was physically capable of doing so and also had any designs to that regard).

Ridley debated whether he should tell anyone about what he and Smeek had seen. But the positive reasons for doing so were far outweighed by the negative consequences, not least of which would be all that bother with his house insurance, and the likelihood that, should he ever want to sell his home in the future, few buyers would be encouraged by the knowledge of what could lie underneath it.

He convinced Smeek that it would not be in his interests either. If he started talking with his friends about huge creatures in tunnels under Mr Ridley's house, Ridley would just deny it. Smeek may then find himself ostracised as a fantasist or a liar, which would not be good for business. Indeed, Ridley would regretfully see to it that very little business came his way.

So all in all, it made sense for both of them to pretend this whole episode had never happened. In fact, very much as they had agreed when Smeek first capped the shaft in the garden. For his part, Ridley vowed that he would never resurrect any ideas about accessing those tunnels again, or indeed talk about them to anyone, and he never did.

The years passed. Smeek did not make it through World War One. Ridley did, but succumbed to Spanish Flu shortly afterwards. The house was sold on, and occupied by a new family, who knew nothing of the shaft, the tunnels, or what might occupy them, and it was probably as well that they didn't.

CHAPTER 14

John had perked up a little by the time he got back from the Lion's Head. He'd had a decent evening, all told.

He'd called round at Flat 2 and successfully swapped the bottle of wine. Trey had been more than happy to accept the better wine, and the apologies and explanation that John had proffered had, if anything, painted him in an even better light than if they had just given the couple a decent bottle in the first place.

Then when he got to the pub, Shady Steve wasn't there, which was just as well for all concerned, really - the last thing he wanted was another argument.

So he had enjoyed a game of darts with Freddie and Roy, sampled a few pints, and, when Nicholas joined them an hour in, the four of them had put the world to rights quite effectively, something at which John felt himself to be quite an authority.

The conversation had touched on wives, as it sometimes did, and, given the events of that afternoon, John had found it hard not to paint his other half in an unfavourable light. He was less circumspect than the others, and as time passed, he had found that he cared less that he was. He quite enjoyed being a grumpy old man.

Perhaps he had said too much this time, though. There was always the danger, however well you think you know your drinking companions, that one of them, when subsequently talking to their own partners, could let slip a confidence intended for male ears only. There was then every chance that his loose-tongued criticisms of Mel could swiftly make their way back to her, potentially in an embellished form.

Well, if that was the case, so be it. He would just deny it and blame Chinese whispers, but it might finally get it into her head that being continuously bossed around and having his life run for him wasn't making him a happy bunny. Her knew her rationale though: he couldn't be trusted to run things on his own. It was bad enough when they were working together but in retirement it was even worse.

Nowadays the skills that he had engaged to build up the company were of little use, whereas her enthusiasm for organisation and micromanaging remained undiminished. He now found them focused on him rather than the company. When they sold the business they sold his purpose and a weighty slab of his independence with it.

In retirement she managed him as though he was a minion, although she probably didn't even realise she was doing it half the time. Everything had to have her approval, however insignificant. He couldn't take a dump without having to get her signature. Alright, she was efficient and did have a better organisational brain, but it was like she was his mother, not his wife.

Escaping to the Lion's Head was one of the releases he needed. The other was Doreen.

A widow at fifty-three, she lived on her own, and John had not been slow in noticing her shapely figure when the two of them found themselves alone together in the dentist's waiting room some years ago. A conversation had ensued, a spark lit, and it wasn't long before an arrangement had been formed that serviced their physical needs now and again.

It wasn't easy to organise, and secrecy was the order of the day, but John had a special phone - what he liked to call his burner phone, like in those crime films – that he used when the occasion arose, and walking to the Lion's Head provided him with that occasion.

If Doreen was available and up for it, he would then take a slightly different route to the pub which involved another road or two and a detour to number fifteen, Warren Close.

Thirty minutes later – forty if he was on form – he would emerge, energised and pleased with himself, and continue on to The Lion's Head. No one was any the wiser. Well, not unless they saw him coming out of Doreen's house, but this was unlikely thanks to the positioning of the house in a quiet and well hedged area.

So far, at least, all seemed well. He and Mel had pretty much given up bedroom activities, a situation that both seemed to accept as a natural consequence of a lengthy marriage, so he didn't feel too guilty. After all, a man like him still had desires, even if she didn't. Of course maybe she did, but it felt awkward to ask her that now. It would feel like asking your mother.

It had occurred to him that maybe she had a 'bit on the side' as well, and her regular coffee mornings with her pals were not always what they seemed, but he wasn't going to pursue that, as he found himself not really caring. He knew he should, but for some reason, probably guilt, he'd leave it.

With the pub being the perfect cover for his escapades, it was a slight concern that because it was only half a mile or so from the manor house, Mel could easily wander down and check whether he was actually there or not, but to be honest, most nights he was. If he wasn't, he had a ready-made excuse to wheel out: that he had bumped into an old friend – you know, Roger, lives down the end of Statton Street, likes his real ale, big beard, remember? - who had insisted he come and see his Hornby train set. That, he hoped, would immediately bore Mel rigid and ward her off from asking any further questions. The fact that trainset-Roger had moved away from Hixton more than three years ago would also prevent her finding him to verify his version of events.

On the plus side, the proximity of the pub meant that he did not have to worry about driving and could therefore drink as much as he wanted. Not that this was an instruction, least of all from his dear wife. He knew from regular experience that her hawk eyes never failed to notice if, when negotiating himself through the front door, there were any signs that his legs were less obedient than they should have been.

Mel tolerated his social gatherings, as he called them, for two reasons. Firstly, it got him out of the house and gave her time to watch her favourite TV programmes in peace, and secondly, it was about the only exercise her husband got these days. Provided he did not come back roaring drunk, the negative effects of the alcohol were tempered by the positive effects of walking nearly a mile every night. At least that is what she said she told herself, as the last thing she wanted was to have to look after an obese invalid husband who could no longer do the jobs that she organised for him.

So as John approached the large cast iron gates of Ridley Manor, his mood lifted by good conversation and mild inebriation, his only thoughts now were to negotiate the gravel driveway and the parking area, and then succeed in the task of getting his key to align with the thin slit of the lock, which sometimes required more than one attempt. Even with a manageable number of pints inside him and his own judgement telling him that he was perfectly sober and could hold his drink like a trooper, one foot had a habit of shuddering forward and putting him out of kilter just as he was targeting the lock with the point of the key.

As he passed through the gates his senses picked up a noise – a sort of throbbing sound, seemingly coming from under his feet. It sounded like someone had slowed down a jackhammer and wrapped it in dozens of blankets.

He stopped and peered at the ground, then turned his head to see if perhaps it was one of those confusing noises that appears to be coming from somewhere it isn't. But wherever he stood, the noise remained under his feet, mumbling away, sometimes louder, sometimes softer. Then it faded, and within seconds it was gone.

John remained standing in the middle of the drive, his slightly fuzzled brain trying to process what he had just heard and wondering if the noise would come back. It wasn't the first time he'd heard it in the last eighteen months or so, and each time it confused him.

In the end, as he continued onwards, all he had managed to do was convert his initial question of 'I wonder what that is?' into 'I wonder what that was?', which wasn't going to win him any Nobel prizes for critical thinking, were such prizes to be awarded.

He reached the front door and began searching for his key. He wouldn't say anything to Mel, as he would only get shelled with questions he couldn't answer.

By the next morning he had forgotten about it altogether. Given the events that were to unfold, this was perhaps unfortunate.

CHAPTER 15 - MONDAY

Being on the second floor at the back, Anita was directly above Trey and Lauren's flat, albeit separated by Tony and Suzanne on the first floor. From one side window she could see the parking area at the front, and from the other side she had a view over the garden, and this was where her writing desk was positioned.

She had just sat down at her desk but, easily distracted, got up again to look out of the window. She looked down over the back garden, and from the second floor had a splendid view of the forest on one side, the gardens in front, and, to the far side, parts of the garden of the neighbouring property, obscured at ground level by a waveringly high ancient red brick wall.

Behind the grounds of Ridley Manor, she could just see the silvery glint of the River Derwash, a big flat slug of water which eased itself into a small lake about half a mile down river, before emerging at the other end to continue its journey to the sea.

A movement caught her eye, and her focus turned to the path below where neighbour Tony had emerged, striding purposefully along as he always did at this time of the morning. But why was he carrying a walking stick? Had he succumbed to the frailties of decrepitude? That was unlikely. Ah no, it was a litter-picker, which would explain the bag in his other hand. She smiled. Such a good citizen of the community. She wondered why he should be wanting to pick litter on his morning walk – he never normally did that. It would slow him down, surely, and it was clear that if there was one thing Tony enjoyed, it was a brisk pace.

The good citizen made his way down the path, chest puffing in and out, before turning behind a hedge and heading down to the part of the fallen wall that provided access to the forest.

Anita checked nothing else was going on before sitting down again and opening her laptop, ready for the unlikely scenario whereby inventive and imaginative plot lines came tumbling from her brain.

***

Tony squeezed his way through the narrow gap that had been cleared between the two edges of the broken wall, pleased that he had managed to avoid Norman again this morning. His freshly laundered brown M&S chinos that he had been wearing since 1992 flapped limply in the breeze. He always dressed smartly, no matter his destination nor his objective. Clothes maketh the man, he always said, although manners couldn't be ignored either of course. Smart of dress, smart of mind – that was another one of his little adages. You couldn't go wrong with an adage or two to guide you through life.

So it didn't matter that he was on a mission to clean up the forest and heading off-piste into untrodden territory – his attire remained sharp, clean, and respectable.

It wasn't long before he spotted the red jacket in the distance off to the right, and a bit of reconnaissance left and right established the path of least resistance to reach the offending item of clothing.

He used the stick to slash at the errant bramble spears attacking his shins, and was pleased at his own foresight in bringing such a fearsome implement with him, even though he had admittedly not foreseen this use for it. His logic had been that if the jacket was hard to reach then a stick with a claw on the end of it could save him a modicum of bother, quite apart from not having to sully his hands with whatever unfavourable substances the garment had acquired during its lifetime.

The jacket was not hard to reach however, because although it was resting on a jumble of stringy undergrowth, one arm stretched out towards where he stood, almost entreating him to grasp it.

He extended his litter picker and, with all the focus of a child manipulating a lucky dip crane grab in a fairground, closed the claw on the sleeve before giving it a yank. It caught on the bramble thorns so he used both hands on the stick to push the jacket back a bit and then lift it up. This seemed to work, and he was able to wheel it around until it was above the open forest floor, then drop it neatly in front of him.

The jacket was very red, but also, as he had feared, very dirty. It had a fragrance that Jean-Paul Gaultier would be unlikely to want to put in a bottle. He wrinkled his nose as he opened up his black sack and stuffed the malodorous garment inside, initially using the litter picker but then throwing caution to the wind and using his hands when he realised that it would be a lot quicker. He would just have to wash his hands thoroughly when he got home and not pick his nose or anything in the interim. Not that Tony ever picked his nose. Well, not when anyone was looking.

He tied the bag up and surveyed the area in case there were any other discarded items in the vicinity that he could deal with while he was there. It didn't seem like it. Ah hang on, though, what was that black lump just a little further on? It could be a lump of rotten wood, but perhaps not.

He left the sack where it was and ventured further from the main path, noticing as he went that much of the undergrowth here seemed already crushed and crumpled. That was odd.

He was wise to check - it was a shoe, a woman's black trainer. He poked it with the litter-picker, for no real reason other than that he could. Yes, it was a shoe alright.

Why would there be a shoe and a jacket out here? If you are going to fly tip you would probably chose a slightly easier place to do it, especially for just two items. Why not just put them in the bin? It didn't really make sense.

The forest at this point, heading north to the river edge, had more tree cover here, so less sunlight available for undergrowth and therefore an easier path between the trees.

Tony noticed that the open ground that he was now walking through had been recently disturbed, with quite a few small branches scattered around, gouge marks in the earth, and piles of wet leaves pushed around into random assemblies. But he paid less attention to that and more to the fact that out of the corner of his eye he had spotted yet another object that didn't belong here.

Not fifty yards ahead, leaning against a tree and adjacent to a crumpled pile of branches and twigs, was a large woven-plastic bag, dirty white with red and green stripes. As he got closer he realised that there were actually two of them, the green one behind the red one. They were the kind of bags you buy off the internet to store your sheets in if you have nowhere else to put them, with u-shaped handles at the top.

He looked around him with an increased sense of nervousness. Perhaps he had stumbled across a camp populated by homeless people who even now were watching him, readying themselves for an ambush that would relieve him of his valuables. Or perhaps it was a tramp who lived in the forest and would not appreciate being discovered, particularly if fortified by high strength cider.

But that was a lady's jacket and shoe, and although it was indeed possible that it could be a lady tramp, it would not explain why she had so carelessly discarded perfectly serviceable items of clothing.

Continuing to scan his surroundings, head swivelling like an owl, Tony gingerly made his way forward towards the bags. There were a lot of broken sticks and branches here, as though there had been a fight, and unsurprisingly this did not douse Tony's now-racing imagination with any cool waters of comfort.

He reached the tree, and observed that on the ground next to the green bag was an old scrunched-up brown blanket. He peered into the first bag and saw half opened packets of food mixed up with more clothing and a tin cup. There was also a small parcel of scrappy newspaper tied up with string but he wasn't going to open it. He poked open the second bag with his stick, and found that the contents were much the same as the first one, except for an empty bottle of Johnny Walker whisky, next to another one that was still three-quarters full.

He looked around again, but there was no one creeping up on him. All he could hear was the forest rustling and breathing around him in the same way that it always did, nature guiding soft blowy breezes through the branches in a rhythm of its own design.

He pondered as to whether he should continue exploring and see if he could reach the riverbank, but his general unease at the situation in which he found himself, and the realisation that if something happened to him no one would know exactly where he was, swiftly quashed any emerging adventurous tendencies.

If this was all just rubbish, it was too heavy and voluminous for his single black sack. Then again, if it did belong to a homeless person who had just gone for a walk or to beg in the town, and the unfinished whisky would bear that out, perhaps he should leave it.

He retraced his steps back to the black sack with the jacket in it. Should he take it and throw it away? Or would a poor homeless lady come back from her day in town and be distraught that it was now missing, with Tony the heartless villain for having stolen it from her? But then she would have worn it to go to town, wouldn't she? And she wouldn't leave a shoe behind. Oh, he didn't know; he couldn't decide. It was a 'lesser of two evils' moment.

He left the sack where it was and strode off. He could always come back tomorrow after having discussed it with Suzanne. If they both agreed, and the jacket in the sack was still there, then he would remove it.

But as he returned to the main path, swinging his litter-picker in a business-like fashion, he reflected on the two stripy bags. Someone had put them there, and they did bear all the hallmarks of a homeless person. Suzanne would know what to do. It was one of the advantages of marriages – two heads are always better than one, unless you are talking about a pint of beer – and if you ask advice from a partner you feel much more comfortable in knowing that if anything goes wrong then you have someone with which you can share the blame, and even apportion it to when they are out of earshot.

As he emerged from the forest onto the road, he looked up to see a large dark cloud cover the sun. He hoped it wasn't an omen.

CHAPTER 16

In Flat 3 Jean Edwards woke up and wondered what would be the point of getting up today. She had had the same thought every morning for quite a while now. Each day stretched ahead of her with very little in it to draw her along, meaning that she had to push herself, slowly, past every hour. It was quite exhausting having nothing to do.

Eighty-three wasn't that old, but it was old enough, as far as she was concerned. She'd had a good life, by and large, but it seemed to have petered out. Husband dead for twenty years. One child married off and living in Australia who she hardly ever saw or heard from. Downsized into an apartment that even after all these years still didn't feel like home.

Home was where the three of them had lived for forty one years. Well, for Roger it was only twenty years, then once he had flown the nest, it was just her and Roy, nested for another eighteen years in their three bedroom picture-perfect semi-detached in Bakewell – a house that simmered with memories and good times.

Until Roy's heart attack in the front lounge and all that went with it. The frantic phone calls, the attempts at resuscitation, the ambulance medic shaking his head and telling her there was nothing more that they could do. Suddenly the house became the place where Roy died; she couldn't live there anymore.

She was happy at Ridley Manor to start with. Still active in her 60s and with some people her age in the other apartments, she made friends and settled in. She and Vera used to play Rummikub together twice a week, and sometimes Barbara would join too. But then Barbara left, and Vera had a stroke and ended up in a nursing home. For the last ten years she had been pretty much on her own, surrounded by people who weren't like her.

She peeled back one blanket, ready to brave another day. But it was cold. Much warmer and nicer in bed, just lying there. She pulled the blanket back over. Perhaps just another ten minutes.

Across from the bed, sitting in a chair next to each other, were Neville and Bobby, their shiny button eyes stared brightly at her, unblinking. Their fur was nice and clean now. Even if they didn't really need washing, she did it anyway, every six weeks. It was a routine, and reminded her of when she used to bathe Roger as a child, although he was generally slightly less compliant, as she recalled.

Recalling things was becoming difficult though. Her memory had been failing for some time now and she didn't know whether it had progressed from forgetting the point of a story you were telling someone, to telling them the same story twice.

That was the irony: you don't know how bad you are getting because you can't be certain that you have remembered what you just said. In your head you haven't told them the story yet, but suppose you just have? Other people are too polite to say anything, so you think you are on good form but you might be making a fool of yourself. How can you tell? It was so frustrating.

Neville and Bobby gave her some comfort though. She could talk to them, even if they didn't talk back, and they would never judge her. Most importantly, they were a reminder of Roy. He had won them both at a fairground stall, to the dismay of the coconut shy owner who had no doubt glued the coconuts onto the poles but was mortified to see Roy launch a perfect throw with such force that the adhesive, if there was any, couldn't resist. The coconut was cautiously restored to its perch and Roy only went and did it again, to the same coconut. How about that? Although this time it did seem to topple off with far less resistance. Once was impressive, but twice?

She smiled. She was so proud of him that day. She could recall that, at least. And she remembered them strolling home, arm in arm, her with a grey lemur over her shoulder and him with a brown marmoset. They certainly got some looks.

Her thoughts meandered. Who was she telling about her monkeys? Oh yes, the new people. She strained to think who they were and what they looked like but nothing came to her. Old memories were the easiest – ask her about her life in her twenties and thirties and she could talk for hours.

Oh well, it didn't matter that she couldn't recall her new neighbours. They would bump into her again, and then at least she would recognise their faces, probably.

She looked at her alarm clock. Twenty to ten. That really was a bit late. She braced herself and threw back the covers.

CHAPTER 17

It took Trey and Ned almost the whole morning to get all of the coal out of the cellar, and it was hard physical work. They had to spade it into a wheelbarrow, lift it up the steps, take it around to the front, and then shovel it into the back of Ned's pick-up truck.

Ned was in his early forties and a stocky, well-muscled guy, but even he was suggesting they take a break after about the seventh barrow load. Trey, not used to physical labour and doing a good job of making it appear as though his end of the wheelbarrow was heavier than Ned's, had no hesitation in agreeing to Ned's suggestion and heading inside to make some tea. His back and shoulders needed some recovery time.

"Heavy stuff, coal," said Trey as he handed Ned his cup. They sat recuperating on the low stone wall above the steps down to the cellar.

"Well, it's like rock, really, isn't it?" observed Ned, blowing on the tea. "A barrow of coal is like a barrow of rubble."

"Hope your van's got a good engine."

"It's ok. I've had builder's sacks of sand in it before and it managed."

"Are you a builder then?"

Ned grinned. "Sometimes."

Trey grunted as though he understood but decided not to probe further. He guessed Ned was a 'ducker and diver', picking up odd jobs, buying and selling on, keeping off the government's radar.

They finished their tea, resumed their shovelling and carrying, and by a quarter to twelve they were almost finished, with just a scattering of coals and a thick layer of gritty dust left at the bottom of the blackened wooden pen.

Ned was now inside the wooden enclosure, scraping the floor with the shovel and scooping up the last of the coals into a heap, when he called out to Trey, who was bumping the wheelbarrow back down the steps into the cellar.

"Hey! Look what I've found!"

Trey appeared in the doorframe and pushed the barrow through. "What?"

"Over here. Look, on the floor. There's a trapdoor."

"What?"

Trey stepped quickly over and peered over the pen.

"Oh my God, so there is. A big one, too. What the hell is that doing there? Why did they put the coal on top of it?"

Ned shook his head. "No idea, mate. It's padlocked, look. Huge great lock too. Bet that's clogged up with coal dust now."

He crouched down and blew on it, an action he immediately regretted as a cloud of black soot rose up and attached itself to his face.

"Bugger. That was a mistake."

He stood up, rubbing his eyes, then got out a handkerchief and wiped his sweaty face, which, rather than improve matters, instead served only to evoke the appearance of a coalminer at the end of a shift. He looked at Trey, who was struggling not to laugh.

"Is that better?"

"Not much, no. There's an outside tap in the garden; probably worth using that."

"Thanks, I will. What are you going to do about this trapdoor?"

"Open it, I suppose," said Trey, recognising that this could be easier said than done.

Ned crouched down again, grabbed the large metal padlock, its hasp as thick as his forefinger, and rattled it.

"Well good luck with that. This is one Sherman tank of a padlock. What do you think is underneath it?"

"A wine cellar?" suggested Trey hopefully, before realising that it was highly unlikely that anyone would leave a valuable cache of fine wines down there, lock them away, then build a coal bunker on top.

"I could probably have a crack at cutting this open if you like," offered Ned, who was as intrigued as Trey as to what lay beneath. "I've got a bolt-cutter at home. Although even they might struggle with that....."

"Maybe no need to!" exclaimed Trey suddenly, remembering what Anita had spotted earlier. "Above your head, look - there's a key on a hook, just to your right. Could that be for the lock?"

Ned glanced up and located the key. "Looks promising," he agreed as he reached up and unhooked it.

Trey watched nervously as Ned used the tip of the key to chip awkwardly at the padlock's keyhole cover, a thick sliver of metal secured with a pin but stuck fast after more than a century of inaction.

"You haven't got a chisel and a hammer, have you?"

Trey knew he hadn't, but instinctively looked around in case a toolbox had fortuitously appeared on the floor. His eyes alighted on the old workbench on the far side of the room.

"Might have," he said, heading over to the bench. A row of nails hammered into the frame supported an assortment of oversized implements fashioned solely from wood and rust-coloured cast iron, with many unclear as to their purpose and likely now to be about as useful as a horse with two legs.

As luck would have it, though, one of them was a small hammer with a round flat end for hammering nails, and a screw-bit shaped end for, well, something else. He lifted it off the nails and brought it over.

"Will this do?"

"Perfect," said Ned.

He tapped away at the keyhole cover, loosening it enough to be able to lever it to one side.

"Here we go then," he said, inserting the key and turning it. But it wouldn't move.

"It's stuck fast. Got any oil?"

"I've got olive or vegetable."

"Ah. That's not ideal, they can gum things up. Best not risk it. You've not got any other lubricant?"

They both grinned at what this might imply but then Trey quickly said "no." He had no interest in DIY and as yet no doors had started squeaking so he hadn't need to buy any.

Ned suddenly glanced at his watch and stood up quickly.

"Christ, look at the time. Sorry, mate, I have to go. I've got some oil at home if you need it, but you might be best to buy some anyway. You never know when it might come in handy. Like now, for example."

He clambered over the wooden pen and brushed himself down.

"It's probably only some kind of storage space down there anyway, maybe for animal feed or something, I don't know, and at some point they gave up using it. Anyway, let me wash my hands and face and I'll give you the money. Fifty quid wasn't it?"

"Sixty."

Ned smiled. "Worth a try. You might have forgotten. Right, I'll have to go, I've got someone waiting for this coal."

After a quick wash at the garden tap, the money was exchanged, and they headed back to the truck.

As he eased away, Ned poked his head out of the window and shouted to Trey, "let me know what you find down there, won't you? Just message me!"

Trey gave him a wave. "Will do!"

Whether he would or not depended on what he found, he supposed.

Up in Flat 6, in the shadows next to a half-open window, Anita wondered what it was that Trey might be finding 'down there'. She had seen them loading up coal into that van all morning so knew that they had been in the cellar. How could there be something there that hadn't been found yet? It didn't make sense. She would have to do a bit of finding out herself.

Trey wandered back to the cellar and re-donned his thick workman's gloves, the beige leather palms now black with soot. Next job: break down the wooden pen. It was attached to the wall but the screws were rusted so no sense trying to be neat and tidy. Brute force was in order.

He launched a kick at one side and a few panels came loose. Another jab with his leg and they hung free. He tore them off and threw them in the centre of the cellar. This would be fun.

Thirty minutes later a there was a dishevelled pile of black and brown wood on the floor, and an open space where the coal used to be. A quick sweep with the broom had revealed the big heavy trapdoor in all its glory, hunkered down protectively, daring Trey to open it.

"Oil," muttered Trey to himself. He had no option – he would have to go and buy some. Unless..... would one of the other residents have some? Who looked like they might be handy with an oil can? Definitely not Anita, and he wouldn't have asked her anyway. Not dear old Monkey Jean. Tony, perhaps? He seemed like an organised chap who would have a little drawer somewhere with a selection of DIY essentials.

Or maybe John and Melanie next door. Given the size of him John would be more likely to be able to help him lift up that trapdoor too – that wasn't going to be easy. And they had been very nice about the bottle of wine. Yes, he would try them first.

He headed upstairs and back into his apartment. As he closed the French windows his stomach instructed him that oiling locks and opening trapdoors would have to wait until the afternoon.

With refuelling completed, he waited until half past two in order to ensure that he didn't interrupt anyone's lunch, then headed out into the communal atrium and across to the door to No 1. He stood there for a while, working out what he was going to say and wondering if he was imposing too early on new neighbours. No, it would be fine.

He pressed the bell and waited. There were some muffled noises, then the door opened to reveal Melanie, wearing jeans, a baggy jumper, and a slightly worried expression that eased into a smile when she saw who it was.

"Oh, hello Trey!"

"Hello, Melanie."

"Call me Mel if you like; it's a bit quicker, isn't it? How can I help you?"

Trey shuffled slightly. "Well, this is a slightly odd question, but I don't suppose you have any oil, do you? As in, lubricant that could loosen a seized padlock?"

Mel wrinkled her nose then laughed. "Oil? You're right, that isn't what neighbours usually borrow. John should have some somewhere. Hang on."

She retreated back through the hallway, and through the half open door Trey could see an opulent sideboard with Chinese carvings, topped by a large, ornate gold clock in a glass bubble case and a Capo de Monte figurine of a relaxed tramp on a bench, smiling benignly with a kitbag at his feet. An imposing grandfather clock stood watch a little further down. These people clearly had money.

The front half of John started to appear around the doorway at the end of the hall and Trey quickly stepped back and adjusted his view to a study of the walls of the atrium.

The door opened fully and a thick forearm extended towards him holding a small can of oil.

"Is this what you're after?"

Trey feigned surprise at John's sudden appearance.

"Oh! Hi, John. Yes, perfect. Thank you."

"No problem. Just don't use all of it, eh?"

"No danger of that - it's just an old padlock. Actually, I don't suppose you'd be able to give me a hand?"

John looked at him suspiciously. "You don't know how to oil a padlock?"

Trey laughed. "No, not with that, I meant once the padlock is opened. It's attached to a large trapdoor."

John's eyes widened. "What? Where?"

"In our cellar."

"Really? We haven't got one in ours. How strange. What's under it? Ah, well I guess you don't know yet. How big is this trapdoor?"

"Pretty big. And it looks heavy. I don't think I'll be able to get it open on my own. I reckoned you would need one person on each side to lever it open between them."

John nodded. "One person trying to flip it over from the front could fall in."

"Exactly."

"Right, yes then, no problem. Give me a second to get my shoes on."

A few minutes later they were both crouched over the trapdoor's padlock, Trey squirting in oil and wiggling the key.

"Still won't budge."

John was watching, convinced, as is anyone who is watching someone else struggle with something, that he could do better. "Here, let me try."

It was more of an instruction than a request so Trey shuffled back while John took his place. His hands dwarfed the lock as he gripped the key between his pudgy finger and thumb and carried on where Trey left off.

"Here we go!" he said, as the key turned and he was able to pull up one side of the hasp.

"How did you do that?" Trey felt like the man who had loosened the jar lid only for someone to take over and rake in all the glory.

"You have to pull the key back a bit more, not push it all the way in."

"I'd tried that," said Trey, not sure whether he had or not.

"Well, it's open now, anyway. I'll just squirt a few drops into the hinges and..... right.....ready for the door?"

They crouched down on their haunches like Kung-fu monks, albeit, in John's case, with grunts and noises more associated with age than oriental fighting skills. John took one side, Trey the top initially, so that he could better heave at the recessed handle – a large round metal hoop.

"Hang on!" said John suddenly as Trey started to take the strain. "If I stick my fingers under here on this side, and you let go, I'll have no fingers left. We need a crowbar or something."

"Good thinking," muttered Trey. He rose to his feet and trod a familiar path over to the old workbench to search out the largest bit of metal he could find. It was an enormous spanner, fashioned, it would appear, to deal with the kind of nuts you'd find on a suspension bridge rather than a lawnmower or other home appliance.

He turned and held it up to John, like a proud fisherman. "Look at this size of this!"

"Whoa, that's a big one," agreed John. "Lord of the spanners. God knows what they used it for. That should do it, though. I can stick it in the gap so the door can rest on it and we can get our fingers in there."

Trey passed the spanner over and hunkered down to grab hold of the handle again. With John at the side, poised to thrust his spanner in, Trey pulled upwards but stopped almost immediately.

"This won't work. I haven't got the leverage from this angle, it's too heavy. I need to be standing above it and pulling upwards, one leg either side of the door."

"Right, yes. I'll stand where you were then, then I can get the spanner in at the front."

They moved positions, as though practising a co-ordinated move in a game of twister.

Trey squatted down, keeping his back straight as he remembered he was supposed to do, and grasped the ring, heaving upwards with all his might.

The door rose slightly, but it was more of a flex than an ascent.

"It's no good," pronounced Trey as he let go of the ring. "The bloody thing weighs a ton. Do you want a go?"

John weighed up the fact that he probably tipped the scales a good few stones heavier than Trey against the fact that he was well over twice the younger man's age, with bones and tendons less resistant to intense strain. The last thing he needed was a torn disc or a hamstring tear.

Yet he was a man, and presented with a challenge that involves physical strength, particularly if it offers you the opportunity to prove superior in any way to another man, the temptation is hard to resist.

He grunted dismissively, laying the groundwork of reluctance that would give him cover should he fail to do any better than Trey, then supplemented this with an anticipatory excuse for good measure.

"Haven't lifted anything heavy for years though, so I'm not going to do anything silly."

"Fair enough."

They swapped places and John crouched down, less careful about his posture and more concerned with being able to get his fat fingers around the ring.

"Right, here we go then," he announced.

In the same way that dads can't resist hitting a soaring six when playing cricket with their small children, John's bravado pushed caution aside and, despite telling himself he wouldn't, he pulled with all his might.

Again the door flexed but this time, as John began to go purple, it lifted too. Slowly it rose.

"Keep going! Keep going!" encouraged Trey, poised with the spanner and not in the least concerned at John's short exhalations of breath and increasing likelihood of injury.

John let out a strangulated groan and heaved even harder. More and more wood emerged.

"Bit more, bit more!" cried Trey, not believing that the wood could possibly be any thicker; no wonder it was so heavy. Finally, a gap appeared, a black sliver of darkness, accompanied by a squirt of dank air.

But the spanner was too thick and at that point John could do no more, and let the door fall back with a loud thud, plumes of dust discharging from three sides.

"Arrfff!" he exclaimed, examining his digits ruefully. "Couldn't hold it, too much pressure on my fingers. Look!"

He turned his hands towards Trey, who could see that the undersides of his fingers were completely white.

"Nice," said Trey. "You did way better than me though. This door has got to be at least four inches thick. Hardwood too. Why the hell did they make it so solid? It's like they made it out of railway sleepers. Anyway, if I'd had a crowbar I might have just got some purchase on it but this spanner was too big to fit."

John shook his head as he stepped away from the trapdoor.

"The hinges are probably too seized up for that oil to have loosened them, too. Well, I'm not doing that again."

He was not entirely disappointed though – he had asserted some male dominance with his feat of strength, albeit a pyrrhic victory given that he had failed in the objective of the exercise and potentially given himself at least one evening of aches and pains once the adrenalin had seeped away.

He shook his hands, trying to get the blood back into them. "You're going to need a Plan B, I'm afraid."

Trey got to his feet. "How about a thick metal pole through the ring, then one person on each side, lifting together?"

"Well, yes, that could have worked if the ring wasn't facing the wrong way."

"Ah yes. You're right."

"Whatever you come up with, count me out Trey. I'm not as young as I was and, much as I am as keen as you to see what is under that door, I'm not going to break my back again to find out. Find a younger man!"

Trey smiled and nodded.

"I'll work something out. We almost did it though!"

"The word 'almost' gives comfort to people who fail," sighed John. "If I had almost won a contract when I was running my business, that would be no better than if I hadn't bothered at all. But I know what you mean."

Trey grimaced. "Yeah, I suppose so. But thanks for your help though John, I really appreciate it."

John shrugged. "We did what we could. Let me know how you get on, won't you? In fact, can you tell me once you've got it open? Just in case there's anything down there I need to worry about with my cellars."

"Yeah, sure. No problem."

With that John grabbed his can of oil off the floor, gave a half wave and turned to head back up into the garden.

Trey remained staring at the trapdoor, working through the physics and calculating how best to get the necessary leverage.

He could tie a rope onto the ring, then create a hoop of rope, and run the pole through that, with a person on each side to do the lifting. Then he would have another strand of rope leading to someone at the hinge end, who could pull as well. Then he needed some form of cushioning for the door as it fell back. That should do it. He smiled to himself. He wasn't just a pretty face. Shame he didn't think of all that in response to John.

What he needed first was a really strong pole, wood or metal, and the rope. And a bloke who was a bit of a unit. He knew just the man.

CHAPTER 18

Anita, sitting at her writing desk, heard voices outside. Upon being presented with an opportunity to find out what someone else was doing, it had probably never been known for Anita to sit still, stay where she was, and ignore the distraction. Her self-justification was that checking up on everyone else could spark an idea for a book, but deep down she knew that this was blowing smoke over the reality that she was just nosy.

So the moment she heard noises she leapt up and pressed her face to the glass, banking on it being unlikely that anyone would be peering up to the second floor.

She was right on that account, at least, as she could just make out two heads passing underneath, belonging, she deduced, to John and Trey. She quickly raised her sash window a little, but any conversation from below escaped her as the two men disappeared down the steps into the cellar and were gone.

Why had Trey invited John into the cellar? That was strange. Now that coal had gone there was virtually nothing in there, apart from that old workbench, yet that guy who collected the coal had said that there was 'something down there', whatever that meant. Why is John being let in on the secret and not her? After all, she made the effort to see that cellar before he did.

Twenty minutes later she heard more footsteps and was just in time to see John heading round the corner towards the front of the house. She didn't know why she felt the need, but she swiftly trotted across to the other side of the room, to check that John did actually come back in through the front door, which he duly did.

It annoyed her slightly that she wasted her time doing that, but she couldn't stop herself. She had to know.

She returned to her desk, just in time to spot movement out of the window. It was all go today! This time it was old Jean, in pleated skirt and blue cardigan, walking slowly but purposefully along the path that edged the lawn. She was heading towards the forest, walking stick in hand but more as a comfort than an aide.

Poor old dear, thought Anita, then reflected that her own future held similar promise unless she did something about it. She watched as Jean struggled round the corner, the bottom of the stick being the last part of her to disappear from view. She wasn't a daily walker like Tony so perhaps she was heading to the shops, although she didn't have any bags, so perhaps not.

She sat back down at her desk but five minutes later heard a door closing. She leapt up in time to see Trey emerge below, and watched as he followed the same route back as John. He hadn't come out through his French windows then.

What did he stay behind for? Was there something he didn't want to share with John? He could share it with her if he wanted.

There was something going on in that cellar, and she obliged herself to find out what it was. She just needed to engineer herself an opportunity - an opportunity that involved Trey.

***

Jean picked her way past the fallen bricks of the broken wall, and made her way into the woods. It was a pleasant enough afternoon and she had decided that a bit of fresh air would do her good.

Mind you, just getting up and down the stairs to the flat was a minor challenge in itself these days – her left hip was giving her gyp, as the phrase went, and she desperately hoped it wouldn't get any worse, otherwise heaven knows what she would do. The thought of moving house at her age, with no one to help her, was just too overwhelming.

On flat ground her hip wasn't so bad, and so she could enjoy walking steadily along, looking for squirrels and listening to the birdsong, what there was of it. Unfortunately it seemed to be mostly rooks at the moment, not renowned for the exquisite charm of their calls.

She progressed all the way to the exit onto the road, then stopped. What had she come here for? Was there something she had to get at the shops?

She tried to wind her brain back to when she left the flat. No, that was it - it was just a walk, that's all. Nothing to worry about. Good.

Pleased that she had remembered, she turned and started to make her way back. Shame there were no bluebells. Why was that? There should be bluebells, surely? She tried to remember whether bluebells normally appeared in autumn or spring, but it was like dipping her hand into a swimming pool and trying to pull out a stone that was on the bottom, far out of reach. You whirl your hand around as much as you can, but nothing will bring that stone to the surface. It is so frustrating, because you know it's there, you just can't grasp it.

She gave up thinking about it. The flowers would appear when they were ready, and then she would have a nice surprise.

A little over half way back to the manor house, she heard a strange noise. Her hearing wasn't what it used to be, but it sounded to her like a tractor in a distant field, except that it was closer, much closer, and seemed to be coming from under her feet. A sort of a low grumble.

She stopped to listen more clearly, but at that point the noise stopped. Perhaps she had imagined it.

Jean continued onwards, and as she walked she started to consider what she would do for her tea.

CHAPTER 19

Lauren had been quite surprised, as she returned from the shops clutching a two pint carton of milk and some eggs, to see a police car speed past her and turn into the manor house drive up ahead.

She quickened her pace, her mind racing with possibilities, none of them probable.

As she turned the corner into the drive she was just in time to see a policewoman and a very tall male colleague heading around the side of the house, accompanied by Tony, of all people. Well, he was the last person she would expect to be in trouble with the police. What had he done?

She hung back a little, then followed, intrigued. As she emerged onto the lawned area, there was no sign of them. Ah, no, there they were, just turning the corner off to the right, on the path down to the entrance to the woods.

That's a shame, she couldn't really follow down there; it would be far too obvious, what with her holding essential provisions and the house being in the opposite direction. She wondered why they would be taking Tony down there. He must be showing them something. Perhaps he wasn't a master criminal after all.

She returned to the flat, explaining to a disinterested Trey, who was working on a design, that she would keep an eye out at the window.

After five minutes or so she noticed two contrasting figures heading back along the path from the forest.

One was the unfeasibly tall policeman, the other, looking as though she was half his height, appeared to be Jean, looking somewhat confused. The policeman stopped, had a few words from a stooped position, and then with a little wave headed back the way he had come, leaving Jean to make her way back to the front door.

"I'm just going to go and bump into Jean," breezed Lauren as she made her way to the front door. "Get to know her better, ok?"

Trey grunted, not looking up. It was obvious he didn't care.

Lauren hurried her way across the atrium and opened the big front door to see Jean walking slowly towards her.

"Hello Jean!" she said brightly, going forward to meet her.

Jean looked up with a start, seemingly oblivious to the opening of the door.

"Oh! Hello. Yes, hello. Sorry, I was miles away there."

"I see you had a police escort!"

A faint grin. "I did, didn't I? Bit of a shock that was, when that huge man appeared in the woods. Good job he had a policeman's uniform on."

Lauren probed a little. "What was he doing there?"

Jean looked momentarily puzzled. "I don't think he said. Oh no, yes he did. Something about doing an investigation. Does that help?"

"No, not really."

"He might have said more as he helped me back, I can't really remember. I was concentrating on making sure my feet were in the right place so I didn't fall over. You have to be careful at my age, you know."

Lauren smiled and nodded wisely. "Of course you do."

She wasn't going to get much useful gossip out of Jean, that much was clear. But they probably hadn't told her anything anyway.

There was a noise behind Lauren and Suzanne appeared at the door with a rubbish bag for the communal bin.

"Oh!" she exclaimed. "Hello! You took me by surprise."

"Sorry," replied Lauren with a smile. She flicked her head at the police car drawing all the attention in the parking area. "I see we have visitors, is this normal here?"

If Tony was with them then Suzanne would be sure to know why, so Lauren would just hand her the key and let her unlock all the secrets.

Suzanne laughed. "Goodness no! This must be the first time we've had the police here." Then her face became more serious.

"I told Tony he should call them. You know there's a homeless woman in the town that you see sometimes in the shopping precinct sitting outside the supermarket or sometimes by the cashpoint?"

She continued without waiting for a reply. "Her name is Molly. She's in her mid forties, I'd say. I talked to her a couple of times as I felt so sorry for her. Out in the cold like that while we worry about how quilted our toilet paper is or whether or not to buy new curtains. Anyway, she was given a place in a refuge but she didn't like it so ended up wandering the streets, poor love. She's not helping herself, though – the police are often called to move her on, and if she gets hold of any high strength cider she can become a bit abusive. Such a shame. One thing I did notice though was that she always wears a red jacket, and when Tony came back from his walk yesterday he said he had found a red jacket on some brambles, and some bags with some whisky in them, but there was no one around. So I got a bit worried."

"That doesn't sound good," said Lauren, biting her lip.

"No, exactly. But it could have just been someone dumping some rubbish. We talked about it and ummed and ahhed, and in the end Tony agreed to give the police a ring. They initially told him to ring the council but when he mentioned the whisky, together with the red jacket, the officer suddenly seemed interested for some reason. He said they couldn't send anyone round immediately but now, here they are."

"So that's why they headed into the woods then?" mused Lauren.

"Oh you saw then?"

"Yes, I was just coming back from the shops. Then Jean met them in the forest."

Jean nodded. "Yes, that big policeman was kind enough to help me back to the house, after he'd given me a fright."

Suzanne looked surprised. "Why would he want to give you a fright?"

Jean seemed not to understand, so Lauren, smiling, explained. "Jean just saw a huge man approaching her in the forest, so it was only when she saw that he was a policeman that she relaxed."

"Oh I see. Yes, he must be at least six and half feet, I would think."

Lauren agreed. "Six foot eight, I'd guess. Must be handy for apprehending criminals. Well at least they're not carting Tony off to the cells, so that's good. Presumably he's showing them where the jacket is?"

"Yes. With a bit of luck it isn't there anymore and Molly has come back for it, assuming it's hers of course. That and the two other bags that Tony found. Right, I must get on, I've got a casserole in the oven."

"Oh, right, sorry!" apologised Lauren in the traditional British way, despite having no advance notice of Suzanne's cooking schedule.

Suzanne picked up her bin bag. "Oh don't worry, it should be fine, but the minute you leave something it can start burning, can't it?"

The two other ladies agreed heartily, as they would have done whether this were true or not. The exchange proved a springboard for parting pleasantries, after which they went their separate ways.

Having seen Jean to her front door, Lauren returned to the flat, confident that for once she had something to tell Trey that might actually allow him to express an interest, rather than feign one.

She flopped onto the sofa and threw her head back, talking to the ceiling, as that was no less welcoming than the back of Trey's head over in the corner. "Phew! We've only been here a week and already there's drama."

"What's that then?" Trey's voice was less auto-pilot than when she had left, which was a good sign.

"There's a homeless lady gone missing in those woods next to us."

"And?"

"What do you mean, 'and'? She could be dead."

"True, but what's that got to do with us?"

"Well, nothing, other than a person could have died just a few hundred yards from where we are now. Doesn't that worry you?"

Trey swivelled round on his chair. "Only if she is actually dead. She might have wandered off somewhere. No sense worrying unless we have to. Is there?"

Lauren conceded the point. "Ok, but if they find a body, I'm going to start worrying, believe you me."

"Yeah, well that would be different. Unless she died of natural causes. I'd just let the police get on with it and then I'm sure we'll find out soon enough." He turned back to his laptop, resuming focus on his artwork.

"Not a nice thing to happen, though," said Lauren, primarily to herself. "Let's hope they find her alive."

But hope does not always spring eternal – sometimes it lives only briefly, before the weight of evidence snuffs it out.

Later that night, Lauren rested her head on Trey's shoulder as the TV flickered and chattered in front of them. It was a political discussion show and they weren't really sure why they were watching it, other than that it was nearly time to go to bed and not worth launching into a drama or a film.

"That trapdoor in the cellar. I suppose I could help," she suggested, apropos of nothing.

Trey, who had started to doze off a little, roused his brain. "Could you?"

"Yes. Not to lift anything, but I could pull the rope while you two are doing the main humping. Well, not humping, that's not what I meant at all. Heaving, you know - lifting."

Trey smiled. "If you expect me and Hoggo to start humping for your entertainment, you're not the woman I thought you were."

"I wouldn't be the woman I thought I was, either. What time did you say he was coming round tomorrow?"

"After lunch some time; I couldn't pin him to an exact time. You know Hoggo, his timekeeping is legendary for the fact that it doesn't exist. He'll turn up whenever it suits him."

"Being unreliable isn't his only character flaw. Did you have to turn to him?"

Trey sighed. "Kind of, yeah. He's a big lad and he's got the hardware. Poles and rope."

"And you didn't know anyone else in the whole world who might have poles and rope?"

"No. Well no-one local, anyway. No good asking Dave Johns, he lives about 150 miles away."

"At least he's not a clown. And he's a builder."

"I know. But after school people move away, don't they? Out of our class there's only about five guys left that I know of who live anywhere near Hixton, and the others weren't really friends at school anyway. At least I know Hoggo. Be fair though, he doesn't work in a circus, even if he acts like he does sometimes, and there's no shame in what he does."

"Scrap metal? That's dodgy isn't it?"

"No, no, it's all above board. He's licensed."

Lauren sniffed, then was silent for a while.

"You'd think he'd prefer to be called Darren."

"Maybe he does. But we all called him Hoggo and to us that's his name now. That's what you get with a surname like his."

"Hoggsmith....," mused Lauren. "It's not the loveliest of names is it?"

"Better than Boghead or .... Piddlebutt, or.... well, anything like that."

Lauren laughed. "Imagine being called Boghead and having your name shouted out in a busy doctor's surgery. Anyway, don't keep him here too long though, will you? Just get the trapdoor open, see what's inside, then say thanks and goodbye."

Trey twisted to face her.

"You really don't like him, do you?"

Lauren gave a brief shake of her head. "Not much. He's too in-your-face and loud. And he drunk too much at our reception."

Trey couldn't argue with that, so judged it wise not to defend his school-days acquaintance too much.

"He definitely doesn't lack confidence. Says what he thinks and often doesn't think before he says it."

"That doesn't make sense. If he doesn't think before he says something then he can't say what he thought because he wouldn't have thought it yet." She looked puzzled. "I think that's what I meant."

Trey stretched out his arms and yawned.

"Man, that's deep. It's too late for philosophy for me. Shall we go to bed? We're not watching this."

He grabbed the remote and pointed it at the TV. Lauren nodded and he pressed OFF. A sudden blanket of silence fell over the room, almost willing them to stay in their seat and fall asleep.

They sat there for ten seconds, staring at the blank screen.

Lauren, despite being the more exhausted of the two, shook herself out of her lethargy and pushed herself to her feet.

"Come on, old man. We need to sleep. I've got a day off tomorrow to prepare for."

Trey grinned up at her. "Less of the old - we're the same age, remember."

"You're nine months older, which makes you old compared to me. Therefore, old man."

She smiled sweetly at him.

Trey stretched out an arm. "Help me up then. Can't manage on my own."

Lauren frowned, knowing that if she grabbed his hand he would just pull her back onto the sofa.

"I'm not falling for that. I'm going to bed."

She ambled off into the corridor that led to the bathroom. As she disappeared from view Trey couldn't prevent his thoughts straying back to that trapdoor and the mystery of what lay beneath. Tomorrow, all would be revealed.

CHAPTER 20 - TUESDAY

Suzanne looked up expectantly from her jigsaw table as her re-invigorated husband burst back into the living room, his morning walk completed.

"Fresh air, can't beat it!" exclaimed Tony, not for the first time.

"Well?" came the reply.

Tony savoured the rarity of a conversation where his wife would be hanging on his every word.

"It's all cordoned off. I had to walk along the road and as I got to the point where the path emerges I saw an officer just leaving. I explained who I was and he said that they would have the dogs in there soon, looking for traces of her."

"So it's definitely Molly then?"

"He couldn't say as much, obviously, but I got that impression. He did reveal they were looking for a woman who's been wanted for questioning for three days now over an incident of shoplifting and assault. She stole some Johnnie Walker whisky."

"So that was why they were interested," said Suzanne. "Otherwise it could have just been some old fly-tipped clothes. It has to be Molly, doesn't it?."

Tony nodded. "You would think so, and it's obvious they can't find her. We may..." and he paused for effect, "... have a murder on our hands."

Suzanne shook her head sadly. "Oh my. How dreadful. That poor girl. Already an awful life, and now this."

Tony grabbed his newspaper off the coffee table and eased himself into his friendliest armchair. "Right on our doorstep too. That's a bit of a worry, I'd say."

"Gosh yes, I hadn't thought of that. There could be a knifeman lurking in the woods. Oh, lambchop, you can't go walking in there anymore. Not until they've caught him."

"Or her."

"Well, yes, possibly. Funny isn't it, though, how no one says 'knifewoman'."

Tony opened up his paper. "Highly amusing."

"As are you. I'd better let the other residents know not to take that route to the shops."

Tony peered over his gold-rimmed reading glasses. "They couldn't if they wanted to – it's all sealed off. And if there is a murderous criminal randomly stalking through the woods, which I would suggest is highly unlikely, then the police would have found him, or her, by now anyway. Our neighbours will find out soon enough. It's going to be on the local news, isn't it? Perhaps even the national news."

"The press might come and interview you!" realised Suzanne suddenly. "After all, you found her clothes. Oh, you won't make a fool of yourself, will you?"

Tony lowered the paper onto his lap - it being clear now that he couldn't read and conduct this kind of conversation at the same time - and frowned at the temerity of his wife's unfounded accusation.

"Now why would I be making a fool of myself? And just how, exactly?"

"Coming across all self-important. You know what you're like."

Tony considered that he really ought to know what he was like, seeing as he was in the closest position to make that assessment, and in his view, he wasn't self-important. Slightly opinionated, granted. A little assertive perhaps, but self-important? Absolutely not.

"I will conduct myself in a manner befitting of my age, experience, and wisdom," he replied self-importantly.

"I need say no more," countered Suzanne as she completed the chimney of the picture postcard cottage with a piece that was mostly sky. "Aha – it fits!"

"Well, it might not happen anyway," Tony grumbled, shifting in his chair. "They'll want to focus on the search for the body, I expect."

"They don't even know she's dead yet, surely?"

"What other explanation can there be?"

"She might have been kidnapped."

"For a ransom of two old plastic bags full of rubbish?"

"No, not for money, for, you know, other things."

Tony looked puzzled, then the penny dropped. "Ah, right, I see. I would be very surprised though, given her appearance. And smell."

Suzanne exhaled loudly. "Alright, perhaps she wandered off down to the river and fell in, and was washed up further downstream."

"And threw her jacket on some brambles before she went, and took off one shoe?"

Suzanne sighed. "I will admit that that is unlikely. I'm just clutching at straws I suppose."

Tony nodded. "That's all we can do."

The ensuing silence gave Tony the green light to raise his paper again, the tranquillity afforded to the occupants of that affluent living room a marked contrast to the fortunes of Molly Baines, the unfortunate lady who had already lost her home and her dignity, and now appeared to have lost her life.

***

It was shortly after half past two that Anita heard the sound of a car engine. She always made it her business to check who was coming in and out, just in case. In case of what, she didn't know, but that didn't really matter.

It was not the first car engine that day. Some police cars had commandeered a couple of the parking spaces since about nine o'clock, but this came as no surprise to Anita as she had caught most of what Suzanne had told Jean and Lauren. She really did have quite a useful aspect to her apartment, and although she would have been closer to the action if she was in Tony and Suzanne's flat below her, she quite liked being top of the pile, surveying all who came and went below. If the wind wasn't against her she could generally hear all that was being said at ground level.

Norman the gardener had driven off early this morning so Anita was mischievously hoping the police cars would stay until they got back, so she could watch his confusion as he found his space filled by the Old Bill. Mind you, there was plenty of room to park further up so it wouldn't be the drama that she would have preferred.

She wasn't going to rush down and pump a policeman for information – if they found the body of that poor woman then the world would know soon enough. She had other hares to follow at the moment.

The car that had just arrived was a dirty looking light blue Ford Mondeo estate. Both ends of the front bumper were heavily scratched, and the roof, beneath its roof rack, looked as though someone had fried a huge egg on it and taken a layer of paint off as they spatula-ed it onto a plate. She guessed that it had not seen the wet end of a sponge for a very long time.

The driver trundled past the police cars and up to the still-gravelled area near the detached garage. Once used for carts, the gable-roofed garage was now a store room, where deckchairs and croquet sets shared space with spare roof tiles and old drainage pipes.

The car parked at an angle and didn't attempt to straighten up. The car door opened and Anita saw a large man get out. He was in jeans, a white polo shirt with a logo she couldn't read, and a scruffy brown jacket. Luminous red trainers betrayed a man who didn't care what others thought about him, and his hair was shaved tight at the sides but lengthened into wavy blond curls on top.

He strolled round to the boot and brought out some short poles and a plastic bag, then stood back to look up at the house. Anita quickly slunk back into the shadows, moving forward only when she heard the crunch of gravel up to the front door.

She watched as the man rung one of the bells and waited. She was pleased when she heard Trey's voice.

"Hoggo!"

"Mate! You alright?"

"Sound. You?"

"Yeah, good, mate. Good."

Hoggo held up the bag. "I've got the merchandise. Lead the way!"

And with that he was gone, the two of them disappearing inside.

Anita's mind raced. Merchandise? Was Trey on drugs? Interesting. But then that Hoggo chap could hardly have been less discreet, so it probably wasn't that. Also, that bag was large and bulging, so even if Lauren had joined Trey, they would have to be consuming substances like it was going out of fashion to need that much. She returned to her desk on the garden side of the apartment and had only just sat down when she heard voices emerging, just below her.

It was Trey and Hoggo again, this time accompanied by Lauren, looking a little apprehensive and not saying much. The two men sounded like they were talking about someone they had known at school, but they were all heading for the cellar. Hoggo was still carrying his poles and plastic bag.

Trey went down the steps first, Hoggo next, almost as though Lauren wasn't there.

"So this is it, mate?" she heard Hoggo exclaim, his voice loud enough to hear should she have been five floors up rather than two.

"Yep," said Trey, "prepare to be amazed."

And with that they were gone.

Anita couldn't write anything now. Her imagination was running away with her, but not in a literary way. Prepare to be amazed? Merchandise? What in hell's name was going on down there? It was just an empty space with a rotting workbench in the corner! Yet both John and this Hoggo chap had been especially invited to see a wondrous item that she had somehow failed to spot herself. Even that chap who came to collect the coal and asked to be kept abreast of whatever Trey found down there. So maybe he had found it! What though? This didn't make sense.

She racked her brains, thinking of an excuse to barge in on them all and catch them in the act of whatever act it was that she would catch them doing.

She looked at her computer screen. The paragraph staring back at her was depressingly familiar as it bore all the hallmarks of ones she had written before, in previous books. Descriptions of tall dark lotharios, their taut torsos straining to emerge from their tightly buttoned freshly laundered white shirts, might have excited her when she first put pen to paper, but now? She sighed. They were just tired old clichés. She was writing for the sake of it, not because she wanted to.

Yet here she was in real life caught up in an intriguing tale that might actually stretch her creative juices a bit, if juices could be stretched. A woman murdered in a forest, a mysterious cellar with a dark secret – yes, this was much better.

Her new agent, Julie, didn't really know her yet, and probably hadn't read all her books. Supposing Anita switched genres and surprised her? All she had to do was create a story around the elements, and the more information she gathered the better armed she was.

She stood up and went to get her coat.

CHAPTER 21

A section of blue nylon rope had been knotted onto the trapdoor handle, and a circle of the rope created just above, through which were threaded both the metal poles Hoggo had brought. They were about four feet long and an inch thick, and had come from some old farm machinery that had made its way into his scrap yard.

He crouched on one side of the trapdoor, Trey the other. A longer piece of rope, tied to the handle, stretched back over the trapdoor, where Lauren was standing with the end wrapped around her wrist and clutched in both hands. Beneath her was piled the rest of the rope, to act as a cushion for when the heavy door flipped over.

Trey glanced at Hoggo. "When you're ready?"

Big white teeth grinned back at him. "I'm good. Count of three?"

"Ok. One.....two..... lift!"

The two of them brought the bars up to their chests, pushing up with their palms, gripping both rods tightly, and used their legs to lift. Trey could tell who was doing most of the grunt work and it wasn't him. Hoggo was used to humping heavy bits of metal around all day and by the look of it could probably have attempted the trapdoor on his own, even accounting for the stiff hinges. The door rose steadily, Lauren pulling on her rope almost as a nicety, as it angled up towards the vertical.

It really was a colossal lump, far heavier than a trapdoor needed to be. Both men were too focused on pushing the door over to be able to look at what lay under it, and as it began to tilt back, Trey shouted at Lauren to move right back. The last thing you need as a nurse is ten broken toes. But Lauren was already scuttling backwards as the big door fell back, collapsing onto the piled rope like a felled redwood.

"Yes, mate!" exclaimed Hoggo, grinning. "Easy!"

But Trey was already turning to see what they had uncovered and what he saw shocked him. "Oh. My. God."

Lauren rushed over and peered in.

"It's a hole!"

Hoggo crouched down to get a closer look. "Buried treasure, has to be. Look how deep it is! Can't see the bottom. And all proper lined with bricks too. Got a torch?"

"An old one, in the apartment," said Trey. "Not sure if it works though. What about our phones?"

He started scrabbling in his pocket.

Hoggo did the same. "I've got a flashlight in the car, but for now maybe if we all shine our phone torches down there together...."

The three of them all switched on their phone lights and held them over the hole.

"That's a bit better," said Trey. "It's so deep! There's something down there I think, like a floor – can you see it?"

Hoggo nodded. "Just about. That's like a mine shaft, it's ridiculous. Why would they.....?"

He stopped talking as he squinted and tried to angle his phone to get a better light.

"Nah, this is rubbish, we need a proper torch, mate. I'll get mine from the car, yeah?"

"Sure, why not?"

"Right you are. Hold tight."

Hoggo stood up and was halfway to the door when there was a double knock. He stopped in his tracks and looked round at the other two. For once his voice was a whisper.

"What do you want to do?" he hissed.

Trey and Lauren looked at each other. There's no way they would have time to close the trapdoor and at this stage they didn't really want everyone knowing what they had found before they really knew themselves. Yet whoever was knocking obviously knew they were in there so they could hardly pretend they weren't.

"You answer it," suggested Trey, knowing that Lauren could put someone in their place and send them scurrying away far more effectively than he could.

Lauren knew this too so she didn't argue.

"Ok," she said, rising to her feet and brushing past Hoggo. She opened the door just enough to be able to see who it was, and was not happy to see Anita standing there with a hopeful expression on her face.

"Oh hello Lauren, sorry to disturb you but could I have a quick word with Trey?"

"Could this be another time, Anita, we're just in the middle of something at the moment."

"Oh, I won't be long, I promise." She smiled enticingly, which didn't entice Lauren at all.

Lauren turned to look at Trey with a 'nothing I can do' expression. "Do you want to come and talk to Anita?"

Trey winced, as he obviously didn't, but it seemed he would have to. Lauren stood back, but as she did so Anita took her chance and stepped forward, pushing the door open and inviting herself in.

"Save your legs, Trey, I'll join you. I've been here before! Oh hello, nice to meet you!"

Hoggo looked a little embarrassed at immediately being the object of her attention and his usual bravado subsided into a muted "alright?"

Before Anita could reply Lauren jumped in.

"That's really rude, you know, Anita, you can't just barge in to other people's property like that!"

Anita smiled as though it was nothing. "I'm sorry, I didn't mean to be. You'll have to excuse me, I'm not known for my reticence. It's just the way I am, and we can't change the way we are!"

"Well, we can, actually," said Lauren, still angry.

But Anita wasn't listening – her darting eyes had spotted the trapdoor and the hole next to it.

"Oh my goodness, what's that?"

She started moving past Lauren to have a look.

Lauren was having none of it and flung out an arm to stop her. "No you don't – we haven't even looked properly ourselves yet. Please leave and if there is anything we want to tell you we'll let you know. You can talk to Trey later."

"There's no need to manhandle me!" exclaimed Anita, suddenly affronted, "I'm only looking, there's no harm in that."

She pushed Lauren's arm away.

Trey and Hoggo exchanged glances. Trey felt he really should step in, but if he started restraining Anita that could go horribly wrong and all kinds of accusations could fly. So instead he stood frozen to the spot, as husbands often do when two women are altercating.

Lauren's red mist had now descended. Who did this woman think she was? She'd made overtures to her husband and now she was barging into a private space, poking her nose into something that was nothing to do with her, and making out that it was nothing. So she started firmly pushing Anita back towards the door.

"There's every need to manhandle you!" she fumed.

Anita was a couple of inches shorter than Lauren but she was a lot stockier, and she was not used to being literally pushed around. That wouldn't do at all. She grabbed at Lauren's arms and swivelled herself around, the two women performing a brief dance of defiance and ending up where the other had been.

Then she let go and stood there angrily, now with Lauren between her and the door. "No one pushes me around!" she shouted.

"Oh yeah?" screamed Lauren, "how about this then?"

She gave Anita a firm shove to the shoulders.

Anita had not expected that and stumbled backwards, catching her heel on a little pothole in the uneven cement floor. Unbalanced, she fell backwards with a little shriek, and the momentum took her straight towards the hole in the floor.

Before Trey or Hoggo could even move to reach out and stop her, she had landed on her bottom where the trapdoor should have been, but wasn't. Her head hit the side of the shaft with a sickening crack and her legs went up in the air, before the whole of her disappeared from view and plummeted to the bottom, landing with a distant thump.

Lauren's hands went to her mouth. "No! No! No! This can't be happening! Please no!"

She rushed to the edge of the hole and knelt down, peering in. "Trey! Is she ok? Oh God, oh God, this is not good. This is so bad. Anita! Are you ok? Anita! Trey, what do we do? We've got to get her out, we've got to...."

Her words died, and she just stared sightlessly at the hole. No noises came from below, not even a groan.

Hoggo stood with his mouth open; Trey hurried to Lauren's side and put his arms round her, rubbing her shoulders.

"It wasn't your fault, it was an accident. She brought it on herself, anyway. You weren't to know she would stumble like that."

Tears had started streaming down Lauren's face. "I've killed her, haven't I? What am I going to do? I'll go to prison. I can't go to prison, all I've ever tried to do is help people. You have to help me!"

"Of course I'll help you, of course I will. Why wouldn't I?" Trey looked up despairingly at Hoggo, who had quickly closed the half-ajar door and come back over, his mind now working.

"Listen mate," he said, "we need to check on her, she might still be alive. I'm going to run round and get my torch, that'll light everything up and we'll be able to see her. Just stay there, ok? Don't do anything!"

Two minutes later he was back with the kind of large cylindrical torch you see police holding in that strange grip above their shoulders.

He slammed the door shut and rushed over to the shaft. "Right, here we go."

A bright white light immediately illuminated everything below them, the lines of the brickwork picked out in clarity right down almost to the bottom, a good twenty feet below.

Anita's crumpled body lay completely still, a growing pool of dark red blood creating an undeserved halo around her head, which seemed to be at an unnatural angle. Her mouth was half open and her eyes stared unblinkingly at a spot half way up the vent.

"Oh Christ," said Hoggo softly. "I think she's had it, mate. Must have landed on her head. Maybe broke her neck."

Trey looked across at his friend. "She's not breathing is she?"

"Don't think so. Hard to tell from here though."

Lauren spoke, each word a struggle. "I'm a nurse, I know what a dead body looks like, and I don't think she's alive. But we need to call an ambulance anyway. We have to. Oh my God. Oh my God, this can't have happened."

"And we'll need the fire brigade to get her out," Hoggo pointed out.

"And the police I suppose," said Trey.

Lauren looked up, her eyes red and watery. "Do you think there is any way we could not call the police? I don't want to go to prison."

"If any of the emergency services turn up, then the police have to be involved," said Trey. "We can't just get her dragged up out of this hole and say she fell in and that's all anyone needs to know."

"No, but if it was an accident, and she just slipped. If we all get our stories straight, you know?"

Hoggo shook his head. "Hey, guys, I'm sorry and all that, but I've seen that on TV. They split you up and then they ask clever questions that bring out little inconsistencies between the accounts, then they claim one of us has said something that they didn't, just to get the other two to change their story, then bam! They've got you, and suddenly you find yourself locked up for perjury, or whatever it is when you lie about evidence. Plus then once they've worked out we are lying, which we all will be, they know we're covering something up..... no, mate, sorry, I can't do that. I only came to open a trapdoor."

Lauren looked crestfallen. "But if we don't do that, then we have to tell them the truth. That I pushed her. It wasn't an accident, was it? I did that deliberately."

"She provoked you!" protested Trey.

"Enough to push her down a hole?"

"You didn't mean to."

"No, I can't do it, Trey, I can't! I can't go through a court case, losing my job, going to jail, I can't!"

There was a few seconds of silence before Lauren added quietly, "also my DNA might be on her clothes where I pushed her. How would I explain that?"

"Ah," said Trey. "I hadn't thought of that."

"Who else knows?" exclaimed Hoggo suddenly.

They both looked at him. "Knows what?" asked Trey.

"Knows that she came in here."

"No-one, probably."

"Has she got family?"

"Well, she lives on her own. I don't know what relatives she has."

"She lives on her own. That's good. Ok, right..... now listen."

Hoggo hunkered down to be at their level and studied them earnestly.

"I might not want to go to a court and stand there telling porkies, but I'm not going to see my mate's wife go down for something she didn't mean to do, with all the knock-on effects that would have on you too, mate. I don't wanna speak ill of the dead or anything, but that woman down there was an arse, from what I could see. If I was a woman being talked to like that I'd have pushed her too. What was her job?"

"Author," said Trey.

"Even better. No one's going to miss her for a while. Listen, I've had a few scrapes in my time, alright? Only minor stuff, but I've spend my fair share of nights in the cells. I've got previous. I know I'm in the clear this time but I'd still rather not get involved in anything if I don't have to, ok? With my record they'll probably think Lauren is covering for me or something, I don't know."

"So are you saying what I think you're saying?"

"We leave her there. We close this door back up and you never open it again. No one will be any the wiser."

Lauren had been listening intently. "Yes, but when they find out she's disappeared and no-one can find her, they'll want to search the house, and they'll find the trapdoor. And they'll open it....."

Hoggo conceded the point. "Ok, yes, that could happen. And then because it's your cellar.... it's not likely though, is it?"

"It's possible. Probable, actually," said Trey. "In any case, we can't just leave her down there, it's not right. We have to bring her up."

Hoggo sucked his breath. "Yeah but then what do you do with the body?"

Trey's shoulders slumped. "This is a mess. We're stuffed whatever we do. Is she still not moving? Shine your torch down there again."

Hoggo picked up the big torch and turned it on, pointing it straight down. Anita's body was still completely motionless.

"She's definitely dead, must be."

The other two nodded, and silently contemplated the tragic absurdity of what had just happened - that a living breathing person who they had been talking to just ten minutes ago had, in an instant, gone, forever.

"There is one other thing," said Trey suddenly.

Lauren looked at him hopefully. "What?"

"We still don't know where this hole goes or why it is here. Down where Anita is, can you see how it looks like the walls of the shaft stop just before the ground, like there might be a cavern down there, or a tunnel?"

Lauren groaned. "I'm not sure I care. I've got bigger things to worry about. I thought you had come up with a solution."

"Sorry, no."

Hoggo, torch in hand, stood up. "Shall we close it then?"

Trey stood up too, helping Lauren to her feet. "We need to think about this. I'm still not happy. Can we sleep on it?"

Hoggo nodded. "Ok, it's your call. Just keep this cellar door locked though, yeah? Don't tell anyone or let anyone in. And if the police start sniffing around let me know. Actually that's the other issue, they're already sniffing around outside aren't they? You said they were looking for a woman in the woods?"

"Ironically, yes, another dead woman, possibly. Well, that's what Tony told Lauren anyway when she saw him cleaning his car, although until they find a body they don't know she's dead."

Lauren sniffed back some nasal tears. "Yes, some homeless woman, he said. I'd forgotten about that. That's two women in a week, died or gone missing in or around this house. This is just terrible."

Her eyes opened wide. "They won't have heard anything will they?"

"No, if they had they would be here by now."

Hoggo clapped his hands firmly together, making them jump. "Look, really sorry guys, but I need to make a move," he said, as though everything was normal again. "Ring me tomorrow, let me know what you've decided."

They nodded and gave a half hearted wave. As Hoggo opened the cellar door, Lauren called out.

"Hoggo!"

He turned.

"What?"

"Thank you so much. You've been.... well, you know.... great."

Hoggo looked a little sheepish.

"No problem girl. And it wasn't your fault, ok? Remember that. See ya later."

He closed the door softly. When he had gone Trey turned to Lauren.

"He's not as bad as you thought, is he?"

She nodded. "Maybe I was wrong about him. What are we going to do though, about all this?"

"I don't know. I really don't know. Let's get back upstairs. This place is giving me the willies."

Lauren gave a little shiver and sniffed. "Me too. I don't think I ever want to come in here again."

"I don't blame you. This is a nightmare."

"She is definitely dead, isn't she? I mean, she looked dead, she wasn't breathing, but supposing......?"

Trey put his arm around her. He couldn't say it, but they both knew that if Anita survived, perhaps with catastrophic injuries, their lives were unlikely to be a lot easier than if she didn't. And at least with the 'she didn't' option, they had a possible escape route. If they brought her up alive, the life journey in front of them didn't bear thinking about. Lauren would be guaranteed a serious prison term.

"You said it yourself, she was still, not moving, not breathing. I know she's twenty feet down, but that torch lit her up like she was a few feet away. Her eyes never blinked, even in that torchlight. She can't be alive."

"Maybe take one last look?" Lauren couldn't decide what she wanted Trey to see, but all her nursing instincts were still telling her that if a life could be saved, it should be, whatever the cost.

"Hoggo took his super-strength torch with him, so that doesn't help." He let go of Lauren and went back over to the hole. Peering in, and with the help of his phone light, he could vaguely make out a dark lump at the bottom of the shaft. He turned back to Lauren.

"Still there."

"Well I wasn't expecting her to have got up and run off. Is she moving or making a noise?"

"Hard to tell, but doesn't look like it."

"Ok." Despite everything it was probably what she wanted to hear.

Trey put his phone back in his pocket, walked over, and took her hand.

"Come on. Let's get out of her."

They took one last look back at the open trapdoor, walked slowly out of the cellar and locked the door behind them. They didn't see Norman the gardener, screened by a bushy lemon plant, weeding. And watching.

A day that had started with excitement and anticipation had, in barely an instant, ended in unimaginable disaster and tragedy. Fate, with all its intricacies and complexities, had once more flicked a signal switch and pulled a lever. In an instant Trey and Lauren had found themselves diverted onto a new track, heading in a direction they did not want to go, watching helplessly as the track they were on before veered away out of sight. Where they were headed for now was anyone's guess.

CHAPTER 22 - WEDNESDAY

Wednesday dawned grey and damp. A steady drizzle lazily washed the windows and the miserable clouds hung low to better do their work.

Lauren had phoned in sick. She sat at the kitchen table, head in hands, staring at her cereal but not eating it. She was still in her nightclothes.

"I've not slept a wink," she said, seemingly addressing the cereal.

Sat opposite, Trey looked up from spreading his toast but, not catching her eye, returned his concentration to the margarine.

"I did hear you snoring last night," he ventured. "For a little while, anyway."

"I don't snore."

"How does anyone know that? You're asleep so how can you tell?"

Lauren just shook her head and pushed her chair back, then got up and shuffled over to the sofa.

"I'm not hungry," she said as she flopped down on it. Her unruly blonde hair looked as though it was having a shambles-contest with a well known British prime minister, and she had traces of shadows under her eyes. She was a mess inside and out, and she knew it, but she didn't care.

"Are you going to check?"

Trey knew what she was asking. "As soon as I've had my breakfast I'll go down and have a look. At least the police cars aren't outside this morning."

Lauren picked up a magazine from the coffee table, opened it, then after five seconds threw it back down. Nothing was going to take her mind off Anita and yesterday's events.

She had run it through her mind a thousand times. Could she have behaved differently? Why did she push Anita? Why didn't she just grab her instead of push, or maybe ask the two men to escort her out? Everything she did was wrong, but it was too late now. It was done, and they would have to live with it. Well, she would anyway. Anita's death wasn't Trey's fault, or Hoggo – they were blameless. The fact that Anita was lying at the bottom of that shaft was all down to her.

She watched Trey eat his toast, biting and chewing as though his life depended on it; he always ate too quickly.

"If she's still there, and hasn't moved, we'll close that trapdoor, won't we?"

Trey took another mouthful, nodded, then swallowed. "Yep. I think we'll have to. Although I'd have liked to have known what's down there. There must be a reason they sunk a huge shaft like that. Like Hoggo said, there could be treasure down there."

Lauren sighed. "This isn't Pirates Of The Carribean. You're not going to find a big old chest dripping with gold sovereigns and guarded by a dragon."

"That's Lord Of The Rings."

"Ok, whatever. The point is if there was anything valuable they wouldn't have left it down there before they covered that door with all the coal."

Trey swigged down the last of his apple juice and got up to take his plate and glass into the open-plan kitchen area.

"We don't know though. People have left valuables hidden away all through history. Maybe the owner deliberately covered the entrance with coal, and was going to come back and move it all and get his treasure back, but died before he could. And his well-guarded secret died with him."

Lauren shook her head a little, then pushed away some stray hairs that had fallen over her face. "It's academic though as you can't get down there anyway. Where would you get a twenty foot ladder?"

"Hoggo. He has to go up roofs and things, he must have one. I noticed there were markings all the way up one wall, where it looked as though they might have secured a ladder once. Shame they didn't leave it."

"What about Anita's body? You'd have to step down on to her."

Trey winced. "I know. That's the bit I haven't thought too hard about yet."

Lauren blanched suddenly, her eyes widening.

"The smell!"

"What smell?"

"Of a decomposing body. If we leave her down there, the stench will be putrifying. I hadn't thought of that."

"Would you smell it in the cellar with that great heavy door over the hole?"

"I'm not sure. Possibly."

"That coal we kept - maybe if we spread it over the trapdoor?"

"That would look weird in the middle of the floor."

"Doesn't matter, though, does it? It's our cellar, we can do what we want. Anyway, after a while don't the maggots get rid of the body?"

Lauren thought back to her training. "It's a couple of months, I think, before a body becomes dry and there's just bones and husk left. But that's not underground – they didn't teach us that, so I don't know if it makes any difference."

"There must be maggots underground. Or worms, anyway. Do worms eat humans?"

He glanced at Lauren, who shrugged weakly, as though her brain no longer had room for questions that ordinarily would sound absurd.

Trey continued. "Anyway, provided we leave her down there for a few months and don't let anyone into the cellar, we might be ok. Oh, no, hang on, the police might want to search there once it's confirmed she's disappeared. And they can be pretty thorough if you believe the TV crime dramas. Oh Christ. This is just crap, isn't it?"

Lauren swung her legs up onto the sofa and laid down, her head on one arm rest, one eye half-closed. "That's putting it mildly. Are you going to check now?"

"Oh, yeah, right, sorry. I'll do that now. Sod's law it had to be raining. I'll go out the front way. That will save you the bother of telling me off for walking on the carpet in wet shoes."

Lauren nodded tiredly and closed her eyes. Normally she would have come back with a witty retort but she couldn't be bothered.

A few minutes later Trey was shaking the rain off his umbrella in the style of a shaggy dog, and throwing it on the floor by the cellar door. Out of his jacket pocket he pulled the old torch from the apartment that new batteries had fortuitously brought back to life. It was a lumpfish to Hoggo's shark of a flashlight, but it would do.

He strode over to the hole in the floor, careful not to trip like Anita had, although he did have the useful advantage of being able to see where he was going.

The hole gaped at him like a gateway to hell, and he was almost afraid to look down it. He got to his knees, switched on the torch and pointed it at the blackness below. The beam was much narrower and weaker, but it reached the bottom.

There was no body there. Anita was gone.

A surge of fright-charged adrenalin shot through Trey's body – it felt like his heart had been given an electric shock. Oh my God. This can't be real. How? How can her body not be there? Had she miraculously recovered and wandered off?

He waved the torch around helplessly, picking out nothing else in particular but hoping that maybe it was a trick of the light and a different angle would reveal her. All he could see was a stony floor, seemingly rounded, not flat. And it definitely looked as though there were open spaces on either side, like a tunnel.

He sat up, stunned. Maybe they just dreamt what happened yesterday. Was it just one big hallucination? No, that would be ridiculous – they couldn't both have the same recollections and be dreaming it.

There was no way up from the bottom and in any case no one else had the key to the cellar. This didn't make sense.

He stood up quickly. He had to tell Lauren. This changed everything.

***

"What did they say?" asked Suzanne, as Tony ended the call and put the cordless phone down on the kitchen work surface.

"Just that they'd finished searching the woods and will be issuing a statement in due course."

"Did they find her then?"

"He wouldn't say."

"I think that's a no then. There'd be no reason not to let you know if she was alive and well, would there? Who's the statement to?"

"The press, I suppose."

"It's my day at the charity shop today so let me know if you hear anything won't you? Just send me a text. I'll have to go in a minute."

Tony grunted. He doubted he would remember, and anyway she would find out soon enough when she got back.

Suzanne put the last fork from the dishwasher in the cutlery drawer.

"I wonder when they'll open up the woods again. Seeing as they've finished searching....."

"Probably today, I'd have thought. Hope so – walking along the road isn't the same."

He came across to get a glass of water, getting in Suzanne's way as he reached over her head to get a glass out of the cupboard.

Suzanne ducked under his arm, brushing her hair on it. "Could you not wait two minutes? Or even ten seconds? I would have been gone by then!"

Tony looked befuddled.

"I gave you plenty of space," he inaccurately pointed out in a wounded tone, "and how was I to know you were about to move suddenly like that?"

"Because I just told you I'd be leaving for the charity shop in a minute. You only didn't whack me in the head because I realised your arm was there."

Tony harrumphed at the perceived injustice of this invention. "Nonsense! I was conscious of your head at all times."

"Well I'm glad you are at least conscious of something. Anyway, as I said, I have to go. Don't forget to eat that leftover salad for lunch."

Tony's mouth began to dry at the thought of ingesting the now-limp and blackening lettuce leaves that had looked so much nicer in a plastic pouch in the shop.

"I know," he said automatically, even though he would only have remembered when he opened the fridge door and saw them staring sadly at him from a cling-filmed bowl.

Suzanne, now at the door, nodded. "I'm off then," she said, "don't forget to put the phone back."

"I know," called Tony again as he sat down, but she had already gone. What phone, anyway? He glanced over at the table. Ah yes, he had left it there. He sighed, eased himself up again, and went to put it back on its charging base.

***

As soon as Trey had told Lauren about Anita's missing body, and convinced her he was not attempting some terrible and very badly judged prank, she quickly got changed and the two of them shared the umbrella back down to the cellar door. She had to see this for herself.

"I don't understand," she said, staring down the hole and waggling the torch around. "It's just not possible. Where's she gone?"

Trey shrugged. "Search me. Wait – shine it right to the bottom again?"

Lauren aimed the torch straight down.

Trey pointed. "See that dark patch? Isn't that where all that blood was?"

"Yes. Why?"

"There's no straight edge to it. See? It's all smeared, like she was dragged over it."

Lauren focused on the different shades of the floor deep below.

"You're right, it is."

She looked up at Trey.

"That would imply she hasn't just got up and walked off. I don't like this. Something or someone has taken her. We should cover this up again."

Trey got to his feet. He still wanted to know what was down there, but his enthusiasm was rapidly waning. What had happened to Anita, though? They couldn't just leave it like this.

"Come on, let's get back the flat and call Hoggo. He's the only one we can discuss this with. Maybe there's something we're missing."

Lauren reluctantly moved away from the hole. "I can't see what, though. We all saw her body – there's no way she could just have got up and walked off."

"Unless she dragged herself – that could explain the blood marks."

Lauren looked thoughtful. "But even if by some miracle she wasn't dead after all, why would she move away from the light of the shaft?"

"To escape? I shouldn't think there's any light with the cellar door closed and the light off. Especially at night."

"Yeah, I suppose. So she might have recovered consciousness, forgotten what happened or why she was there, and just tried to escape by pulling herself......." Lauren stopped herself. "No, this is daft, she was definitely dead. The eyes, the mouth, the blood. There's no question. She must have had broken bones too."

"She didn't look too lively, I agree."

"And even if she was alive she would probably have heard us talking just now, too, and called out."

"Not if she'd dragged herself a long distance away, although that would be a medical first if she'd done that while she was dead. Should we shout, though, just in case?" Trey peered back into the hole.

"What if she answers? What do we do then? No, we know she was dead, there's no point shouting. Also, we don't know what's down there."

"How do you mean?"

"It's a flipping great big hole into the depths of the earth! Anything could be down there!"

Trey laughed. "What, like a big worm or something?"

"I don't know. I just don't know. Can we go now?"

Lauren was getting upset and Trey couldn't blame her. He put his arm around her shoulder.

"Of course we can. Come on, let's go and phone Hoggo."

CHAPTER 23

John pulled aside the net curtain and stared out at the parking area. The few remaining cars stared back at him, their headlamp eyes slowly weeping at the wet dreariness of a soggy grey day.

It really was a miserable morning, and it didn't help his mood. Mel hadn't yet come back from a session swanning around with some girlfriends drinking coffee and talking about their useless husbands, and he'd spilled a raspberry smoothie down his best shirt at breakfast.

Now he'd just finished the last chapter of his John Grisham book and he was bored. When you didn't have enough hobbies and it was too wet for golf, the sunlit uplands of retirement ended up taking you on a path back to your childhood in the days before TV and the internet, when you had to make your own entertainment and very often couldn't.

To be fair his childhood thankfully did not involve trips to see any Doreens, but their arrangement was usually for evenings only, as she still worked. During the day, he was on his own.

He probably had an odd job to do but he couldn't remember what it was, and even if he did remember, the less you have to do, the less easy it is to get around to doing it. General Lethargy has taken over and given orders to stand at ease.

He noticed that Trey and Lauren's little car was still there – that was two days running. It reminded him that Trey hadn't updated him on what was under that trapdoor - he'd helped him on Monday and it was Wednesday now.

He wandered back over to the sofa. He could watch some TV, he supposed. The big 65 inch screen obeyed his directions and leapt into life. A balding man in an unnecessarily red jumper was standing in front of a pebble-dashed house explaining how the poor woman inside was owed money from a garage that had sold her a malfunctioning car but wouldn't take it back. The seriousness of the injustice, soon to be righted, was enough to cause the man to wave his arms in a very expressive manner as he talked. This, he explained, pausing before resuming the sentence, was a job for the bailiffs.

Photos then appeared of a selection of large, frowning men sporting black uniforms and folded arms, each with a resumé down one side explaining how Dave's favourite food was a cheeseburger or how Andrew liked collecting paving slabs.

John had seen enough and flicked over. He'd watched so many of those programmes before – it was a side-effect of retirement, especially in the UK where outdoor pursuits are limited by the weather. You become far too well acquainted with daytime TV, to the extent that your brain starts telling you to go and do something else because it is dying.

Now he was watching a game show where a tanned and excitable host with very white teeth was asking lamentably easy general knowledge questions to a bunch of bewildered contestants. The more questions they got right in two minutes, the more tokens they would win that they could then use to place on the Wheel of Wonder. Build a link along a spoke and that gets them into the face-off showdown, which..... John flicked over again. What a load of dross.

Another game show, adverts, someone walking through a dirty field pointing at a herd of cows, an old romantic film, a person cooking something, another game show, an American sitcom with canned laughter...... no, none of this was for him.

He switched it off, got up, and walked to the other window. Still raining. In the distance by the trees a white bird swooped and circled poetically, buffeted by the gusts of wet wind. John squinted a bit harder to see what bird it was and realised after a while that it was a plastic bag. He really ought to get some new glasses.

His thoughts went back to Trey's cellar. He'd checked their own cellars yesterday and there were definitely no signs of trapdoors or secret openings anywhere, but that was hardly surprising as it is the last thing you would expect to find, and in any case he would have been very disappointed with himself if it had turned out that he had been walking over trapdoors and had not noticed them before.

When he was younger he'd stayed in digs in an old converted house, and there was a loft that had a loft hatch that led into another loft above it, but that was only because the lower one was a false lowered ceiling, so it didn't really count. A cellar inside a cellar, though, if that is what it was, that was just bizarre.

He walked into the snug that they had converted to an office space, sat down at the desk and switched on the iMac. He typed Ridley Manor into google. The first two and a half pages of entries were all for an apartment block in Delaware County, but following that was a link to a 'fine buildings' website, which contained a brief reference in a lengthy paragraph of small dense text, describing Ridley Manor, Hixton, England, and explaining that it was built in 1892 by Herbert Ridley, an industrialist. But that was it.

He typed in Herbert Ridley. A very short Wikipedia entry explained what he did and how he died, but didn't mention the manor. This wasn't proving very productive, but then he wasn't sure what he was actually looking for. Just a small clue, he supposed, as to why a large Victorian home would have a trapdoor in its cellars. Did any others have them?

He searched for '19th century manor houses' and clicked on the photos tab. Lots of grand looking houses appeared before him, slightly less grand for being thumbnails.

He clicked on one, and like the gun going off to start a blindfolded three-legged-race, he launched himself into a rabbit warren of mindless exploration and directionless travel through the stately homes and manor houses of the United Kingdom, clicking aimlessly on whatever link caught his eye. And it was by this unstructured method that, twenty five minutes later, he came across an article on priest holes and hidden rooms. Perhaps that was it!

Could there be a stepladder down to a secret room where anyone hiding from the authorities wouldn't be found? Then he remembered that he was in a house from the late Victorian era, not the middle ages. Queen Victoria, an elderly lady at the time, wasn't going to be sending troops on horseback to flush out and hang a dissident nobleman or members of the clergy. No, he had got his centuries all wrong.

It was no good, there was nothing for it - he would just have to ask Trey. He'd nip round after lunch.

He wondered over to the fridge, wondering what Mel might have planned for lunch. Along with so many other things, that was her domain – deciding what he should eat. Perhaps he could take a bite out of something and disguise it so that she wouldn't notice.

As he went to open the door he heard gravel crunching under sharp braking. He temporarily abandoned thoughts of food and walked swiftly into the main bedroom, which gave the best view of the parking area.

A bulky young man with blond hair was climbing out of a Ford Mondeo that had a large ladder tied to the roof rack. Wasn't that the same car he had seen here yesterday, but without the ladder? The man was hunching his shoulders against the rain, keeping his head down and grimacing. John watched as the chap glanced at the ladder, as though considering whether or not to untie it, then evidently thought better of it.

He quickly locked the car door before trotting up to the front door in the kind of loping stride people choose when they don't want to go too fast and get a face full of rain, nor too slowly and be rewarded with sodden clothes.

John's curiosity got the better of him. He padded into the hall and across to the front door, pressing his ear against it. The intercom system buzzed and John heard the man coming in, muttering some choice words about how wet he was despite his brief exposure to the skies.

Then there was the sound of a door opening and Trey's voice saying "hello mate, thanks for coming so quickly".

"No worries," came the reply, the voice fading as it moved into the apartment opposite, "I've got the ladder but best to have a look first, eh? In case it won't fit in……."

The door closed and John heard no more.

What could Trey suddenly need a huge ladder for, one that has to fit into something? Surely there could only be one answer.

He walked over to the lounge window, close enough to be able to see along the path beneath the windows. Just a few minutes later he could hear a bolt being rattled and then both his neighbours and the blond man emerged from the French windows in jackets and hoods, before dashing along and down the stone steps into the cellar.

His suspicions were confirmed then, and he felt a bit left out. After all, he was the one who had tried to help first. Why were they now ignoring him and bringing in this other guy? Then he recalled how he had said something like "count me out Trey, I'm not as young as I was" and noted that the blond chap was around Trey's age, so he supposed that was fair enough.

Perhaps he had been a little hasty to withdraw his services though. Whatever was under that trapdoor appeared to need a very large ladder, in which case he wanted to be counted back in again. This was getting more and more interesting.

He debated what he should do. He couldn't just bundle into the cellar and catch them discussing their find. But once they had come back in, he could knock on the door and try to join in. After all, as chairman of the management committee he of all people should have some oversight on anything of interest affecting the fabric of the building. Yes, that could be his tactic. He'd need to monitor their movements then.

He selected a large hardback book from the bookshelf – the kind you never read unless trying to fill some time. Volcanoes Of The World, this one was, with lots of dramatic photos accompanied by paragraphs of small text that only a volcanologist would enjoy. A gift from some relative or another, the round discount sticker carefully removed but leaving a faint sticky residue that he could see if held up to the light.

    He placed a dining room chair by the window where he had a good vantage point, sat down, and began paging through the brightly coloured photos of fire and brimstone.

CHAPTER 24

"That's just mad. How could she just disappear?"

Hoggo switched off his torch and stood up slowly, shaking his head. Trey and Lauren waited on the other side of the cellar, Lauren no longer wanting to get too close to the hole in the floor.

"I thought you was joking at first, didn't I? Well, you know, not a funny joke or anything, just pulling me leg. But can't argue with me eyes. She's not there. There's something spooky going on here, mate, really spooky."

"What do you think about the ladder?" asked Trey.

Hoggo glanced at the hole again despite not needing to. "It would fit, I suppose, but there's nothing to attach it to, so you'd need a good footing on the ground. And it has to go straight down, up against one side – it won't work if it's slanted. Also........" he looked up to the ceiling and back to the floor, "might not have enough of an angle to get it levered into that hole, you know? It's 8ft with three sections, so slides out to 24ft."

Lauren gave a little shiver. "I don't think we should go down there."

Trey nodded but the desire to find out what happened to Anita was bolstered by the lure of hidden treasure that kept tugging at his shoulder. The shaft had to lead somewhere, didn't it? No one would just sink a dirty great hole into their cellar for the fun of it. There had to be something down there, a good reason for digging it.

"How about......," he suggested carefully, "we just climb down once, shine Hoggo's torch around, then come straight back up? There can't be any harm in that. Anita's body might just have been blown a few yards along by a strong gust of wind or something."

He realised how unlikely that was as soon as he had said it.

"You'd need a hurricane to do that, mate," Hoggo was quick to point out. "More likely she regained consciousness after we all left, then dragged herself a few yards with her dying breaths, trying to escape. Her body's probably just out of sight." He looked at Trey. "You volunteering then?"

Lauren jumped straight in. "No, Trey, don't! Please."

Trey looked at her, then looked at Hoggo, who looked back at Lauren, then back at the hole.

The big man scratched his chin, then ruffled his hair. "Ok, ok. I'll do it. Straight down, quick look, straight back up again, alright?"

Trey walked over and shook him by the hand. "Top man. I'll hold the ladder tight at the top."

Hoggo grimaced at him. "You'd better. I'm only doing this cos I'm curious, ok. And I get a cut of anything we find down there, yeah?"

Trey looked shocked that he had to ask. "Oh God yeah, three-way split."

"Or two-thirds to you two, in other words. Not born yesterday mate!"

Trey grinned. "That's fair enough though, isn't it?"

Hoggo shrugged. "S'pose so. It's your cellar, innit."

Lauren stared at them as though they were still schoolboys. "Stop making deals! There's nothing down there except a dead body, and no one's going exploring down there, least of all you." She gave Trey an arched-eyebrow glare.

Trey held his hands up. "I know, I know. A quick look, that's all. We need to know what happened to Anita. Whether she's in that tunnel, if that's what it is."

"I'll get the ladder," said Hoggo, slapping Trey on the shoulder. "Wanna give me a hand?"

Trey glanced at Lauren.

"Well I'm not staying here on my own," she said quickly.

Hoggo shrugged. "No worries, you both stay here then, nice and dry." He grinned as he opened the door, trying to keep their spirits up. "I'll manage. Looks like it's easing off a bit though anyway. Back in a sec."

As the door closed Trey turned to Lauren.

"You alright?"

"Not really. This just all feels like a really bad dream that's only just started."

Trey looked thoughtful.

"I think," he said, "we were always going to have to go down that hole after what's just happened."

"Why?"

"Ok, once Anita is reported missing, as we said before one of the first things they are going to want to do is search this place. Maybe they'll use dogs, I don't know, and pick up a scent of her in this cellar. So what will they find at the bottom of this shaft? A great big splodge of her dried blood. Then what do we say?"

Lauren clutched at her hair and rubbed it distractedly. "Oh for Christ's sake, this just goes from bad to worse. What do we do then?"

"We clean it up. Get some bleach or something to get rid of it. But obviously it means going down there."

"But we don't know what else is down there."

"No, so we go prepared. Take a knife, just in case."

"I can't believe we're having this conversation. A knife? To stab someone, or something with?"

"Well, theoretically, but it shouldn't come to that, should it? Supposing there is a tunnel down there, then it must lead somewhere, right?"

Lauren nodded.

"Ok, so all tunnels have exits and entrances, right?"

"I guess so."

"So what if someone already has access to that tunnel, and they were the ones who found Anita's body and.... actually this isn't helping is it?"

"No, it isn't. That person would then report where he found the body and we'd be arrested."

Trey scratched the back of his neck and walked slowly over to the workbench, kicking at the ground as he thought.

"Then we'd have to get rid of the body somehow, if it is still down there. Or find out where the tunnel comes out."

"How would that help?"

"Maybe if it is gated off and padlocked and we can find out who holds the keys, then explain to them that Anita wandered into our unlocked cellar on her own, because she was nosy....."

"Which is true."

"Yeah, and then she didn't see the hole and fell in."

"A bit unlikely isn't it?"

"Yes, but could anyone disprove it?"

Lauren thought for a moment. "They'll be able to work out when she disappeared from her unopened post, phone records, computer access, all that stuff. Hoggo's car was here that day, and they'll ask him why he was here, did he go in the cellar and so on. Someone might have seen him arriving, carrying those poles and the rope. It's like Hoggo said, all it takes is one careless answer from any of us..... I'm a bad liar, Trey, you know that. If I have to be grilled in an interview room for hours at a time I'll let something slip, I know I will. Hoggo was right."

"So you're saying that the better option is for there to be no trace of the body so they can't even begin to suspect us of anything."

"I suppose I am, although God knows I wish I wasn't."

"So effectively that is what I was just saying, then, about going down there and removing all traces of her."

"Maybe." Lauren rubbed her face, then tousled her hair again. She was so conflicted, but there was no easy way out of this. It had come down to which was the lesser of a collection of evils, all of which had red eyes and brandished pitchforks.

"Let's see what Hoggo finds first, shall we? See what he thinks too."

Trey shrugged. "Ok. We'll have to decide quickly though. Interesting that he's been thinking about what might be down there too."

"What do you mean?"

"Already dividing the spoils, in case there's anything valuable down there."

"Maybe that's why he's being so nice all of a sudden."

"I don't think that's fair really, he's putting his neck on the line by not reporting you. He was always a decent guy at heart. He was just very good at playing 'one of the lads'. Also he's older and wiser now. Well, older anyway."

"I know, I'm being mean, but only because of how he behaved before."

"At the wedding? Yeah, well, drink doesn't help either. If we keep him sober we should be ok."

"What about when he *is* drunk though? Down the pub with his mates and eight pints inside him, he might let something slip."

Trey winced. "It's always possible. We'll need to drill it into him to never, ever, say anything about this to anyone, especially when he's had a few."

Lauren shook her head. "More stress and stuff to worry about for the rest of my life."

"Maybe not, though. I mean, whose going to believe a drunkard? Also, if all the evidence has gone by then, it would just be his word against everyone else's, and then when he'd sobered up he could just pretend it was the drink talking. In fact, that would be another reason to see if we can find anything valuable down there, because if he got a cut of it, he'd have another major incentive to keep quiet!"

Trey congratulated himself internally on this sudden burst of helpful logic. If there was an ancient wooden chest down there, stuffed full of banknotes and gold bullion, it would be criminal not to try and find it, despite what had happened. They just had to be careful. It could change their life for the better in so many ways. A white sand beach with palm trees swaying in the breeze floated into his thoughts.

"Possibly."

Lauren's unconvinced reply brought him back to the present.

"I'd say more than probably. The number of times he's started conversations with 'what would you do if you won the lottery?', so he must think about it a fair bit."

"A lot of people do….." replied Lauren, just as the clang of an aluminium ladder against the steps outside announced the return of Hoggo.

The door burst open and the H-shaped end of the silver ladder appeared, followed four feet later by Hoggo, supporting it in the middle.

"Stopped raining now!" he announced a little too cheerfully as he slid the ladder onto the floor and closed the door behind him. "Right, shall we give this a go?"

***

John had become too engrossed in his volcanoes to hear or notice that the large blond man had come out of the cellar, but he vaguely heard some crunching of gravel around the front, so rapidly put the book down and moved into the front bedroom for a better view.

The man was taking his ladder off the roof rack, and after a few minutes of struggling with wet rope knots and stretchy elastic hooks, he freed it, hoisted it onto his shoulder, and set off round the back again.

John watched from the lounge window as the man angled the ladder down the cellar steps and shortly afterwards disappeared.

Well, that proved it then. You couldn't possibly need a ladder in a cellar unless it was to climb down somewhere, and a ladder that size would indicate a very deep hole. He had to find out more.

***

It was fortunate that the cellar ceiling was reasonably high, as the insertion of the ladder into the hole was not a straightforward exercise. In fact it was very nearly impossible. As they angled one end into the vent, the other became stuck on the underneath of the floor above, wedged between the beams. So Trey found a hammer and a block of wood and set to work, placing the wood up against the ends of the ladder and hammering as hard as he could, while Hoggo forced the other end to scrape down the brick sides of the vent. At one point they almost gave up, but finally, one last blow did the job and the ladder was fully upright.

Hoggo then fed the ladder down into the depths, releasing the catch to allow it to extend to its full length. He felt it touch the floor below and let go. The fully extended ladder only just stood proud of the hole. "That's a long way down alright."

He looked at Trey, who was standing on the other side of the shaft. "You sure you don't want to…..?"

Before Trey could open his mouth Lauren had answered. "No he doesn't."

Hoggo raised an eyebrow at his friend. "The lady has spoken. You ok with that?"

"Your ladder, your torch. Only fair you have first use of them," replied Trey with a hint of a smile mixed with some barely-disguised relief. "Got that kitchen knife, just in case Anita's turned into a zombie?"

"In me jacket pocket. Thanks for that thought though. Just make sure you remember my sacrifice, eh?" He pulled the ladder tight against one side of the shaft. "Here, hold this, will you? Just here, nice and tight so it doesn't move."

Trey moved round, knelt down, and gripped the sides of the ladder hard, pulling it towards him.

Hoggo checked his torch was easily accessible from his pocket, then placed one foot on a rung.

"Wish me luck. I'm just going to get to the bottom, shine the torch around and have a look, then come straight back up, ok? Don't go off and make a cup of tea or anything."

Trey nodded. "Good luck, mate."

Hoggo grunted and began his descent, lowering himself into the darkness of the shaft. Soon his head was below floor level. Lauren moved over to the edge so she could watch as he clambered down, the ladder creaking and squeaking as he went.

Half way down, Hoggo looked up. "Still there? Just checking." He grinned. "You can feel the draught down here, this isn't just a cave."

"You're doing well!" called Lauren instinctively, before wishing she hadn't said it, as it sounded patronising.

Hoggo looked back down, checked his footing, then continued downwards. With the top of the tunnel approaching, he stopped and got out his torch, pointing it down with one hand and holding onto the ladder with the other.

From above it now looked like a ghostly light show, the brightness of the ground masked by a big lump of a moving silhouette. They saw Hoggo complete the final few rungs and step onto the floor, somewhat cautiously given the fresh bloodstains.

Immediately they could see him crouching down and flashing the torch left and right, and up and down a bit. He looked up at them and from twenty-four feet below hissed "It's a tunnel! A big one!"

"Can you see Anita?" called Lauren.

"No. Hold on!"

And before they could say anything he had taken a step to one side and disappeared from view.

CHAPTER 25

From the window Suzanne was pleased to see some lighter grey clouds pushing away the black ones, and the heavy, gusty rain turning to light spits.

In the distance she could just make out a boat on the river with some figures moving around on it. There was some large writing on the side which she couldn't decipher.

Thankfully on the window ledge beside her were some binoculars, not often used but handy for checking out the occasional interesting bird. She grabbed them and grappled with the focus. One eye always seemed to be blurred, even though she adjusted the ring every time and was sure that Tony hadn't been using them.

Gradually the boat on the river snapped into sharp relief. Ah! It was a police boat. And the black figures were scuba divers, frogmen – never the kindest of job titles, she felt. She watched as one sat on the edge of the boat, straightened his mouthpiece, and tumbled backwards into the water with an ungainly splash. Another followed soon after.

She wondered what they were looking for. Oh, hang on, could it be....? She turned her head and called out. "Lambchop! Can you come here a minute?"

It took a couple of minutes for Tony's frowning head to appear at the door.

"What do you want? I was in the loo. And can you not shout from a different room? I keep telling you. Come and find me. Then you won't have to shout."

Suzanne ignored him. "I was looking out of the window just now and I can see police divers out on the river. Do you think this could be connected to the Molly case, in the woods?"

Tony walked up beside her and squinted his eyes, before taking the binoculars and studying the scene like an army general. "I'd be amazed if it wasn't. They're bound to look for her in the water. It was still all cordoned off this morning, but I couldn't find anyone to ask. There were a couple of police cars up at the other entrance to the woods, parked on the verge, so they must still be searching for her, but maybe the signs all led to the river. The poor girl."

"Terrible."

"Annoying I have to walk along the road now, too. It's not the same."

Suzanne pictured her furious husband puffing along the pavement getting facefuls of fumes and spray instead of gentle woodland breezes. She took the binoculars back and had another look. Half the boat was behind the top of an intervening tree now, but she could see a black head bobbing in the water and heading towards it.

Once the rain had completely stopped, and after lunch, she would catch some fresh air and maybe go and buy a local paper at the newsagents. They might have an article on it, not least because Missing Molly, although potentially tragic, had a bit of a ring to it when it came to a headline.

***

"Hoggo! Come back!"

He'd been gone at least a minute and Trey's hissing down the shaft was having no effect.

"He said he'd come straight back up!" said Lauren, her face stretched with worry. "He'd better not disappear too."

Trey nodded grimly. "I know. At least Anita wasn't our friend. The big idiot. Come on mate, come on, show yourself."

Lauren jumped suddenly. "Look, it's getting lighter isn't it?"

Trey peered down intently and watched as a flicker of light blinked below, then another, then a steady beam. The torch was returning, hopefully with Hoggo behind it.

At last a blond head appeared, the owner of whom stood up into the shaft and looked up.

"Hold the ladder mate!" called Hoggo.

Trey shouted down. "Ok! Ready."

The ladder shook as large feet began the ascent, and a minute later Hoggo was sitting on the cellar floor, breathing more heavily than a man of his age should.

"Why did you put us through that?" asked Lauren angrily. "We were worried sick when you disappeared. Anything could have happened to you."

Trey had a different agenda. "What did you see, what was down there?"

Hoggo held up a hand. "Yeah ok, sorry about that, but I had to have a look, once I was down there. It's a tunnel ok. And no sign of a body. I thought I'd just check a little bit further just in case she was lying there just out of the light, further ahead. So I headed the way it looked like the blood had been smeared."

"How far did you go?"

"Oh not that far, about fifty feet I suppose. I had to crouch so it wasn't easy – my thighs are killing me."

"So what's the tunnel like?"

"Very smooth. But just a big round tube, basically, about five foot high. Where I turned round and came back, the torch just showed it carrying on straight ahead for about eighty feet then it curved to the right. Could have gone on for miles for all I know."

"No chambers full of treasure then?"

Hoggo chuckled. "Bad luck mate. No, just tunnel. Although further down, or at the end of it, who knows?"

"Mines," said Lauren randomly.

The two men looked at her. "Eh?" they said, in unison.

"Mines! You know mines, for digging – not the explosive ones obviously. This county's famous for them. That tunnel could be part of an old mine."

"I did say it looked a bit like a mine shaft when we first saw it," said Hoggo. "Probably a lead mine. Now that could be handy in my line of work. A good piece of lead's worth money."

Trey shook his head. "It doesn't come out of the ground like a strip of lead roofing does it? I guess you'd have to process it and have all the right machinery."

"Also, they'd have mined all they could find," added Lauren. "They'd have stopped mining because it wasn't economic any more."

Hoggo drew a deep breath and sighed. "Bugger. Bang goes my Lamborghini then."

Lauren brought them back on track. "Never mind your Lamborghini, what about Anita? If you couldn't see her, where the hell did she go?"

"Mining?" suggested Hoggo, before clocking Lauren's expression. "Sorry. Joke."

"Maybe that's a good thing though," said Trey, "that she's disappeared. It means we won't have a body to dispose of. We'd better clean that blood up though like we agreed, before we put the hatch down."

Hoggo got to his feet, his thighs sufficiently rested. "I wouldn't mind having a quick scout in the other direction too, just in case, you know?"

"Yeah, good point," said Trey. "Anita might have been moved one way and then the other, so the blood marks might have been a red herring. Or, you could be right – despite everything maybe she did regain consciousness and drag herself off in the other direction, and her body is just around a corner. Also the hidden chambers with all the gold sovereigns for us and strips of lead for you might be that way."

Hoggo smiled. "Finder's keepers, I reckon. Shall I go back down? Seems safe enough. I'm guessing you still don't want to."

"No, he doesn't," said Lauren quickly, again. "But you'll need a bucket of water mixed with bleach and a scrubbing brush. And gloves. I'll go and see what we've got, if you want."

Hoggo exchanged glances with Trey. "I've drawn the short straw here, my friend. You are both going to owe me big time."

"We already do," said Trey.

Lauren nodded. "You can say that again. You've been, well, immense. Really, we can't thank you enough."

Hoggo grinned sheepishly, evidently slightly wishing now that he hadn't forced them into thanking him. "No worries. Off you go then girl, get me that bucket!"

Ordinarily Lauren would have bristled a little at being called 'girl', but she just smiled and headed out of the door, thankful that this big lump had come to their rescue.

She returned five minutes later with a bucket half full of steaming hot water mixed with bleach, a wooden handled scrubbing brush, and a pair of pink rubber gloves.

"I'm not wearing them!" cried Hoggo as soon as he saw them.

"They're probably too small anyway," pointed out Trey. "What size are they? Medium?"

"Large. Always buy a size bigger than you think otherwise you can't get them off. Here, at least try one."

She threw one of the gloves across to Hoggo, and he reluctantly attempted to stretch it over his right palm, rolling it up to get the fingers in first, then fumbling to unfurl it over the rest of his ape-ish hand. Lauren stepped in to assist, as a mother would when watching their child unable to get a pullover over its head.

"Aagh, hold up, that's too tight!" complained Hoggo, although as Lauren was in nurse-mode his words fell on deaf ears. "I've never going to get this off when it's wet."

He held up his bright pink plastic-coated hand as though it was covered in blood.

"We'll peel it off for you," reassured Lauren. "I'm still not happy about you doing any more exploring down there, though."

Hoggo felt in his pockets for his torch and the kitchen knife, checking they were both still there. "Nah, I'll be fine. I can handle myself. But I'm just going to do the same, alright, quick scout up that side for about fifty feet, then back again. Any further, you'll need to be kitted out with head torches and stuff."

Lauren nodded. "Ok, be quick though."

"Yeah, I will."

Once again Trey gripped the ladder while Hoggo sat on the edge of the hole and supported himself on the edges. He placed his feet on a rung further down, and grabbed the cleaning bucket with one hand.

"Right, see ya later, people!" he said under his breath as he looked down. Then he began to descend.

CHAPTER 26

Norman Baston was not a people person. Although biologically a human being himself, he much preferred the company of animals and plants. At least they didn't talk at you, and judge you.

When it came to a choice of career, anything involving an office, or meetings, or handshakes and back-slapping, was not for him. School was bad enough, being surrounded by taunting kids who didn't understand him, but it was obvious that the adult world of work would be no better – it had humans in it too. He had needed to find something where he could work alone, and gardening suited him down to the ground, if the humour of such a phrase can be forgiven.

This had allowed him not only to work with plants, but also with animals too – insects, mainly, like beetles, bees, and butterflies, and birds too of course. They all had plenty in common, and it wasn't just that they started with a 'b'. They were an integral part of the harmony of nature, helping to create and sustain all the gardens he worked on. They were his friends. Well, apart from the slugs and aphids – he could do without those little buggers, to be fair.

Were it not for the fact that he lived in an attic, he would have got himself a dog. That kind of companionship he would be happy with. But it wouldn't be fair on the creature to be cooped up in a pokey one bed apartment, and he knew some of his clients might complain were he to bring a slavering, barking hound along while he worked, defecating in their gardens. The hound that is, not Norman.

So a dog would have to wait. He had to weigh that up against the unarguable benefit of having a lovely garden where he lived, and the fact that all the other residents not only kept out of his way but were also more than happy for him to look after the grounds for a nominal monthly fee charged to the maintenance accounts. When work was light, or even just on a day off, he could tend to his own gardens just for the fun of it. At least that is how he viewed them, even though they were shared between all of them.

The plants knew him better here than at client's sites – he could talk to them and encourage them, and unlike the other gardens, he was there for them almost every day; he felt they knew that.

It was surprising what you heard though, being outside. People didn't always realise that you were crouching at the back of a flower bed, doing the weeding or pruning a bush. He knew more than people might think, yet their secrets were safe as he didn't really have anyone to tell about what he had heard.

He knew something was going on in that cellar – people going in and out all the time. He'd even see Anita going in there with that new guy in the ground floor flat. That seemed odd.

He also knew about Molly. He knew quite a lot about Molly, actually. More than anyone, probably. He'd spotted her once, peering through the gap in the wall - that red jacket wasn't the best camouflage. She'd retreated as he approached, but for reasons he couldn't explain he had followed her into the woods and saw where she had gone.

He knew she wasn't like the others – she was on the fringe, like him. After initial hostility and wariness they became friends, and Norman understood, for the first time, what it was like to have an adult friend. He brought bits of food out for her in the evenings, even when it was dark. In fact it was easier when it was dark because then no one saw him.

She had made herself a little shelter out of branches and sheets, and he helped her make it stronger, and gave her a blanket. In the winter she would go back into town and find somewhere more sheltered, but through summer, her home was the woods. Sleeping in the forest, clothed in nature, was a little scary sometimes, yes, but actually not such a great hardship, and on warm nights sometimes Norman envied her a little.

Last Sunday he'd been out working all day. In the evening, he waited until dusk started to fall, and everyone was inside. Then he crept out of the house, edged around the garden, and made his way into the forest, his torch lighting the route he knew so well, carrying a packet of biscuits for Molly.

Suddenly he stopped. He had heard something. It was a low rat-a-tat-tat kind of noise, but muffled. It seemed to be coming from the direction of the river. He held his breath and listened harder.

The noise got louder, very loud, and then he had heard a cry. Molly. He began to run to help but then she screamed. It was a terrible scream, but it was cut short, like someone had clamped a hand over her mouth.

He turned off his torch, panicking, and stood stock still. The rumbling noise continued, and he heard what sounded like branches snapping, before it quickly receded, fading to nothing. All that was left was a rustling stillness as the leaves of the trees whispered about what they had just seen.

He stood there, motionless and afraid, for fully five minutes, weighing up self-preservation against concern for Molly, then cautiously moved forward. His torch, switched back on, swept back and forth, looking for the slightest movement. His eyes had never been so alert.

As he came to the area around the shelter he saw Molly's red jacket, flung on top of some undergrowth. Close by was one of her shoes. The shelter was destroyed, just a few sticks in a pile, the rest scattered far and wide. Her bags remained, by the tree.

"Molly!" he hissed, not wanting to shout. Silence. He shone his torch in a long slow arc, but there was no sign of her.

The darkness of the night felt as though it was closing in on him. Suddenly there was evil in the air. He didn't like this, didn't like it at all. His heart was beating fast enough to sustain two men, and beads of sweat were forming on his brow. He had to get out of here.

He turned and started to retrace his steps, tripping on a tree root in his haste and sprawling onto the floor. Feeling sure he would be pounced on in his moment of vulnerability, he scrambled frantically to his feet.

Right, that was it, no standing on ceremony. He took off, running and jumping as fast as he could, his eyes focused on the ground lit by the torch, until, panting furiously, he emerged back into the safety of the gardens of Ridley House.

Quickly he loped around the edges of the grounds, glancing nervously behind him as he went, then along the single width slab path that encircled the house and enabled him to avoid crunching on gravel as he headed for the front door.

A wave of relief washed over him as he closed the big solid door behind him. He stood there for a while, breathing heavily, listening out for anyone or anything that might have followed him. But there were no unusual sounds from outside, so after a couple of minutes he crept upstairs, his mind racing.

Back in his flat he fumbled for the mobile phone in his pocket and began to dial 999. Then he stopped. Perhaps he'd better think about this. Molly was in trouble, but if he called the police surely they would immediately suspect him. Creeping around in a dark forest isn't normal, and it was awkward having to explain to other people why he was avoiding other people. He couldn't really prove that he had been helping

Molly because no one could back up his story – he'd told no one. Very convenient, they might say.

He'd been picked up once before on suspicion of shoplifting, just because he had a beard that made him look like the guy who had done it. Two hours in the cells before they let him go, shouting at him like he was a criminal. Then when they let him go they didn't even apologise. He didn't like that, and had never forgotten it.

So who's to say there couldn't be a terrible miscarriage of justice this time? If they couldn't find any other suspects, he would be an easy target. Weird loner guy, says he was going to give her a packet of biscuits. Yeah, right, pull the other one. No proof but plenty of circumstantial evidence, and the prosecution would no doubt invent a motive for him.

He looked at his shoes. They might even find his footprints all over the crime scene, a scene which he had now fled. But then who wouldn't have run away after going through something like that? Oh Lord, this was ridiculous. What should he do?

This all assumed something bad had befallen her, but how could it not have? Someone or something had flattened her shelter, and clearly attacked her. She could be fighting to escape her captor right now, in another part of the woods, or maybe they bundled her into a car.

A thought occurred to him. Neighbour Tony always went on an early morning walk through the woods – he often saw him when down in the gardens early of a morning. Tony might spot the jacket and shoe, and think something was amiss. But would he put two and two together, or think they were just rubbish that needed clearing up?

He owed it to Molly though, didn't he? How could he leave her, and not call for help? He would want her to do the same if the roles were reversed. Although.... not if she got unfairly accused of his death. But then if he was dead, or she was dead, it wouldn't matter what the other one thought, and it would be more important not to get banged up from something you hadn't done.

Was she alive then? That terrifying scream, cut off suddenly, then not even a whimper, was not encouraging. And that noise – what was that? If he mentioned that would the police think he was making things up? Or off his head? They'd soon find out he wasn't averse to smoking a bit of weed now and then, and that wouldn't help him.

He paced up and down the centre of his lounge, ducking his head below the central light each time. The attic ceiling was low, the lightshade even more so, and the walls rose upright only to waist height before they angled inwards to follow the roofline and meet at a central beam. If you wanted to walk up and down, your only choice was the middle of the room unless you wanted a crooked neck. But the pacing helped him think.

He needed to calm down though, so he changed tack and collapsed into his only comfy chair. He rolled himself a joint, and concentrated on inhaling.

After a while he realised that the decision had been made for him. Two hours had passed since he heard that noise and the scream, and if he phoned now, they might later be able to pinpoint the time of the incident, or perhaps someone else heard the scream too, and then they will be asking him why he waited two hours, and what had he got to hide?

This was a nightmare. He walked into the bedroom, and slumped back onto the bed, still fully clothed. His eyes closed as he tried to retrace what had happened in his mind, and before he realised it, he was asleep.

Now it was Wednesday and there had been police everywhere since Monday afternoon. He had tried to avoid them but on the two occasions he had crossed their paths they had looked at him with an air of such obvious suspicion that he felt it was only a matter of time before they launched a dawn raid on his apartment. It was one of the drawbacks of being an outsider and looking like one too.

It was way too late to tell them now, though. Even if they believed him they could probably do him for withholding evidence or something.

So he kept his head down, although he did trim his beard a bit to make it look less wild man, more Victorian explorer, just to help counter any prejudices.

He'd had a half day on Tuesday and in the afternoon, looking out of his dormer window, had seen the police frogmen on the river. That wasn't a good sign.

All in all, this was a terrible week.

CHAPTER 27

Hoggo stepped down onto the damp floor of the tunnel and put the bucket on the ground. He flashed the torch left and right, and all was as before. No zombie Anita lurching towards him, nor even a dead body Anita, just empty tunnels in both directions.

Glancing upwards, he saw two heads silhouetted against a square of light, staring down at him. "This'll look like new when I've finished," he said, as much to himself as to the heads. He crouched down and fished the brush out of the water in the bucket.

With the torch resting on the floor and spreading lengthy shadows he set to work. It was hard to tell completely in the strange light, but after five minutes of hard scrubbing he felt the traces of blood must have diluted and disappeared. The whole area of the floor just looked wet now.

He looked up to see one head – Lauren must have lost interest.

"Mate, I'm done!" he called up. "Gonna have a quick butchers up this other way now."

"Ok," replied Trey. "Be careful."

Hoggo nodded. He placed the bucket behind him and got up into a semi-standing position. Progressing along a five foot high tunnel would have been so much easier if he had been five foot three rather than a foot taller, but there was nothing he could do about that.

He leaned forward, bent his legs, and waddled forward. He had only gone about thirty feet when he noticed something odd. The blackness in the distance looked different, as though it had a texture. He carried on forward and soon the torch had revealed what it was – the end of the tunnel. Why would it just end there?

Then he saw it. A massive hole in the floor, right where the tunnel stopped.

"Jesus!" he said under his breath. "What the……..?"

With great caution he got nearer, his torch now picking out the far wall of the top of the hole. Water was running down from above here – he could see it glistening on the wall and there were drops coming from above. Sweeping his torch upwards he was astonished to see that the hole continued upwards. Yet there was no light.

He hurried forward, intrigued, and as he got within six feet he shifted down onto his hands and knees to edge towards the shaft, not worrying about his jeans getting damp.

Leaving about a foot to the hole, he peered up, and the light from his torch rested upon some solid wooden beams about fifteen feet above him. In his head he orientated where he was and realised that this must be somewhere in the garden, and people were probably walking over this covered shaft without even realising. He shivered, even more so when he looked down.

The strong beam of the torch flung its light into the depths of the darkness, and revealed more darkness far below. As he waggled the torch around, he could see that the sides of the shaft were much like the tunnel he was in – quite smooth but scored and pitted, whereas as the shaft above him, heading up to the surface, was much rockier and more uneven. He also noticed that another thirty feet or so down, there appeared to be different tunnel emerging into the shaft from the opposite side.

He scrabbled around for a stone. Strange how few there were – it was mostly grit and dirt. So he got the knife out and prised a small chunk of loose rock from the wall, about the size of a cherry tomato.

Then he got himself very still, held his arm over the centre of the shaft, and dropped the stone. He listened, hard. Nothing. Just an eerie, echoing silence.

Man, that was deep. Too deep. Certainly worth not falling into. He quickly shuffled backwards, deciding in remarkably quick order than he had seen enough.

Returning a lot faster than he had gone, he grabbed the bucket and almost took Trey by surprise as he stood up and shook the ladder.

Trey quickly clutched the top rungs of the ladder so that it didn't fall backwards, and Hoggo manoeuvred himself one-handedly back up to the cellar floor.

Lauren had come over to watch now. "Well?" she said as Hoggo's head appeared.

"Hang on." He offloaded the bucket then heaved himself up and into the cellar. "Right, you're not going to believe this. I think I know what might have happened to your neighbour. Say she did somehow regain consciousness....."

"I can't see how," interrupted Lauren.

"Yeah I know, but go with me on this ok? Suppose she did, and it was pitch black, and she didn't know where she was. The natural instinct is to try to move, yeah? She probably called out a few times but got no answer, so maybe she dragged herself a bit in one direction, then felt a bit of a breeze coming from the other way."

"Where you've just been."

"Yeah. So she hauls herself back and heads off down the tunnel towards where the air's coming from, thinking it's an exit. She gets about fifty feet and then 'whoosh', she's gone."

Trey and Lauren glanced at each other. "What are you talking about?" asked Trey.

"There's a bloody great hole up there. Massive. She'd have not known it was there and gone straight over the edge. And it's bottomless, goes down for ever. I dropped a stone and didn't hear a sound."

"She's not had much luck with holes, then, has she?" said Trey. "Falling down two in one day."

Lauren looked sceptical. "I still think she was dead."

Hoggo started to rub his hands together, which reminded him that one of them with still encased in pink rubbery plastic. "Well have you got a better explanation? Here, pull this bloody thing off for me will you?"

"Maybe clean round the edges of the hole first though?" suggested Trey. "Don't want any traces left where she hit her head, right?"

"Yeah, good point," said Hoggo, crouching down to dip the brush in the bucket. He gave the top edges, where the bricks met the concrete, a good scrub all the way round.

"Right, done. Stinks a bit – hope that smell goes. Want your face scrubbed too, mate?"

He waved the brush in Trey's face.

"Another time, eh?" said Trey, finding it hard to smile right now.

"Suit yourself. Here you go then, girl."

He held his hand out to Lauren, who grabbed the cuffs of the glove and peeled it back over Hoggo's clammy hand, leaving it inside out apart from the tips of the fingers. She pulled it back into the right shape and balanced it on the edge of the bucket.

"There's no other rational explanation than what you said, I suppose, for her not being there now. Might help us, too - at least we'll know she probably won't be found down there, and is definitely 100% dead."

Hoggo chuckled. "If she got up and walked off after falling down that one, then I'm a rocket scientist."

"But why the big hole down there?" asked Trey.

Hoggo's eyes widened. "Oh yeah, I forgot! It goes up too, up into your garden! It's been blocked off but you could be walking over it. Must have been originally accessed from there. And there's another tunnel further down the shaft."

"So it's probably an old mine then, like Lauren said?"

Lauren tried not to look too smug as Hoggo replied.

"Looks like it. And you can access it from your cellar! How smart is that?"

Trey scratched his head. "But that doesn't explain why anyone would build a little shaft like this one in the cellar to access a mine, when they had access from outside."

"Ventilation?" said Hoggo.

"Yes! Good thinking! That could be it. Then when they came along and built this house, it was easier just to put a trapdoor over it than fill up the hole. I think we've cracked it!"

Hoggo raised an eyebrow. "We? I think you'll find I've just proved I'm the brains of the operation here, my friend." He grinned. "But buy me a few pints and I might let you take some credit."

"We still can't tell anyone," said Lauren flatly, picturing the two men in a state of inebriation, proudly regaling the whole pub with tales of their find. "Anita's down there, and if you get mining specialists poking around, they might find her. Then we're in the frame again."

Hoggo winced. "Fair point, don't want that. We'll all keep schtum then. We've no idea where that woman went."

He touched his nose conspiratorially.

"Exactly. Can we close this trapdoor now?" She looked at Trey.

Trey thought for a second. "Now that there's no evidence of Anita left, do we need to? I'm thinking maybe we could explore further in the other direction, where the tunnel bends round."

Lauren looked at him open mouthed. "Why would you want to do that?"

Trey gave a half shrug. "Dunno really. In case there's something interesting."

Hoggo concurred. "I'd be up for that."

Lauren put her hands on her hips. "Are you two mad?" She lowered her voice. "Have you forgotten there's a dead woman down there, and I killed her? I just want this whole thing over with, and that bloody trapdoor closed for ever, so…… so I don't have to worry about it any more. Well, not as much, anyway."

The two men looked at each other, then looked back to Lauren.

"But you already don't have to worry," said Trey. "She's at the bottom of a hole which could be hundreds of feet deep, and we've removed any evidence that she was ever in this cellar. Supposing there are some big rooms or caverns further down that tunnel. How cool would that be?"

Lauren shook her head. "And if the police start searching the house?"

"Then they'd find the trapdoor, whether it was open or closed."

"But Anita wouldn't have fallen down it if it was closed."

"But we could have closed it afterwards, as you are suggesting we do. Doesn't matter either way really, does it? Also, wouldn't they need a warrant? They'd have to have a reason to suspect us before they could enter our property, wouldn't they?"

Feeling herself manoeuvred into a corner, Lauren picked up the bucket and headed to the door. "I still don't want you going down there," she said, before adding "ok?"

"It's not just about what you want, though," said Trey, as Hoggo began to wish he was somewhere else. "We need to talk through the pros and cons."

Lauren turned round and glared at him. "There are no pros! It's a stupid idea. You're both just trying to have a boy's adventure without thinking through what might happen. Just…. just don't even think about it!"

She opened the door and stormed out, slamming it behind her.

"Should think the whole house heard that," observed Hoggo.

"Yeah, not helpful," said Trey. "She'll calm down though. When you think what she's been through it's hardly surprising she doesn't want anything more to do with this hole."

"What about me ladder then?"

"You going to need it for anything else?"

"Hardly use it, to be honest. I've got a smaller one I use most of the time. Up to you, mate, if you wanna keep it there for now. I can shout if I need it."

"Thanks. Maybe keep it there for a little while. We can't close the trapdoor then, can we? It would be good though, wouldn't it, if we found some hidden chambers or something like that."

"Still reckon there's treasure down there, then?"

"Might be."

Hoggo hitched up his jeans and headed for the door. "We can dream, eh? Come on. I've got to be making a move."

CHAPTER 28

John had moved on to My First Book Of Wonder, a reminder of his childhood with surprisingly accomplished hand-drawn illustrations of what the most exciting parts of the world looked like in the 1930s.

His father had given it to him and despite it being a children's book he was finding it much more interesting than photos of volcanoes. So much so that he had almost forgotten that he was supposed to be keeping an eye out for what might be going on outside.

A sudden bang shook him out of a renewed fascination with the jungles of Borneo and he glanced out to see a grim faced Lauren marching back into her apartment. A few minutes later she was followed by Trey and the other chap, both looking far more relaxed.

He closed his book and put it back on the shelf. Time to find out what was going on.

***

Trey watched Lauren in the kitchen area as she briskly rinsed out the bucket and began putting everything away.

"Hoggo's going to come back on Saturday morning," he said, trying to make it sound as though this was of no consequence.

Lauren made a noise but it was not clear what it meant. The two men looked at each other.

"I'll get away then," suggested Hoggo, "let you two sort things out, eh?"

Trey forced a smile that didn't reach his eyes. "Yeah, maybe best, mate, if you don't mind."

The door bell went.

Hoggo uttered an expletive. "Always as I'm just about to leave!"

"Hang on, I'll get rid of them."

Trey headed to the front door as Lauren emerged from the kitchen, wiping her hands on a towel.

Trey opened the door to find neighbour John looming in front of him. "Hi John, how can I help you?"

John rubbed his hands together as though applying hand cream and leant forward slightly. "Do you remember you told me that you would let me know what you found under your trapdoor?"

He looked around to make sure there was no one eavesdropping behind him then turned back to Trey. "I guess you must have opened it by now?"

Trey groaned internally. John could not have come at a worse time.

"Ah yes," he said, thinking frantically. "Er, I'd invite you in but I have a guest, and I'd better not say anything with the door open. Can I let you know later?"

"So you do know then?" persisted John.

"Er, yes."

"I need to know too, you see."

"Do you?"

"Yes, in my role as Chairman of the Management Committee, you understand. In case there are any structural implications. Was it just a wine cellar or a storage area, something like that?"

Keen to get John off his back and also not get him involved in the secret of the tunnels yet, Trey made his first mistake.

"Yes, just a kind of storage hole, nothing spectacular."

"Nothing too deep then?"

"No, no. Just a few feet."

John nodded.

"So not anything you would need a long ladder for then?"

There was something about the way he said this that told Trey that John knew more than he was letting on, and the penny started to drop. He must have seen Hoggo bringing that huge ladder into the cellar. There was no way Trey could explain away that one.

"You'd better come in," he sighed.

Trey led a grimly-smiling John through to the lounge from where Lauren and Hoggo had been listening in.

"John, this is Hoggo, an old school friend," said Trey.

The two nodded and exchanged how-do-you-dos.

"Now then," said John, confident now that he was on the right track, "perhaps you had better explain what's really under that trapdoor."

Lauren aimed a targeted glare at her husband that he knew was beaming the message 'don't mention Anita'. He gave her an almost imperceptible nod to assure her that he wouldn't, and that would have included the subtext 'I'm not stupid you know' if a nod could do such a thing.

"It's a small shaft," he said.

"How deep?"

"Judging by the ladder, about twenty four feet to the bottom."

John gave a low whistle. "That's not small, that's deep. Does it lead anywhere?"

Trey looked at Lauren and Hoggo. All three of them realised John would have to have a look at the hole so they couldn't avoid him knowing.

"There's a tunnel down there."

"What? Really? Where to?"

"We don't know yet. Hoggo's gone about fifty yards in both directions." He looked at his friend, inviting him to take over.

"Yeah," said Hoggo, "on one side it just disappears round a corner to who knows where, but the other side, it leads to this massive shaft. We think it comes up in the garden somewhere but it's been capped off."

John's eyes widened. "An old mine?"

"Yep, that's what we think. I dropped a stone down it but heard nothing. It's really deep."

"Can I see it? If this house has been built over a mine I need to assess whether we need to be worried or not."

"It's been fine for the last 130-odd years," Lauren pointed out.

"True," said John, recalling something he had just read, "but volcanoes can be fine for hundreds of years and then suddenly they erupt. Who's to say that we don't have a minor earthquake that we don't notice, but which causes your tunnel to collapse and brings the house down with it?"

Hoggo only half succeeded in suppressing a snort. "Unlikely, though, mate, isn't it?"

John gave him a look that could not be mistaken for admiration.

"There have been plenty of natural disasters that were unlikely," he said coldly. He was going to go on and give some examples but decided not to, mainly because he couldn't think of any, but the point was made. "We have to err on the side of caution," he concluded.

Trey and Lauren glanced at each other. They both knew they had no choice.

"Alright, John, we'll show you. Hoggo, you wanted to get off?"

"Yeah, cheers. Need to dash. See you Saturday, alright?" Without looking at John he gave a little wave and then was gone, the door slamming behind him.

Trey looked at Lauren. "You coming?"

Lauren sighed. "No, you go. I don't need to." She turned back to the kitchen. It was clear she had just had enough of the whole thing.

Not really surprising, thought Trey. What happened to Anita would haunt her for the rest of her life, and the immediate aftermath hadn't even begun yet. His next job was to find a way to persuade John not to go public with the news of the old mine and end up getting professional people down there mapping it out and stumbling across dead bodies.

The two of them went out through the French windows. The rain had stopped completely now and a few blue patches had started to appear between the clouds.

Trey led John down the steps and into the cellar.

"There you go," he said, turning on the light.

John hurried over and peered into the hole.

"Oh my good Lord. I can't even see the bottom."

"Oh, right, sorry. There's a torch over here if you want."

Without waiting for a response Trey went over to the workbench and grabbed the old torch that he had left on it, handing it to John, who was now crouched down next to the shaft.

"Yes, I see what you mean about the tunnel," said John, angling the weak beam past the ladder to get the best view of the void below. He switched the torch off and stood up. "We'll need to get a survey done of course."

"Why?"

John looked at him as though Trey had asked why you would milk a cow.

"To assess the danger to the house. There could be a whole honeycomb of tunnels and caverns beneath us. Also we need to know exactly where that mineshaft your friend talked about comes up."

"We can work that out ourselves."

"Well, yes maybe."

"And Hoggo and I are going to check out where else the tunnel goes, on Saturday. It looks as though it heads straight out under our bedroom and off towards the road. If we can confirm that, seems a waste of money to pay big bucks to get a survey done. Also, what would their report state? Just what we already knew."

John looked thoughtful, so Trey, on a roll now, hammered home his point.

"Then what would their solution be? If anything needed doing, it would involve either re-enforcing the tunnel or filling it with cement or something. Either way the cost would be colossal. All for preventing something that hasn't happened in a hundred and thirty years and has very little chance of happening in the next hundred and thirty either. Doesn't really seem like a good use of everyone's money, does it?"

John handed the torch back to Trey to buy himself some thinking time, before concluding that Trey was broadly right.

"That's a fair point, I suppose. And it is quite a long way underground. I'm not entirely convinced though – I'll need to do a bit of research myself; see what the risks are. Just in case."

"I'd say the risks are pretty low based on what's happened so far."

"You're probably right, but I'll check anyway. What are your plans for Saturday then? How far in are you going to go?"

Trey shrugged. "Haven't really discussed it yet. As far as we can, I suppose."

"May I ask why?"

"Just to see what's there. In case there are caves and caverns too, that kind of thing."

"Are you sure you know what you're doing?"

"What do you mean?"

"Have you got experience in caving or potholing?"

"I went potholing in France once when I was a kid. One of those adventure activity holidays. It was good fun actually."

"That doesn't make you an expert."

"No, but at least I know I'm not afraid of enclosed spaces."

John rubbed his chin, not sure what to say. "Well, it's up to you I suppose. Just don't go too far in. We'll have to let the other residents know about this, of course."

"No!" said Trey rather too loudly, before tempering this with "I don't think we should worry them. Also, they'd probably tell all their friends and then it would be all round town, and Lauren and I don't want to be fending off requests all day from nosy people wanting to come and have a look."

"You could charge an entrance fee. Nice little earner."

"Good idea but no thanks! We'd appreciate it if we just kept it between ourselves for now. Or at least maybe until we know a bit more about what's down there."

"Yes, I suppose we don't really want hordes of strangers marching up our drive every day. Ok if I tell Mel though?"

Trey felt himself backed into a corner. He wanted as few people to know as possible, but if he said no it would imply he didn't trust John's wife. His reply perhaps didn't entirely eliminate this possibility.

"She'll not tell her friends?"

"Not if I tell her not to," John assured him, more out of hope than confidence. Experience told him that he could bark orders at her as much as he liked and it wouldn't make any difference unless she agreed with him. What else could he say though?

"Ok. That's it though, just the five of us. Deal?"

John smiled grimly. "I wasn't aware this was a business transaction, but yes, deal. You'll need someone up top to summon help if needed."

"You think? We'd be careful."

"Supposing you have an accident? Who's going to call for help?"

Trey paused. That was a good point. Lauren would be working, assuming she was up to it by then. Perhaps they did need someone to keep an eye out for them. The chances were high that mobile phone reception wouldn't be five bars down there.

"You're right. I don't suppose.....?"

Conscious that he had not enjoyed being left out of the action over the last few days, John decided he wanted back in.

"Ok. I'll keep watch."

"Thank you John. We'd be grateful for your help. I'll give you a shout when Hoggo arrives if that's ok."

"What time?"

"Mid morning, probably around eleven. You won't get anything more precise than that out of Hoggo."

"No that's fine. I'm not doing anything else on Saturday. Golf is on Sunday."

"Excellent! Until then, we say nothing. It's our secret."

Despite his misgivings John found himself rather pleased that he was in on the secret, even though, being a gentleman of advanced years, he was not supposed to have feelings more suited to those of a child.

"Indeed," he said gravely, in a manner befitting of a distinguished adult.

There was little else to be said so the two of them returned to the flat, and once John had gone, Trey put his arm round Lauren.

"I think it's all going to be ok, you know," he said.

Lauren turned to face him.

"You think? What happens when they find that Anita is missing?"

"Nothing! Well, not unless you go running up to them and tell them you pushed her down a hole. They'll have no reason to suspect any of us, will they? Think about it. You barely knew the woman, so you wouldn't have a motive. They're more likely to suspect people who've lived here for longer and knew her better."

Lauren nodded slowly. "I suppose. It's so weird that none of them know yet."

"I wonder when they'll find out she's missing."

"Whenever it is, I'm not looking forward to it. I'm scared, Trey."

"Why?"

"If I say the wrong thing, let something slip, you know? I'll have to be on my guard the whole time as soon as people start talking about her. I'll be thinking everyone knows it was me."

"Yeah but how long will that be for? Get through that and then after a few weeks it won't be a hot topic anymore and something else will be the new talking point."

"But until they find her body – which they won't – the case will be open. There won't be any closure."

"Yeah but loads of people go missing every year and never turn up – more than you think. I've never understood why only a few of them get all the publicity. It's only if they find a body that it cranks up a notch, 'cause then it's usually a murder they're dealing with."

"Right, so all the more reason to close that trapdoor then."

"After Saturday, we will, I promise."

Lauren gave him a shot-across-the-bows warning look. "You'd better. I'm not sure how much more of this I can take - my nerves are torn to shreds."

"Yeah, I know." He leant over and kissed the top of her head. "We'll get through it though. Also, I don't think it is medically possible to tear your nerves to shreds, is it?"

Lauren couldn't help smiling. "We've had no cases of that at the hospital, no. Maybe they're just frayed then."

"That makes more sense. Frayed is treatable, shredded less so. Are you going back to work tomorrow?"

"Not sure. Do you think I should?"

"It might take your mind off things. But you've got to be comfortable you won't spend all day moping around and looking worried about something, as that isn't going to act in your favour if the cops start asking questions."

"I'm not going to be Little Miss Sunshine though, am I? How can I be happy after what I've done?" She lowered her voice. "I'm a murderer, Trey. I've killed someone. How do I ever live with that?"

"I can't answer that because I don't know. All you have to keep thinking and telling yourself was that it was an accident, because it was. You didn't mean to kill her, did you? It was a complete accident."

"Of course."

"Well you're not a murderer, then, in the legal sense. It was manslaughter."

"It's just semantics though, isn't it? Anita's dead, and she wouldn't be if I hadn't pushed her."

Trey tilted his head. "Hang on though, now we know that you didn't actually kill her, did you? Turns out she probably crawled off and fell down that hole in the tunnel. So all you did was injure her! That's a whole different ball game!"

"Yes but we left her down there. If we had rescued her she might still be alive."

"Exactly. *We* left her down there, not just you. So me and Hoggo are as much to blame for that as you."

Trey realised only after he had said it, that this was not such a good thing as he was making it sound, at least not for him and Hoggo anyway. Leaving a dead body and not phoning the police is one thing, but leaving an injured person to die? They'd all done that, not just Lauren. They all could possibly have prevented her final demise, but they didn't. He'd phone Hoggo later and point this out.

At least it appeared to be giving Lauren a crumb of comfort. She smiled weakly and gave him a brief hug.

"We're all in this together, aren't we? That does make me feel a bit better actually. I was thinking, though......... can I tell Mum and Dad?"

Trey stood back, shocked. "Good grief no, that would be a terrible idea. Why would you want to do that?"

"I've always confided in them. It's just that I might need someone else to talk to, when you're not around."

"But I'm always around, I work from home! Also, why give them that burden? Imagine being told that your daughter has killed someone. It would ruin their lives. You don't know how they'd react."

"Mum would be supportive, I know she would."

"And your Dad?"

Lauren wasn't so quick to answer this time. She winced a little.

"Well, yeah, ok, he might not be quite so understanding. He'd probably say I should go to the police and tell the truth, and if I didn't he'd do it himself."

"Exactly. And you can't tell your Mum and not your Dad, that would put all sorts of pressure on her. No, definitely keep them out of it, for everyone's sakes. Promise you won't tell them."

Lauren sighed. "Ok, you're right. It wouldn't be fair on them. It's just that...."

"I know, I know. But you've got me, haven't you? We'll support each other through this. And there's Hoggo too, so there's three of us who know the truth. You're not alone."

"Suppose so."

"Good! Ok, I really need to get back to that album cover illustration I'm doing – I've only got 'til Friday. You gonna be ok if I do?"

"Yeah sure." She ran her hands through her hair and stretched her arms. "I'll check Facebook then work out a colour scheme for that dining area. Not that my heart's in it, but...."

She turned and padded off into the kitchen area, from where an adjacent room served as a place to eat as well as a temporary place to store packing boxes. Sometimes conversions of old houses resulted in unusual layouts, and this one was definitely odd, or to use estate agent speak, quirky.

Trey wandered over to his desk and wiggled his mouse to reactivate the laptop. He wasn't sure whether he was looking forward to Saturday or not.

CHAPTER 29 - FRIDAY

Julie Bingham was worried. It was Friday morning now, and the deadline for an answer was looming fast, but it was like Anita had disappeared off the face of the earth. All day yesterday she'd been ringing and emailing her, but nothing. Silence.

It wasn't like Anita at all. Julie hadn't represented her for long but in that time Anita had never been backwards in coming forward, and was always straight back at her if she contacted her, like she was just waiting for the message. Yet now, just when it was most important, she'd clammed up. Something wasn't right.

The slot she'd secured at a prestigious London book fair was too good a chance to miss, especially as it had only come up after another author dropped out due to illness on Wednesday. It was one of those 'confirm within two days or we give it to someone else' ultimatums, and if nothing else it would prove to Anita that Julie was doing the business for her. But only if she responded!

By mid-morning Julie, already not one of life's calmest people, was getting stressed. She looked up Anita's address and started calculating travel times. If she left her Northampton office early and got the train back to her house by half past two, she could pick up her car and be in Hixton by four o'clock. Half an hour with Anita and then she'd be heading back against the traffic and should be home by six. It was a pain, but it was a plan.

She got approval from her manager and at ten to four she was standing outside Ridley Manor, ringing the buzzer to Anita's flat.

It was Suzanne, putting the sheets back on the bed in the front bedroom, who had heard the strange car cautiously approaching the house, and then watched as a nervous looking young woman parked and got out.

She saw the woman, long blonde hair tied back in a bunch, stand back from pressing the intercom button and peer up to the floors above, her eyes scanning the windows as though hoping to see someone waving down at her. Suzanne could not recall seeing an expression of such worry in a long time, and when the woman started walking around in jerky movements as though she didn't know what to do next, or was perhaps in need of a toilet, Suzanne felt compelled to help.

Tony was engrossed in an old war film, so she slipped out, down the stairs, and opened the front door.

"Oh!" said Julie, startled but relieved. "Hello! I don't suppose you could help me?"

"That's why I came down," said Suzanne. "I saw you looking anxious."

Julie smiled nervously. "Yes, well, I am, actually. I've just driven up from Kettering to find out what's happened to Anita. I'm Julie Bingham, her agent. She's not answering her phone or her doorbell. It's quite important."

"That's odd," said Suzanne. "My husband mentioned that for the last three mornings when he's got back from his early morning stroll he saw her window open, even though it was still quite chilly. Let's have a check."

She walked out onto the drive and the two ladies looked upwards.

"It's that window there look, at the end. Do you see it? Still open. You quite often see her looking down at you actually but come to think of it I haven't seen her for a few days. Shall we go up and knock on her door?"

"Please, yes. I'd really appreciate that."

The two of them went inside and up to the second floor. Their repeated knocking elicited no response, meaning that there was every chance that Anita could be lying unconscious on the floor having had a stroke or something. They agreed that they really ought to do something.

And so it came to pass that later that evening, after the police had gained entry to Anita's apartment and found it in a state of abandonment, that Anita Rackman joined Molly Baines on the missing persons list, and senior police officers began to consider the possibility that the two were linked.

CHAPTER 30 - SATURDAY

Saturday morning found two young gentlemen crouching at the bottom of a shaft, with another older gentleman looking down at them from above, suddenly worried that they would not come back and he would be the one left answering awkward questions. Lauren, glad if she never saw that hole again for as long as she lived, had returned to work, keen now to take her mind off the awful events of Tuesday afternoon and reassured that John would be the adult in the room on her behalf.

They'd agreed that Trey could have a quick look at the bottomless shaft before they headed in the other direction along the tunnel, so Trey led the way, Hoggo guiding from behind.

"Can you see it, mate?"

"Yeah, I think so. It looks blacker up there."

"Be really careful, yeah?"

Trey resisted the temptation to say that this hadn't occurred to him, and slowed his pace.

"Don't worry, I'm not planning on falling down it. Oh my good Lord, will you look at that."

His head torch had picked out the edges of the hole, and as he got closer, his anxiety levels rose. Still ten feet away, he stopped. "I'm not sure I want to go any further, mate. Don't need to really. It's a big hole, let's go."

"You can see how it goes up as well as down?"

"Yeah, I can. Right, turn round, chop chop."

"Alright, keep your hair on, it's not so easy for me."

Hoggo crushed himself into a ball and swivelled round 180 degrees, grunting a little to demonstrate the complexities of this manoeuvre. Trey did the same behind him, with a little more finesse.

"We'll call up to John," said Trey as they shuffled back.

Hoggo said nothing, presumably judging that no reply was needed.

They reached the vent, Hoggo passing under it so that Trey could stand up and see John.

"Everything all right?" called John as he spotted Trey's head emerging. "Did you see the shaft?"

"Yeah, good thanks," Trey called back. "Saw all I needed to see. You ready with the stopwatch?"

"Yep, you've got thirty minutes!" Any longer than that and he would be calling the authorities. Well, perhaps not immediately, but sooner or later. That might be easier than he had envisaged actually as he had noticed a police car parked in the drive just before he came across to Trey's flat – perhaps they were going to have another search of the woods.

"Ok!" replied Trey, crouching back down. He knew the score and didn't need John to remind him. The last thing he wanted were the authorities poking around, so he checked his watch, now set to stopwatch mode, and held his arm above him so that John could continue to be in no doubt as to the fact that he had a time measuring facility on his wrist.

"Starting the countdown now!" he said, pressing the screen. The thousands of a second started to cycle through at an alarming rate.

"Right, come on then, big man." He gave Hoggo a gentle shove on his back.

Hoggo was forced to jut his foot out to regain his balance. "Hey! Cut it out will ya? I'm adjusting me head torch."

"Sorry. The clock's started though."

"Only cos you started it." He got the angle of the beam as he wanted it then started to shuffle forward. "Ok, let's do it."

Trey was pleased that Hoggo was going first, but less so that he couldn't really see anything other than a big fat backside, keenly illuminated by his own head torch. He hoped Hoggo hadn't had baked beans or left-over curry (or worse, both) for breakfast, although knowing him that was extremely likely.

They had agreed to keep going for about 14 minutes, then turn back. Depending on what they found, they could always return another time. This was a sort of a test run.

As Hoggo had previously described, the tunnel, shiny wet in places but bone dry in others, soon began to curve to the right. The air was surprisingly fresh, seemingly being drawn from somewhere up ahead to the vent behind them, but after a while they were both breathing heavily thanks to the awkward way they were having to edge forward.

Trey was just about to tell Hoggo that they had reached ten minutes on his stopwatch when he heard "Hold up!" from the man in front.

"What's up?" he asked.

"Fork in the road, mate. Keep going."

Another thirty seconds and Trey saw what he meant. The tunnel split in two. It gave Trey enough room to draw alongside his companion.

"Wanna get your flashlight out?"

Hoggo rummaged in his pocket. "Yeah, let's get some proper light down there."

It was like switching from dipped headlights to full beam, virtually doubling the distance they could see down the left hand tunnel. It was clear now that about fifty yards ahead the tunnel abruptly plunged downwards, the roofline disappearing behind the ground level like an escalator.

"Don't like the look of that," said Hoggo. "Let's have a look at this one, then."

He swung the torch round to the right. Both men gasped.

Trey blinked. "Oh my God. Is that what I think it is up there?"

Hoggo glanced at him. "Depends what you think it is. I'd say it's a bloody great cave. We're definitely going this way."

Keeping his torch switched on now, Hoggo led the two of them through a section of tunnel before emerging into a circular cavern shaped like a large doughnut. It was approximately thirty five feet in diameter, and the roof was probably fifteen feet high.

This was much more rough-hewn, the rock having been hacked away with considerably less care than might be taken by a sculptor of Greek statues. Two more slightly larger tunnels, big enough to stand up in, led off it on the far side, the three passageways all roughly equidistant.

But this was not caught their attention as they stood upright and stretched their spines. It was the bones.

Scattered all around the open space, they gleamed white in the beams of their lights, thousands of them. Some were quite large, but most were small, and all around the edges of the cave they were pushed up against the walls in huge piles.

Trey could see that some were skulls – some small, once belonging to creatures unlikely to be much larger than a rat – but many of them a lot larger, the sort that could feasibly have once been covered by the face of a dog or even a deer.

"Shit," whispered Hoggo slowly, his eyebrows raised in horror. "This isn't good."

Trey swallowed. "No. It's really, really bad. We need to go back."

"Wait, what's that?" Hoggo pointed his torch at something black that was lying close to a larger pile of bones nearer the centre of the cave.

"Looks like a shoe," said Trey. "It can't be though."

They glanced at each other.

"Quickly, eh?" said Hoggo.

They picked their way through the bones, crunching some of the smaller ones underfoot.

Trey crouched down to get a closer look. "Oh my God. It's a black trainer, all chewed up. What was Anita wearing?"

Hoggo shrugged. "No idea. These bones though...... look, that one's like half a pelvis."

"Yeah, and that could be a thigh bone there, not that I'm an expert."

"Maybe from a horse?" muttered Hoggo. "Or a cow?"

"How would they get down here?"

"Maybe the miners in the old days cooked their meals in here."

"What, and dragged horses and cows through five foot high tunnels so they could cook them on an open fire? Then asphyxiate themselves with all the smoke?"

Hoggo shrugged again. "Alright mate, just a suggestion."

"Yeah I know. Also, though, some of these bones look almost new. Look, there's still bits on them."

"Don't say that. You're right though, it's gross. Can't see a human skull, though. That would confirm it."

"Not sure I want to. Could be under one of these piles. Let's go, eh?" Trey checked his watch. "We're twelve minutes in already."

"Try and stop me. I've seen enough to....." He stopped suddenly. "Did you hear that?"

Trey nodded. "It's coming from behind us. Could it be John?"

They stood stock still, listening. It was a low, distant, clacking rumble, but very rapidly getting louder.

Hoggo shook his head. "Nah, the volume wouldn't change if it was John. It must be coming from one of these tunnels."

"I think it's ours," said Trey, "where we've come from."

Curious, they started to retrace their steps, but the increasing volume of the noise quickly changed their minds. As one they stopped and then started backing away, looking around for cover.

"We've no choice," hissed Trey, "down one of these tunnels."

Hoggo shone his torch down each in turn. Neither one appeared to offer any great advantage. "Take one each!" said Hoggo. "Then if one of us gets in trouble the other can help. And turn your light off!"

"Yes, but if we both....." Trey began, but Hoggo was already leaping across the piles of bones and heading for the tunnel closest to him on the right.

There was no time to think. The rattling, rumbling noise was getting louder incredibly quickly, and definitely heading towards them. Trey was nearest the left hand tunnel so he veered over to it, kicking bones noisily in his desperation to escape from whatever was bearing down on them.

Each man reached their respective tunnel and fumbled to turn off their head torches. Stumbling any further would not only be too hard in the complete darkness, but also make too much noise; they had to stay where they were.

The sudden darkness amplified the feeling of overwhelming peril that now enveloped them, and Trey was experiencing a level of fear that was completely new to him - his 'flight or fight' adrenalin levels were like nothing he had ever experienced. Even though he couldn't see anything in the pitch dark he tried to focus his now useless eyes on where he thought the other tunnel entrance was, in the vague hope that as his vision adjusted he would be able to pick out some detail of whatever was about to enter the cavern.

As the thing got closer he could now hear a clamorous scrabbling that was accompanying the staccato rumbling, and he found himself pressing himself even harder against the side of the tunnel, trying to make himself less noticeable, in case whatever was coming could see in the dark.

He felt the breeze increase, as though air was being pushed forward, then with a sudden crescendo of noise and scattering of bones, something entered the cavern, and the rumbling noises abruptly stopped, replaced by a sticky silence. Then, slowly, a quieter, but scarier kind of sniffing, snuffling, and low grunting filled the cavern. It was obvious that this was some kind of animal, and a big one too.

He cursed himself internally for their stupidity in not bothering to bring any weapons with them. It hadn't seemed worth worrying about after Hoggo had come back safely from his first explorations.

Now there was a scratching noise, like someone running a metal whisk up and down a piece of slate, but accompanied by the sound of more bones slithering around the floor - scrabbling feet.

The sniffing grew louder, accompanied by more low grunts.

Trey closed his mouth, not wanting to breathe out any kind of odours that might give away his presence, particularly now that he could start to smell something himself. It was bitter, slightly rank. It reminded him of when his class at school went to an animal farm and they were taken to see a pen of pigs. It wasn't pleasant.

The noise stopped suddenly, as though the creature had detected something and was listening for the slightest of sounds.

Trey had never felt terror like he was feeling now. This was no computer game or film; it was real, undiluted fear of an imminent, violent death. A bead of sweat started running down his temple. Even raising his arm to brush it off might make a slight rustle, or displace the air such that this creature could sense it. He stood stock still, barely breathing. Still silence.

In the close, intense blackness his mind superimposed Lauren's tearful face, as she stood over his own still, mutilated body. His eyes started to well up, which was the last thing he needed right now. He brought his focus back. Should he run? All his survival instincts were telling him to, but his brain knew that this would seal his fate. He couldn't out-run this thing, especially in the dark. By the time he had switched his torch on he would be.....

An unexpected noise broke his train of thought. From the other tunnel Hoggo had broken wind. It wasn't a small, exquisite squeak either, but a real low, long snorter. The kind you can do nothing to prevent, and if you do try to stop it, it just makes it last longer.

Trey groaned internally. One of Hoggo's catchphrases was "Incoming!" shortly before letting one rip, but it wasn't so funny now. Whatever was in this cavern would know it had company, and where that company was. Trey could only imagine the panic Hoggo must be feeling now.

The silence held. Then without warning, there was a flurry of scratching and flying bones, some of them hitting Trey on the legs. From the other tunnel there was a loud thump, and almost immediately the cavern was filled by a dreadful, howling scream that could only have come from Hoggo.

Trey froze even stiller than he already was, his head pounding with panic. If he switched his light on, the creature would probably turn on him and he would be equally defenceless. There was nothing he could do to help his friend without putting himself in the same danger.

He flinched as some raucous scuffling was followed by a series of short yelps from Hoggo, then the sound of something cracking. A last despairing, rasping cry died in the air, chilling Trey to his core.

The scrabbling of feet instantly resumed, as did the guttural rumbling and ka-ka-ka noise. It grew quicker, but then rapidly more distant as it headed down the other tunnel. Within thirty seconds the sound had gone, and the humid, dark silence had returned.

All Trey could hear now was his suddenly-released heavy breathing, his chest heaving as he tried to control his state of mind and his terrorised emotions. There was no sound at all from the other tunnel, not even any groaning. He wanted to go and help his friend, but at the same time he couldn't afford to attract the creature back with a noise. He gave it another minute before turning on his head torch. His arc of light picked out a scene not dissimilar to the one they had seen before – bones all over the floor, although most now swept aside at the entrance to Hoggo's tunnel.

Feeling as relieved to still be alive as was possible when still clenched in a suffocating overcoat of fear, he crept across the open space of the cavern, desperately trying to avoid stepping on any other bones and so potentially alerting the now-distant creature to his presence. Who knew how good its hearing was?

As he neared the entrance of Hoggo's tunnel, he took a deep breath. Tears were blurring his vision. His mate Hoggo, who he'd been chatting with just minutes ago, could be lying there, broken and bloodied, and probably dead. This couldn't be happening.

His head torch illuminated the inside of the tunnel. It was empty. No sign of Hoggo at all. That was a sixteen stone man, carried off down that tunnel and out of sight in a matter of seconds. Whatever that creature was, it wasn't lacking in strength.

He directed his beam as far as he could up into the darkness, in case he could make out the shape of a body further on. But there was nothing other than the pitted ground surface. There was also nothing he could do, and he knew he had to get out of there, as quickly as he could.

He turned and swiftly but carefully picked his way through the bones on the floor until he got to the tunnel they had emerged from. Without stopping he stooped to enter it and stumbled along at as fast a pace as he could manage, hands outstretched on either side to steady himself against the cold, hard, scratchy walls.

It seemed so much further coming back than it had been in going. His breath was starting to appear in little puffs before his face as he put more and more exertion into forcing his legs forward.

He stopped a couple of times to listen, and see if he could hear that tell-tale rumble coming after him. To his relief there was just an eerie but extremely welcome silence. He did not wait any longer than he had to before continuing on his way.

All the while he was thinking of Hoggo: what had happened to him, how it could have happened, whether he was really dead or not, how his family would feel, what that creature was. His mind was falling over itself with competing thoughts, all of them awful.

At least he saw a patch of light up ahead, like heaven shining down a shaft of deliverance; his way out. The bottom of the ladder, sideways on to him on the left hand side of the tunnel, glinted enticingly in the light. He wanted to call out to John, but he dare not risk it, so he continued to focus on moving his feet as quickly as he could in short, fast steps.

The brightness was closer now, just yards away. He was sure he could hear that noise again, or was his brain playing tricks with him? He reached the ladder, squeezed round it and stood up, shaking the rungs gently.

"John!" he hissed. "I'm here. Quick!"

Nothing moved in the square of light above him. At least he must have imagined the noise – just standing there it was still quiet in the tunnel. He put his right foot on the first rung and started climbing but without anyone holding the top, the ladder fell backwards and clanged against the opposing wall. He didn't have enough of an angle to make it work.

But then a face appeared above. Thank God for that, thought Trey.

"Back already?" boomed John down the shaft. "You've only been twenty five minutes. I thought you'd want the full thirty. I was just looking at those tools on your workbench, sorry."

"Can you hold the ladder please?" pleaded Trey, annoyed that John couldn't see the urgency even though there was no reason why he should.

"Hang on. Right, there you go. Come on up."

Trey had never climbed a ladder so quickly in his life, and, watching him practically leap onto the cellar floor, it did not escape John's notice.

"Your pants on fire or something? What's the rush? And where's your friend?"

The look on Trey's face immediately told John that something bad had happened and now wasn't the time for jokes.

"What is it? Are you ok?"

Trey shook his head. "No, definitely not ok. It's Hoggo. He's almost certainly...... he's probably dead. He was attacked."

"What? How? By who?"

"There's a bloody great thing, an animal, down there. It attacked Hoggo. It must be huge."

"Didn't you see it?"

"No, we had to turn our torches off when we heard it coming. It made this sort of staccato grumbling noise. Didn't you hear it?"

"I did hear a noise like that actually, yes. At first I just thought it was a plane going overhead or something. It's funny, I remember hearing a noise like that before actually, but outside, round the front. Anyway, I was over by the workbench looking at those old tools. Then the ladder suddenly rattled quite violently just as the noise was loudest. I rushed over and looked down but there was nothing there. It didn't last very long. I thought maybe it was you, but obviously not. So I reckoned it must have been a gust of wind rattling the ladder."

"Well that was it, the animal. It lives down there. There's a sort of cavern that we got to, full of bones."

"Bones?"

"Yes, thousands of them. Mostly small ones, but a few big ones too, and get this, a shoe."

"What? A human's shoe?"

"What other kind of...... yes, a person's shoe! A black trainer, all chewed up. Anyway, then we heard the noise, we took cover in separate tunnels, and the animal turned up, sniffing for us. It was pitch black, couldn't see a thing. Then Hoggo goes and farts."

John had been carefully backing away from the shaft while Trey was speaking.

"Why did he do that?"

"It wasn't deliberate. Often with him it is, but there's no way he'd have let one rip deliberately like that, in that situation. It was a loud one, too. Nothing he could do about it, I guess. Then this creature hears it, of course, makes straight over to the tunnel Hoggo's in and attacks him. The screams....... it was terrible, John. Just.... terrible."

"My God. I'm so sorry. You said he was *probably* dead, though. Don't you know?"

Trey scratched the back of his head and ruffled his hair. "That's the other thing – he's not there anymore. He's gone."

"Gone? What do you mean?"

"The animal must have taken him."

"But he's a big guy."

"Exactly. And it was so quick. One minute, he's attacking Hoggo, the next minute, they're both gone. Whatever that thing is down there, it's incredibly strong. And it's carnivorous."

John leaned back on the workbench to support himself. "Oh my good Lord. This is unbelievable. We need to shut that trapdoor."

Trey looked across at it.

"To be honest, mate, whatever that thing was it has to have been too big to fit up there. When you hear it close up, it just sounds huge, like a bear. And we can't close it until we've got someone down there to find Hoggo."

"Absolutely. We have to call the police, and quickly."

John's words were like a bucket of cold water over Trey's head, as realisation dawned. Maybe Anita didn't drag herself off in the dark and fall down the big shaft – maybe she was grabbed by the animal and carried off to be eaten by it. That seemed much more likely now. Was that her shoe down there? If so, the police would find that and Anita's remains, and then it was all over for him and Lauren. Questions would be asked as to how she got down there, and there was only one obvious entrance. Maybe if they blamed Hoggo? But then why would Trey have gone down the shaft with him a few days later – that would make him an accessory to murder. This was all way too difficult. And in any case, there was no way Hoggo could have survived that attack. That rat didn't take prisoners. He changed tack.

"Trouble is, no-one's going to want to head down that vent, are they? Not with that thing down there."

John pursed his lips.

"You're right. I can't see the police or the fire service would want to rush down there after what you've just said. Professional cavers wouldn't either. That only leaves the Army, really, doesn't it?"

Trey paced over to the wall and back. "Look, I'll do it. I'll go and get a knife, a big one, and find that thing and kill it. And find Hoggo."

"So you do think he could be alive then?"

Trey let out a huge sigh and his shoulders slumped. "No. Not after what I heard. And with all those bones in the cavern..... me going down there again isn't going to bring him back. I'd just be trying to find what's left of his body. So what do we do then?"

"Start with the police I suppose and take it from there. Let them sort it out."

"I'll need to give Lauren a ring first."

"Why?"

"Just.... so she knows. That's all."

John paused before replying. "Alright. Come on then, no time to waste."

He headed for the door, Trey right behind him.

CHAPTER 31

"A giant *what*?"

"I don't know what it was, it was pitch black. But it was big enough to attack Hoggo and..." – his voice was cracking – "sorry......carry him off."

There was a short silence at the other end of the line as Lauren processed whether or not her husband was winding her up.

"This isn't a joke, is it? If it is, it's not funny."

"It's not, I promise. It's real. Honestly. It was horrific."

"This can't be real..... you said you're with John now?"

Trey looked across at a grim faced John, the very picture of impatience.

"Yes. And he wants to phone the police."

"Listen, I don't know what's going on, but I'm coming home," said Lauren in a tone that Trey knew would brook no argument. "Don't decide anything yet, ok? Stall him. Just…. just wait. I can't think straight at the moment – this is just terrible. You're not making that up about Hoggo?"

"No."

"Oh my God, poor Hoggo. That's just awful. We need to talk about what to do though, if John's there. I'll be as quick as I can. I just can't believe this, it can't be happening. Ok, right, I'm leaving now. See you later."

"Don't drive too qui….." started Trey, but the beep of the phone told him not to bother finishing his sentence.

He looked up at John. "Guess you got the gist of that. She's coming back. Said not to do anything until we've talked it through with her."

John looked at him strangely. "Why would she say that? Your friend has probably died, and she is asking that we don't do anything? And she's a nurse? How long will she be?"

"About forty minutes."

John shook his head. "That's too long. What is so vital that has to be discussed with her before we call the police? We can't wait. I know it's unlikely by the sound of things, but your friend could theoretically still be alive, badly injured."

Trey acknowledged the point with a wince and turned to face the lounge wall to give himself some thinking time. What the hell was he supposed to do now? If that shoe did belong to Anita, and, as it seemed likely, and the only working access to the tunnels was via their cellar, one way or the other it would be obvious that he and Lauren would have realised she was down there even if they denied pushing her, and they'd said nothing for four days now.

Hoggo's point about three people under interrogation not keeping to the same story was less valid now if there were only two of them left, but it was too late now. They'd done the equivalent of a hit and run, and would be facing a police tape recorder and an angle poise lamp in their eyes before you could say 'lengthy jail term'. Why hadn't he brought the shoe back with him? What an idiot. Unless he went back..... no, not with that creature down there, that wouldn't be worth the risk.

But then there was the blood, too. Yes, Hoggo had cleaned the large patch under the vent, but what about the rest of the tunnel? If the animal had been dragging her roughly along, there would be traces left everywhere. They hadn't thought of that.

As soon as they brought the cops in, all this would be forensically raked over. That wasn't good.

"Trey?"

It was clear that John didn't have to be Hercule Poirot to detect that something was up. It would be obvious something was up otherwise why was Trey even having to think about helping his friend?

Trey turned back to face him. "Sorry, John, I......"

He stalled.

"Yes?" prompted John. He was getting impatient.

"I'm in a dilemma. I don't know what to do."

John pulled his own phone out of his pocket and held it up in front of him.

"Dilemma or not, I'm calling them right now unless you tell me what's going on. I don't know about you but I don't want the death of a young man on my hands."

As Trey grimaced John raised his forefinger to his phone and started dialling.

"Wait!"

John looked up and paused.

"Are you going to tell me then?"

Trey let out a cry of frustration.

"I've got no choice, have I? This just goes from bad to worse! Why the hell did we ever go back down there? Lauren was right. I'm such an idiot. And now she's going to kill me for telling you."

"Telling me what?"

Trey sighed and took a deep breath. "What happened to Anita."

The hand with the phone in dropped slowly to John's side.

"You know what happened to Anita? Mel told me she had gone missing. But what's that got to do with……"

"Have a seat," said Trey, pointing at the sofa, "you might need it."

***

Being on the top floor, and in a converted attic with sound insulation installed very much as an afterthought, Norman was all too aware of any unexpected disturbances that occurred on the floor below.

Thus when, on Friday afternoon, some loud and repeated knocking downstairs started interfering with his enjoyment of the snooker on TV, he felt obliged to put it on mute and go and see what the fuss was about.

As 'getting involved' was not his forte, he merely eased open his front door a little to better hear what the commotion was about. In that way he became aware that Anita had gone missing, and the arrival of the police later that evening, forcing their way into Anita's flat with a loud bang, told him that his life was about to get complicated.

And so it was not a complete surprise when the following morning, just before ten o'clock, Norman spotted a police car crunching up the driveway. Weeding the border on the front lawn was supposed to help take his mind off Molly but it wasn't really doing that, and the arrival of the police did not really help in that regard either.

He watched out of the corner of his eye as a male and female officer emerged from the vehicle and gave him a quick glance before heading for the front door. They probably thought he was just the gardener, he thought, which of course was factually true.

He really didn't want to speak to them though. He didn't like speaking to anyone, let alone the cops. He'd probably get flustered and say the wrong thing and end up in handcuffs. He felt his heart rate rising and realised he was actually quite scared. Perhaps if he avoided them, they would leave him alone.

As Tony opened the big oak door and let them in, Norman started gathering up his tools and slowly placing them in his garden trug, where they nestled amongst the plucked weeds. Rising to his feet, he ambled around to the back of the house; he would be less conspicuous there.

He chose a spot behind a low wall, where an assortment of flowering shrubs and perennials jostled for supremacy. From there he could see over the wall towards the back of the house, but could also duck down a bit if he had to.

He wondered how long the police would be inside the house, presumably questioning all the residents, and hoped they would be done before lunch otherwise he was going to get hungry. With deliberate languor he began removing a few weeds; no sense in rushing.

After a while he wandered off down to the lower gardens, but the sound of voices brought him crouching back up to the low wall. From there he could see Trey and John, accompanied by a large blond chap, heading into the cellar.

There seemed to be a lot of things going on that cellar. Why was John involved? He can't be best friends with Trey already – the newcomers hadn't been here that long. Odd.

About half an hour later he was alerted by the noise of Trey and John, without the blond guy, trudging up the cellar steps to the back path, both looking extremely glum and saying nothing. They disappeared into Trey's flat. Curiouser and curiouser. He returned to the lower gardens, thinking he would leave it for another hour before going back around the front to see if the police car had gone yet.

***

"Well," said John, more as an exclamation of considered shock than a precursor to anything. He shook his head sadly. What Trey had told him was possibly the most incredible thing he had ever heard, if you took the word incredible by its literal meaning. He threw his hands up in the air slightly to register his befuddled state of mind and slapped them back down on his thighs.

"I don't know what to say."

Trey had been perched on the front edge of one of the dining chairs but now he stood up and walked over to the window, his stomach churning with worry. He had had to tell John; he had no choice. He had to protect Lauren, and himself too. Bring the police in now and he wouldn't be able to explain why Anita fell down a hole in their locked cellar, or why any of Anita's clothes that might be found down there had

Lauren's DNA on them - that was another thing. It all depended on John now. He turned back to look at the older man.

"You can see the dilemma. Look, John, Hoggo can't have survived that. Honestly. The way he screamed, then stopped suddenly, and the sound of bones cracking…….. whatever that thing is down there, it eats meat. It eats people. Hoggo's dead, he has to be."

His voice wavered at the finality of those words, and he realised that a one cheek was wet, so he quickly turned back to the window and brushed the tear away. How could he not be emotional now that the initial shock was starting to subside?

He had just lost a good friend, a guy who had put his neck on the line to help them. But despite that, this was no time for grief. He still had to convince John not to tell the police about Anita, especially with Lauren on her way home now.

He returned to the chair and stared intently at John.

"If we tell the police, they find that shoe, and no doubt some bones, and probably traces of blood along the tunnel, then put two and two together…. then that's the end of me and Lauren. One or both of us in jail for a very long time."

John, who had been staring at his lap, looked up slowly.

"It's not going to work. You can't hide Hoggo's disappearance too. He's probably told people where he went. His car's outside in the drive, for goodness sake. How do you explain that?"

Trey felt like someone had just closed the lid of a coffin on him as the sharp pang of realisation struck him in the solar plexus. John had a point. He hung his head.

"Shit," he muttered. "You're right. Ok. Ok. Maybe we've got no choice. But we don't have to tell them about Anita. If they find her shoe, we'll just have to cross that bridge when we come to it. Maybe it isn't even her shoe. Maybe….." his head started back up and his eyes widened "John, maybe that shoe belonged to the woman who went missing in the woods!"

John stared back at him. "I'd say that's entirely possible, but only if there was another entrance to that tunnel somewhere."

Trey's excitement ebbed out of him again.

"Oh. Crap. I hadn't thought about that. It would need to be a big entrance too, wouldn't it, and someone would have noticed it by now. Can't be then. No, hang on, that's wrong – there must be! How else would all of those bones got there?"

"I don't think it matters anyway."

"Why not?"

"If the police find human bones down there, they'll do DNA tests on them, won't they? If they match to Anita and find that blood you were talking about, that starts right under your vent, it won't matter whether that's her shoe or not."

Trey exhaled slowly and scratched an invented itch on the back of his neck. "You're right. So the only way out of this is to close the trapdoor, cover it up again, and.... No, that wouldn't explain Hoggo coming back to the cellar with a ladder. There's actually no frigging way out of this, is there?"

"Can't see one, I'm afraid."

"Unless......"

"What?"

Trey paused, reconsidered what he was about to say, then decided to say it anyway.

"We could say that Hoggo just wanted to store his ladder somewhere, which is why he came down to the cellar with it, then he had gone for a quick walk in the woods to stretch his legs, and not come back. That way he could have met the same fate as that other woman who they haven't found yet. And if they don't find him, no one is any the wiser. That would work! What do you think?"

John shook his head. "No. You should tell the truth."

"And send Lauren to jail? Or, more likely, both of us? Why would I do that?"

"Well, just because it is the right thing to do. Oh, and also because you might struggle to get that trapdoor closed again."

"What would you do in my shoes then?"

John grimaced and thought for a few seconds. "The same as you, probably."

"Exactly. You can see....."

The doorbell went.

Trey jumped, his heart suddenly racing.

"Who the hell is that?" he hissed rhetorically. "Can't be Lauren unless she's borrowed a Formula 1 car. Anyway, she has her own key."

John started to shrug but then realised that the visitors were probably the two words Trey least wanted to hear. "The police? That would explain the car outside. Maybe they're asking questions about Anita."

"Oh for Christ's sake, this is ridiculous. What do I do?"

"They would probably have heard our voices. If you don't answer...."

Trey nodded. This was it. Crunch time. Either John would back him up, or he would drop him in it.

"Think of Lauren, please, John," he pleaded as he backed out of the room before turning and walking into the hall. He slowed as he approached a front door that had now taken on the mantle of Gateway To Hell.

The doorbell rang again just as he put his hand on the door knob, urging him to get a move on. He took a deep breath and opened the door.

As John had predicted, two uniformed officers stood in front of him in their lumpy uniforms, looking appropriately grave.

The female officer, who could not have been much older than her mid twenties, was first to speak.

"Good morning, sir. We're just doing some enquiries regarding a lady who has been reported missing. She lives in this building on the second floor. Anita Rackman – do you know her?"

Trey tried his best not to look shifty.

"I met her briefly, yes," he replied. "We're new here, only moved in about ten days ago."

"Oh, right," said the police woman. She glanced at her colleague as though this was an unexpected development that they hadn't planned for. He nodded imperceptibly back. She turned back to Trey.

"Do you mind if we come in, just to ask a few routine questions?"

"Er, yes – I mean no. No I don't mind, that is. Sorry!"

He internally cursed his stumbled reply as he beckoned them in and closed the door behind them. Hardly the confident reply of an innocent man.

"Through here?" asked the policeman, his somewhat stout frame not flattered by an overjacket covered in pockets full of gadgets.

"Yes, straight ahead," said Trey. "My neighbour John is here too."

"Aha, two birds with one stone then!" said the police woman without looking at him.

Trey clocked their name badges as he showed them into the lounge. John was standing uneasily by the table, presumably hurriedly deciding on what he was going to say. He had the appearance of a man unsure as to whether or not he needed to go to the toilet, and smiled unconvincingly as the police officers came in.

"I'm John Firwell," he said, having heard Trey mention him and hoping to head off any immediate interrogation. "I live at number one, just across the atrium there."

He waved a hand in the general direction of the front door in case the officers were in any doubt as to how best to reach his apartment.

"Very good, sir," said PC Davis in the style that only policeman do, and certainly not because John's ownership of the apartment opposite merited a compliment.

"We'd just like to ask you both some general questions about Ms Rackman if that's ok."

"Yes, of course," said John, "fire away. Not literally of course."

Trey was not surprised that neither officer dissolved into fits of laughter at this well-worn wisecrack, and could tell that John immediately wished he hadn't said it.

"Shall we sit down?" asked PC Rakowska in a manner that favoured instruction over suggestion.

"Oh, yes, sorry," said Trey, "there's the sofa over there. John, you take the armchair, I'll grab a dining chair. Tea, anyone?"

PC Davis hurriedly shook his head as he sat down. "No, no, we're fine thanks. Shouldn't be long anyway. Now, can I ask you both when you last saw Ms Rackman?"

Trey hung back, willing John to speak first. Should he mention Anita coming down to ask him about doing her book cover? That was last weekend now. It might look a bit suspicious, him being alone with her. But then someone would have seen her after that, surely. Yes, that should be ok, as long as he didn't mention the cellar.

Fortunately John had caught their eye first and was now in the process of racking his brain. "Well we had that housewarming party back whenever-it-was but since then I'm not even sure I've seen her at all. It's usually just chance if we bump into each other."

PC Rakowska looked up from her notebook. "Housewarming party?"

"Last Saturday," interjected Trey. "For us. Anita was there. All the residents, in fact, except Norman."

"That's the chap in the attic flat, isn't it?"

"Yes."

The two officers exchanged glances.

"And you, Mr Clark? Was that when you last saw her too?"

Trey's insides jumped slightly, and not just through surprise at the formality of being called Mr Clark. He cleared his throat.

"I did see her once after that housewarming. She came round the day after, on the Sunday, to see some of my work. I'm a digital artist. She was an author."

"Was?" PC Davis looked curious.

Trey's stomach dropped. "Sorry, is, yes. Hopefully still is. I just thought that if she was missing then, well, you know. It's normally not good news."

"There's always hope, Mr Clark."

"Yes, of course; course there is. Sorry."

"She has only been missing a few days. So how long were you with her on the Saturday?"

"I'd say about ten to fifteen minutes, not long. I just showed her some of my work. Then she left."

"Did you agree to work with her?"

"No, she hadn't formally asked. She was going to go away and think about it."

"Did you notice anything unusual about her behaviour, anything that now you think about it could have been relevant to her disappearance?"

Trey appeared to think deeply before replying.

"Not really, no, but then I'd only known her a day. Also, her behaviour was already unusual, it seemed to me."

"In what way?"

"She was very in-your-face, you know? Didn't seem to know when to stop talking, or worry about what people thought. John?"

John was not expecting to have the conversation flung back in his direction.

"Anita? Oh, well, yes, she certainly didn't hold back. Bit batty if you ask me."

The two officers turned their focus back to John.

"Didn't not doesn't?" queried PC Davis. "You seem to be referring to her in the past tense too, Mr Firwell."

John blinked. "Did I? Oh, sorry, didn't mean to. Just a turn of phrase... you know." He did his best to hold the officer's gaze.

PC Davis gave him a curious look. "So, that being the case, was there anyone in the building who she might have annoyed?"

John shifted in his seat. "Possibly, but not enough to kill her, if that's what you mean."

He hadn't told them yet. And the fact that he hadn't told them, Trey thought, meant that he wasn't going to, surely, as that would look very odd indeed if he suddenly revealed the news now. He felt his armpits starting to get a bit sticky.

PC Davis stuck to his line of questioning. "So who might she have annoyed?"

John shrugged. "Anyone, really. She didn't seem to find it very difficult to do."

"Including you?"

John realised where this was going.

"Sometimes, yes, at our management meetings - the freeholder board meetings for the building. I'm the chairman, and it could be hard to get her to shut up or stick to the subject. That's all really, though."

"Any decisions that she objected to that might have peeved someone else?"

"If she was the only one it wouldn't matter anyway as we pass things on a majority vote."

"Supposing she had the deciding vote?"

"She doesn't – it's done on a show of hands. There's seven of us so we always get a decision. I think you're clutching at straws here, officer."

"If you pull at a short straw, sir, you sometimes find it is longer than you thought."

PC Rakowska turned to look at her colleague. "That's very good! I might write that down! Very profound, for you."

PC Davis's mask of formality briefly dissolved and the human emerged from underneath. "Thank you. I'm not just an ugly face you know."

He turned back to his two interviewees, his police demeanour switched back on.

"Right then gentlemen, is there anything else you could tell us that could be of assistance? Have you noticed anything strange in the last week or so? I appreciate that you will have seen police around the place due to the lady who went missing in the forest last weekend, so you don't need to refer to that. You will also appreciate that this is an additional reason why we need to follow up on what has happened to Ms Rackman."

"You think the two might be linked?" asked Trey hopefully. That could help throw them off the scent a bit, as he had not been anywhere near the woods.

"We are not ruling anything out at this stage."

Trey looked at John, hoping he wouldn't say anything. But he did.

"There is one thing."

"Yes?"

He looked at Trey, who was trying his best to send messages with his eyes that the officers wouldn't see.

"It's Trey's friend. He was here this morning."

Trey felt his stomach turning. This could be the sliding doors moment where his life veered onto a slippery slope he could never crawl back up.

"And....?" prompted PC Davis, not hugely impressed with the information provided so far.

John sighed. "Trey, you tell them. He's your friend, not mine."

Trey tried not to look relieved. Thank you John, thank you, thank you.

"Yes, it's my mate, Hoggo. He's not come back."

"What do you mean?"

"He went out for a walk in the woods to clear his head about an hour ago. Said he'd only be ten minutes."

"You said Hoggo? Not his real name I take it?"

"No, sorry, it's Darren Hoggsmith. He's a big guy, about 6'3", blond hair. To be fair, he's not the world's best timekeeper, but he should definitely have been back by now."

"Did he come by car?"

"Yes."

"Is his car still there?"

Trey only just stopped himself saying yes and then being unable to explain how he knew.

"I can have a quick look if you like."

"If you would."

Trey avoided looking at John and retreated into the bedroom. There was no point looking out of the window but he did so anyway, just so that he could say that he had. By pressing his face up against the glass he could look far enough along the parking area and sure enough, there was Hoggo's Mondeo, now freshly bereaved.

He walked back into the lounge.

"Still there. Although I don't think he'd have just driven off without saying goodbye."

PC Davis grunted and levered himself to his feet. His colleague immediately followed suit, as did Trey and John, as to do otherwise would have seemed strange.

"Well," he said, "we do seem to have a lot of people going missing around this place, don't we? We'll have a quick scout round and see if we can find your mate, but if we can't, and he hasn't returned by the middle of this afternoon, give us a ring at the station would you?"

"Yes, of course," said Trey. John just nodded silently, his face impassive, his thoughts less so.

"Now, Mr Firwell, we haven't spoken to your wife yet. Is she at home?"

John seemed surprised that they would need to speak to her. "She's not, no, but I can assure you that she has nothing to do with...."

"Yes, no doubt," interrupted PC Davis, "but she may have seen something you haven't."

"I'm sure she would have told me."

"Quite probably, but that won't stop us asking her a few questions."

John realised that he wasn't sure why he was arguing other than for the inconvenience of having the police knocking on his door again, so he backed down.

"She'll be back around mid-afternoon, probably. So any time after that would be fine. Or tomorrow – I don't think she's going out."

"Thank you," said PC Davis, managing to make it sound like an admonishment.

PC Rakowska folded her notebook and tucked it into a pocket. "There's one household we haven't spoken to yet. Mr Baston on the top floor. His van's still in the car park so I don't suppose you know where he might be?"

"Probably in the garden," said John. "He maintains the grounds here in his spare time."

"Oh! Right. Was that him we saw in the front garden, then, when we came in? Brown hair, big beard?"

"Yes, that's him. He doesn't say much, just so you know. Keeps away from people. Amiable enough, though, and does a good job with the garden."

Trey could almost see the cogs whirring in the officers' brains as they added all the clues together regarding the strange man who lived in the attic. Poor old Norman might end up as a suspect, but what could Trey do? He could only stop that happening by confessing everything and throwing his wife under the bus, to use an unfortunate metaphor, and he wasn't going to do that yet.

"Thank you," said PC Davis. He looked at PC Rakowska. "Right then, time for a wander around to see if we can find this friend of yours. And Mr Baston, of course. We'll be in touch if we need to speak to you again. We'll see ourselves out."

When they had gone Trey whistled softly.

"Thank God for that. John, thank you so much. Lauren will be so grateful." He glanced at his watch. "Actually she should be here soon. Do you want to stay on until she gets back?"

John had been staring at the floor, looking troubled.

"No..... no, I won't," he said. He moved towards the door, then stopped and gave Trey a long hard stare.

"I'm not happy about this you know. I'm effectively perverting the course of justice by going along with this. I'm not being funny but I've only known you both for a week or two and, no offence, but we aren't best friends or anything. So I'm questioning what I'm doing. Just so as you know. After all, what happens now?"

"What do you mean?" Trey's heart was beginning to sink again.

"Well, they won't find your mate, will they? His car will still be here tomorrow, and the day after. When they declare him missing that will be three people in quick succession who've all disappeared into thin air around this building. And we – us two, and Lauren - know what happened to at least two of them. It stinks, Trey, it really does. How I've got myself dragged into all this I don't know. Well, I do, obviously, it's that bloody trapdoor."

"Wish I'd never sold that coal," muttered Trey.

"When Lauren gets back you two have a serious chat. Think about what you are doing here. You're digging yourself a huge hole, and that's not meant to be funny. And we haven't even talked about that bloody great animal thundering around under the foundations of our building. That needs investigating too, if it's dragging people out of the forest."

"We don't know that."

"No, but it would be a remarkable coincidence otherwise."

"True."

"So my guess is that there must be another exit somewhere, possibly in the woods."

"The police would have found it, wouldn't they, with all the searching they did?"

John sighed. "You would have thought so. Anyway, think on, and let me know what you decide."

"You won't tell Melanie will you? The fewer people know about this the better."

John ran a hand through his hair. "I don't know. I might need someone to talk it through with."

Seeing a look of horror start to appear on Trey's face he added "but if I tell her then she becomes an accessory to the crime too unless she calls in the police immediately. And then that puts me in the frame too for withholding evidence in our chat with the cops just now. I'm going to have to weigh this all up. Whichever way you look at it, it's not good. In fact, it's bloody awful."

"I appreciate the position you're in, but please, for Lauren's sake, don't tell Mel."

"I'm sorry to say this but I don't really owe you or Lauren any favours, Trey. In fact at the moment you owe me. So all I can say is that I'll think about it, ok?"

He raised a schoolmasterly eyebrow for emphasis, then turned and disappeared into the hall before Trey could respond. The front door clicked shut.

Trey stumbled back into the lounge and collapsed onto the sofa as though someone had thrown him onto it. What had happened to his life? One minute exciting new home, everything ahead of them, the next, well, unmitigated disaster. And it felt like it was only going to get worse.

CHAPTER 32

"Tell me this isn't true, please, babes. Not Hoggo as well! Please say you've found him and he's ok."

Lauren had flown through the front door and was flinging her coat on the table as she spoke.

Trey stood awkwardly in the middle of the room and shook his head. "No, he's gone. The animal got him."

"Oh my God. So you're telling me there's a giant animal living in a tunnel under our house, and it's killed Hoggo? That's what you're saying."

"Yes. I know, it sounds mad, but honest, there is. I was lucky to get out of there alive."

"How did… I mean, Hoggo's big enough to fight it off, isn't he? I can't believe it. I was hoping… well, you know. I was driving back and I could hardly see for the tears…. praying it wasn't true. This is awful."

"I know."

"And what's this about you telling John? What happened? He didn't phone the police, did he?"

"No, but….."

"But what?"

"I had to tell him about Anita."

Lauren's eyes opened wide. "What? Why?"

"I had to. He would have phoned the police otherwise."

Lauren walked over to the sofa. "Yes, but, and I don't feel good saying this, without Hoggo that means there are no other witnesses to what happened to Anita – just us two. We could have shut that trapdoor and come up with any story we wanted. How could you be so…. so stupid to tell John? This is all we need!"

She grabbed a cushion for no particular reason other than to throw it forcefully back onto the sofa, which she now duly did, emitting as she did so an anguished cry of frustration. "It's just one bloody thing after another!"

Trey wasn't going to back down on this one. "What would you have done then, eh? John, with his phone in his hand, about to dial 999? Twenty minutes later police turning up in force and swarming all over the place, interrogating us? I had no choice. How would you have stopped him, then?"

The question hung in the air for a few seconds as Lauren processed it. "I would have made something up," was the best she could muster.

"What?"

"I'd have thought of something." She wasn't shouting so loudly now.

"There was no time! It had to be weighty, too. I couldn't just say 'oh we would rather you didn't report Hoggo's horrible death, John, because Lauren is allergic to policemen,' or something. I had to say something plausible, and quickly; give him a damned good reason why we'd rather not bring the cops in right now. The truth was all I could think of."

"And where's John now? What did he say?"

"He's back in his flat, thinking about it. He's not happy, obviously."

"So we are not out of the woods yet."

"No."

Lauren walked over to the armchair and flopped into it. "Look, I'm sorry I shouted at you, ok? My emotions are all over the place. I can't believe I'm saying this but Hoggo's dead, and all because you had to have your harebrained boys' adventure, which I warned you not to do. He'll have a family – parents who brought him up, probably a girlfriend. Think what that's going to do to them! Then you nearly get yourself killed too, and you tell me there's a man-eating creature under our flat. That's bad enough, but now…. now you've told John. And he'll tell Mel. He's bound to, isn't he? Or he'll decide to phone the police anyway. And once that happens, I'm in jail. I murdered Anita, Trey. I'm a murderer!"

"Keep your voice down will you? Do you want the whole house to hear? Jesus! And you're not a murderer, it was an accident, and you know it was."

"Yes, but we didn't tell the police."

"I know. We all agreed though."

"We should have told them. Why did we ever agree to hush it up? You're right, it was an accident – we could have said that."

"They'd still have done you for manslaughter though. Pushing someone back right next to a mining shaft – they'd argue that you should have known she could have fallen down it."

Lauren began to look indignant. "How could I have known that….. oh sod it, you're probably right. It's a mess."

She had returned to normal volume now, slumped back in the chair, head up, staring at the ceiling.

"Unless we had just said that she had stumbled of her own accord and fall in. Why did we not say that?"

"Remember we talked about that with Hoggo after it happened? He was saying that if you come up with a lie like that, and there are three of you all telling the same lie, the cops are good at wheedling out inconsistencies when they interview you separately. If our accounts don't exactly match up, they get suspicious. That's why he didn't want to go down that route – too risky. Even with just the two of us now it's dodgy. Also, the chance they'd find your DNA on her clothes."

Lauren sighed. "I remember now." She said nothing for a while, then brought her gaze back down to the carpet. "I can't believe Hoggo's gone, can you? I'm so sorry. He was your friend. And he was being a friend, too, helping you out like that. He didn't have to go down that shaft."

"Yeah, I know. If I'm honest, I'm really struggling with it. Being there, too, when he screamed. It was so bad, babes, really bad."

Lauren brought her gaze back down from the ceiling and looked across at her husband. She got up, walked over, and gave him a hug.

"I'm sorry. I hadn't really thought about what you are going through. I'm just so tied up in my head with this. Me going to prison. I couldn't do that. Just couldn't."

Trey stroked her hair. "I know. I know. We can't let that happen."

That was easy to say, less so to action – they both knew that. The two of them stood there, holding each other, each thinking how this could be the last time they could do this if John had now spilled the beans and the police suddenly burst in and arrested them.

Lauren pushed herself gently back and looked at Trey. Tears were streaming down her face.

"What are we going to do?"

Trey was also struggling to stay composed, and his eyes were moist. "We have to stop John telling anyone. We can still run with the story about Hoggo taking a walk in the woods then disappearing. That ties in with the tramp lady who did the same thing."

Lauren nodded eagerly and a tear from an eyelash splashed onto Trey's shirt.

"Yes, and then all that's left is to close that trapdoor and cover it up again. Then no one will be any the wiser."

"Right. Except for John."

"Yes. John......."

There was a silence as each tried to read the other's mind, not wanting to say it first.

Trey felt obliged to at least air the thought.

"If John was out of the equation.....?"

Lauren pretended to be shocked, even though she had very briefly entertained the same thought before immediately dismissing it.

"No, Trey, you can't say that. If that's what you mean?"

Trey's hands had slipped down to the nape of Lauren's back but now he let go, stepped back, and instead grabbed her hands, his eyes focused on hers.

"I love you. I can't lose you, and I'll do anything to make sure of that. Anything."

Lauren attempted a smile through her tears.

"That's so sweet, thank you. But what are you saying?"

Trey glanced up at the ceiling, wondering how he could possibly be saying what he was about to say. He looked down again, back into Lauren's eyes.

"The trapdoor. We can't close it without getting that ladder out and I can't do it on my own. I'll need some help and John is really the only person we can ask. Supposing, as we were getting the ladder out, that he were to accidentally slip and fall down the hole? Then we close the door and that creature will do the rest."

Lauren shook her head emphatically.

"No, we can't do that. Definitely not. That really would be murder. That's wrong, so wrong. He's done nothing to harm us."

"No, but he could. And we will have that hanging over us for the rest of our lives. One little slip when he's downed a few too many pints and that could be it for us, game over, just when we thought it was safe to breathe again. We'd probably both end up in prison and not see each other for years."

"I know, but I couldn't live with that on my conscience."

"You already have Anita on your conscience."

"But this would be deliberate. That's different. Oh my God, what's happening to us, even talking about stuff like this? We're supposed to be good people!"

"Are we though? We deliberately left Anita down there without being a hundred per cent certain she was dead."

"She did look dead though. She must have been. Look, I'm just playing devil's advocate about John, looking at every option. There's no way I want to be a murderer, and it sounds mad even saying that. It's just.... well, you know."

Lauren shook herself free and wandered over to the lounge window. She watched a robin dart from wall to bush and back again, its little head constantly flitting from one direction to another, always alert to danger. Suddenly it was gone, flown away in an instant. Free as a bird, she thought. That meant such a lot.

"Do you think John will tell Mel?" she asked without turning.

Trey shrugged. "No idea. But if he does, I can't see Mel doing nothing about it."

Lauren said nothing and Trey knew not to prompt her. She needed time. When she did speak, it was not what he expected to hear.

"There are two police officers coming up from the woods. And they've got Norman. He looks like he's handcuffed."

CHAPTER 33

Norman had crept round to the front of the house and the police car was still there. Should he risk heading up to his flat? Perhaps the police had already knocked on his door and were now inside another apartment. But then they could come out just as he was creeping up. The thought scared him. He had nothing to hide though, did he? He'd done nothing wrong, not really.

Trouble is, he'd seen police dramas on TV. He knew how they could 'fit you up' and he had given them a head start because he was in the woods when Molly went missing. And then he didn't tell anyone. So maybe he had done something wrong after all. No, better that he avoided them. Then, by the time they got round to seeing him, they might have found the real murderer.

He reversed back into the rear garden, an idea forming. He'd go for a walk in the woods, now that the police had opened them again, and then hopefully they would be gone by the time he came back. He moved carefully around the edges of the garden and headed towards the gap in the wall that led to the forest.

***

"Yep, they're the two that interviewed us," said Trey, his head pressed up against the window next to Lauren's. "They went to look for Hoggo. Wild goose chase, obviously, but looks like they found Norman instead."

"But why would they handcuff..... oh, you don't think they think Norman's killed Hoggo in the woods?"

Trey watched as the group of three marched up the path. Norman had an expression of startled bemusement.

"Poor guy, he was in the wrong place at the wrong time. How was he to know they'd be searching the woods again? Not sure what he was doing in there, though."

"Mmmm," said Lauren, "maybe he was hiding from them. Why would he do that though? Let's go and have a look out the front."

The two of them made haste to the front bedroom and watched as Norman was bundled into the back seat of the police car and the door closed on him.

"Perhaps he did have something to do with that lady in the woods who disappeared," said Trey. "They wouldn't arrest him just for having a walk."

"Maybe he did. It's not likely though, is it? Not with those creatures down there."

"Creatures? There's only one of them."

Lauren looked at him as though he were a primary school pupil.

"You do know how biology works? There won't be just one of those things."

That was a good point; he hadn't thought of that. He watched the police car crunch down the drive and out of the entrance gate.

"It could be the last one of its kind. Like Nessie."

"You know there's no proof that the Loch Ness Monster is real. This thing is, according to you. Whatever they are, they've probably been down there for centuries, breeding away."

"How did they get so big, though? Underground animals are pretty much all small, aren't they?"

"I don't know. I'm sure there were big burrowing things in the age of the dinosaurs."

Lauren turned from the window and headed back to the lounge, continuing her train of thought as Trey followed her.

"Maybe these creatures are like crocodiles and survived the meteor that killed off all the other dinosaurs. They were underground so weren't affected. And they've somehow carried on for millions of years without mankind being aware of them."

"Seems unlikely, doesn't it?" said Trey, "especially seeing how big they are."

Lauren reached the lounge and turned suddenly to face him, stopping him in this tracks.

"You haven't actually seen it though, have you? So you don't really know how big it is."

"No," admitted Trey, "but nothing small could have moved Hoggo that quickly down that tunnel. It has to be colossally strong. The noise it made, too. And I could sort of feel it as it scuttled around in that cavern, breathing and grunting. No, it was big and scary. Definitely not small."

Lauren shuddered slightly. "We need to get that trapdoor closed."

"Yes. Although if it's any consolation, I don't think there's any way it would fit up that shaft."

"There might be baby ones. Or juveniles, anyway."

Trey's eyes widened. "Oh shit, I hadn't thought of that. You're right. Although it's been open all this time – we'd be unlucky if a teenage animal came rushing up that ladder in the next hour or so. I doubt they can climb ladders anyway."

"They've got themselves up that bottomless hole you talked about haven't they? How would they do that?"

"No idea. Must be through gripping the sides with their claws somehow. That's probably what's smoothed the sides over the years. A smaller one could have trouble doing that. Although.... it could come from the other direction I suppose."

Lauren plonked herself onto the sofa and flung her head back with her mouth open, before focusing back on Trey.

"This is just so ridiculous, isn't it? Nothing makes sense. Massive carnivorous underground animals the size of bears roaming around in tunnels under peaceful Derbyshire villages? It's like something out of a horror film, not real life. Also, they can't have been down there for thousands or millions of years if those tunnels were originally mines constructed in the last few hundred years. Why didn't the miners come across them?"

"Maybe they did, and that's why they closed the mine."

"What, and said no more about it?"

Trey fell into the armchair and shrugged. "Maybe the animals found the mines after the men had left. Maybe they've got a bigger network of tunnels somewhere else, that they constructed themselves and they just happened to dig into the mines recently. I don't know. None of us know."

Lauren nodded. "Yeah, that's a lot of maybes. We just know that we don't know."

Trey thought for a minute. "We should give it a name, really, shouldn't we?"

"What, like 'Dave'?

"No, something official. Like the Clarkosaurus – named after us."

"That sounds terrible."

"Yeah, it does. Scratch that, then."

"Also, it can only be a 'saurus' if it's a dinosaur. I've not heard of any living sauruses."

"This could be the first one. But yeah, ok, maybe that's unlikely. You'd think it must be a mole or a rat of some description, or a cross between them."

Lauren shrugged. "I don't really care what it's called, to be honest."

"Ok, well I'll name it then. I need another word for 'big'. Massive, colossal, huge, gigantic..... massamole. No. Gigantarat?"

"Look, just keep it simple and call it a gigarat, ok? Hard 'g' though, not like a jig. Like computer storage. There, done."

Trey smiled. Despite not caring what it was called, Lauren had quickly come up with a good name for it. The beast was now a gigarat until some scientist decreed otherwise.

"I like it! Gigarat it is."

"Good." Lauren, accustomed to being on her feet all day and slightly on edge sitting down during the day time, rose to her feet. "So what do you want to do now?"

"Eat! I'm starving – can we have lunch first? Then I'll have to get John over to help with that door, if he'll do it. Should be a bit easier to close it than open it."

Lauren checked her watch. "Yeah, it's 12:30 already. Pot noodle ok? I don't feel like making a sandwich."

"Yep, thanks, that's fine, anything will do. Need a hand?"

"Strange how you only offer when there's nothing to do."

Trey smiled. She was right, he hated cooking, and wouldn't have volunteered his services if there'd been much more to the recipe than switching the kettle on.

He shrugged. "At least I offered."

"Better than a poke in the eye, I suppose. Not by much though."

Lauren flashed him a tired grin then headed into the kitchen while Trey gave some more thought about what he was going to do about John.

***

The glossy white tiles of the wall opposite reflected a grim silence. Norman stared at them from his built-in bench seat. The police cell was functional in the sense that it had four walls to prevent you wandering off and a heavy metal door with a viewing hole in it, but not so functional that it allowed you to perform any function other than to sit there and reflect on your misdeeds. A grilled window looked out onto something, but he didn't know what, as the glass was obscure.

There was a shiny metal toilet in the corner that could not be seen from the door. Norman gained momentary amusement from considering what a guest to your home would think if they visited your bathroom and discovered one of those models awaiting them.

But mainly he thought about what had happened in the forest. How he had been on his way back along the woodland path when he saw two figures approaching in the distance. By the time he had worked out that they were police officers, they had spotted him.

If he sprinted off, he knew his fate would be sealed – they would be straight after him. He decided to bluff it out and hope they hadn't remembered him from when they first arrived at the house, but that tactic hadn't worked, as they had.

They even knew his name. Then they bombarded him with questions and he got flustered. Why was he out here in the forest? Why didn't he go to that housewarming party? What was his relationship with Anita? Did he know Molly? How often did he come to the woods? Who had he bumped into this morning? Had he seen a tall guy with blond hair?

So many questions, one after the other. It reminded him of when he was bullied at school and he didn't like it. He got mixed up and stumbled to reply. He couldn't tell them the truth now, it was too late for that, so he said the first things that came into his head, and even as he said them he realised that they weren't very plausible.

It was clear these police officers weren't impressed either. "Doesn't add up," said one of them, and before he knew it they had handcuffed him and started marching him towards the house, to be taken in for questioning. That wasn't nice. Especially when he had to walk past all those windows – he was sure that every resident was watching.

And now here he was, an innocent man, feeling very guilty but not sure why, imprisoned in a cell. He wondered what his mother would think if she were still alive. She was the last person left who he could really confide in – he wasn't that close to his younger sister and when they were both very young their father had upped sticks and started a new life in Thailand with some other woman he met on holiday. Much younger than him, apparently. For Norman being lonely had become a way of life but, apart from not having his Mum for the last six years now, he preferred it that way.

Perhaps he should call his sister, if they would let him. But what would she do? Tell him he was a fool, probably, and he didn't need that. He decided that there was only one way out. He would have to tell the truth.

Then if they believed him, great. If they didn't, well, they had no evidence to show that he had killed anyone, did they? Surely that meant that they couldn't lock him up?

Yes, that is what he would do. He glanced up at the window then back at the wall. Not much of a view wherever you looked. Not even any plants he could look at out of the window - even a few weeds would have been better than nothing.

He stood up, walked around a bit, then sat down again. How long did they say they would be? He couldn't remember. The bench had a very thin blue plastic mattress on it so he lay down, and within five minutes had drifted into a troubled sleep.

CHAPTER 34

John checked his watch.

"Mel's going to be back soon. Well, in about half an hour anyway. Oh sod it, ok, I'll come. We need to seal that tunnel off. The last thing we need is some man-eating rat-mutant emerging into your cellar and rampaging around Ridley Manor."

Trey doubted it would do that but he went along with it.

"Thanks John. Lauren's going to help too so between the three of us we should be able to get the ladder out and the trapdoor levered shut. It'll be easier than opening it."

"It better be. Hang on, I'll just get my shoes on."

The door closed slightly and a minute later John emerged, suitably shod and jacketed. "Let's go!"

Trey nodded and the two of them walked across the atrium floor, into his apartment, and out into the garden, having collected Lauren on the way.

As Lauren opened the cellar door, Trey looked at John.

"Have you decided yet?"

"Decided what?"

"Whether or not to tell Mel about Anita."

John hesitated. "Let's get this trapdoor closed first, eh? Then we can talk about that."

Trey nodded but he didn't like the sound of it. To him that implied bad news, that John was going to tell Mel. That was not the right answer, John.

The three of them cautiously entered the cellar, wary of being assailed by a ravenous four legged visitor.

The room was empty though. The hole in the floor was no longer the portal to an exciting adventure, but a dreadful pit, an opening into a nightmare that had to be closed and sealed forever. The two men walked over to it.

Trey found himself whispering. It could have been noise that brought the creature hurtling along the tunnels and shafts to find them, so who knew how acute its hearing was.

"If you go that side, then I'll lift the ladder up and you can pull up the overlapping sections and turn it into an 8 ft ladder again."

John grunted an agreement. Between them they hauled up the lower sections and hooked them back into place.

"Right," said Trey, "if you can angle the ladder forward and hold onto it, I'll pull it from this end and try to scrape it along the ceiling here, between the beams. I'm hoping it will come out more easily than it went in."

John nodded. "Right."

Trey pulled at the top of the ladder then angled it diagonally as much as he could until the top reached the underneath of the floorboards. Naturally it became stuck, as before. As with almost all situations like this, the process of getting it out appeared even less straightforward then when getting it in.

"This is ridiculous," muttered Trey as he tried a couple of fruitless and slightly painful punches with the palm of his hand. "It went in, so it must come out. I thought we'd created a path for it."

"Hammer?" suggested Lauren.

"Yeah, go on then. I'll use that piece of wood again, too – just there, on the workbench."

"And maybe quickly too," suggested John, who was now kneeling on the hard floor as he held the ladder up, and was regretting the effect it was having on his knees.

Lauren dashed across to the workbench and back, and handed the hammer and wood to Trey. He lined the little block of wood up against each foot of the ladder in turn, striking hard with the hammer and adding to the gouges in the wood from last time as the struts jarred and scraped their way along the wood. Five minutes of hard hammering and increasing moans form John, then suddenly it was free and could be pulled up and out of the shaft and laid on the floor.

"Success!" exclaimed Trey, rather unnecessarily. "That was painful. Shall we have one last look down, now that nothing can get up?"

He walked over to the workbench and got the torch.

"No thanks," said Lauren, stepping back.

Trey stepped over the ladder and shone the torch down the shaft. It was highly unlikely a slavering creature would be down there looking up at him – for a start they would have heard it coming. But you never knew.

As expected all that the torch picked out was the floor of the tunnel below. John, peering down from the other side, looked up at him.

"I suppose you want to close the trapdoor now?"

"Yep," said Trey, ignoring the tone in John's voice. "Let's do it."

On the other side of the hole, John began getting to his feet, announcing this manoeuvre with a series of bad-tempered grunts. It was bad enough that getting up off the floor took longer every year that his body aged and waistline expanded, but the task had also been exacerbated by how long he had been forced to stay kneeling. He didn't realise that he had developed a nasty case of dead leg, and as he pushed up on his right leg, it buckled.

A look of alarm spread across his face as he fell forwards and assumed the shape of a man kneeling, but with only the black gape of the shaft below him. As his knees descended he instinctively threw his arms forward, the right hand successfully latching onto Trey's ankle, the left hand grasping the edge of the hole. He held position, with elbows on the edge of the shaft, for less than a second before they were scraped off and downwards by the weight of his own body, such that only his clutching, white knuckled hands remained visible above ground.

Trey felt his left foot being yanked from under him, and he fell hard onto his back with a loud cry as the torch went flying. Instinctively he dug his right foot into the ground and the slight lip that was the edge of the shaft, pushing as hard as he could to stop himself sliding any further towards the hole. All thoughts of saving his neighbour became secondary to saving himself. "Let go!" he shouted, "you're dragging me in!"

With a scream Lauren rushed forward and grasped one of Trey's hands, simultaneously reaching out with her other hand and grabbing the handle of the vice attached the workbench.

This gave her just enough leverage to hold Trey still, and therefore John as well. For a few moments they all held their positions, straining every sinew. As thought fought to overcome panic, John began scrabbling his feet against the walls of the shaft, and with a Herculean effort he managed to haul himself a little upwards by pulling hard on Trey's leg and the edge of the shaft. His head and one elbow appeared above the hole.

"Grab my arm," he grunted, although it was not clear who was in a position to do this.

But Lauren was struggling now to hold the weight - her fingers were slipping from the handle of the vice. "I can't hold on!" she screamed, "I'm going to have to let go!"

Trey braced his right leg even harder against the floor of the cellar. Could he still hold John when Lauren released her grip? He couldn't see how. And if she let go of the vice and kept hold of him, he had visions of all three of them being swallowed into the shaft. He had to act fast, in the last moments that Lauren's grip was still giving him some leverage. He clenched Lauren's hand even tighter, then brought his right leg back and launched it, hard, into John's face, twice in quick succession.

The second kick broke John's nose and he cried out in pain, screaming an obscenity. In an instinctive effort to defend himself from the leg attacking him, John's left hand let go of the edge of the shaft, but this immediately transferred all of his considerable weight onto Trey's ankle. Lauren had no choice but to immediately let go of the vice, and, as she was pulled violently forwards, Trey too. John, still holding onto Trey, disappeared downwards, causing Trey to be sucked in after his neighbour like a log going over a waterfall. He slapped his chest painfully onto the opposite wall of the shaft, his nose just missing the lip of the shaft before he plummeted after John into the darkness.

Shock turned to panic as Trey felt his hair brushing the edge of the shaft, heard Lauren's cry of horror, felt the rush of air and the drop in his stomach, and then.... nothing.

Lauren rushed to the side of the shaft, screaming.

"Trey! Trey!"

She grabbed the torch that was lying on the floor and fumbled to switch it on, tears streaming down her face.

"No, no, no. Not you too. Please, no. Trey!"

Frantically, she aimed the torch down the hole, not wanting to look but having no choice. A jumble of arms and legs were lit up, some of them twitching and moving slightly.

"Trey!" Then she remembered. Noise could attract the creature. And that was the other thing now. Even if the two men had survived the fall, they were still in mortal danger. Sobbing uncontrollably, she moved the torch around, trying to focus on her husband, who seemed to have landed on top of John but was facing down, his head lying on John's upper back. His legs were moving slightly – he was still alive, thank God.

"Trey" she hissed, softly. "Trey!"

His right arm was moving a bit more now.

She had to get him out. But now they'd gone and removed the ladder! A rope, maybe.... but she didn't have one and in any case how would he attached himself to it if he was unconscious, or conscious and injured?

She needed help. Her own situation didn't matter any more. She wouldn't care if she went to prison if it meant saving Trey's life.

She heard a groan from down below.

It was definitely Trey - from what she could see John wasn't moving at all. And now Trey's head was lifting slightly.

"Trey!"

Another groan, some more movement, then he was still for a few seconds. Suddenly, he was awake, jump-started by his consciousness. He weakly attempt to scramble into a seated position, perhaps still to realise, in his dazed state, that the seat was John's body.

A wave of relief washed through Lauren, her tears now suffused with hope. He was ok, he'd survived! Realising he would not want to look up into a blinding torch light, she aimed it to one side.

"Babes, are you ok?"

She could see him rubbing his head, dazed and confused. He raised his head and tried to speak but only a croak came out. He cleared his throat and tried again.

"My head hurts. And my left arm. And my hip. That really hurts. And my chest is painful too."

"Have you broken anything?"

"Don't think so. Mostly bumps and bruises I think. Oh God – John."

He'd realised what he was sitting on and tried to stand up, but his legs wobbled underneath him and he sat back down with a thump on John's back.

"Is he dead?" whispered Lauren as loudly as she dared.

She could see Trey leaning over and looking at John's face, then looking despairingly back up at her. "I think so. Oh my God, this is a nightmare. How can I tell for definite if he's dead?"

"Check his pulse."

"Don't think I want to."

"Don't be a wuss. Just hold his wrist and see if you can detect anything."

Trey nodded and reached out to John's right arm. Tentatively, as though feeling a tarantula, he put his fingers on the inside of John's wrist and pressed down. After ten seconds or so he called up.

"Nothing. I must have landed on top of him."

"I doubt that killed him on its own – I heard the crack of his head hitting the ground from up here. Although you arriving on top of him wouldn't have helped."

Trey looked at John's still, bloodied face, with its freshly angled nose. Was it the fall that killed him, or Trey kicking him instead of trying to help him? He might have been able to save John but in the heat of the moment, he'd instead hastened his death. Had there been a devil on his shoulder screaming 'OPPORTUNITY!', or was it just self-preservation? Or a bit of both? His mind was all mixed up, and this wasn't helping him focus on his current predicament.

Lauren was calling down from above. "We need to get you out quick. I'm going to call the police."

"No! You can't do that. Once they've found this shaft, they'll find what's left of Anita and Hoggo, as well as John and his broken nose. Then we're back to square one again. If John hadn't grabbed me and pulled me down, we could have closed the hatch, covered it up, and no one would ever know. We still can – you just need to get me out."

"How?" Lauren had started crying again.

"I don't know. Maybe... hang on, what's that?"

"What?"

"Ssshh!"

Trey cocked his head.

"Oh shit. It's coming."

"What?"

"The animal.... The gigarat. I can hear it, coming up that big shaft. Drop the torch down here, quickly!"

"Ok, ok. Ready?"

She lined it up with Trey's outstretched arms and dropped the torch. Trey caught it perfectly.

"Right, listen. I'm going up to that cavern. Hopefully it will concentrate on John and leave me alone. Stay here, wait till I come back. I don't know how long I'll be. Love you."

"Love you too," said Lauren, although the last word didn't come out. She watched as Trey hurried out of sight, the glow of light from the torch fading as quickly as the sound of his scuffling footsteps.

Then she began to hear the animal's noise. Trey had described it but it was another thing hearing it. Almost without thinking she got to her feet and dashed across to the cellar door, opening it just a few inches, and then hastened back to the edge of the shaft. She'd seen horror films where pursued victims couldn't open a door, and she just wanted to be sure.

But she had to see this thing. Without the torch all she could really make out down there now were dark shapes, the main one of which was John's body.

Taka-taka-taka, with that low underlying grumble, getting louder and louder – it was terrifying. She could see what Trey meant. Please let him get away, she thought, please let him be safe. She wasn't even sure how far away that cavern was. How long had he got before the creature caught up with him?

A flash of an idea struck her and she struggled to get her phone out of her pocket. The fingerprint scanner wouldn't work – her fingers were probably too sweaty – so she stabbed at the screen to get her code in, but made a mistake. 'Please try again'. Come on, come on, get it right! She tried again, concentrating, not glancing down the shaft as the creature approached. 1-7-1-1-9-1. Trey's birthday. Not the most secure password but at least she could remember it, provided her fingers worked and all those 1s didn't derail her. This time, success.

She flicked to the camera function and set it to video, and started recording. Even if it picked up nothing else, it would record the sound. She would have some evidence should she need it. Her hands were trembling as she held the phone over the shaft, knowing that, above all else, she mustn't drop it.

The noise below, now at a decibel level perhaps akin to one of those road sweeper machines that sprays water along gutters, suddenly slowed and the grumble lowered in tone then stopped. Lauren held her breath, her heart beating furiously. It felt like it was right there beneath her but she couldn't see it. She heard some snuffling, then something moved.

The grey down below shifted and turned browner and shinier. There was a sudden crunching noise, then some slithering and scraping, before the noise level dramatically rose again and barrelled up the shaft, causing Lauren to involuntarily jerk her head back. The staccato clicking that accompanied the rumble was slightly higher in pitch - perhaps that was a signal that it had found food.

Almost immediately, though, amid the sound of something - John - being dragged or pushed along the ground, the noise receded into the tunnel again, heading in Trey's direction. The movement below had gone.

Lauren held the phone over the hole until the noise had completely gone, then slowly brought it back towards her and almost without thinking stopped the recording. She put the phone back in her pocket, then sat back on the floor, her mouth open, breathing heavily.

What had just happened? This was mad. Trey, her husband, was now being chased by a giant mole or rat or something, in a tunnel under their cellar. And she could do nothing, and not tell anyone. She would have to sit here for as long as it took, waiting for Trey. Waiting and hoping.

But then what would they do if he did make it back? She couldn't get the ladder back down on her own. This was hopeless.

She drew her knees up, scrunched herself into a tight ball, and sobbed uncontrollably.

CHAPTER 35

"John?"

Mel had been surprised to find the front door locked, and there was no sign of John in the apartment. She wondered why she was calling him as it would have made no sense for him to have locked the door from the inside.

She went back into the hall and saw his indoor brogues lying askew, hurriedly kicked off by the look of things, and in the space on the floor where his outdoor shoes normally resided.

Well, he had evidently gone out without telling her. Probably off to see his fancy-piece; maybe thought he would get back before she did. She knew about Doreen, despite the old fool thinking he'd kept it quiet. She'd followed him once and then watched from a distance as he furtively emerged from her house after the deed was done, looking unusually pleased with himself. She'd had her suspicions, but if she was honest, it was no great surprise.

They didn't even talk about sex any more, let alone suggest that they should partake in it. Neither of them wanted to do it with each other – those days were long gone. They had been falling out of love for a long time and had now completed the fall, picked themselves up, and walked off in different directions. They co-existed, just about tolerated each other's presence, but no more than that. He was more of a nuisance than a husband, and he probably felt the same about her.

So she could understand why he might have wanted to get his excitement elsewhere. In fact, it gave her the perfect riposte were he ever to discover that she was doing exactly the same thing. So she had kept her detective work under her hat, stored away to reveal in a flourish should she ever be caught in flagrante with Jim.

She sometimes wondered why they both went to so much effort to keep their affairs secret – why not just come out with it and agree to an open marriage? She just couldn't bring herself to take that first step though, to admit that she was being adulterous, even though he was too.

It didn't help that Jim was married too, otherwise they could have just eloped together, and to hell with John. They'd talked about that, even to the point where they'd jokingly thought about bumping off their respective partners. Neither was entirely sure the other wasn't serious, though, so it was a little awkward. They didn't talk about that again, but the thought seed had been sown, and had been sprouting little green shoots in Mel's mind however much she didn't want it to.

The whole thing was just too complicated. So much for retirement being a golden road of relaxation and happiness along which they would stroll hand in hand.

She rang John's mobile but it went to voicemail. She needed to speak to him though. Her brother had just texted to say that Mum had had a fall in the care home. Nothing major, but she wanted to go and see her. Mum had always got on well with John, bless her, so would be upset if John wasn't there too. Who knew how long she had got left. That was another reason for sticking around with John for now. Wait until Mum has passed on.

Perhaps he'd actually just gone for a walk in the garden, now that the sun was out. She put her coat back on and headed for the door.

***

Lauren had been thinking things through, or at least trying to; her brain was fighting a scramble of emotion and panic.

John's body had disappeared, hoovered up by the gigarat in the same way that it had evidently disposed of Anita. A fleeting worry occurred to her: if this underground monster thought that someone was now regularly throwing big tasty meals down the shaft it might head this way more often.

She needed to get Trey out, but if she called the emergency services, that would lead to them finding Anita, Hoggo, and now John. Investigations would begin and there was only one way it would end – her going to prison for a very long time, and possible Trey too.

Yet now, as things stood, there were no bodies at the bottom of their shaft, and no witnesses or evidence that could link her and Trey to any of the deaths. The only thing linking Lauren and Trey to any crime would be if evidence was found in the tunnels, be that of human origin or clothing, which could only have ended up down there via their cellar.

So if they swung the trapdoor back over it and buried it under some coal or something, no one would be any the wiser, because they would never find the tunnels. Unless there was another entrance of course, and from what Trey had said about all those other bones, that did seem quite likely. And if there was actually another entrance, then surely Anita, Hoggo, Molly the homeless lady, and John could all have been dragged in through there.

This was a glimmer of hope. But all of that would mean nothing if she couldn't get Trey out, and how could she do that without help? There's no way she could get that ladder back in on her own.

Trey had said that his left arm hurt – supposing he couldn't haul himself up a rope? If he tied one end around his waist, though, then….. no, no, that wouldn't work either. Lifting up a patient with the help of other nurses was not the same as hauling a twelve stone man single-handedly out of a twenty foot hole. She'd need to be Wonder Woman to do that, and the last time she'd checked, she wasn't.

Maybe Trey's arm wouldn't stop him climbing the rope though, in which case she could tie one end to the leg of the workbench. The dilapidated workbench looked back at her with an air of 'are you sure you really want to do that?' and she realised that if the leg broke as Trey was half way up, that would make things even worse.

Not that she had a rope anyway. Where did you get one of those when you needed one? Perhaps there was one in the communal garden shed, where Norman kept all his stuff. But why would he keep a rope? Gardeners didn't need to abseil down buildings or anything.

She let out a long, low groan of frustration mixed with despair. What was she supposed to do? She held her head in her hands, then raked her fingers back through her hair, slapping the back of her head with both hands as though this could bang some ideas into her.

She became aware of movement and looked up quickly. The door was opening. She scrambled to her feet.

"Who's that?"

A head poked round the corner of the door.

"It's me, Mel. Oh my God, Lauren, what's happened? You look like you've been crying! And what's that?"

Mel was in now, walking across to Lauren, who was standing next to the shaft. It was too late now – she'd seen it. Lauren's mouth opened but no words emerged. Mel grabbed her hands.

"Love – I was out looking for John and I heard a moan coming from your cellar. Then I saw the door was open. Are you ok? Where's Trey?"

Lauren looked at Mel and could only think of John. Tears welled up and streamed down her face.

She couldn't stop herself. "I'm so sorry, Mel. It wasn't meant to happen. Everything's gone wrong. It's all gone wrong."

Mel moved forward and gave Lauren a hug.

"What has?"

She pulled back and glanced to her left. "And what on earth is that? Did John know about this? He never mentioned a bloody great hole. He just said that that you couldn't lift the trapdoor when he tried to help you. Never said what might be under it."

Lauren sniffed and wiped her face with her sleeve. That seemed such a long time ago now, but it was just a few days. She nodded.

"Yes, that's right. We didn't know. But then we opened it later."

Mel leaned over slightly, trying to see the bottom.

"How deep is it then?"

"Twenty four feet to the ground, Trey said."

"Where does it go? What's at the bottom?"

Lauren paused. What was she supposed to say? All of this was because they didn't want John to tell Mel, because she was bound to go to the police even if John didn't. Now here she was, and the situation was even worse.

"It's a long story," said Lauren.

Mel looked at her blankly.

"Wait a minute. You were saying you were sorry just now, and 'it wasn't meant to happen?' What wasn't, Lauren? What's going on?"

She stepped back a few paces. "And can we move away from this hole? It's giving me the willies."

A terrible thought glinted in the recesses of her mind. Mel was a slim lady, probably weighed less than she did. Perhaps.... no, no, definitely not. Lauren Clark was not a killer. Anita was an accident. She could not end someone's life deliberately. Never, never, never - no matter what the consequences. There had been way too much of that already, and it hadn't gone well. She moved away from the shaft, over to the workbench, and leant on it, giving herself time to think. Mel had folded her arms now. She wanted answers.

"Mel, they fell down the hole."

"They?" Mel didn't understand.

"Trey and John."

Mel started to blanche. "What? Where are they then? How did they fall?"

Lauren wiped her nose again and sniffed loudly. "John was kneeling next to the hole and he sort of tripped as he was getting up, like his leg went from under him. Anyway, to stop himself falling he grabbed hold of Trey's leg, and they both went down the hole. It was awful. I tried to stop it but I couldn't."

"Oh God. No, that can't be right. Where are they then?"

Mel rushed back over to the shaft, got on her knees and peered down, her eyes adjusting. "I can't see them. They're not down there."

She looked back over her shoulder. "Lauren, what the hell is going on? If this is a joke it's not funny."

Lauren briefly mused again on the opportunity that had presented itself there. The fact that she could have walked over and pushed Mel in, but had decided not to, gave her some comfort that she hadn't completely lost her sanity. She was oddly pleased with herself for that, when she had no right to be. After all, the default behaviour for all humans is not to kill each other, and to adhere to that principle should be an expectation, not an option. What did that say about her husband though? She pushed that thought away.

"Mel, John's dead," she said simply. "He landed first. Trey landed on top of him. And then the creature came."

Mel rose unsteadily to her feet and walked slowly back towards Lauren. She didn't appear quite as upset as Lauren had expected.

"Oh my God. Sorry, I thought you just said 'creature'."

She'd asked about the creature rather than John. Strange.

"I did. There's something down there. We've called it a gigarat. It took John. Trey escaped but now he'd hiding down there and..... and...... I don't know if he's going to come back."

Mel's mouth was slightly agape but she wasn't crying. She closed it, like a fish in a tank, and took another step forward.

"Escaped? Escaped where?"

"There are tunnels down there. And a cave."

"Look, Lauren, I don't know you very well, and I don't know if you've got any..... well, you know..... mental issues, but this sounds....."

"There is nothing wrong with my mind!" Lauren interrupted. ""I'm perfectly sane, ok? I know it sounds unbelievable but it's true. There's a man-eating rat-mole thing down there and my husband is down there with it and I need to get him out!"

She realised she had been shouting. "Sorry. I'm just upset, that's all."

She also realised that focusing on the fortunes of her very much alive husband, having just informed Mel that her own partner was decidedly dead, could have been viewed as a trifle insensitive.

Yet Mel didn't seem too bothered. Only now did she enquire further.

"So this rat animal dragged John off down the tunnel."

"Yes. Trey had already checked his pulse and there was nothing. I'm so sorry."

Mel took a deep breath, metaphorically taking it all in. "Just so you know, I'm having a bit of trouble believing this thing about the gigarat. How could a big rat move a man John's size? I don't buy it."

Lauren smiled grimly. "I don't blame you. Doesn't sound possible, does it? But honestly, it really.....oh my God, what an idiot."

"Who?"

"Me! I recorded it! It's on my phone."

She started rummaging in her pocket, then jabbing at the phone that emerged.

"Look, here, see the date and time? Just over ten minutes ago. Now, watch....."

She maximised the display and gave the phone to Mel, who squinted at the grainy dark picture.

"What's that noise?"

"That's it, the animal. You can hear it coming. You might be able to vaguely make out John's body at the bottom."

Mel nodded, angling the phone to try to get the least reflection. The noise abruptly stopped.

"Oh my good god, I can see it. Something moving, glistening a bit."

Lauren moved round beside her to get a better view. She hadn't even seen it play back herself yet. As she did so, they both heard the sickening crunch, followed by the sudden burble of noise as the gigarat started moving again, somehow taking with it the grainy blur that was John's body. The noise receded, the picture jerked back up to briefly show the cellar, and the video stopped.

Mel slowly handed the phone back to Lauren.

"Right," she said. "Ok. I can't believe I'm saying this, but I believe you."

"You didn't before, then."

"I wasn't sure."

Lauren just had to say something. "You don't seem as upset about John as I was expecting."

Mel looked at her with an expression of pained melancholy.

"I know. I should be wailing and gnashing my teeth, shouldn't I? And I don't really know why I'm not. Well, that's not strictly true. I do know – firstly, I'm probably still in shock, and secondly, our marriage was a sham. There, I've said it."

Lauren was shocked. "What do you mean? Why was it......?"

Mel shook her head slightly and a little laugh fluttered out. "You and Trey and still so young, not married long. Me and John? Forty one years and counting. Well, stopped counting now, obviously. Fell out of love yonks ago. We only stayed together because of the business. Then since we retired we've just spent our time arguing, getting under each other's feet. He was seeing another woman, you know."

"No! Really? And you knew about it?"

"Yep. Kept it back as a bombshell torpedo, if there is such a thing, should I ever need it. Don't suppose I will now, will I? I think both of us were contemplating divorce but neither wanted to be the one to throw the first stone or admit fault. It was only a matter of time though."

"I had no idea. I'm so sorry."

"Thank you. Doesn't matter now though. I wanted John out of my life and now he is. Not like this, though, obviously. I may have grown to dislike him but I didn't really want him dead, however much I might have thought about it. Certainly not like this. As I said, I suppose I must be in shock at the moment. Maybe I'll grieve later. It's weird, I just don't feel anything really. Maybe the relief is cancelling out the grief. What about Trey though? Look, we need to dial 999. The fire brigade will know what to do."

The mention of his name spurred Lauren back to the issue at hand.

"No, we haven't got time to wait for them. Trey could be heading back now with that animal behind him. We need a ladder or a rope right now, not whenever a fire engine can get here. Even a short ladder is better than nothing - at least he can get half way up, where that animal can't get him."

"Rats can climb ladders though."

"We don't know for definite it is a rat. Also it's too big to get up the shaft, Trey said, and from what I saw I think he's right." She shivered. "Gives me the creeps just thinking about that thing. We just have to hope that there are no smaller ones down there who can scramble up. Have you got a ladder?"

Mel pointed at Hoggo's ladder, now lying on the floor up against a far wall. "What's wrong with that one?"

Lauren thought back to the effort and force that it had taken two grown men each time to get it in and out again.

"We wouldn't be able to get it in. The angle wasn't right. They were hammering away at it for ages and almost gave up. I don't think we'd be able to do it. Have you got anything else?"

"An old stepladder, yes. Used it for some decorating. It might be an A-frame one, though, not a slidey one that extends - can't remember. Either way it's not long enough."

"Doesn't matter, it's better than nothing if it can get him some of the way up and maybe out of the clutches of that animal. Can you get it?"

"Of course. Wait there."

Mel hurried out of the cellar as Lauren decided not to point out that she was unlikely to go and wait somewhere else. Her main role now was to listen out for Trey.

CHAPTER 36

Trey realised, as he staggered forward in the darkness, that holding a torch was a lot less convenient than having one strapped to his head. Previously, he could use both arms to propel himself along, one on each side wall, but now his right arm was fully occupied pointing the torch, and this was slowing him down a little.

Behind him that grumbling, rattling noise grew louder. He resisted the urge to look back – he knew he had to focus every second on going forward.

His left side hurt and he was hobbling slightly thanks to the pain in his hip, but they were the least of his worries. Being caught and devoured by a giant rat monster gave him plenty of incentive to move faster than any mild pain could hinder him.

He felt water on his face and brushed at his cheek, only then realising that it was the dampness of tears. Stress, yes, but mostly the enormity of the terrible, awful thing that had befallen him. He had helped kill John, effectively, in order to save his own skin, yet the end result had been the same - they had still both fallen down the hole. Could he have saved him, though, and helped John clamber out? Maybe, maybe not. If he had, then perhaps John would have been more inclined to help him and not tell the police about Anita.

As he stumbled onwards John's smiling face came into his head, handing him a bottle of wine. He shook his head. He had to think of something else; just focus on his escape. Block John from his mind.

It had taken them about ten minutes to walk to the cavern last time, but he hoped to do it in half that. He got himself into a fast rhythm of steps, taking deep breaths between every three strides to make sure he was getting enough oxygen. How good the air was down here was another matter, but as long as he could breathe, he was ok. He pictured the cavern ahead in his mind and focused on that.

Still that noise grew louder behind him. He pictured a ravenous mouth with huge pointed incisors, bitty little squished up eyes, probably now redundant, and a fat snub nose designed for burrowing.

It obviously couldn't see in the dark, he thought, or it would have spotted both Hoggo and himself last time, hiding in their tunnels. It seemed to be attracted to noises from quite a distance away, so must have acute hearing.

But perhaps, somewhat surprisingly, its sensory acuity didn't extend to smell. Otherwise why wouldn't it have found them almost instantly? It only reacted when Hoggo let one rip, and however powerful Hoggo's anal emissions might be, the smell would not have reached it before the noise. It definitely reacted to the noise. If anything the smell should have acted as a deterrent, one would have thought.

So perhaps it relied almost entirely on touch and sound. Meaning he stood a chance. He just had to get to that cavern.

He was well past the curve of the tunnel now and so was out of sight of what was behind him. His left palm and fingers were grazed from repeated clawing at the tunnel wall as he hauled himself forward, over and over, pulling with each step.

Suddenly the noise stopped, and it felt as though his footsteps and heavy breathing had immediately compensated and were now booming around him, echoing back to alert his pursuer. He couldn't stop though; he had to keep going.

It must have found John's body – that was the only explanation. So he knew where it was, but it also probably knew where he was, and it was quicker than him even when pushing a body along, given the speed that it disappeared with Hoggo. John was no lightweight, though, probably even heavier than Hoggo; that should help.

He raised the weak beam of light from where his feet were going to look directly ahead, hoping to see the tunnel forking in two – the first sign that the cavern was within reach. But all he saw were the tunnel walls, stretching into the distance.

He was getting tired now and his legs, moving in an unnatural gait, were begging him to stop and rest, but he wasn't going to do that. Resting so that you could die wasn't a great plan.

The grumbling and rattling started up behind him again, not so loud this time. He wondered why it did that. Surely it would alert any prey? Maybe it was some kind of hypnotic noise that worked to scare and disorientate its victims. Maybe … but it didn't matter right now. Just move, fast. No time to think of anything but escaping. Step, step, step, breathe. And again. Come on, cave, where the hell are you? Step, step, step, breathe. That noise behind was building up again, getting closer.

It would know he was here, so it would be coming after him. He was doomed. Step, step, step, breathe. This was hopeless. Unless it was too pre-occupied with John – that was the wisp of hope that he had to cling to.

He thought of Lauren; he might never see her again. How would she cope without him? Oh great, he'd not told her the new password for their savings account – they'd forced him to change it this morning. Not there was much in the account, but she would need it. That wasn't good. And what about his clients? How would she know who they were? And they hadn't done a will yet – would that matter? So many thoughts going through his head; he couldn't stop them. After all, they could be his last ones, ever, so how could he not think them?

The pain in his hip was getting worse, and he knew the gigarat was closing on him. If it was pushing or dragging John like it did with Hoggo, how could it still move so quickly? It must be immensely strong.

At last he saw the fork where one tunnel became two, the passage to the left plunging downwards, the one to the right opening up into blackness.

He kept to the right, and as he got closer the white specks of the bones on the floor began to come forward from the gloom, like gravestones in a midnight cemetery.

He stumbled into the cavern, kicking bones and almost falling as he pulled his tired legs across the floor towards the tunnel entrance where he had hidden last time. It wasn't that much of a hiding place, though. All he could do was rely on the 50/50 chance that the animal would choose the other tunnel first, perhaps remembering the meal it had found there last time. He saw quite a large bone on the floor, about the size of a baguette, so he quickly scooped it up. It wasn't much of a weapon, but it might be better than nothing.

Lurching his way through the other bones, he reached the furthest tunnel and positioned himself about ten feet into the mouth of the entrance, stopping when the noise of the gigarat felt as though it was about to burst into the cave.

He couldn't afford to keep moving in case he made more noise and attracted attention. He had to be still, and quiet, very quiet. He switched off his torch, and pressed himself into the darkness of the wall.

Realising that he was still breathing heavily, his chest rising and falling, he clamped his mouth shut and tried to regulate his breathing as quietly as he could.

He had indeed only just made it in time. Taka-taka-taka, rising to a crescendo, building and building, a big slithering scattering of bones... then silence.

It was here now, in the cave. He couldn't see it, or hear it, but he could feel it. The hairs on his arms began to rise. Where was it?

The hush gave way to some sniffing and low grunts. It sounded about twenty feet away. Could it actually smell him after all? It was game over if it could.

This time there was no sound of scrabbling paws rushing around on stone, so it was not searching around the cave yet. Instead he heard a swishing noise, then another – the sound of something large being nudged and pushed along the ground as though it was being arranged - John. He shuddered.

He felt the weight of the bone in his hand. It wasn't really heavy enough to do anything other than administer a light rap. Even if Trey brought it down on the skull of the creature with the power of a kangaroo's tail, he doubted that the effect would register anything more than mild irritation. It would be like attacking a tank with a stick.

There could be another use for it though......

If it went away, down the other tunnel, fine. If it didn't... he waited.

The sniffing and grunting continued, but now bones were sliding around on the floor as it started shuffling. Looking for the source of the noise it had heard before, no doubt.

A bone skittered down his tunnel and past his feet. Trey froze even more rigidly than before, desperate not to make any noise whatsoever. He couldn't afford a Hoggo moment now, whether it was from his downstairs orifice or indeed any other.

That rank smell started to assail his nostrils as the animal got closer. Too close.

Trey panicked. Swiftly raising his arm he took aim and, despite being unable to see, launched the bone in his hand as hard as he could in what he calculated was the direction of the cavern, trying not to throw it too high in order to avoid hitting the roof of the tunnel. He hoped it wouldn't hit the animal, and to his relief he heard it clatter against the far wall and fall to the ground with an echo-y rattle.

A wrenching screech pierced the air and with a scurry of claws the gigarat turned and scrabbled back to the other side of the cavern, bones flying everywhere in a frenzied ruckus of aggression.

Trey debated whether or not to make a run for it, but in the dark, what would be the point? He would barely get fifteen feet before he was caught and attacked. He stayed flattened against the wall of the tunnel, wishing so much that his eyes would work in the coal-black murk of this terrible death cave, so that he could actually see his enemy.

But then the noise stopped. The gigarat must have realised that there was nothing there, no potential meal waiting for it. It was silent now, then began moving slowly back towards him, bones pushed to one side like the parting of the seas as it resumed the position it had been in before being so rudely distracted. Then it slowly came even closer.

Trey could hear it's short, sharp breathing, and could smell its rancid breath. He could almost picture its evil little face as it closed in on him. It was just a few feet away now, virtually next to him. Surely it knew he was there; and if it didn't, it soon would.

Trey knew now that he had just seconds to live. He had no options left. He couldn't just stand there and wait for it to tear unto him like it did with Hoggo. If this thing was going to kill him, at least he wanted to see what it looked like before he died.

Taking a deep breath, he stepped back into the middle of the tunnel, switched on his torch, and let out a huge roar, a screaming bellow louder than anything that had come out of his mouth before.

In front of him, barely six feet away, lit up now, he saw the gigarat, and it wasn't far off what he had imagined. It was huge, the size of a grizzly bear. Its matted brown-black fur shone damply in the light. Up its chest and presumably under its belly was a thick, scaly, pitted skin that reminded him of a worn leather sofa. The two legs he could see were short and squat, splayed sideways to allow the belly to rest on the ground, and sheathed with hooked claws that did all the work in propelling it along. Its expressionless face reminded him of a beaver, but the mouth was larger and sported four enormous front teeth, yellowed and worn, with two incisors sticking upwards from the lower jaw.

Surprisingly, it had eyes. They were jet black and small, much too small for its face, but their very presence was what saved Trey's life.

Faced with a beam of light aimed directly at them, the animal stopped in its tracks, screeched loudly, and hissed through its teeth, shuffling backwards into the cavern as it did so. Emboldened, Trey wiggled the torch and roared again. He wasn't sure which was having the greatest effect; perhaps his roar was giving the impression of a huge adversary who would put up a fight, but he doubted it. More likely the gigarat couldn't handle the brightness.

It hissed again, saliva dripping from its front teeth. Then it abruptly turned round and scuffled off down the other tunnel, click-clacking as it went. The noise quickly receded, and silence returned.

Trey stood transfixed, the release of tension allowing him to now replenish his lungs with noisy gulps of air. What the hell happened there? How was he not dead? Light must be its weakness. If only he had known that when he and Hoggo were down here; that could have saved his friend. But it had saved Trey, and for the moment that was all that mattered. Now he had to get out of there.

Still in shock and not ready to process what had just happened to him, he stumbled back into the cave. Shining the torch around he saw a dark, crumpled lump in the middle of the floor. He didn't want to look; John was likely to have been badly disfigured on his journey through the tunnel and Trey had no wish to see that. Also, the body might as well have had a big sign on it stating 'partly killed by Trey', and the sooner it was out of his sight the better.

He quickly picked his way through the bones on the floor, and was just about to duck into the tunnel leading to the shaft when he had a thought. The shoe – the black trainer. While he was here, he could quickly grab it, like he wished he had done last time.

Scanning the space with his torch, he spotted it about fifteen feet away mixed up with a small jumble of larger bones. He hurried over and was about to pick it up when something in his head told him to be careful. The situation had changed now.

If he emerged with the shoe, and it eventually got into the hands of the police and he was questioned about it, how would he explain why he had it? That wouldn't look good. He would have to admit he had been down here. Plus with John now gone, perhaps he and Lauren still had a chance to cover their tracks and claim that none of this was anything to do with them. All they had to do was close that trapdoor and hide it again.

Whoever's shoe it was, whether Anita or the homeless woman, or even some other missing person, they were indisputably dead. The discovery of their shoe wasn't going to change that. So he really should leave it there, and he had better not get his DNA on it either.

He shone the torch right up close to it. On the inside of the heel area he could see a label sown onto the side and make out a size. 'Made in

Vietnam' it said, above the wording UK 5 EUR 38 US 7. About average for women, he thought, so no real clues there. Could Anita have been a size 5? From the look of her, yes, no reason why not, so it might not be the homeless lady's shoe. He'd need to talk it through with Lauren, so he got his phone out and with one hand held the torch and with the other took a photo of the trainer where it lay. At least then he could show her.

Right, that would do, if he hung around any longer the gigarat might return with a few of its mates.

He turned back towards the tunnel, desperately hoping Lauren had found a way of getting him up that vent. Otherwise his relief at not being rodent food could be short lived.

CHAPTER 37

Mel clattered through the cellar doorway dragging an aluminium stepladder that wasn't much more than six feet tall.

"Here you go," she announced as she laid it on the ground next to the hole, "that's all we've got. Can't see that it's going to help much, is it?"

In Mel's absence Lauren had come to the same conclusion.

"No, you're right. At first I was thinking that if we drop it down there, at least Trey could climb up into the vent so his feet are above the tunnel, but if that beast comes along he'll just knock the ladder out from under him. So sorry, but I'm not sure that's going to be any use after all."

Mel looked slightly pained. "I did think that as I was lugging it down here. Although maybe he could use it to fend the thing off. Poke it in the face, you know?"

"I suppose. It would be better than nothing. Shall we drop it down then?"

"As long as I get it back." Mel smiled. "Only kidding. Yes, let's drop it."

The two women lifted it up between them and peered over the edge into the vent.

"Trey?" called Lauren, not too loudly but enough that Trey would hear if he was approaching in the darkness. The last thing she wanted now was for him to miraculously escape from the creature only for his wife to drop a ladder on his head.

There was no response. "Right," said Lauren, "over it goes then."

They held the ladder over the middle of the vent and with a joint nod, let go. A second of silence, then a terrible racket as it caught the side of the shaft and scraped and banged its way down to the bottom, where it landed on its feet, then toppled over with a final metallic thud.

The two women looked at each other.

"That maybe wasn't such a good idea," said Lauren, her eyes wide with realisation. "If that animal is attracted by noise...."

Mel stepped back from the vent and winced. "I know, but we had to, didn't we? We just have to hope it doesn't come back."

"It's still not going to get Trey out though, is it?"

"Look, we have to call 999 now. My phone's in my bag in the flat, we'll have to use yours."

Lauren looked at Mel blankly, her mind now a whirling mix of emotions wrestling with reasoning and motivations. She just couldn't think straight. Was it ok to involve the authorities now? Everyone who knew about her and Anita was dead, apart from Trey, hopefully. Only she and Trey knew that he helped John fall; Mel thinks it was entirely an accident and no one can prove otherwise.

But she had to keep reminding herself that if the authorities are brought in and start exploring the tunnels, they might find evidence of Anita, Hoggo and now John, and traces of Anita's blood along the tunnel leading to their vent.

Yet if she now refused to call 999, that would look suspicious and Mel would realise that not all was as it seemed. Then she would have to tell her the truth, and their experience with John had shown that almost certainly wouldn't end well.

Mel prompted her. "Lauren?"

Lauren started. "Oh, sorry, yes, let's call them." She flashed a tired smile. "My mind's all over the place."

Mel reached out and touched her on the arm. "Course it is, love. Don't you worry about that."

Lauren gave her another smile, and got her phone out. With a sense that she was about to unleash a whole new episode of uncertainty, she dialled 999.

***

Trey stopped in his tracks. He had heard something up ahead, a couple of seconds of distant banging. Could that be another gigarat, heading up the main shaft?

He stayed rooted to the spot, heart racing, holding his breath, listening acutely for that tell-tale rumbling tak-a-tak noise. Nothing. Just a damp, heavy silence.

What on earth was that noise then? Maybe something Lauren was doing? But she knows not to make noises. His anxiety levels rose another notch, if that was possible. He had no choice, though, he had to carry on to where the noise had come from and just hope it was friend, not foe.

He began breathing again, and resumed his progress.

***

Lauren abruptly ended the call before the first ring, her head still full of panicked thoughts about whether bringing the emergency services into this situation could still end up with her in jail. There must be another way. "Wait, this isn't going to work."

"What do you mean?"

"Ok, so the fire brigade turn up, and Trey isn't there yet. They're not going to just hang around for hours waiting for him, are they? They're only going to come and rescue someone who needs rescuing, not someone who might need rescuing. We'd be wasting their time unless they just happened to turn up just as Trey makes it back to the bottom of this hole. How likely is that?"

Mel's face fell. "And I suppose you can't expect them to go down there and probably get themselves killed."

"Yes and if we tell them the situation they probably won't believe us."

"So, what, we wait until Trey appears and then call them? Suppose that creature is chasing after him? That's no good. What do we do then? Actually, on reflection, I do think...."

"Hose!"

"Pardon?"

Lauren was suddenly excited. "Hose, garden hose! Why didn't I think of that before? They're easily long enough, aren't they? Norman would have one, wouldn't he?"

"Well, yes, he does. He's always watering the garden with it. It must be in the garage store room. Are you thinking....?"

"Yes, we could pull Trey up with that!"

"It might not be strong enough, though. If it stretched and snapped while he was half way up......"

Some of Lauren's enthusiasm waned.

"Well, yes, but it might be ok. We can test it out, can't we? See how strong it is. Do you think you could get it? I'd come with you, but...."

Mel waved a hand. "No, you need to stay here. Right, back soon I hope."

She ran over to the door and was through it and up the steps in an instant. Lauren heard her hard heeled shoes clopping along the stone slabs like a departing horse, then turned her attention back to the vent.

She shone the torch down, hoping to see Trey's head peering up at her, but all she could make out was the silvery stepladder, lying prone, another victim of a fall down this cursed shaft.

Six minutes later Lauren heard footsteps and Mel's voice. Why was she talking to herself? Down the outside steps, then the door swung open and Mel reversed in, holding a large reel of hose on a cart that was supported on the other side by the arms of a man.

The arms revealed themselves to be attached to Tony, who was looking puffed but also surprised.

"Here we are!" announced Mel, in case Lauren had somehow failed to notice them coming in. "It was too heavy for me, there must be at least 60m of hose on here, Tony reckons. I was so lucky he was just coming out of the house."

Tony snorted as they lowered the cart to the ground. "Not so lucky for me though. Shouldn't be carrying heavy things at my age, you know. What's this all about then? You said it was urgent, matter of life and death, you said, but carrying a garden hose into a cellar isn't..... hello, what's that?"

He had spotted the vent.

"Careful!" warned Lauren as Tony strode towards it. "It's really, really deep. Also, explanations later, please, we need to get the hose down there."

Mel had already started unwinding it, and while Tony peered down the shaft and whistled at its depth, Lauren rushed over and helped Mel direct the end of the hose into the vent. Being the younger of the two, she took over the winding of the handle, as fast as she could, while Mel got the torch to see how much had reached the ground.

"We'll need about 6 ft of spare hose at the bottom," suggested Mel. "No more than that or it will slow things down. Right, slow down a bit. Bit more. That's it!"

Lauren stopped winding and stood up.

Tony, stepping back from the hole, looked at the two women with the expression of a man who thought he was attending a conference on holiday homes but has just realised it's for neurosurgery.

"I'm sorry," he said, giving his head a little wobble, "but can someone tell me what in heaven's name is going on?"

Lauren glanced at Mel – she'd take this one.

"Tony, we found this shaft in our cellar. To cut a long story short, John slipped and fell down it and grabbed at Trey as he fell, so the two of them went down it."

"Oh my good Lord!" exclaimed Tony before Lauren could go any further. "Are they alright? Where are they then? All I could see was what looked like a ladder at the bottom."

"John died instantly, Trey was hurt but ok."

Tony staggered back a little. "What? John's dead? Oh my good Lord. Really?"

He looked across at Mel, who nodded.

"Oh Melanie, I'm so sorry. I can't believe that. I know he and I didn't always see eye to eye, but it was nothing personal. This is the last thing I..... it's just too...."

He mumbled to a halt and rubbed one eye.

"And Trey? Where is he?"

Lauren continued. "He survived the fall – he landed on John. There are tunnels down there, Tony. An old mine, we think. And there are animals too, large ones. One of them took John's body and chased after Trey. We don't know what's happened to him." A tear ran down her cheek. "He might be dead too."

Tony's mouth opened and shut like a fish. "Animals? That took John's body? What are you talking about?"

"Show him the video, Lauren," said Mel.

Lauren nodded, pulled out her phone, and played the clip to Tony, whose mouth fell open again. When the clip ended he straightened up and tugged at the ends of his jacket, trying to get some order back into his affairs.

"A bit grainy but that was this shaft alright and there's something down there, isn't there? My goodness, this is unexpected. Sorry but I'm finding it a bit hard to take all this in."

"Join the club," muttered Mel.

"Have you called the police? Or at least the fire brigade."

"No," said Lauren firmly, "they might not get here in time, and anyway we'd waste even more time explaining about that animal down there. With this hose now, if Trey makes it back to this shaft, we should be able to pull him up."

Tony looked doubtful. "It's only plastic and rubber though. If I were you I would pull it back up, then lower it in a loop so you have two lengths to give some extra strength. He can also loop it under his shoulders then."

Lauren and Mel looked at each other – why hadn't they thought of that?

"You're right!" said Lauren. "Right, quick let's pull it up. Mel, can you unwind another equivalent length?"

Immediately they set to work, Tony and Lauren pulling the hose back up until they had the end in their hands, then pushing the coils back in like an unwanted snake, while Mel carried on unwinding the hose on the cart until the two lengths in the hole were the same size.

Tony clung onto the end of the hose, looking a little uneasy.

"Whatever you do don't let go of that end," pleaded Mel.

"I wasn't intending to," Tony replied, trying hard, given the circumstances, to moderate the level of sarcasm he would normally have applied to such a statement of the obvious.

"Although," he continued, "I can't stand here holding this all day. How long do we wait? Suzanne will be wondering where I am. I only went out to post a letter. And now I haven't posted it."

"I think what you're doing now is slightly more important," said Mel pointedly.

"Granted," replied Tony with a sniff. "But I don't want Suzanne worrying."

"You can ring her, can't you?" suggested Lauren. "Have you got your mobile?"

Tony passed the end of the hose to Lauren and rummaged in a pocket. He squinted at the screen, expecting no signal, but was pleased to see one bar.

When Suzanne answered it quickly became clear to Lauren and Mel that Tony was not one for a lot of sentiment.

"John's dead, dear, and Trey's missing. Yes, John Firwell. No, I'm not kidding. I'm with the two wives now, in the outside cellar. I know, yes, terrible. I might be here a while now – Trey is down a mine shaft and we'll have to haul him up. Just thought you should know."

They could faintly hear Suzanne's reactions but not make out any words, just Tony's responses.

"Yes, in the cellar. A mine shaft. I know. No, there's no need. Right. Ok. Ok. Yes. Have to go now. Yes, I know. Alright then. Ok. Bye. Yes, I'll do that. Bye. Bye."

He ended the call, slightly embarrassed that he had been overheard.

"She expects me to ring her after thirty minutes and if I don't she will come down herself."

"Why not?" said Lauren wearily. "The more the merrier, eh?"

She had just about given up on trying to keep the tunnels a secret now. Far more important to get Trey out. She walked over to the hole and peered down it.

Was that her imagination or did it look a bit lighter down there? The lighter shade of black disappeared suddenly, then was back.

She looked up at Mel and Tony, her face wreathed in hope. "I think it's Trey!" she hissed. "Get ready!"

CHAPTER 38

Trey stopped again, briefly, his ears straining to hear anything above his own heavy breathing. Still silence, thank God. But that could change in an instant. He picked up the pace again.

The tunnel started to curve round to the left – the sign he needed to tell him that he was nearly there. His hip still hurt, although adrenalin was masking some of the pain, keeping him walking.

Finally he saw a blur of light ahead, coming from the vent. As he got closer he could see a flash of silver-grey, suddenly illuminated by a torch from above. Lauren.

He started to cry out, then thought better of it. No sense attracting the gigarat back to him now. He shone his own torch ahead and saw two tubes hanging down – too smooth for rope, but better than nothing. Below them the silver thing appeared to be a small stepladder lying on the ground. What was the point of that? That must have been the noise he heard.

With a flood of relief he reached the vent, pushed aside what he could now see was garden hose, and looked up. A grinning but tearful Lauren was looking back at him from high above.

"Trey! Thank God! Are you ok? Where's the animal?"

"It's ok, it's gone for now," he hissed, trying to keep his volume to a minimum. "Am I supposed to climb up this hose?"

He felt a wet drop land on his nose and smiled. Lauren's tears were raining on him.

"Put the loop of the hose under your arms and hold tight onto both tubes, or whatever you want to call them. When you're ready give me a thumbs up."

Trey quickly did as he was told and grabbed hold of the hose, bringing the two tubes together and wrapping his hands round them. Realising that made a thumbs up trickier, he instead nodded his head and called "Ok, ready!"

Lauren's head disappeared, and a few seconds later the hose stretched thin until it became taught, and he began to feel himself being lifted. Surely Lauren couldn't be this strong? He dangled for a bit but as his legs came level with the top of the tunnel he spread them apart and started pushing against each side of the vent in a gangly climbing motion, taking as much of his weight as possible off the hose.

The hose was stretched alarmingly thin, and he didn't like the thought of it rubbing over the rough edge of the hole with all that pressure on it, but still he rose. Lauren must be superhuman, a secret Wonder Woman; how was she doing this? Then he heard voices. Ok, that made sense, there were at least two people pulling him up. But who had Lauren found? How much did they know?

His feet scuffed against the bricks; the hose was biting into his armpits now, and really not at all comfortable. But it was working – he was still rising. Now he could hear a man's voice, and another woman, cursing and shouting and evidently expending a lot of effort. He could imagine them up there like a tug-of-war team, pulling hand over hand and getting in each other's way.

"Keep it going," he heard Lauren urge, "we're nearly there. Oh!"

A sudden slip, accompanied by cries from above, and Trey juddered back down a good five feet before the hose went taught again. His heart rose from his stomach as he hung there, waiting.

Then he heard it. That terrible noise was back, distant but heading his way. It was coming. They were coming. Who knew how many of them were down there? And was there a smaller one who could get up this vent?

He shouted up above him, urgency now overtaking caution. "Hurry up, it's coming back!"

He heard Lauren call back, panic in her voice. "Ok, ok got that! Sorry about the slip, we're just knotting the hose round the leg of the work bench."

He wished they had thought of that before, but maybe they didn't have time. He heard Lauren give the command "heave!" and the upward momentum resumed.

He could hear the taka-taka-taka getting louder, coming closer, and his legs pushed even harder against the sides in a sort of an upward breaststroke leg kick motion.

He was rising faster now, and as his head finally emerged above the cellar floor he was amazed to see that the tug-of-war team, leaning backwards and gripping the hose with white-knuckled hands, comprised an exhausted-looking Tony and a furiously-straining Mel, with Lauren now released to help haul Trey over the edge.

Not first choices for such an endeavour, but they'd done it. As Trey collapsed onto the cellar floor, the two neighbours let go of the rope and also sank to the ground, panting.

"I won't be doing that again," gasped Tony, although it is doubtful that anyone had supposed that he would.

"Thank you guys, you were brilliant," gasped Trey, scrambling to his feet. "That was some effort. And the hose didn't break either."

"Thank God for that," Lauren said as she grabbed him in her arms and gave him the tightest hug he could remember. "I can't believe you made it. How did you escape that thing?"

Trey squeezed her back. "I'll tell you later. Can we just move a bit further away from this hole for now? It's not far away now – you can hear it."

He manoeuvred her back to a safe distance and watched as Tony slowly got back on his feet again, vigorously dusting the seat of his trousers in the knowledge that Suzanne had only just washed them.

"Right," he announced, still catching his breath slightly, "let's have a look at this thing for real then. Hard to see much on the video." He edged towards the vent.

Trey looked at Lauren. "Video? What video?"

"I took one looking down the hole as that thing went after you. When it, er, collected John."

That was quick thinking, thought Trey, proud of his wife's calmness under pressure. "Nice one. I can look at it later."

"It wasn't very clear though."

"I'm not surprised. I know what it looks like now, though."

"You do? Didn't you turn the torch off to hide?"

Trey was just about to respond when he noticed that both Tony and Mel had now crawled across to the hole and were on their hands and knees, very carefully peering down as the noise got ever louder. Mel had picked up the torch and was about to turn it on.

"I'm not sure that's wise, guys," he said, breaking away from Lauren. "The thing making that noise is a man-eater. It shouldn't be able to squeeze up that vent but you never know. It could be like an octopus."

"Wouldn't it have come up before now, then?" asked Lauren.

Trey thought for a second. "I suppose if it could climb up, it would have tried when the trapdoor was closed, found it was a dead end, and not bothered to try again. We might be ok though, with it lit up."

Tony and Mel had begun reversing back and standing up at the thought of an octopus slithering up the vent to attack them. "What do you mean?" asked Mel, brushing the dirt off her palms.

"The only reason I got out of there alive was because when I shone the torch in its face, it didn't like it. Turned right round and ran off."

The sound from below was very loud now, probably only about fifteen seconds away. Trey strode over to the cellar door and flung it wide open to provide a quick escape route.

"Right!" he announced, striding back towards the vent. "We need to test this out. Mel, when you see the gigarat down the bottom and I give the signal, switch the torch on. I'll do the same with mine. Lauren, can you film it like you did before. If it starts trying to climb up, run like hell. Through the door and up into our apartment. I'll go last and close the cellar door. I think it will react against the light though, so we should be ok. Get ready!"

He ran to the vent, got his torch back out, and he and Mel held each of them just over the edge, forefingers ready to press the 'on' button. Lauren fiddled with her phone to get the video function back.

Tony looked around nervously and wondered how quickly he would be able to get back to his feet and out of the door. He didn't want to be the 'expendable' extra you see in films meeting an untimely death so the rest of the well paid cast don't have to, but if there was a creature down there he was keen to see it.

The noise below had stopped abruptly, and the small stepladder was being pushed slowly forward by a huge brown snout, now snuffling and sniffing to see what feast this was that had been delivered down the vent for it on this occasion.

Trey glanced at Mel, whose eyes were like saucers.

"Oh my God," she whispered under her breath. She looked quickly up at Trey. "Now?"

"No, it needs to be looking up at us."

Mel nodded and returned her gaze to the shiny brown blob below as it noisily wiggled the unfortunate step ladder violently from side to side in its mouth, and appeared to make the wise decision not to try and eat it.

Perhaps its acute hearing had heard the whispers above, or perhaps it just sensed that there were other living things in the vicinity, but without warning it froze, standing stock still, such that without clear light or motion it could hardly be seen. Suddenly it moved, using the rounded tunnel sidewalls to twist itself up and round, and poked its head up into the vent, spitting between its fangs like an angry cat, but thankfully unable to squeeze itself any further up.

The four humans above all involuntarily pulled their heads back a fraction as though hit by an electric shock.

"Aagh!" cried Tony, forgetting that he should not be trying to attract attention.

"Now!" hissed Trey, and he and Mel switched on their torches. Two beams of light pierced the gloom below and were aimed at the aggressive yellow-toothed face below.

Immediately the gigarat hissed, dropped down, and disappeared back the way it had come.

"Yes!" shouted Trey. "Have that, you bastard!"

Lauren started, not used to her husband shouting aggressively. But she could understand why Trey hated this creature so much after what it had put him through, and of course, because of Hoggo. That seemed so long ago but it was only this morning that Hoggo had been standing here helping them. And now.....

She brought herself back to the moment and pressed the red circle on her phone to stop recording. "I got it all on video," she announced, without a hint of triumph, "including that last bit about the bastard."

Trey looked slightly sheepish. "Sorry, I just had to say something. After what it's done. You know."

He didn't go into details. How much had Lauren told Mel and Tony? He needed time with Lauren alone.

Mel stepped forward.

"We need to call the police. We're so pleased that you've made it back, Trey, but we need to report what happened to John."

A flood of realisations struck Trey simultaneously. Mel hadn't reacted when Lauren mentioned John being 'collected' by the gigarat, so she obviously knew he had fallen down the shaft and was dead – Lauren must have told her. And although it could be argued that he had just helped to kill Mel's husband, that must mean that Lauren sensibly hadn't mentioned that bit, otherwise Mel would have been going absolutely mad at him. But despite knowing that John was dead, she wasn't an emotional mess. If anything, she seemed quite calm and controlled.

"I've just realised Mel, I haven't said how sorry I am about what happened to John. It's was just terrible."

Mel smiled weakly. "Thank you Trey. Don't suppose it was much fun for you either by the sound of it. I was saying to Lauren, I guess I'm still in a bit of shock – it hasn't really sunk in yet. Especially with that creature down there too. It's all a bit overwhelming."

"You can say that again," agreed Lauren.

"Mel's right about the police," interrupted Tony, cutting to the chase, "we need to get them here pronto. Tell them about that massive beast down there. I'll call them now."

"You'll get a better signal outside," said Trey hastily, trying to delay the inevitable. Could he and Lauren still be suspected of the murders of Anita and John? All the people who knew anything were dead now. They might still actually get away with this, especially if they can find the other entrance where all those bones had come from. The only other potential issue he could see tripping them up was if anyone had seen Anita or Hoggo go into the cellar, but then how would they know that they hadn't come back out again later?

No, there was definitely a chance now that they would be ok.

He put his arm around Lauren as they followed Tony and Mel out of the cellar, and gave her shoulder a squeeze. "Time for the police?" he whispered.

She nodded. "No choice now, really. We'll need to talk before they get here though."

"Definitely."

Ahead of them, Tony had already dialled 999 and had his phone to his ear as he climbed the steps up into the garden.

CHAPTER 39

Norman closed the door behind him and limped across to his favourite old chair.

They'd not beaten him up or anything, he'd just stubbed his toe on the stone step coming in the front door of the house, thanks to his mind being on other things, and it really hurt. Just one thing after another today.

Good thing he had no jobs today – with the luck he was having he would probably have gone to the wrong house or something. Mind you, he had very few jobs these days. The financial crisis was hitting everyone in different ways, and some people had started cutting their own grass and pruning their own bushes as an easy way to cut back spending a little. He seemed to be spending more and more time in Ridley House gardens these days.

The chair welcomed him into its bosom. Worn yellow fabric, once bright as a dandelion on a sunny day, and now the muted colour of dirty sand, took him in and comforted him with a gentle rocking motion. The dark wooden rocker frame was scuffed from every angle, little nicks and pockmarks painting its neglected history. Much like its owner, thought Norman; scuffed mentally as well as physically.

He'd done what he'd promised himself that he would and told them the truth, but of course they didn't know he was telling the truth. To them, all he'd done was change his story.

"Did you know that one of your close neighbours is also now missing?" they had asked him, and like a fool he had said yes, because he had been listening through a crack in his door when they were breaking into her flat yesterday afternoon. What an idiot, why didn't he just say no? But of course that answer attracted further intense questioning, and it was obvious that they were looking for a link between the two missing ladies.

They had to let him go in the end, as they had nothing they could charge him with and no further questions to ask, but he felt their eyes boring into his back as he walked out of the police station just two hours after they had brought him in.

"We are keeping all our lines of enquiry open at this stage," he was told when he asked if he was in the clear now. So he assumed they had not ruled him out of Molly's murder; if anything he was probably their number one suspect now. After all, who else would have been out at that time of night in the forest?

This was all so unfair. He was the one trying to help Molly and here he was, being repaid for his kindness by having the fingers of the law pointed at him, scratching at him to see if they could reveal anything underneath.

He sat brooding in a cloud of self-pity, until he realised that the pain in his toe had eased. Well, this wasn't solving anything, and he was hungry. He stretched his arms over his head in a wide arc, and breathed out slowly, trying to release some tension and prepare himself for replacing comfort with actually doing something useful. That done, he flopped his arms back down and introduced them to the arms of the chair, so that all four arms could work together in propelling him to his feet.

He'd been given a tuna sandwich for lunch at the police station, but it wasn't enough. He padded into the kitchen. After he'd eaten, he'd find out who or what had actually killed Molly. Yes, that's what he'd do. He owed it to her, and he owed it to himself not to be framed for a murder he had no part in.

How he would do this, he had absolutely no idea. But if the cops were going to build a circumstantial case against him, he needed to be one step ahead.

Perhaps Anita was the key. If they were both dead, they may have been killed by the same person. That seemed likely. The last time he had seen Anita was..... with that new guy on the ground floor. They had gone into his cellar on the Sunday, but Norman had gone off to get some compost out of the shed after that, so hadn't seen them come out, but then on Tuesday, he had seen Anita go in there again, on her own this time, but then not come out again. He might just have missed her, but now, in hindsight, the whole thing was looking suspicious. What if her body was in there, lying in a corner next to Molly's. His imagination started to get the better of him as he pictured the two corpses propped up against a wall.

The big question was why Anita would be enticed down into the Clark's cellar in the first place. Twice, as well. Presumably they had only just met her, so that was odd.

He had to find out.

The major problem he faced, though, in trying to clear his name, was that it would involve talking to people, and he didn't really know how to do that. Not like everybody else around him – they seemed to be able to strike up conversations just like that, and keep them going too. How did they do that? He might get one sentence out, possibly a second, but after that he'd be struggling. Oh Lord, this was not going to be easy.

***

"Ok, thank you officer, we'll be here waiting. Goodbye."

Tony pressed the 'end call' button on his phone as though prodding a peach in a shop to see how ripe it was.

"There," he announced, adding somewhat unnecessarily "the call is made."

The four of them stood in Trey and Lauren's lounge, all with the same thought. What happens now?

"How long will they be?" asked Lauren.

Tony shrugged. "He just said 'as soon as they can'. I don't blame him but I think he thought it was a prank call when I started explaining what happened to John. Kept repeating back what I'd just said to him. But I suppose the fact that people keep disappearing round here meant he couldn't just ignore it. Two women and now John."

He shook his head sadly.

"And Hoggo," said Trey.

Tony and Mel both looked up sharply, and replied in unison. "Who?"

"My friend, Hoggo. Big guy, blond hair. He came round this morning, went for a ten minute walk in the woods, and hasn't come back. His car's still in the drive. We told the police and they said they'd look for him."

Lauren's eyes widened. "They haven't come back to us, have they? We kind of forgot about that while everything else was going on. We saw them going off with Norman, but since then, nothing."

"Maybe they did come back but we didn't hear the doorbell. Hang on though, didn't they say we should ring them if we didn't hear anything and Hoggo hadn't returned?"

"Did they? I can't remember." She ran a distracted hand through her hair. "We should maybe fit a doorbell buzzer in the cellar, though."

"How often are we going to be down there? It was just bad luck if we missed them."

"Good point. Never again if I can help it." Lauren shuddered. "Nothing but bad things have happened down there since we arrived."

Mel nodded. "I'd be the same in your shoes. Really sorry to hear about your friend. Four people gone and two in one day now, that's ridiculous. Maybe he's just fallen over a tree root or something and broken his leg."

"The police would have found him by now," pointed out Tony. "Apart from anything else he'd be screaming in pain. My word, this whole area seems to be cursed right now. You don't think……." he paused and looked round the room in the style of a conspirator, "you don't think that maybe Anita and Hog... your friend, that maybe they fell down that hole too and got taken away by the animal?"

Trey felt his pulse rising. Every step he took on this sticky web of lies now risked him getting trapped.

"I can't see how," he replied as innocently as he could muster, "that door is locked except when one of us is down there." Realising that this immediately made them sound like prime suspects, he hastily added, "and they didn't fall down that vent when we were in there."

"No," confirmed Lauren. The catch in her voice as she spoke didn't help her cause, so she quickly cleared her throat and added some emphasis. "No, definitely not."

Tony nodded, seemingly satisfied.

"It was just a thought," he said.

Mel was looking troubled though. Was she putting two and two together? Trey was starting to realise that both he and Lauren, previously citizens of good standing, had now not only now both been involved in the deaths of their new neighbours, but, even if they avoided prosecution, would be spending the rest of their lives holding a guilt-lined shield of deception in front of them, and hoping that neither one of them stumbled and dropped it at the wrong moment. No wonder some criminals turned themselves in after a while – the mental pressures were going to be crushing. He waited for the first accusation to arrive.

To his relief, though, Mel had other things on her mind.

"Look, I need to go and, er, perform my ablutions, before the cops come," she said.

"Good idea," agreed Tony. "They'll probably want to speak to us separately in any case. They always do, don't they?"

Mel glanced at Trey and Lauren. "As I said, I'd best be going. I'll need to tell John's relatives too; that's not going to be easy. I'll see you later."

She turned and headed back to her flat.

"Thanks for everything, Mel," called Lauren after her.

"No problem," came the voice from the hall, almost too brightly. Was Mel already contemplating the new life ahead of her?

"I'll be off too then," said Tony. He reached the lounge door, stopped and turned, waiting until Mel had closed the front door behind her.

"Melanie seems surprisingly sanguine about her husband's demise, does she not?" he remarked in a low voice.

Lauren was careful not to break too many confidences. "I think they had grown tired of each other. It was a bit of a loveless marriage, I think, more a case of them tolerating each other towards the end."

Tony raised an eyebrow. "And now the end has been reached. They hid it well, then. Still, glad you made it out, though, Trey. At least John had lived a life – you're still young."

Trey smiled. "Thanks Tony. Not feeling quite so young at the minute though, I have to say."

"I can imagine, after what you've been though." Tony shook his head in wonder. "Anyway, I'll be off. Prepare to answer questions!"

With a perfunctory wave of his hand he turned on his heel, and moments later they heard the front door slam.

Lauren padded over and closed the lounge door.

"Right," she said, "quickly tell me what happened down there, then we'll make sure we know what we're going to say to the cops."

Trey nodded, but found that he was shaking. "I think the adrenaline's wearing off – look at my hands."

He held them up – they were trembling uncontrollably. Suddenly his brain buckled under a burst dam of emotions, flooding through him, taking over. He stumbled over to the nearest chair and fell into it. His eyes were wet as he looked up imploringly.

"I killed John, babes. I kicked him in the face, deliberately. Not like you, you didn't mean it, but I did. Only for a second, you know? But that's all it needed. I just did it in the heat of the moment, thinking he'd pull me down, but maybe he could have got out if I'd dug that leg in and held on so he could get out. I just thought..... well, I might have thought I could stop John telling the police. That might have been part of it. I don't know. It all happened so fast...."

Lauren rushed over and sat on the arm of the chair to give him a hug. Her tears ran into his hair.

"You did it to save yourself, babes, and me too maybe. I'm sure most people would have done the same in your position. I know you said John would have told Mel, and probably the police, and so I'd have ended up in jail, and maybe that was in the back of your mind, but that wasn't the main reason you kicked him, was it?"

Trey looked up at her and smiled through his tears. But the more he thought about it, the more he questioned his own motives from that split-second moment, as he tried to get John to let go of his leg rather than helping him. Was Trey was now in the same position as his wife? Perhaps not a bona fide murderer, but almost certainly a manslaughterer, if such a word existed. Two hard working, decent members of the public, now like something out of Bonnie and Clyde.

She gave him a kiss on the forehead. "I know it's hard but we've got to get ready for the cops. Can you do this?"

Trey looked at his beautiful wife, her eyes redder than his. To do what he had done, and then muck it up now, would be ridiculous. She was right, he had to pull himself together.

"Yeah, of course. Sorry. It just hit me, you know? Not just what I've done, but what I've escaped from. Ok, so after I heard the gigarat coming after me and said goodbye to you......"

Urgently but quietly he recounted his escape from the animal.

"I was that close to dying," he concluded, holding up his finger and thumb, millimetres apart. "Still can't believe I got out."

Lauren grabbed him and gave him a long hug, her face buried into his shoulder.

"I thought I'd lost you. I thought I'd be on my own for ever. I was so scared."

Trey thought he could feel the wetness of her tears through his shirt. He stroked her shoulder, his protective instincts taking over from the delayed shock. "I know. I know. I thought I was done for too. But hey, no sense thinking about that. You can't get rid of me that easily!"

He eased her away and held her out at arm's length. Her eyes were moist and her lips quivering at the thought of what could have happened to her husband, but there was a trace of a smile too.

"Yeah, you're right," she sighed. "We need to think about the future now, not what just happened. First thing is to make sure we don't end up banged up in jail for the rest of our lives."

"You're not wrong there. Let's sit over there and talk."

They got up from the chair and walked across to the sofa, flumping into it in unison. They didn't know how long it would be before the police turned up, so they would need to make the most of it.

Lauren rushed through how much she had and hadn't told Mel and Tony, then they quickly synchronised a creative recollection of events based on a meld of fact and fiction, with the sole objective of ensuring that the reason for the deaths of Anita and John, and to some extent Hoggo, could not in any way be attributed to them.

Anita bursting in on them in the cellar now hadn't happened. As far as they were concerned, she had seen the cellar with Trey on Sunday, when the coal bunker was still in place, but that was the last time she had been down there. Who knows what happened to her after that? And if there was any of her blood in the tunnel under the vent, that was just coincidence – the gigarat may have dragged her along there from wherever he had found her. It was stretching credulity, yes, but if they couldn't definitively prove otherwise……

Then there was Hoggo. It was too late now to admit any involvement in his death, as John and Trey had told the first two officers that he had gone for a walk in the woods, and Lauren had repeated this to Mel. If they now suddenly admitted that the gigarat had killed him, they'd be as good as inviting the police to charge them. It could not be changed now.

So…. when he turned up in his van on Wednesday, apart from John, had anyone noticed him removing the ladder from it, and bringing it into the cellar? Maybe, but there was no time to check that.

So the story would have to be accurate in terms of Hoggo helping open the trapdoor and bringing his ladder round on the Wednesday. But after that, they mustn't give the police any suspicions that Hoggo went down to have a look, or that Trey and Hoggo might have ventured into the vent for an adventure a few days later, as that would mean they had lied to officers Rakowski and Davis, and why would they have done that?

No, instead, the cops must be told that when the top of the ladder wedged up against the underside of the floorboards and wouldn't fit into the hole, they gave up, and put the ladder to one side. Hoggo agreed to leave it there while they decided what to do.

Hoggo then returned this morning to collect his ladder, but after saying he felt ill and wanted to clear his head, went for a walk in the woods and hasn't been seen since.

As far as John was concerned, yes, he did come and have a look at the closed trapdoor on Monday, but then didn't confront them on the Wednesday and see the hole then. No, his first sighting was today and of course it turned out to be his last too after he fell in and took Trey with him down the vent.

The hospital will know that Lauren left her shift early after a phone call from her husband, but thankfully she hadn't given them any detail of why she had to rush off other than that it was urgent. The actual reason had been Trey telling her that Hoggo had been attacked by the animal, but of course they couldn't say that. They had to come up with another reason. Man, this was getting complicated.

They hadn't much time to think, so settled on something random: Trey had developed a terrible pain in his stomach and thought it might be serious. Luckily, by the time Lauren got home, it had gone. A pretty lame explanation, but it would have to do. They were just trying to save him having to call an ambulance, after all.

However, almost everything after that, including the near-death experience Trey went through escaping from the gigarat, could be truthfully explained, as Tony and Melanie would know about this already, and there was no reason to keep it secret. It was just the manner of John's death that had to be altered.

"This is a whole steaming pile of poo," concluded Lauren with a loud sigh. "We're never going to remember all this and which bits we have made up. Maybe we should just give in and admit everything."

Trey lowered his voice but raised its intensity. "What, and see you sent down for manslaughter and not reporting a death? And something else I've just thought of – assuming the gigarat leaves some of John behind, do they have the technology now to find traces from the soles of my shoes attached to John's face? How would I explain that? On top of which, I didn't report Anita's death either. Or Hoggo's. Neither of us did that."

"We've dug a hole for ourselves with Anita and just kept digging ever since."

"Exactly. No, we're in too deep now. Let's see if we can get through whatever these officers want to ask us, then we'll have to sit down and go over our story again and again until we know it off by heart. Ok?"

Lauren nodded. "I suppose so. What a mess."

Trey was about to agree when the doorbell went. He gave Lauren a look of weary resignation, took a deep breath and went to answer it. "Here we go then", he muttered as he padded across the lounge.

When he opened the door, he was confronted by the last person he had expected to see.

CHAPTER 40

"Hello," said Norman.

He had a strange, lopsided smile, that looked as though he was forcing it out very much against his own wishes, which may well have been the case. His hair was wild as usual, his ragged beard exploring the collar of an old tweed jacket that appeared to have been re-homed from a 1970s charity shop.

Before Trey could overcome his shock at the fact that his vision of a couple of uniformed police officers had been usurped by the wild man of Borneo, Norman offered some information.

"I'm Norman," he explained. "From upstairs."

Trey tried to recover his composure. "Yes, hello. I know who you are."

That sounded rude, so he clarified with "I've seen you in the garden. Nice to meet you."

Norman nodded, searching for words.

"Yes," he said, followed by "er...."

Trey didn't want to appear impatient, but he did have things to worry about at the minute, and Norman's sudden appearance wasn't of great assistance.

"Is there something I can help you with?" he prompted.

Norman took a small step back, then forward again. He had lowered his head since his initial greeting and didn't seem to want to look Trey in the eye.

"Do you know Anita?" he mumbled at last.

"I met her, but only twice. Why?"

"I saw you with her."

"Did you?" Trey quickly put two and two together. "The day after the housewarming party, presumably, in the garden? Last Sunday?"

Norman appeared slightly non-plussed, as though that was not the answer he was expecting.

"Yeah," he replied. "I saw..."

The doorbell above Trey's head rang again, giving both of them a start. Norman looked behind him, then back at Trey with the kind of 'shall we run?' expression of a man who had just seen a leopard creeping up on them.

Trey really didn't help matters by announcing that "that'll be the police".

Norman had had enough. This had been a bad idea, and as he expected it had not gone well. In a way he was thankful for the doorbell as it had saved him having to say anything else, but this was countered by the revelation as to who was apparently waiting outside.

"I'll go then," he said hurriedly. "Yeah, ok, er, thanks. Bye."

Trey watched him lope across the atrium and up the stairs. What was that about? Why was he asking about Anita? Weird guy.

He looked behind him. Lauren had drifted into the hallway and heard the conversation. She shrugged at him as if to say 'no clue either'.

As Trey walked across the atrium to open the main door, he had a sudden thought. Had Norman been about to reveal that he had also seen Anita go into the cellar on Tuesday afternoon and not come out again? His heart sank. It was entirely possible of course. Even in the short time they had been here Trey had often checked out a movement in the garden and been relieved to see that the potential trespasser was always Norman, tending the plants. He was like a camouflaged CCTV camera.

Well, that was just great, terrific. No sooner had they thought they were in the clear than another possible fence to jump looms up in front of them.

That would have to wait though; they needed to get through the next hail of arrows first.

Detective Sergeant Erica Collins looked hard at Lauren, then handed her phone back.

"Well. That first video wasn't conclusive, but the second one....... I don't know what to say. It looked terrifying, if I'm honest. That thing was chasing you? Rather you than me, I have to say. It's definitely real? This isn't a prank, is it, some manufactured video or some film clip you've downloaded off the internet?"

Both Trey and Lauren shook their heads. "Absolutely not," said Lauren.

Collins studied their reactions, looking for a glimmer of uncertainty or taunting, but finding nothing.

"And you, sir, came face to face with that thing in a tunnel down there?"

"Yep," replied Trey.

"Ok. Well, I'll admit it's not something I can explain. The video doesn't look manufactured, but then I'd half believe Godzilla was real if I wasn't told it was CGI. You just can't tell half the time these days. Anyway, we'll need you to forward those videos on to us if you can."

She fumbled in her pocket. "Here's my card; there's an email address on it."

Lauren nodded, took the card, and began typing on her phone.

Collins turned to Detective Constable Bartrum, whom Trey judged to be no older than himself. "What do you think?"

Paul Bartrum straightened his back and gave his verdict.

"I've certainly never seen anything like that before. It wasn't nice, was it? Those big teeth. Ugh. I'm finding it hard to believe, to be fair. I think we should go and check out this hole, m'am."

Collins nodded. "I agree." She waved an arm at the young couple opposite. "Lead the way, please, if you would."

"Sure," said Trey, pleased that so far neither he nor Lauren had said anything that they shouldn't. Early days, but their story was holding up.

He led the detectives out through the French windows, Lauren bringing up the rear. Interesting that the detectives had been wheeled in now – clearly the police had realised that this was becoming a major event and they needed to apply some investigative expertise to establish what was happening with all these missing people.

At least now they had a genuine death to contend with – John was missing, yes, but the first to be reported as definitely dead.

They descended into the cellar and Bartrum whistled as the beam of his torch picked out the pattern of the bricks all the way to the bottom.

"Whoa. I've never seen anything like that before. That's incredible."

He wiggled his torch around.

"It does look like the hole in the video. And I see what you mean about the tunnel down there at the bottom. See that, guv?"

Collins grunted, more conscious of the need to maintain a professional veneer. "Yep, it checks out. Any idea why it's here? Why build a shaft to a tunnel system under a house? Seems a daft thing to do."

"It would be," agreed Trey. "So we reckon it must have been a ventilation shaft for the old mines below, then when they dug the foundations for the house they found it, and rather than try and fill it in they just put a heavy door over it. Don't know that of course, we're just guessing."

"Seems a bit dodgy to me. Tunnels can collapse, can't they? If something happened down there it could be like a sinkhole appearing. The whole house could go down with it."

Trey recalled the debate he had had with John on this very subject. "It's been there for over 120 years and that hasn't happened," he pointed out.

"Nonetheless, we'll need to get some Health and Safety advice on this before anyone else goes down there."

Trey gave a little snort. "I was going to say I can vouch for the fact that it's safe enough, but then of course it's not safe at all with a man-eating animal chasing after you."

"Indeed. I would also suggest," said Collins, "that your method of accessing the tunnel wasn't that safe either."

Trey was about to object that a ladder was perfectly safe but remembered just in time that as far as the police were concerned, he'd never used a ladder to get down there.

"Yeah, true. Not by choice, of course."

"Of course. Looking at the depth of this shaft now I find it amazing that you weren't seriously injured."

"John was a big guy, he must have been a good cushion. I've got a load of bumps and grazes though, and I did hurt my hip too."

"I noticed you were limping a bit."

"Just a bit, yeah."

"Do you need medical attention?"

"He's ok," said Lauren. "I'm a nurse so I'm keeping an eye on him."

"She always does," smiled Trey. "The pain is going, though; it was pretty intense when I was down there, especially when I was trying to get away from the gigarat. I was hobbling like an old man."

"What did you call it?"

Trey let out an embarrassed cough. "Gigarat. I made it up. Just so it had a name."

He could see Bartrum suppressing a smirk, but Collins simply raised a painted-on eyebrow and pressed on with her questioning.

"And you're quite certain it can't climb up?"

"Like we said before, it could only get its head wedged into the vent, not its body. You saw the video."

Collins didn't answer, instead smoothing back a loose hair that had escaped from her ponytail and found the corner of her mouth, whilst continuing to scan the room for anything else that might require a question. Her gaze settled on the trapdoor.

"That's a weighty block of wood. You said earlier that you found it under the coal, so how did you lift it up?"

"With difficulty. My friend Hoggo helped us. Strong guy."

"The chap who went for a walk in the woods and hasn't come back?"

Trey lowered his head. "Yeah."

Lauren stepped forward. "You've not found him then?"

Collins turned to Lauren. "Shouldn't that have been the first thing you asked us?"

Trey could see Lauren trying to mask the whirring thoughts in her brain as panic threatened to strangle a viable answer. He cut in.

"We've just got a lot of stuff going on – we're a bit stressed out, you know? I've only just escaped death myself."

Collins viewed him from the corner of her eye. "You think he's dead then?"

Now it was Trey's turn to escape from a self-laid trap. It was proving so easy to fall into them – they'd have to be so much more careful. "No, I used 'myself' in the sense that…. well, I meant that was why it's hard to think straight, when you've just been through such a traumatic event. So many things happening at once. We'd not forgotten about Hoggo, but, well, Lauren nearly lost me, and that's been more important to her….."

Collins gave a curt nod. "I understand. You're in shock, I would imagine, after what you say you've both been through. There's no sign of your friend, though, and that's a worry. We've now got four people either dead or missing within a few days, all in or around this house. Quite a coincidence, don't you think?"

Trey and Lauren both mumbled in agreement, Trey feeling he had to add something.

"It's not good," he heard himself saying rather lamely, then noticed Collins fixing him with a gimlet eye for longer than was strictly necessary, hanging out an invitation to elaborate. This was psychological pressure and he was feeling it. They knew what they were doing, these detectives, trying to wheedle out the smallest sign of potential guilt or uncertainty. He held her gaze. To look down or to one side now would be a 'tell' – he'd watched enough TV to know that.

After a few moments Collins sniffed and turned away, apparently satisfied there was nothing more to see in Trey's face. For now.

She pointed at the vent.

"Can you tell me which direction Mr Firwell was coming from when he fell down this hole, and where you were standing? Describe what happened."

Ok, thought Trey. Remain calm. They'd talked about this, agreed a viable account of how John could have fallen without assistance, taking Trey with him. All he had to do was describe it and make it sound real. Don't, under any circumstances, think about what actually did happen up until the point where they both fell in, or some crucial inconsistency might slip into the account of the incident. No mention of the ladder. Right, here goes.

"We'd just come into the cellar. I went round this side of the trapdoor, and John went round the other side. He was quite keen to see what was down the hole so kneeled down, and we talked for a bit. Then when he got up, his right leg sort of buckled underneath him. He fell forward towards me, over the hole, and as he fell he grabbed my ankle. Then it all happened so quickly. Both of us cried out and he dragged me down with him. One minute I was standing here, the next minute I was being pulled downwards. I tried to grab the edge of the vent as I went down, but John's a heavy guy so I had no chance. After that, I don't remember much except waking up and finding myself at the bottom."

"There was a loud kind of a crack," interjected Lauren, "after they fell. It sounded pretty bad. We think it must have been John's head hitting the floor." She gave a little shiver. "Thankfully Trey landed on top of him."

Detective Bartrum had remained crouched by the vent, repeatedly glancing down, perhaps in the hope of catching sight of the scary creature in the video. He looked up as Trey concluded the description of John's demise.

"Poor bugger," he commented, "what a way to go, eh?"

Detective Sergeant Collins rewarded him with an icy glare. The subtext was: 'you can make casual comments when the public are out of earshot, but save it until then, eh?'

Bartrum took the cue and rose to his feet, thinking of something useful to redeem himself with.

"Was the deceased still alive after the fall?"

"No," said Lauren. "Because I'm a nurse, I could guide Trey in checking for any vital signs, but John had no pulse. I would guess that he died instantly when his head hit the ground, but I'm sure that Trey landing on top of him didn't help."

"Indeed," remarked Collins. "So what happened then?"

Trey explained how he had heard the gigarat coming, and the rest of the drama from then until when he was pulled up by Lauren, Mel and Tony.

"Quite a story. You're a lucky man. Who else has access to this cellar?" Collins fired in another arrow.

Trey pulled the large iron key out of his pocket and held it up. "This is the only way to get in. There's only one key."

"Do you always lock the door?"

"Yes. To be honest, we've only been here just over a week so we've not been down here that much ourselves."

"So no one could have wandered in here when your back was turned and fallen in?"

A hummingbird of an idea flitted into Trey's brain, darting around but not staying still long enough for him to cover every possibility. If he said they'd left the door open then any of the missing people could have their disappearance explained if they had gone into the cellar and fallen down the vent.... But no, that wouldn't explain Hoggo, as he knew the hole was there. How likely is it that two or three people would all stumble, trip, and fall to their deaths? No, keep the story as they had agreed.

So having appeared to think hard, Trey replied firmly. "No. No, we did lock it, every time we went out."

Collins nodded. "Alright." She glanced at Bartrum. "I think we've seen enough. We had better go and speak to Mrs Firwell. I would imagine she is in quite a state."

"Actually no," said Lauren, briefly explaining the fractured relationship status of the couple.

Trey watched the detectives taking in this information and no doubt immediately marking Melanie up as a possible suspect in arranging for John to somehow fall down the hole, with Trey and Lauren as collaborators.

How little they knew.

As they all left, Trey was careful to lock the cellar door behind them. They came back up through the French windows into the apartment, and before the detectives moved on to Mel, Collins had a last warning.

"There may be some interest from the press which I would strongly suggest you ignore. If any journalists come sniffing around, tell them to speak to us. Anything you say to them could be mis-reported and prejudice our enquiries, and that would be a serious matter. Do you understand?"

"Yes," they both replied, then thought about what Collins had just said. The last thing Lauren needed was reporters stalking her at work, trying to catch her out with dumb-fool questions.

"Is that likely?" she asked. "Have they been informed?"

Collins gave a wry smile.

"Even if they weren't they have ways of finding these things out. I suspect we will need to give a press conference soon but that decision's above my pay grade. The problem we've got..." she paused, working out how best to explain this "...is that this could become a big news story. One person goes missing, big deal, happens all the time. Two people missing, apparently not connected other than they are in the same vicinity, is pretty unusual. But here, you've now got three missing and one dead in the space of a week. That's potentially front page news. We're talking the national press. So actually that brings me to a really important point. If they get wind of the fact that there's a huge rat that eats people under your house, you'll have not just the UK press, but the world press here too, besieging your apartment and making your life hell."

Lauren clutched Trey's arm.

"Oh! No, we don't want that. Definitely not."

Collins smiled humourlessly. "Well, you know what to do then. Whatever this animal is, it's going to be big news unless we manage what information is released. We'll make this clear to Mrs Firwell too, and you said that there was another gentleman helping to get you out?" She flicked open her notepad. "Tony, you said. Tony Wilson."

"Yes," said Trey, "but you might need to get round there fast. Suzanne will know too."

"His wife?"

"Yes, and for all we know she's phoning a friend as we speak."

Collins shot a glance to Bartrum.

"Nip up there now would you, Paul? Catch them before they spread it any further. Which flat are they? I assume it's upstairs."

Trey looked at Lauren.

"Flat 4," she replied instantly. "On the first floor." How did she do that? He had no idea which number flat everyone was in, apart from the Firwells, and that was only because he walked past their door to exit the building. Well, Mel's door, as it was now.

"Thanks," replied Collins, flicking her head at Bartrum by way of an instruction.

Bartrum nodded and was quickly out of the front door and heading up to speak to Tony and Suzanne.

Collins, having now seen for herself that this was not the fantastical nonsense that her brief had indicated, was well aware of the importance of containing the situation. Potentially four people dead, and all eaten by a massive rat? This was science fiction, surely. But if not, and the truth got out, there would be complete chaos, and their investigations would be significantly hampered by having hundreds of reporters everywhere. As soon as she had spoken to Mrs Firwell, she'd give the guv'nor a call and seek his guidance. This needed to go all the way up the chain.

"I make that five of you that know about this now, and that's already too many. I may be back, so don't go anywhere."

She turned on her heel and was out of the door before Trey or Lauren could confirm that they wouldn't go anywhere.

Lauren collapsed onto the sofa.

"Oh my God, thank God they've gone. That was so stressful!"

Trey suddenly widened his eyes and held a forefinger to his lips, suggesting silence. He put a knee on the sofa and knelt over to Lauren, whispering in her ear.

"What if they've bugged the room?"

A look of horror dawned on Lauren's face. "When?" she whispered back.

"While we were telling them what happened. One of them might have been quietly attaching a device to the underneath of the coffee table or something."

They both looked at each other, then Trey got down on the floor and peered under the coffee table. Nothing. He got up and walked round the room, checking every chair, lampshade, sideboard – even the TV. Still nothing. He gave Lauren a thumbs up.

"I suppose," he said, "that it is a bit early in the day to start suspecting us to that degree. Also, they probably need a court order or a warrant or something, as it's a pretty invasive thing to do. We could sue them otherwise."

Lauren let out a long sigh. "This is not showing signs of getting any better. And what about Hoggo's family, his girlfriend – we need to let them know what's happened. Well, you know, not everything, but…."

She looked nervously around the room, now concerned that Trey had not spotted a listening device that was transmitting her every word.

"I don't have any of their details," said Trey. "They must be getting worried by now, or at least his girlfriend would be. Knowing Hoggo he wouldn't have given her our details either. Not a detail man, was he?"

"I guess the police will do all that. Probably best they do, too."

Trey checked his watch. "Just coming up to five o'clock. This day seems to have gone on forever. There is one thing that's still bugging me, though."

"Just the one?"

"Ha, well, one in particular, anyway. Old Hagrid upstairs - Norman."

"He does look a bit like Hagrid, doesn't he, apart from the brown hair. Why do you need to see him though? I didn't catch everything he was saying when he was at the door."

"He didn't say much, and that's the problem. All he said was that he had seen me and Anita together, and why was he saying that? Why had he come round to ask questions, when normally he doesn't interact with any of us? Seems a bit random. But maybe he saw something from out there in the garden. One revelation from him and we could be toast. I need to speak to him, find out what he knows."

"When?" Lauren kicked at a bit of fluff on the rug, frustrated that yet another worry was emerging. The fluff seemed attached to the carpet so she left it and got to her feet to begin pacing around.

"Before the police get to him. They'll be busy with Mel and Tony for a while, so I'm thinking maybe I'd go up now....."

"Shall I come too?"

"No, probably best there's only one of us. He seemed quite jumpy earlier. You might scare him." He grinned. "Although maybe if you put some makeup on......"

Lauren couldn't help a tweak of a smile, but she wasn't really in the mood for humour.

"Go on then, Columbo, go and find out what he knows. Don't be too long though, that detective said she might come back. I'll man the fort."

"Ok, see you later."

Lauren watched him go, then realised she really needed to go to the bathroom. Sitting on the loo, a place where a variety of random thoughts are always likely to take the place of a focused concentration on what is happening down below, she tried to fathom what had happened to them both.

How were she and Trey, an ordinary, slightly boring couple, now effectively both murderers, evading police capture and lying through their teeth about the death of three people? As for the fourth, she wondered what had actually happened to Molly the homeless woman. It would seem far too much of a coincidence if her disappearance was nothing to do with all this.

Her shoulders slumped. She wasn't sure she could keep this up for much longer. All the deception and stress. They'd agreed they couldn't even confide in their parents, so it was just her and Trey against the world, pretending everything was fine when it so definitely wasn't.

At least if Norman turned out not to know anything important, perhaps the world wouldn't win. Perhaps they could make it. Come on Trey, bring back some good news.

CHAPTER 41

Trey's progress up to Norman's apartment was impeded by an old lady negotiating her way up the final few steps of the stairs. Trey remembered who she was but not what she was called. It was a short name, he knew that much. Edna, was it? Betty? Hilda? No, these were just all old lady's names. Didn't it begin with a J? Jane….Joan… no, Jean, that was it. He felt strangely proud of his brain's ability to rescue him eventually.

Not that Jean had noticed him. Her focus was on holding onto the banister and raising each leg in turn as though a puppet master above her was in control of them.

Trey bounded up behind her, manufacturing a cheery 'hello' as he went so as not to give her a scare, followed by 'would you like a hand up the stairs?' She glanced round.

"Oh, hello young man. That's very kind of you, but no, I mustn't rely on anyone. You're the new neighbour, aren't you?"

Trey presented a polite smile as he drew level.

"Yes, I'm Trey. Hello Jean."

Jean's watery grey eyes looked up at him. Her eyelashes were white, he noticed.

"How are you finding it here, then?" she asked, pausing with two steps left.

Trey briefly considered what she would think if she really knew how he was finding it. Instead, he lied. "Oh, good, thank you. Yes, very nice."

He couldn't really leave her with that dull platitude before heading up to Norman, so added "how are the monkeys? Keeping you busy?"

Jean looked at him with an air of puzzlement.

"Well, not really, no."

"Oh, that's lucky. Well-behaved then?"

Jean smiled now. He was joking, obviously.

"Yes, very well behaved."

"Are they quiet then?"

"Oh yes, they don't make a sound."

"Really? What do you feed them?"

"As little as I can!"

Trey laughed but realised that this confusing conversation about her monkeys was going nowhere, and he really needed to be hurrying up.

"I don't blame you. The food must be expensive. Anyway, I can't stay Jean, I've got things to do, but lovely to see you again!"

"You too," said Jean, completing her ascent as Trey made for the next flight of stairs. That was too brief, she thought, even though she didn't understand what he meant by the food being expensive. Conversations were a rare treat these days, however peculiar they were, and to have one finish so quickly was a little depressing but not unfamiliar. Her apartment door creaked open and she prepared herself for another evening alone.

As he made himself a cup of tea, Norman wished he was somewhere else. He could have been finishing the planting on that rockery in Holland Drive, or cutting the grass for old Mr Doughty in Ferndale Avenue. But they were both booked in for Monday. He only had one job tomorrow afternoon and it was a small one, trimming a wayward hedge for the Gold family in Harford Road. Couple of hours, tops.

Other than that his weekend was regrettably free, with no excuse not to be mooching around Ridley Manor, a big archery target on his back as the local police patrolled the grounds brandishing their bows and arrows. Far better had he been gainfully employed somewhere else.

He'd been brought up to trust the police, but they didn't seem to want to trust him and believe his story, and that wasn't right of them, because he was telling the truth. Well, the second time around, anyway. Why couldn't they see that? And if they couldn't see that, how could he trust them to find the real killer and not blame it on him? He knew people had been sent to jail for crimes they did not commit, and he had a worrying feeling that he would be next.

Now they were back in the building. The fact that they hadn't come chasing up the stairs after him was a good sign. They must have been going to see Trey, otherwise he wouldn't have known it was them at the door. But then where would they go?

They'd done enough damage as it was by interrupting his investigative work interviewing Trey. He'd had to summon up so much courage to do that, but he'd got precisely nowhere after he was so rudely cut short. It was extremely annoying.

The door bell rang.

Norman dropped the teaspoon of sugar with a start, leaving a pile of white granules on the worktop surface. Oh great, here they were again. And now they'd think he was a druggie no, as well, no doubt, unless he cleared this up. He roughly swept the sugar off the surface and into his cupped hand before tipping it into the cup. Want not waste not, as his mother often used to say. Also, don't give the cops anything to get suspicious about. She didn't say that, of course, but it was still good advice in a situation like this.

The doorbell buzzed again. Alright, hold your horses. He'd make them wait a bit, get his own back. But supposing they broke the door down? On seconds thoughts maybe they'd waited long enough.

He squeezed himself out of the small galley kitchen, and wove his way through the furniture obstacle course that littered the cramped lounge. Heart in mouth, he opened the door, expecting to see two stern faces sitting atop some hi-vis jackets.

But it was Trey from downstairs. He relaxed a little, but only a little. What did he want? Had he come to have a go at him for asking intrusive questions?

"Hey, Norman," said Trey, "hello. Again! Sorry we got interrupted down there. Shall we carry on from where we left off?"

Norman's expression of nervous surprise twisted into an awkward smile.

"Alright," he replied, then waited for Trey to say something else.

"Can I come in then? Probably easier to talk in private, you know." He swivelled his eyes to indicate the presence of potential eavesdroppers with notebooks elsewhere in the building.

Norman started into motion. "Oh, yeah, right, ok." He opened the door wide and as Trey inched his way past into the cluttered room, Norman immediately regretted letting him in. Not only was the flat a mess – what was the point of keeping it tidy when only he saw it? – but now he had a man in his home who, though appearing to be outwardly friendly, might have murdered people.

After all, Anita had ventured into that cellar twice, and now she had disappeared, so who's to say there weren't two bodies in there? And now here the man was, who was with Anita both times, in Norman's small flat. He seemed pleasant enough, but that could all be a façade. Underneath, a hardened murderer, a psychopath. His heartbeat rose a few notches. This wasn't good. He was going to have to be careful. He closed the door and turned to face his potential assailant, hands knotted together in front of him, ready to release and ball them up into fists should that be needed.

There was only one faded yellow chair available for Trey to sit on, the historical dent of Norman's rear quarters clearly pressed into it. Norman, hoping this conversation wouldn't take long, made no effort to clear any of the old newspapers and discarded clothes that had buried the re-purposed sofa opposite, so Trey remained standing.

"You were asking me about Anita?" prompted Trey.

Norman nodded and lowered his head, only raising it half way through his reply. "Yeah, she went into the cellar with you. I saw you. And now......."

Despite not finishing his sentence, the implication hung in the air. He had effectively accused his new neighbour of murder with his first utterance. That wasn't very polite, but he remembered Molly screaming and how urgently he needed to find out what had happened to her. It was no time for niceties. He tried to keep his eyes on Trey, not really knowing what signs of guilt he might spot, but more worried that he would suddenly see the flash of a knife coming his way.

Trey seemed slightly taken aback at how abrupt Norman had been, but replied calmly.

"That's right, on Sunday. She came round and wanted to see what the cellar looked like. She was only in there about five minutes. Did you not see us come out again?"

"No."

"Well we did, both of us."

Trey's eyes bored into Norman's bowed forehead. Norman was around the same height as Trey so when he looked up their eyes met directly.

"What about Tuesday?" asked Norman, playing his trump card.

Shit, thought Trey, as his heart rate quickened. He knows. He's seen Anita go into the cellar and not come out again. This is bad. Quick, think of something. He played for time.

"What do you mean?"

"There was something going on."

"Where?"

"In your cellar."

"What makes you say that?"

"Just what I saw."

"What did you see?"
This was like pulling teeth, but he needed to know.

Norman made a face that could have been interpreted as insouciant, but masked a feeling of considerable unease.
"People going in and out."
He had seen that blond guy go in there with them. Quite a while later he'd seen Anita flit across the paving and descend the steps, followed by some raised voices, then silence. He couldn't see the door from where he was as it was mostly below ground level. But later on he had noticed Trey and Lauren coming out with the blond chap. He wasn't able to tell whether or not they had locked the door. But what about Anita? Just because he hadn't seen her leave the cellar didn't mean she hadn't left a bit earlier. He had been moving between flower beds so he might easily have missed her when his back was turned.

All of this activity had been mildly interesting at the time but no more than that. Now he wished he had been more attentive to what was happening, perhaps moved a bit closer so he could better hear what was being said when voices were being raised. Maybe even seen if he could get into that cellar too, and ask if everything was alright. Although that was probably wishful thinking - he would never have summoned up the gumption to do that, and anyway, back then he had no reason to do that.

He felt now as though he had won the toss and opted to bat on a sticky wicket. He had hoped to trap Trey into admitting something, but if that didn't work, he couldn't just blunder into an outright accusation. There was the small matter of evidence, and the fact that he didn't have any. He could hardly complain about the police trying to accuse him of Molly's murder and then apply the same tactics to Trey. Also, he had to consider that he was standing very close to someone who would then suddenly have a reason to bump him off too. Maybe telling Trey everything he saw wasn't such a good idea.

"Not sure who I saw," he added. "I was quite busy, you know, gardening."

"Right. Ok. So then, what was your question? Were you just wondering what was going on?"

"Yeah."

Despite feeling he was now on top of the situation, a small bead of sweat had started to form on Trey's right temple, and he disguised its removal as the scratching of an itch. Stressful situations did that to him and it was so annoying. It was like when otherwise calm looking people develop red blotches on their neck so that you know that they are churning up inside, however well they think they are disguising it. He hoped Norman hadn't noticed.

He now had to think quickly as to what he should tell Norman. The vent was no longer a secret so he might as well enlighten him on that. Everyone would know about John's death soon, so he could reveal that too. Norman was being cagey, but he could well have seen Hoggo going in and out. In fact he probably had, so he'd have to admit that. Even if he had seen Hoggo come back yesterday and go in there with a ladder, that would be fine. The story was that the ladder didn't fit so they gave up, then Hoggo went for a walk in the woods. Nothing about the gigarat though, and no admission that Anita was there on Tuesday.

"There are things going on down there, yes. We've found a vent in our cellar, leading to some old mine tunnels. So we brought a friend round to have a look and see if we could get down it. That was on Tuesday. But do you know about John?"

Norman's face had presented a slightly befuddled expression as he tried to align Trey's account with his own recollections. On hearing about the vent and the mines, he nodded slowly but without surprise, as though he had just been told that grass was green, then changed that to a shake to answer Trey's supplementary question.

"John downstairs?" he clarified.

"Yes. He died today. Fell down that vent."

"Oh."

Norman considered whether he ought to say a bit more. That was a shock, sure, but one benefit of not getting to know anyone very well was that he didn't get attached to them, and so if a terrible thing befell them, as had happened to John, it seemed, it wasn't really his concern. He had no real feelings for other people. They were there, around him, but as he would not expect them to feel anything for him, and generally they didn't, so he returned the favour.

"Another person dead, then?" was all he could come up with.

Trey nodded gravely, appearing a little surprised at how nonchalantly Norman was taking this news. "Yep. Hit his head on the bottom. He grabbed me and took me down with him but I survived and got out, as you can see."

Norman said nothing for a while, contemplating what he had just been told. It didn't occur to him to ask if Trey had been hurt.

"Is it deep then?"

"The vent? Yes. About 24ft to the ground."

Norman gave a strange low moan of appreciation. "That's a long way down."

"Yes, it is."

A silence settled as Norman considered his next move. Everything Trey had said so far had checked out with what he had seen, but one huge issue remained. On Tuesday he had seen Anita go into that cellar, on her own, heard raised voices, and then she had not come out again. Or at least, he hadn't seen her come out. Trey had studiously avoided mentioning her in his answer.

"Why did Anita go into your cellar again, on Tuesday? If she had already been on Sunday?"

"We didn't see her on Tuesday."

"She went into the cellar. You were already in there."

"I don't think so. Maybe you're confusing it with Sunday. Why are you asking all these questions, though? What's it got to do with you?"

Feeling Trey's tone, Norman took a precautionary step backwards but gently bumped his head on the sloping ceiling. He looked up angrily it as though it was a surprise that it was there. He suddenly felt hemmed in, and wanted Trey to leave.

"Nothing," he replied, sounding defensive, then realising that this wasn't really the best answer he could give. "Well, it's because I want to know what happened to Molly."

"The homeless lady?"

"Yes."

"And you think it had something to do with us?"

"No," said Norman quickly, as he was obliged to do, even though he wasn't sure whether he did or not. "But she disappeared, like Anita did. Seems odd."

"It does," agreed Trey, "but you know as much as I do on that, I'm afraid. None of us know anything about it. Didn't even know that Molly lady existed until we heard she's gone missing. And Anita..... she went back up to her flat, then the next thing we know, she's gone."

Norman, now mentally exhausted from too much conversation, saw an exit route. He reached for the door handle.

"Yeah, looks like it's a mystery. Thanks for coming."

He opened the door wide, welcoming in some cooler, fresher air.

Trey stood still for a minute, wondering whether he needed to quiz this strange man further about exactly what he had seen. He was conscious though, that the more he talked, the greater the chance of him pressing open the metal bar of a man trap, then shortly afterwards stepping in it. He'd leave it at that for now, but he still felt uneasy.

Squeezing past the pungent tweed jacket of the figure next to him, he remembered that police were in the building, so lowered his voice a little.

"That's ok, glad I could help answer your questions. Believe me, we had absolutely nothing to do with Molly."

Norman grunted an acknowledgement as Trey headed back down the stairs. He quickly closed the door and pondered over whether his questions had been answered or not.

He wasn't stupid – he'd noticed how Trey had denied that Anita was in that cellar on Tuesday, but then quickly turned the questioning round on him to avoid further discussion. That was a bit suspicious. So if Anita had gone in that cellar on Tuesday, like he saw, then not come out again, did that mean Molly could be in there too? Had both of them been thrown down this vent that Trey had mentioned?

There was nothing for it. He would have to find a way into that cellar.

CHAPTER 42 - SUNDAY

The fact that Sunday had turned the first page of daylight and revealed a shaft of sun, with the promise of more to come, was not enough to brighten the thoughts of the occupants of Flat 2, Ridley Manor.

Trey and Lauren felt only gloom and foreboding. They didn't know exactly what Norman knew about them. They weren't sure what the police were thinking either. Every day laid out before them was a minefield, with either one of them capable of stepping into an explosion at any time. And although they knew they had got off lightly when compared to the three, possibly four, people who had died, they also knew that they now had to focus on their own self-preservation. Their story had to be watertight.

And so they had spent almost an hour going over it, trying to put themselves in the minds of the police. What would the cops be looking for, what techniques might they have for truffling out inconsistencies?

It helped that much of the couple's version of events was actually true, but that left a large enough chunk that was not. Mixing the two together was not the easiest of tasks, but if they kept going over it, so they were both saying exactly the same things, they might just hold their heads above water.

The main outstanding worry was whether Norman would poke another stick into the spokes, were he to have seen something that they didn't want him to have seen.

But as well as that, Trey now had two additional traumas to deal with: the fact that he had helped someone to die instead of helping them to live, and the awful death of his friend Hoggo. He hadn't dreamt it, he really had been there yesterday as Hoggo had met his grisly end, and on top of that he was having to lie about it. His head was so fogged up, so muddled with emotion, so shocked, so conflicted.

He had tried to catch up on some work that morning, but he just couldn't concentrate. A bit of artwork on a screen seemed so unimportant and pointless. His friend had just died, and then there was John too. Everything else was just..... trivial.

Lauren tried to distract herself by catching up on some of last night's TV, headphones on so she didn't disturb Trey, sitting with his back to her on the other side of the room. She usually liked Saturday night quiz shows, but this time they annoyed her. How could those people be so carefree, laughing and joking like that? Chances are none of them had inadvertently murdered anyone - they were so lucky.

She sighed and switched it off. She had a late shift today, starting at 2pm – should she go? Probably. It was better than moping around at home. But then she'd gone to work yesterday and look what happened. Almost straight back home again when Trey phoned with the awful news about Hoggo. Going in and leaving suddenly was almost worse than not going in at all.

Surely that had to be it now, though. No one else was going to die, were they? Yes, she'd go. If nothing else it might look suspicious if she didn't.

"Trey?"

"Yeah?" He didn't turn round, pretending to be hard at work but with his artwork barely changed since he had sat down.

"The police will probably come back today, won't they?"

Trey gave up the pretence and let go of the mouse, turning to face her.

"I guess so."

"Will it matter if I go to work then?"

"They didn't say you couldn't."

"What about the press? They could come here, or to the hospital."

Trey thought for a moment. "It depends if the police have told them anything. To be honest, I'd be amazed if they released details of the gigarat at any press conference. No, they'd be mad to do that. So that being the case…. they'd not want to mention our cellar either. Or us. All they would probably confirm to the press is that one person is dead and three are missing, but leave it at that."

"But giving press conferences means answering questions."

"Yes, but they don't have to say much. Just that they are following various lines of inquiry and can't say much more at this stage. I reckon that detective was just covering all bases when she said not to tell the press anything. I'm less worried about that than what Norman will do. We need to go over that again."

"How do you mean?"

"As I said last night, he's got it into his head that Molly's disappearance is related to Anita, and he saw Anita go into our cellar, twice. If he says anything to the police…."

"But Molly was nothing to do with us."

Trey lowered his voice. "Yes, but Anita was."

"And we told them that the last time we had seen Anita was on the Sunday."

"Exactly. If they believe him when he says he saw her joining us in the cellar on Tuesday, we're toast."

Lauren let out a gasp of exasperation and flung her arms down on the sofa. "This is ridiculous. Every time we take a step forward some other stupid thing pushes us back where we started. What do we do about Norman then? And don't say anything about killing him. I'm just not going there. Don't even think about it."

Trey got to his feet and walked over to the window. A tear of condensation trickled down the glass in front of him.

"What do we do, then?" he asked softly.

He turned to face Lauren.

"I'm not sure I could get through to Norman. He's a strange character. Maybe autistic or Aspergers or something, I don't know. Problem is, I told him the same as we told the cops, like we agreed. The last time I'd seen Anita was on Sunday. Then he goes and says he saw her go in the cellar on Tuesday and not come out again."

"Has he told the police yet?"

"If he had, they'd be straight round here, so I guess not."

"Well that's one small mercy. But it doesn't solve the problem. He'll tell them at some point."

"Exactly."

A fog of troubled silence weighted the room with a minute of silence, as both of them tried to find a way to engineer themselves out of this new mess. Trey spoke first.

"I could speak to him again, and this time admit she did briefly come into the cellar on Tuesday because she heard us in there and wanted to ask me something about her book cover. We can say we forgot about that as she was only there a couple of minutes. And just because he didn't see her come out doesn't mean she didn't – he'd have had no reason to be staring at our cellar door constantly. He'd only have to look down at his weeding for a couple of minutes and he'd have missed her. So that's what happened. She came out, he didn't see her. Simple as that."

"Yes but when he tells the police, they'll want to know why we lied to them. We wouldn't both have forgotten."

"Yeah, good point, and then we look like we're hiding something. Which we are."

Trey strode over to the armchair, flopped into it and let out a cry of frustration, striking the arm of the chair with his fist in three short raps. "This is so annoying! Such a small thing yet so crucial. It could be what brings us down. We'll just have to keep trying to persuade him that he has got himself mixed up with what he saw on Sunday. And we could show him the cellar, I suppose."

"Why?"

"Just to prove we weren't lying about the vent, and also that Molly isn't in there."

"If she was, then the police would have seen her. Anyway, if we had murdered her we would have thrown her down the hole. We wouldn't have just laid her out on the work bench and left her there, would we?"

"No. But he might not have thought about that. He probably doesn't even know that the police have already had a look. It could just get him off our backs."

Trey stared up at the ceiling. The dust on the light shade had highlighted a few strands of spider's web. He'd have to deal with that later. One day.

"I'll do it. I'll take him down there."

"No funny business though?"

Trey found himself pausing. "No."

"Promise?"

"Yes."

"Just persuade him he was imagining things. See if that works. Make him think he was confusing what he saw on Saturday with Tuesday. If you deny it enough maybe he'll start to think he must have been mistaken."

Trey let out a long sigh. "Yep, he might. Guess I better go and find him now, then."

"Probably best. Before the police get to him."

Trey grunted and rose reluctantly to his feet. The last thing he wanted to be doing was dealing with Norman again, but it had to be done.

As she heard their front door click shut, Lauren felt an uneasy concern beginning to gnaw away at her. Trey had killed a man before, to save her from going to jail. He had that in him, and so who is to say that he wouldn't do it again? Could he be tempted to dispatch Norman too?

He might think that if he could get away with one killing, why not two? She shivered. This was just unbelievable, that she was thinking about her Trey like this.

She would have to come with him to the cellar with Norman. They were in this together, but more importantly she could keep an eye on things then. If Norman went missing too, and Trey and Lauren were the last people to see him, they really would have trouble explaining their way out of what would be turning into a literally unbelievable coincidence.

No, far better to focus on convincing Norman that he was barking up the wrong tree if he thought they had anything to do with Anita's disappearance, let alone Molly's.

She guessed she probably just had time to empty the dishwasher. But she'd barely got through the cutlery when she heard noises outside, and there through the kitchen window were the tops of the heads of Trey and Norman heading down the stone steps to the cellar. Damn, they must have gone out of the main door and round the building rather than coming through the apartment.

She rushed into the hall to put some outside shoes on and grab a coat. But what if they were down there for a while? She really needed a wee. Great, perfect bad timing. She ran back to the toilet as fast as she could, sat down without closing the door, and tried to force it out quickly. No, that wasn't working. Come on, relax, relax.

There was a bump from down below, a kind of clang, and a shout. Trey and Norman. Oh shoot, that wasn't good. She squeezed out what she could, waved her hands under the tap, and hurried back to the hall. Probably could have lasted anyway, after all that.

Her outdoor shoes weren't that dirty so once they were on she ran back through the lounge and unlocked the French doors, flinging them open and bursting through.

She pictured Trey standing by the vent, on his own, looking guilty. Or both of them wrestling on the ground, grunting and panting. Please God no. Quickly down the stairs, through the cellar door, and……

"Hi!" said Trey. He and Norman were standing by the workbench; Norman was holding the big rusted iron spanner in both hands as though it was a newborn baby.

"Norman was just admiring the size of this spanner."

"Oh! Right. Hi. Pleased to meet you," said Lauren a little breathlessly, although in all honesty she probably wasn't too pleased at all.

Norman looked up at Lauren with an expression of cautious guilt, as though the spanner belonged to Lauren and she was going to grab it off him. "Alright?" he said.

"Yeah, good, thanks." She turned to Trey. "What was that noise just now?"

"Noise? Oh, yeah, I dropped the spanner as I was handing it to Norman. It bounced and hit his shin."

"Hurts," said Norman, lifting and shaking his leg, as though this proved it.

In as casual a fashion as he could engineer, Trey moved in front of Norman, so the gardener couldn't see his face.

"He's seen the vent," said Trey, "and he can see that Molly's not here, and nor is Anita. After all, if either one of them had fallen down the hole, they'd still be there at the bottom, wouldn't they?" He winked and pulled a face, to re-enforce the cleverness of this plot device.

Lauren gave nothing away in her expression, but internally relaxed. Nice one, Trey.

"Yes, exactly," she replied, "and they're not."

Norman put the spanner back in its place wedged between two nails, bent down and rubbed his shin, then leant back against the edge of the workbench.

"John's not down there either. You said he fell down that vent, so where is he?"

Trey, still with his back to Lauren, widened his eyes into a face of mild panic, conveying that he hadn't seen that one coming.

"The police brought him up," said Lauren. It was all she could think of to fill the silence. Should she have said that? How did they do it? Oh Lord, they were digging another hole for themselves, as if they did not have enough holes to worry about already.

But.... hang on, this was ok! The police had told them not to tell anyone else about the gigarat, so she was lying for a good reason, and could justify it. She took a step to one side so that Trey's head shielded her from Norman's gaze, and gave Trey a wide-eyed expression together with a slight nod of her head, as if to say 'leave this to me'.

Continuing her walk, she circled round to face Norman, Trey turning round too.

"They sent someone down on a rope," she said, "tied it around John and hauled him up. We couldn't use that ladder over there as it wouldn't fit. Then they took the body away. If either Molly or Anita were down there too, do you think Trey and I would be standing here? We'd be banged up in a police cell."

Norman, fresh from his own visit to a police cell yesterday, shifted uneasily. Being a man of few words, he looked up at Lauren and wrinkled his nose as his way of saying 'fair point'.

Lauren was on a roll now. "And you must have been mistaken about Anita coming in here on Tuesday." A thought occurred to her. "Or maybe you weren't! Maybe she walked down the steps, heard voices inside, stood there for a while, then decided not to come in. We might have been arguing about something. So then she came back up and left, without us ever knowing. And you wouldn't have been staring at our cellar steps the whole time, would you?"

Norman scuffed a foot back and forward on the floor. "No." It would have been odd if he had.

"That must be it then!" Lauren folded her arms, as though the matter was settled. "Right, was there anything else?"

Norman shook his head. "I need to know what happened to Molly though."

"Why?"

There was a ten second silence. Then, "they're blaming me. The cops think I done it."

Lauren and Trey exchanged glances. Lauren spoke first.

"Sorry to keep saying 'why' but....."

Norman gripped his hands together and kneaded his fingers, clearly not comfortable with holding the stage. His gaze remained focused on the floor.

"I was the last one to see... well, hear her. She screamed." He shook his head. "Wasn't nice, that. Not nice."

"Was this in the woods?" prompted Lauren. She felt sorry for him now.

"Yeah. After dark. I used to give her food. I went out that night, and I was maybe a hundred 'n fifty yards away when I heard this noise, sort of a grumbling, with a kind of a clicking beat. Hard to describe."

Trey and Lauren looked at each other. They knew exactly what that noise was.

"Then she screamed. And the scream got further away, like she was being carried off....."

He stopped, trying to control his emotions.

Lauren gave a subtle hand signal to Trey. They can't tell him what they know. Not yet. Trey nodded. But both of them now knew what had happened to Molly. And both of them now realised that the gigarat was not confined to the tunnels – it had somehow got into the woods too. That wasn't good.

"How awful," said Lauren. "I'm so sorry. But why do the police think you were responsible?"

Norman gave a little snort. "I was in those woods when she was attacked, wasn't I? That's good enough for them."

"I'm not sure it is," offered Trey, "they have to have evidence too. Don't they?"

Norman carried on as though Trey hadn't spoken. "I lied to them too, told them I didn't know her. In, like, the heat of the moment, not deliberately. Just to get them away from me." He smiled ruefully. "Didn't work."

"Was that when they handcuffed you and took you away?" asked Lauren. "We saw you yesterday morning, being marched off."

"Yeah. Then I had to tell them the truth. That I knew Molly and had been visiting her to give her food."

"And I'll bet they reckoned you made that up to cover for what you told them the first time," said Trey.

Norman nodded but said nothing.

There was an awkward silence and a realisation that they were all in a similar position: under suspicion for murder. The difference between them was only obvious to Trey and Lauren.

"I'm sure they'll soon realise it wasn't you!" said Lauren brightly, primarily because there was nothing much else she could say.

Norman shook his head, his shaggy brown hair still moving after he stopped. "Nah. They think it's me. I know they do. That's why I've got to find out what happened to Molly."

"You told the police about the noise you heard, though, yeah?" asked Trey.

"Yep."

Trey glanced at Lauren, who nodded. That was what would save the shambolic man in front of them. They couldn't say too much, but she could at least throw a lifebelt.

"That's the biggest clue – the noise. I think you'll be alright. I wouldn't worry. Just let the police get on with it. They'll work out what killed Molly."

Norman looked up at her with a strange expression.

"What, not who?"

Trey jumped in. "Well, that too. They need to know how she died and who killed her, obviously."

"You know she's dead then?"

"It's hard to be believe she's not," he stuttered. "I mean, how long is it now?"

"A week," said Norman, before Trey could think it through.

"Well there you go then. She would have turned up by now, wouldn't she? If she was still alive....."

Norman said nothing, eyes now back on the floor, thinking of Molly. Then, suddenly, "she could have been abducted. She could be tied up in someone's basement. Or something."

"So you thought that's what we had done? Abducted her and brought her down here? Anita as well?" Lauren wasn't angry, as she didn't need to be. After all, what Norman was thinking they might have done would have been preferable to the reality. She sounded almost sympathetic.

"Maybe," muttered Norman.

"Well now you know. We didn't."

"No."

Another awkward silence.

Norman stood up straight. "I'll go now."

He walked past them before they had even had time to reply, then stopped and turned.

"If you hear anything........ I don't want to go to prison."

"Of course," replied Lauren instantly, "of course we'll let you know."

As Norman closed the cellar door behind him she looked at Trey with the expression a mother would give when their child has just cut its finger. "Aww, poor guy."

"Yeah," said Trey, "maybe we've misjudged him. Seems like he's just a misunderstood soul. And now we know how Molly died too."

"You think she's definitely dead?"

"Without a doubt. That thing doesn't take prisoners."

"Do you think the police have worked that out?"

"If Norman told them what he told us, then yes. If they haven't, they're in the wrong job."

Lauren brushed a hair back behind her ear. "And we're ok with Norman now, do you think? He'll believe us?"

Trey came closer and gave her a little hug.

"Yeah, I think so. And if the police ask why we lied to Norman about John's body, we just say they told us too. Well, not in so many words, but as we can't mention the gigarat what else could we do? You did great there by the way. That thing about Anita standing outside the door but not coming in – brilliant!"

Lauren smiled. "I know, it just came to me on the spot. You're a very lucky man, Mr Clark, being married to me."

Trey squeezed her even harder. "Don't I know it. Right, well, hopefully that is one less worry now. You still going to work this afternoon?"

"Yes, I feel up to it now."

"Good. Come on then."

As they locked the cellar door behind them and returned to their apartment, neither could have known that Norman was still not entirely convinced that what they had told him was true.

CHAPTER 43

Jeremy Stanton-Davies put his phone down slowly and took a deep breath. He wasn't expecting a call from work on a Sunday, and he certainly wasn't expecting it to be from Mr Webber. It must have been at least two and a half years since they had last spoken. But when Mr Webber called, you paid attention. He may not have the title of Home Secretary, but he may as well have done. His orders often came directly from her and were not to be challenged.

Despite having Deputy Director on his own business card, Jeremy still had three levels of high ranking officials between him and the Home Secretary, and orders from on high ordinarily trickled down via his immediate superiors - The Permanent Secretary, the Director General, and the Director. But when Mr Webber called, whatever Mr Webber said took precedence.

And if it involved action, as it usually did, then his managers would be informed that Jeremy's services would be required immediately, but not told exactly why. They would just have to absorb the impact it would have on Jeremy's day job, and Jeremy could only imagine how pleased they would be about that.

But then he had, almost uniquely, a security clearance that they did not have. That came from knowledge and great age really – he just happened to be in the right place at the right time when the previous incumbent, Charlie Grayson, retired back in the 1980s.

Charlie had been looking for someone trustworthy, competent and well spoken, with proven investigative and man management abilities combined with a sharp intellect, in order to take on one particular part-time responsibility that was to be performed with scrupulous secrecy.

Feelers were put out and words exchanged at senior level over glasses of whisky in the dark recesses of members-only drinking establishments. In those days it wasn't quite so tediously bureaucratic when it came to promotions and appointments; managers were given more licence to trust their instincts about people. Jeremy had been one of those suggested – he was a promising young cub, respected for his mastery of detail, organisation and people management, and earmarked as showing great potential. It was noted that he had been to Eton, and without him even knowing he found himself at the top of nomination list.

He was duly summoned to Charlie's office under the auspices of a discussion about mentoring, at which point he was told that he had been chosen to take on a new responsibility that had the highest of security clearances, unless he objected. All he had to do was impress Charlie at an interview and then sign a few seriously worded forms and promise to hang himself if he told anyone, or words to that effect.

Once Jeremy had nervously confirmed that he was still interested, an interview of sorts was duly conducted. At the end of it, Charlie produced a slim folder with the word D.U.S.T. stamped in big black writing across it, and laid it in front of Jeremy but with his hand still resting on top.

"In here, young man," he announced, "are things you will not believe. Things you will not have heard about. And the fact that you have not heard about them is one of the measures by which I have been judged, and by which you will now be judged. Secrecy is of the utmost importance, and your primary mission will be containment. This is your last chance to back out now - are you quite sure that you are in no doubt that you wish to take this on?"

Jeremy remembered mumbling something about it being tricky to say you want something when you don't know what it is, but then also that it would be an honour and he was keen to progress with the handover.

Charlie then let go of the folder and reached for a piece of paper.

"Alright, good. First things first. Sign this form please. It's your pledge not to breathe a word of this to anyone who doesn't need to be involved."

Jeremy looked at the piece of paper in front of him, then up at Charlie.

"What happens if I let something slip? By mistake? Not that I would of course, but...."

Charlie gave a little snort. "Probably best you don't know."

Jeremy smiled, pulled the form closer, and signed it.

"I have some meetings now," said Charlie. "Stay in my office and read everything in here. Formulate whatever questions occur to you. I'll be back in an hour and a half." The door closed softly behind him before Jeremy even realised he had gone.

The folder was made of that thick yellowish paper that gives aspirations of legal authority to otherwise ordinary documentation. It was stamped CLASSIFIED beneath the title, as though this would be enough to deter a foreign spy or nosy employee, rather than encourage them. There was a black ribbon band around it that had to be snapped back before he could open it.

From the minute that Jeremy began reading the first entry, there was no turning back. He had spent the next ninety minutes absorbed by the content, turning each page with an eagerness and interest that had been earned by no government document before it.

These were not stories of paranormal visitations or unsubstantiated UFO sightings. There were no accounts of human-shaped aliens or tea cups leaping off shelves. The common theme for the events concerned was that not only was there no rational or scientific explanation for the events or items described, but also that there was actually some hard physical evidence. Something you could touch. Not a photograph, not even corroborated accounts, but actual hard-arsed proof of something very odd indeed. Something that could not be explained.

A large, perfectly smooth metallic ball about a metre in diameter had been found deep in a forest in Scotland. It was made of a metal that hadn't been seen before, and carbon dated as being more than 7,000 years old. No one could determine what it was or why it was there.

A woman in Birmingham, in 1967, had died in childbirth giving birth to a stillborn child with what looked like hooves instead of feet and hands. Small stumps on its head appeared to be the first signs of horns. Internally, the organs were in the wrong places and there were cells in the bloodstream previously unknown to science. Subsequent DNA analysis performed years later was inconclusive. There was effectively no medical explanation.

A fossil had been found on the Norfolk coast that revealed a creature from the Jurassic period with three heads yet missing most of the organs you would expect from any creature that has lived on this earth.

In 1971 two hikers in the Yorkshire Dales had been killed by a barrage of small rocks that suddenly started firing out of a small cave about ten feet away. A third hiker managed to run for cover and reported seeing an ape-like scaly creature subsequently bursting out of the cave and disappearing into some trees. Imprints of footsteps in the earth confirmed his account but could not be matched to any known animal. The recovered rocks appeared to be fragments of a meteorite. The creature was never seen again.

Washed up on a Welsh beach in 1972 was the corpse of a form of squid new to, but unexplainable by science, as it had a skull made of honeycombed bone, a brain ten times the size, relative to its head size, of any other squid, and eye lenses that facilitated optical magnification. That made no evolutionary sense, so where had it come from?

There were twenty seven such incidents logged, all in great detail. All of the physical artefacts relating to these accounts had been swiftly removed and taken to be stored away in a secure vault.

The last section in the folder had come as another surprise. Just one side of A4, headed 'DUST Team'. What was DUST? Anyway, at least there were other people who were in on this – he wasn't alone. Only four, though. He recognised one, Alice Hepburn, as keeper of the records down in the basement. Richard Bellweather just had 'police' against his name. Then there were two scientists, Mr John Carval and Professor Edward Bean, presumably cleared to perform the initial study of the artefacts and subsequently engage any new technology that might squeeze out some valuable clues.

When Charlie returned he had asked who Richard Bellweather was and what DUST stood for.

"A police Chief Constable," he was told. "We need someone in the know to cover that side of things and work with you where necessary. As for DUST, they needed an acronym for the team, so just made one up. Declared Unexplainable Specialist Team, it stands for. Yes, I know, it's a bit lame. It makes it sound like the team is unexplainable. But it's stuck now. I think they came up with the name then made the words fit. You have read everything in there then?'"

"Yes. Quite the eye-opener."

"Indeed. Can you imagine the panic that most of those incidents would have caused to the general population if news had spread? The government doesn't want people to be alarmed. History tells us that alarmed people can do alarming things. That then becomes an unnecessary distraction to the business of government. So when something unexplainable occurs, we have to keep a lid on it, you know?"

"There'll always be some people who know, though, won't there? Local officials, whoever found the object, that kind of thing...."

"Of course. There's an element of luck involved, obviously, that once you have impressed the importance of secrecy upon those people, that they comply. But we have a three pronged approach to this. Firstly, we are authorised to issue incentives."

"Really? How?"

"There is a budget. Not a huge one, in the scheme of things, but you will be cleared to approve the promise of funds, as it were, to certain individuals who find themselves in the know. An increased pension, for example." He tapped his nose to signal the sagacity of this tactic. "A carrot in the distance. Nothing they can spend immediately then go back on their word."

Jeremy nodded slowly. "I like it. What's the second prong?"

Charlie got up from his chair and walked to the door, opening it slightly before closing it again.

"Just checking," he said. He ambled back over to the desk, sat down, and leaned forward, lowering his voice. "We outline what could happen if they talk."

Jeremy was now feeling slightly worried.

"And what could happen, exactly?"

"There are some options that you will have at your disposal. I don't like to call them threats – encouragements is a nicer word. But they could involve some fairly unpleasant experiences, believe you me."

"Such as?"

"Temporary financial ruin could be arranged. A spell in prison, perhaps, for tax avoidance, which covertly amended records could prove. An accusation of child abuse from a child whose identity has to be protected. There are a number of possibilities that could be arranged by the Home Office."

"But that's immoral! How could I possibly….?"

Charlie held up a finger. "Ah-ah! You forget one thing."

"Which is…?"

"We never follow through as we haven't needed to. They are encouragements, my boy, that's all. Together with the incentives, that is a powerful package. It works."

"We do make good on our promises when it come to the money, though?"

"Absolutely."

"But definitely not on the threa…. encouragements?"

"No."

Jeremy relaxed a little. That wasn't so bad then. He would have to be a good cop / bad cop in those situations, but the bad cop would turn out not to be so bad after all. He could live with that.

"And the third prong?"

"Denial. Once we have collated all the physical evidence and taken it away, if anyone says anything, we just deny it. You know, the usual 'we do not recognise that account' type of thing. Usually the claim is so fantastical that, even though it might be true, it's unlikely that anyone one else would believe it. Especially if they have no proof."

"Supposing they've taken photographs?"

"Then we find the photos and remove them, negatives and all. We are usually on the case before anyone has had time to go and get a camera, though. It's not our biggest problem, generally."

Jeremy could not have foreseen back then how comprehensively that would change – now, with mobile phones, that was his biggest problem.

A little later he was taken downstairs to meet Alice Hepburn. She looked to be in her mid-thirties, with short wavy brown hair and a slightly pinched face that fitted an older person. Draw a few wrinkles on and she could be sixty five. She moved in sharp, short, thin bursts. Like a sparrow, thought Jeremy.

Her handshake was small but firm and she was clearly already aware of the succession plan and why the two men were there.

"Follow me!" she instructed. Quick, clickity footsteps on the polished wood floors became more muted as she unlocked a door set so flush into a panelled corridor that you would only know it was there if you knew that it was there.

"Through here quickly please," she urged Jeremy, ushering the two men in before locking the door behind them. They were now in a dimly lit grey-carpeted tunnel, the padded walls and ceiling closing in on them.

Jeremy's eyes adjusted to the gloom, and as they walked in single file along the sound deadened corridor, he saw ahead of them a larger, more imposing barrier to their progress, in the form of a set of black metal grilled gates, one behind the other.

To one side of the first gate was a key pad.

"There are two codes," said Alice. "You key the first one in, which is 2-4-4-5," – she keyed in each number as she called it out – "then you wait between five and ten seconds before keying in the next code. 7-9-0-1. There."

There was a clank as a latch was released, and the first metal grille slid back.

"Very important to leave that gap between the numbers. Less than five seconds and more than ten, and it doesn't work. So even if someone does manage to acquire the codes, they still wouldn't get in unless they were extraordinarily lucky."

"Clever," observed Jeremy.

The second grille required the same two codes, but in reverse order. Beyond that lay a small chamber of about ten feet square, with three metal doors leading off it.

"This is your door," said Alice, pointing at the one directly ahead of them. "And before you ask - the other two you don't have clearance for." She shrugged. "Sorry!"

"Not a problem," replied Jeremy, slightly deflated.

Charlie nudged him. "I don't know what's in there either, if it makes you feel any better."

It did, and Jeremy flashed a smile at him.

Alice produced another, much larger key. "The handle needs to be upright, then turn the key in the lock, three times, like this..... then pull the handle right down through 180 degrees. There. We're in!"

Charlie helped her ease open the heavy door, and the three of them entered a vault that was about the size of two train carriages if you laid them side by side. It was big.

Along three sides were metal lockers stacked floor to ceiling, like graves in a Spanish cemetery. Down the middle were glass display cabinets, glinting under spotlights.

"This..... is the Vault of the Unexplainable," said Charlie a little over-dramatically.

Jeremy, open-eyed, nodded, somewhat awestruck.

"Bit of a mouthful."

"Just call it the VU," said Alice. "That's what I do. Not that I mention it much. Best not to, really."

"So all the incidents I read about in the file – the evidence is all here?"

"Yes," said Charlie. "Some in the cabinets, some in the lockers. Larger stuff in the lockers."

"Why display cabinets?"

"Just easier to keep an eye on. To make sure nothing is deteriorating too badly with age. Also, this was built decades ago, so maybe there were other reasons for having cabinets back then. Alice checks in at least once a week. Isn't that right Alice?"

"Yes. And if you are wondering why it is so big, the records show that it was originally intended for something else – I can't tell you what I'm afraid - that got moved out of London, so when they realised that they needed to create an archive for the unexplainable stuff, this was available."

"Right. Pretty future-proof then, in terms of capacity. Can I have a look?"

"Of course. Don't take too long though, as we'll have to wait for you."

Charlie cleared his throat. "I've got a meeting at five. That gives you about... er... twenty minutes."

The twenty minutes had flown by, but of course Jeremy had been back in that vault a number of times since then. He now knew what was in each locker and cabinet and how it related to the filed accounts.

After a while he had even convinced Alice that she did not need to accompany him in there every time either. Because there were so few of them, they could suggest their own protocols. All they needed was a rubber stamp from Mr Webber, except back then it had been Mr Hemp. Mr Webber had taken over about ten years ago.

Those weren't their real names, so he had no idea who they actually were. Alice didn't either. She seemed to have clearance for a lot of things, as you would need to have in her position, but even she was officially in the dark about her 'other' boss. However, she had her suspicions. It was extremely likely to be a Permanent Secretary, and she thought she knew which one, despite the voice disguise on the phone calls.

Why their identities were secret wasn't quite clear. Perhaps a legacy from the war years that had turned into a tradition.

Alice was well into her sixties now, and looking very much as he had envisaged that she would. But unlike him she seemed keen to carry on past her retirement age, cradling the power and the knowledge that she held in the same way that politicians often do. The feeling of self-appointed indispensability creates a pride that is only felled when you eventually leave and everything carries on without you, and without the calamity you expected and secretly hoped for.

As for Charlie, even after he had retired, he remained a mentor and a reference for anything in that UNEXPLAINABLE folder, and thankfully had kept himself physically and mentally functional to the grand age of ninety four before succumbing last year to that scourge of the elderly: 'natural causes'.

Now, here Jeremy was, some thirty five years after that handover, faced with one of the very rare occasions when he was probably going to have to insert a new entry into that folder himself. He'd had a number of call outs in his time, but over the last few years there'd been nothing to speak of – just a couple of 'incidents' which turned out to have had rational explanations. Eventually, most things did.

At least he would not be alone this time. Two years ago he had started succession planning, and initiated a stringent vetting and interview process unlike any other, in that you could not tell the applicant exactly what the role was until they accepted the offer to take it on. If a candidate was not dissuaded by this, it was the first sign that they may have the necessary gumption to fit it. And so eventually the replacement had been chosen.

Jason Crisp was in his early thirties, fiercely intelligent, and with a mind that always seemed to be one step ahead of his peers. An Oxford Graduate with a First in Politics and Economics, he'd reached SEO (Senior Executive Officer) level reasonably quickly, and had recently been transferred to the Police Integrity Unit, which was actually quite a useful position as far as DUST was concerned.

Tall, dark haired and half-handsome, he also had a sharp sense of humour that could sometimes come across as slightly juvenile. But that aspect to him was also reflected in how damn keen he was about everything. He saw opportunities to improve wherever he looked, and was a human suggestion-cannon, firing out ideas continuously, often without thinking them through first. But Jeremy liked that. Better air a thought than suppress it and lose it; sometimes the daftest ideas end up being the best.

So Jason had seen the folder. It was all digitised now of course. Some years ago Jeremy had spent an inordinate amount of his own spare time scanning all the sheets of paper and loading them into a security controlled digital vault. Only he and Jason, Alice, Mr Webber, and the Home Secretary had the password to that vault. It was a digital VU, if you will. The original paper folder was in a locker in the physical VU.

Alice told him recently that only three new Home Secretaries had ever requested access to the physical VU. Most of them probably wanted to, but never got round to it – too many other priorities chipping away at them. Only after they had been reshuffled to somewhere else and had their security clearance withdrawn did they no doubt realise they had missed their chance.

The case that Mr Webber had just outlined to him sounded as though it could be one of the trickiest that had ever come his way. He'd described a giant rodent, and by giant he really did mean giant – the size of a bear, by all accounts. The worrying part was that it seemed that one man had already been killed, and three other people were missing. This was going to be very hard to manage.

With people dead and unaccounted for, the press would be sniffing around already. He had to act quickly. It was his number one priority, he had been told – drop everything else you are doing. Jason too. And above all, keep a lid on it.

There was an encrypted USB stick with a couple of videos on it, which a courier would deliver to him shortly, along with a summary of key names and contacts. The videos were the reason that this had quickly passed all the way up the chain of command and ended up with the Home Secretary. It seemed no one was quite sure what to do, which is why it had been given to Mr Webber. And now to Jeremy, where the buck had finally stopped. No pressure then.

He checked the carriage clock on the shelf just over his shoulder. Eleven twenty five. He reflected that he could have just looked at his watch for the correct time, but he preferred looking at clock faces; they seemed friendlier.

Two rooms at the King's Arms Inn, Hixton had been booked for tonight – all he and Jason had to do was get there. He'd let Jason know, then leave straight after lunch. One hundred and fifty miles would take him around three hours – traffic shouldn't be too heavy on a Sunday afternoon.

He'd have to make some other phone calls before he left though, starting with the Chief Constable on the DUST team. He needed all the background and intel on who knew what at this stage. Containment would be extremely important for a case like this. If the general public knew that a man-eating giant rat, or whatever it was, was on the loose, there would be absolute chaos.

Richard Bellweather had long since retired and was probably dead by now – Jeremy's contact now was Sharon Bateman, one of the first female Chief Constables. And her first job would be to get on the phone immediately to her fellow Chief Constable in Derbyshire and instruct him to spread the word down the chain that this was now a containment situation, and anyone who had seen the videos, or been told about the existence of the creature, would be required to sign an affidavit promising that they would, until given permission otherwise, say nothing about this to anyone.

He heard a bump upstairs. Anne putting her sewing machine away, probably. By the time the courier got here, he may just have achieved the objective of weathering her predictably angry reaction, which would be focused on how he prioritised work over his own family.

They had planned on going for a walk this afternoon, down by the river, and the sun was out too. The best he could hope for would be to talk her into a state of irritated acceptance, although it didn't help that not only could he not tell her what the emergency was, but he also had no idea how long he would be away.

Summoning up all his reserves of diplomacy, he climbed the stairs with the slow trudge of a mountaineer but with none of the excitement for what lay ahead.

CHAPTER 44

Norman poured a lumpy waterfall of baked beans over the two pale, microwaved sausages. He sprinkled a few pinches of garlic granules on the beans, and added a squirt of ketchup for additional taste. To complete the dish, a thin square of processed cheese, shiny-smooth and orange, was draped across the hot beans. Perfect.

He doubted it was something that Gordon Ramsey would proudly reveal to an expectant table of lords and ladies, but it was food, it was cheap, and it was tasty enough for a simple palette. And beans were a vegetable, weren't they, even when baked, so that evened up the health score when weighed up against the can of beer that was to accompany the meal.

It was getting dark as he sat down to eat. He'd spent another afternoon in the garden, just mulling over things. Something didn't add up.

If John fell down that vent yesterday morning, that would explain the police car that he'd noticed turn up and park in the drive just after he'd been released from custody and got home. But after that, he'd seen no rescue vehicles, and no ambulances.

Lauren had said that the police had hauled John's body up out of that hole with a rope. Would they really have done that? Pretty undignified at best. It wouldn't have been a quick job either - it would need at least three or four men as John was a large chap - so surely he'd have heard or seen something. They would still have needed a stretcher and a hearse or van, or whatever they carted dead bodies off in. It didn't make sense. There'd be a forensic team too, wouldn't there? That's what happened in all the crime dramas he watched. People in white coats, covering stuff in polythene sheets and poking at things with cotton buds. Where were they?

Downstairs, a similar thought had occurred to the Clarks as they lay in bed, Lauren unable to sleep yet with her mind still bustling after her shift that evening. Why hadn't the police come back with a forensics team, to help verify the cause of John's death? But the two of them, and the police come to that, at least knew something that Norman did not, regarding what lay in wait at the bottom of the vent. There was a good chance that someone in charge at Police HQ had decided that their forensics people were not dispensable, and were instead trying to work out how to deal with this unusual situation. Rushing in without a plan where more lives could be at stake rarely brought success when it came to body counts – almost any Hollywood action film could tell you that.

Also, how hush-hush did the police top brass want to keep the story? Send in a team of people into that cellar and the gigarat could put in an appearance, or at least a vocal performance. Then before you know it, alarming rumours are flying round town, and from there round the country and into media outlets.

"Maybe they're assembling a team of SAS veterans sworn to secrecy, with a mission to hunt down and kill that thing," suggested Lauren.

"Hey, yeah, wouldn't that be cool," chuckled Trey, abandoning a half-started yawn. "I'd favour a flame-thrower as my weapon of choice, I think. Give that thing something to think about."

Lauren twisted her head to look at him. "It's personal with you, isn't it?"

"After what it did to Hoggo? Oh yes. I'd be down there helping them kill it if I was allowed. I'd happily blow its brains out, believe me."

"Well it's a good job you won't be. Leave it to the experts."

Trey sighed. "Yeah, you're right. I've put myself in enough danger already."

Lauren turned her head to look back at the ceiling. "You can say that again."

"I don't think I will if it's all the same to you."

Lauren smiled, then became serious again.

"What's tomorrow going to bring, do you think? They'll not find Hoggo, so they're going to be back, aren't they? Asking more questions. How long will this go on for?"

"I guess they won't leave us alone until they've found the remains of all the bodies and done the post-mortems."

Lauren reached over, switched the bedside light on, and sat up. "Oh no. I've just thought! Suppose they find broken bones? Like, consistent with a fall from just over twenty feet? Not with John, I mean – they know about him. But Anita. Supposing they work out Anita fell into the vent? Oh shit, shit, shit. Just as I was starting to..."

Trey grabbed her hand. "No! That can't happen. Stop worrying. She will have been mauled senseless by that thing, flung about everywhere when it, and I hate saying this, ate her. Her bones will be cracked and broken all over the place. They won't be able to prove any breaks weren't caused by the gigarat, will they?"

Lauren flopped herself back down, head back on the pillow.

"I don't know. I don't know about anything at the minute. This is a nightmare, all of it. It's like we've stumbled into some ridiculous film script, except it's real. God, how I wish we'd never moved here."

Trey gave a little snort. "I'm not going to argue with you on that one."

Lauren reached over and turned the light off again.

"If I get any sleep tonight it will be a miracle."

But twenty minutes later Trey heard her rhythmic breathing - slow, steady, and definitely asleep. He couldn't stop worrying, though, about what Lauren had said. Supposing she was right about the bones?

It was another forty minutes before he finally dropped off, and into a world where no nightmare could be any worse than the one he was already in.

CHAPTER 45 - MONDAY

Jeremy's dreams were disturbed by a knocking sound, that got louder as he fully woke up. A muffled "Jeremy! You up? Coming to breakfast?" permeated the door round the corner.

He opened his eyes and checked the alarm clock. 07:46. What!! Why hadn't the alarm gone off? That was the last time he would rely on a hotel clock radio; he'd use his phone next time. Or maybe ask for a wake-up call, something he'd always refused just out of habit, really. There was probably some hidden switch on the device that he should have clicked into place. No, wait – there was a little PM displayed to the right of the 07:46. Oh Lord, a schoolboy error, why hadn't he checked that? So much for his famous attention to detail.

He called out to Jason, "you go on without me, I've overslept." He didn't want to admit it but his still foggy brain couldn't think of a better reason.

"Alright, see you later," came the voice back through the door, its owner wisely choosing not to risk a comedy answer at this juncture.

He showered at speed, flung on his Italian wool suit, and grabbed his square-cornered, black leather briefcase. Its best days were behind it and there wasn't a lot in it, but he felt it gave him an additional air of authority and was a useful place to store papers and emergency food. You couldn't do that with a mobile phone.

The mirror in the hallway presented him with the image of a still-slim man of ever advancing years, a full head of side-parted white hair slightly at odds with his darkish eyebrows; the small metallic framed glasses adding to the scholastic air of a respected university professor. He straightened his tie. Whatever happened to that young face he used to have? Buried in history, as everything was. He moved on, and was assailed as he opened the door by the familiar musty smell of hotel corridors with patterned red carpets.

Jason was sitting at a table scrolling through his phone, a scrunched up napkin on the table in front of him. He looked up as Jeremy approached.

"Look on the bright side, at least you woke up – at your age there's always the chance you won't."

Jeremy put his briefcase down by the side of the chair. "I'll bet you've been working on that one while you were waiting. My stupid fault though - didn't realise the alarm was set to PM instead of AM. Not the best of starts to the day. Food any good?"

"If you like lukewarm congealed egg and water-flavoured mushrooms, you're in luck. Otherwise...."

"Great. I'll see what I can salvage."

He returned with a lightly filled plate and a cup of thin coffee. Twelve minutes later they were in Jeremy's car heading to the police station.

The introductory meeting had been arranged for 9:00am sharp at Hixton police station.

It was a twenty year old building that, possibly due in part to its relative youth, had not been turned into a pub and therefore remained functional, and a hub for the smaller towns in the surrounding area whose own police buildings had been capitally punished.

A flurry of high level phone calls the previous evening had resulted in Chief Superintendent Rob Berriman drawing the short straw, not least because he was already overseeing the case from a distance, along with his other duties. But now, with the sudden development of the emergence of a frankly terrifying video, he was required to immediately clear his diary and focus all his energies on the Ridley Manor missing persons mystery. First agenda point: team up with some chap from the Home Office called Jeremy Stanton-Davis and his sidekick, who would explain the unusual aspects of this case and how it was to be handled.

The Chief Super was no stranger to Hixton, of course – it was part of his territory. He knew the station well, having spent time there as a Sergeant some years ago. As he sat in the small interview room reviewing his notes and waiting for the Home Office men to arrive, he felt as though he'd been demoted back to his previous role. It was a recurring dream of his, that he was back at Hixton, his promotions wiped out. He would wake up genuinely anxious that he'd been demoted. Not that he would ever share that with a psychoanalyst of course. But now, here he was, stepped back in time, waiting to take orders from someone in his own police station, just like in his dreams.

It wasn't the same though. This was very much a real case, and a big and difficult one, too. Four deaths, most likely, and those videos. The second one in particular, was quite harrowing. How do you police that? Well, hopefully this Mr Stanton-Davies would know. Not that he wanted the guy taking over as such. This was his patch and that meant something.

He heard voices in the lobby, so pushed his chair back and rose stiffly to his feet. He wasn't as young as he once was, he reflected sadly. Takes time to get the old joints warmed up in the morning.

As he went to open the door, it opened for him. Sergeant Piper leaned in.

"Mr Stanton-Davies and Mr Crisp are here, sir."

"Good. Show them in, will you?"

Piper nodded and stepped back, making space for Jeremy and his briefcase, followed by Jason, to squeeze past. The door was closed behind them.

The room was barely ten feet square, with a thin beech coloured desk up against the wall on one side, flanked by two sets of interlocking chairs. A recording device sat grimly upon it, and adjacent to one set of chairs there was a red panic button attached to the wall. If that was needed today then something would have gone very wrong indeed.

At least there was a window on the far side, double glazed and with Venetian blinds tweaked open to shed some light on proceedings.

Directly in front of Jeremy, the outstretched hand of Chief Superintendent Berriman awaited, fingers short and stubby and reminding him of a butcher's unsuccessful sausage display. They shook hands, the process repeated with Jason.

"Hello! Welcome to Hixton!"

Although not being a tall man, his voice was rich and deep.

"Thank you. Nice to be here," said Jeremy.

He didn't mean it of course, and they both knew it. They had a task on their hands, to put it mildly.

Jeremy flicked a hand in Jason's direction. "Jason here is learning the ropes," he explained. "Ready to take over from me when I expire. His role in this case will be to absorb and digest all the wise words that fall from our mouths, and ask the questions we may have overlooked."

Berriman nodded at Jason and sniffed. "Let's hope we can live up to that promise of wise words, eh? Please, have a seat." He beckoned at the two chairs on the other side of the desk.

As they all sat down Jeremy watched Berriman squeeze himself in. His uniform was tight and he looked as though he was starting to outgrow it - the buttons securing his jacket around his belly were doing a lot of heavy lifting, and were a testament to the strength of the thread that secured them.

He had a round face, and where once there was ginger hair there was now a mostly mottled and slightly moist scalp, although a crew cut of white and ginger flecked bristles remained around the edges. Early fifties, Jeremy reckoned.

Once they were all seated, he got straight down to business.

"You've been fully briefed on why we're here, I assume?"

"Yes. I had a call from Sharon Bateman last night. Quite unexpected, that was – I don't even know her, to be frank, although of course I know *of* her. She filled me in on what was going to happen. Said something about a team called DUST?"

"That's right," said Jeremy, "it stands for Declared Unexplainable Specialist Team. Yes, I know, not the greatest of names, but better than any of the alternatives they came up with. I believe Classified Investigations Specialist Team was one of them, but when you said it out loud it sounded like a medical condition. Anyway, the existence of DUST is on a need to know basis only."

"Right. That would certainly explain why I'd never heard of it. Sharon Bateman said she'd cleared it with my Chief Constable with the full authority of the Home Secretary, and told me you'd be coming here today. Read me the secrecy act as well, so don't worry, I've not said anything. I also rang round last night and passed that instruction on to my people. The last thing I need is a panicked population and the world's press on my doorstep."

"Exactly, and believe me that is exactly what would happen, particularly if the videos got leaked. We need to keep it watertight."

"Definitely. Oh, and I've seen those videos too, just so you know. Detective Sergeant Collins had immediately passed them up the chain of command, and as you can imagine that is probably how the Home Secretary got involved. I forwarded them on to Roger straight away. Roger Weston, that is, my Assistant Chief Constable. Good job they were short enough to send as attachments."

Jeremy considered how encrypted pen drives had been couriered to himself and Jason for reasons of security, given that email accounts can be compromised, and compared that to the police approach. But you couldn't blame them; they weren't to know, and hopefully no damage had been done. But he would need to catch up with Detective Collins as one of his first tasks, and double check who else she may have confided in, especially family. The answers that she gave to her boss on the phone last night may have been hasty and designed to tell him what he wanted to hear.

"What was your reaction when you saw it?" Jeremy asked.

"I have to admit I wasn't expecting to see something quite that frightening. Between you and me, I had a bit of trouble getting to sleep last night after seeing that! Any idea what it is?"

"No. No, not yet. We've got one of our scientists looking at it but we'll need something physical so we can do some analysis. Don't suppose you have anything? A few hairs or skin cells, for example?"

"Nothing. No one's gone down that vent yet, and I'm not sending any of my men down there, I can tell you that."

"That doesn't surprise me. Now, I understand that one person has died and three are missing. Do think they are all related to the activities of this creature?"

Berriman sat back and steepled his hands.

"Too early to say, but seems very likely, in my opinion. I'll need your help in confirming that, of course, and eliminating the possibility that any murders have been committed. Let's just review each case to make sure we're on the same page, shall we?"

Jeremy nodded, while Berriman leaned forward and arranged his notes in front of him. Jason, bursting to say something in order to feel useful, sat silent, knowing that his job was to watch and learn.

"Ok, we've got Molly Baines, a homeless lady who according to a local gardener....," he flipped over a page, "... a Mr Baston, was dragged away screaming out of the woods eight days ago at approximately half past ten in the evening, although he claims he was too far away to see anything in the darkness. From what we could make out from trails on the ground and the broken branches, it looks like she was dragged right down to the river. There was a small amount of blood found on some leaves, which has been confirmed as hers. We've had frogmen down there in the water, but found nothing. We had no idea who or what might have done this, but now I've seen that video, one comment from Mr Baston in particular was of considerable interest."

He paused, carefully adding weight to what he was about to say.

"He mentioned a noise, and his description, from what I can ascertain, very closely matches the noise that can be heard on the video."

"Interesting," said Jeremy. "It all leads to one conclusion."

"Indeed."

"Were there any prints on the ground?"

"No, it was pretty much all leaf fall, twigs and grass patches – the team couldn't find anything distinct enough. Obviously they were looking for human footprints, but they'd have noticed animal ones too."

"Especially if they were large ones."

Jason felt the time was right to chip in. "Now that we know what we might be looking for, could it be worth going back to see if there are any traces of this creature still floating around? Hairs, or skin flakes, or something?"

Berriman maintained a non-judgemental expression. "To be honest, Mr Crisp, to find evidence like that on the forest floor the day after the event would have needed more luck than a lottery winner, and since then we've had a few windy days so I'd suggest too much time has passed now."

Jason sat forward. "If it is a big creature though, mightn't you have more luck looking at broken tree branches, in case a tuft of hair has snagged on them? That might still be there."

Berriman abstractedly tugged at his sleeve. The young man had a point, which was good on one level, but annoying on another.

"It's a consideration," he conceded, making a note. "So, where were we? Ah yes, I should elaborate on Mr Baston, the gardener. He lives in Ridley Manor, and when two of our officers went to investigate the disappearance of Miss Rackman – which I will come to in a minute – they found he wandering in the woods with no clear explanation of what he was doing. Then when he was taken in for questioning he changed his story. I've not seen him myself but he is described as being of 'unkempt appearance', and lives on his own. We had to release him, and we have nothing yet that links him to the other missing persons, but I'd say he warrants further investigation even if we don't think he killed Molly Baines. I'm going to get some surveillance on him. Ok with you?"

"It would do no harm," agreed Jeremy. "I'd like to speak to him, as well."

"Of course. Now, next is Anita Rackman, also living in Ridley Manor. We found her flat empty on Friday, but neighbours reported seeing her window open since Tuesday or Wednesday and no one had seen her during that period either. Her agent had been trying to get hold of her since Wednesday to no avail."

Jeremy had started making a few notes, then put down his pen. "Could I have a copy of that briefing when we've finished?"

"Yes, of course. Now, the third missing person is Darren Hoggsmith, known as Hoggo to his friends. Doesn't live at Ridley Manor, but went to school with Trey Clark, who lives at number two with his wife Lauren, and was visiting him on Saturday when he went for a walk in the woods and disappeared."

"Why would you visit someone, then go for a walk on your own?"

"Yes, that did seem odd. The notes here say that it was 'to clear his head', but my detectives felt that didn't quite sit right. They also said that… hang on…" he flicked over a couple of pages, "….. ah yes, here we are. They said that later on in the day the couple were not particularly desperate to ask whether their friend had been found, almost as though they had to be prompted to ask."

"Like they knew he wasn't in the woods?"

"Possibly. Although to be fair, Mr Stanton-Davies, they were in shock, as a result of what had just happened with our fourth victim. Well, first confirmed victim, anyway – John Firwell. So also on Saturday, he was reported to have tripped and fallen down this hole in the cellar of the young couple, taking Mr Clark with him. Clark survived almost unscathed, Firwell died, and was subsequently dragged off by the creature, as the first video just about shows."

"Indeed. Please call me Jeremy, by the way. My surname is a bit of a mouthful."

Berriman chuckled. "I'm Rob then. Also easier."

"And I'm Jason," revealed Jason with a fleeting smile, realising immediately that the two more senior men not only already knew this, but were in any case at liberty to call him what they liked.

Berriman glanced at him and then back to Jeremy, who sat back and folded his arms.

"So this Trey Clark, he is our key witness, yes?"

"Undoubtedly. He and his wife are the only witnesses to Mr Firwell's death. Ordinarily of course we would have brought them into the station and interviewed them separately, but everything got derailed when the videos came to light. I should also say that he has come face to face with this creature, or so he tells us, and lived to tell the tale. Discovered its weakness too, it seems."

"Really? I haven't heard about that."

"Yes, light. Shone a torch in its eyes and it ran off. And you can see it again in that second video. It scarpers when they shine torches at it."

Jeremy rubbed his chin. "That would explain, then, why no one has seen it during the day. And why, if that creature was involved, Molly Baines went missing at night."

Berriman tried not to look too impressed. This guy was sharp enough – he'd caught on quickly. "It seems a logical conclusion," he agreed.

"Yet Mr Hoggsmith supposedly went missing in the woods as well, and it was broad daylight, I assume?"

"Indeed."

"Which sheds further doubt on him having been dragged away by the creature, if that creature is averse to light."

"Yes, very much so."

Jeremy wondered whether Berriman had already worked this out, despite not having mentioned it in his summary. He suspected not, but then to be fair, a lot had happened yesterday and everyone was still coming to terms with it all.

Berriman, who had indeed not yet added this particular pair of twos together, filed it in his memory bank before throwing in another nugget of supporting information.

"And on top of that, we couldn't see any signs of fresh disturbance in the woods. Nothing obvious at any rate. But then I would imagine that such things could easily be missed without an organised search."

"How big are those woods?"

"As I recall, just a few acres. Nothing substantial. I could bring back the search team to look again for any signs of a fresh struggle, of course."

Jeremy sat back and put his hands behind his head – a signal of relaxed authoritative thinking that he had noticed his superiors doing from time to time.

"I would suggest sealing off the woods in the unlikely event that anyone decides to go for a night-time walk in them, but perhaps you should hold back on looking for signs of a second abduction just for the moment. We don't want to waste everyone's time, and I'd like to have some in depth discussion with Mr and Mrs Clark before going down that route. Could that be arranged for me this morning? They seem to be pivotal in much of this."

"Yes of course," said Berriman, reaching across for an azure blue notebook, A4-sized and with a well-worn hardback cover, that had been lying to his right. Jeremy could see as he opened it and flicked through the pages that many of the notes had been decorated with little doodles.

It seemed incongruous but he was sure that the Chief Superintendent probably had to sit through as many dull presentations as he himself did, and exercised some artistic endeavour when he felt his eyes closing.

A pen clicked and an action point was marked in the notebook, before Berriman looked back up. "Although I'd suggest we separate them this time – bring them back to the station and interview them here, one at a time. You can sit in."

"Suits me," replied Jeremy. "We'll go and have a look and the house and this cellar first though, won't we?"

"Yes, of course."

"Thank you. You said 'detectives' earlier. So it wasn't just Detective Collins?"

"No, she was with Detective Constable Paul Bartrum. Just so you know, we had two officers investigating Ms Rackman's disappearance earlier, PCs... er.... let me check... ah, here we are, Rakowski and Davis, but no one knew about this animal at that stage. So they shouldn't know anything they shouldn't, as it were."

Jeremy raised an eyebrow. "It's going to be hard work keeping a lid on this. I'll need to speak to the first two as soon as we're finished here."

"You know that I have already spoken to them about keeping this to themselves, as I was instructed?"

"Yes, of course. I'm sorry, I wasn't meaning that I doubted that, more that I want them to hear it from me too. Just to hammer it home, you understand?"

Berriman grunted. It seemed a weak argument to him but it couldn't do any harm.

"That's fine, but they're on a 12 til 9 shift today – I've already checked."

"Ok, not a problem, I'll catch them this afternoon, after I've been to the house."

"I'll take you there myself – I need to be on top of every development now. I'm keen to see this vent, too."

"We'll send you down first then," joked Jeremy.

Berriman smiled. "I'm not that keen. Just a look down it will be fine for me."

"Me too, I suspect." Jeremy brought his hands back down to the table. "Let's finish here first though. So there are tunnels down there, under the house."

"Indeed. Again we are reliant for the moment on Mr Clark for the detail, but he described one tunnel at the bottom of the vent, with further tunnels and caverns further on, then in the other direction it leads to a massively deep mine shaft that has been capped, but would have an entrance directly under a part of the garden."

"Sounds like our friend the rat-bear has got quite a warren down there. Is it an old mine system? Do you have plans of it?"

"The answers to those questions are 'probably' and 'not yet'. We just haven't had time to do a lot of digging on that, if you'll forgive the pun – maybe that's something you can help with?"

"I can pull some strings, yes. Ok, leave that one with me."

Jeremy paused for a second as he re-opened his notebook and started his list of actions. Jason did the same, using his phone.

"Now, before we go any further, could I ask you to confirm if anyone else apart from the police and the Clarks have seen the videos or know about the creature? I'll need to speak to all of them."

"I'll check with Erica and compile a definitive list. Some of the residents, I believe."

"Thank you. It would be helpful to know before we set off for the house. And from your side it is just the Assistant Chief Constable and the Deputy Chief Constable? And the Chief of course."

Berriman's eyes darted left as he checked his thoughts, then back to Jeremy again. "Yes."

"Fine. They'll all have been read the riot act by Sharon. That's the kind of thing she does in these situations. At least they'll all have some idea why you have been assigned to this and why it is a containment situation. Now before we agree actions, one last thing. I would imagine that there is more than one of those things down there?"

Berriman hadn't even thought about that. He'd not exactly had much time to think after that phone call last night; his time had been spent gathering information and making phone calls himself. Despite a tell-tale scratch of his ear, he again bluffed it out.

"You would have thought so, yes. Unless it is some mutant creation that has escaped from some laboratory. You'd know more about that than me, I assume."

Jeremy suppressed a laugh.

"You think? You'd be surprised how much I don't know actually. I tend to make it my job to find out. Having said that, I'd say that a creature like that breaking out of a lab cage was highly unlikely. I'm aware that we have some experimentation labs, but not doing that kind of thing.

Anyway, my point being, our task could be a lot harder if it turns out that there is a whole colony down there."

"There could be miles of tunnels that they're running around in too."

"Yes, and if they are unmapped we won't know where they are. So we'll have to get a team in to map them. No easy task when you've got man-eating rodents round every corner. Now, next steps. You ready?"

"Fire away."

Thirty minutes later, action plan in place, they were in a BMW marked police car heading for Ridley Manor, Berriman remembering the roads as he drove along them, and only a little surprised that so little had changed. A small cluster of new homes here and there, a new pedestrian crossing, some different shop fronts. Other than that, a trigger trove for memories from years past.

It was a quarter to ten as Berriman crunched the car to a halt on the driveway of Ridley Manor. He turned to his front seat passenger.

"Mr Clark works from home, I'm told, which is helpful for us. His wife's a nurse."

"I saw that in the notes," said Jeremy, holding up the copy of Berriman's summary he had been given before they set off, and which he, like Jason in the back seat, had been reading on the way.

Berriman undid his seat belt. "Ah, right. Yes. I forgot you'd be fully up to speed now. Shall we proceed?"

Jeremy smiled to himself. It had reminded him of the stereotypical policeman in a court of law, telling the judge that he had been "proceeding in a northerly direction". Policemen enjoy proceeding.

"Of course."

The three men emerged into the damp morning air with a synchronised thunk of their car doors. The lawn still glistened with white dew, layered with a wisped icing of cobwebs that sparkled intermittently as the sun concentrated on burning through some gently smouldering low fog. It was strangely quiet, other than the cawing of some distant crows.

Jeremy looked up at the substantial frontage of Ridley Manor rising three, no four floors, if you counted the roof space with dormer windows poking out. He observed all the gothic arch shaped windows, checking each one for anything that might be of interest. Through the lower floor windows he could just about make out some very elaborate plaster coving at ceiling level.

"Impressive house," he murmured. "Right, let's have a quick wander round first, shall we? Lie of the land and all that. Get our bearings."

There wasn't much else to see at the front, so after a quick amble up and down the frontage they checked out the back garden and the route to the woods over the broken wall.

"Do you know if many people pass this way?" asked Jeremy.

Berriman looked around him. "I'd presume only the residents. It doesn't lead anywhere else in this direction."

Jason chipped in. "And on Saturday none of them saw Mr Hoggsmith either heading here or in the woods themselves, according to your report."

"Not as far as we know. Which adds further weight to the fact that he may not have come here at all."

Jeremy turned to look back at the manor house from a different angle. It was all pointy windows, ornamentation and fastidious design; grandly crafted with an attention to detail and aesthetics that modern housing generally can't be bothered with. Yet what price can you put on something that is so easy on the eye, and the pleasure that this brings. He knew that were he to be standing there looking at a block of low rise 1970s flats his emotions would be very different. Everything had its price, though, that's just how life was.

"It's a big old house," he said.

"Certainly is," agreed his uniformed companion. "Don't build 'em like that any more. Must have cost a fortune to run in its day."

They all stood for a moment admiring the majesty of the imposing structure in front of them, but a moment was all they needed. They had work to do.

"Ok," said Jeremy, "let's speak to the residents. Starting with the Clarks."

As they walked back towards the house, there was some movement behind the raspberry bushes as a crouching figure gradually rose, watching the three men as they headed back round to the front door.

CHAPTER 46

It was Lauren who eased open the big oak door and peered out.

"Can I help you?"

Berriman switched himself into 'formal policeman' mode.

"Good morning, madam. I'm Chief Superintendent Berriman and these gentlemen are Jeremy Stanton-Davies and Jason Crisp from the Home Office. We would like a word with you and your husband please. Can we come in?"

"Oh! Right, yes of course."

The door opened wide and the three men followed Lauren in. Through a small lobby area and they were into the wood panelled atrium with its huge glass lantern roof a good thirty feet above them. Shafts of sunlight streamed across the upper walls.

"My goodness," exclaimed Jeremy, "I wasn't expecting that! It's magnificent, isn't it?"

"It certainly is," agreed Berriman, realising he had never actually been inside the building before, but deciding not to make that obvious.

Ordinarily Lauren would be proudly accepting the compliments as though she had helped design the building herself, but her mind was on other things.

"We're in here," she said, leading them to the door to their apartment that she had left ajar. "Trey's working in the lounge."

She spoke loudly enough for Trey to hear, just to give him time to mentally prepare for what was likely to be another high-stress conversation where one false move could expose them. The morning so far had been like watching the waves recede far out to sea and enjoying the unusual quietness of the beach, but knowing all the while that a tsunami was on its way. Well, here it was. And to mix metaphors, these three were the big guns. Chief Superintendent? The Home Office? That wasn't a good sign.

Trey was up out of his chair by the time the three men entered the lounge. After formalities were exchanged, tea and seats offered and declined, and all pleasantries completed, Jeremy kicked off proceedings before Berriman could open his mouth.

"I'm sure you'll understand why we are here. One person dead and three missing, and on top of that a rather large creature running about under your apartment. Not your average police investigation, which is why Jason and I have been brought in."

Trey and Lauren nodded, though not yet through any understanding of why the two men should have been brought in.

"We are part of a team that manages anything for which there is no obvious explanation, and has the potential to cause alarm within the community or indeed the world at large. At the moment, this case falls under that category, due in no small part to what you have told us, and of course the videos that you provided. I appreciate that you have already been interviewed by DS Collins and DC Bartrum, and much of what you tell us may just be repeating what you told them, but it important that the chief superintendent and I hear it from the horse's mouth, as it were. Is that ok?"

He received the expected affirmative responses.

"Good. My colleague here...." he flicked his head at Berriman rather than Jason, "is of course most concerned about the people who are dead or missing, or both, and that is his focus. My primary interest is the animal below us. But of course the two are intrinsically linked, and therein lies our challenge. Now, before we go any further it would be helpful if we were to have a look at your cellar. Then your accounts will make more sense to us."

"Of course, yes," said Trey, his neutral expression hiding a growing panic. "Follow me."

They all trooped out through the French windows, down the brick steps, and into the cellar, Lauren taking up the rear like a second teacher on a school trip helping to keep an eye on her charges.

Thirty yards away, now quietly planting bulbs for next spring, Norman checked his watch. He'd have to go soon – he needed to be at Mrs Whitmarsh's in Holland Drive by 11:00am, and he still had to load up the van. Then at 2:00pm he'd got Mr Doughty's lawn to attend to. As much as he would like to know what those official looking people - one of whom was clearly a policeman - were doing, going into that cellar with the Clarks, he would have to leave them to it. But what if they were working out ways that they could pin the blame on him? He knew their game. If they thought he'd been responsible for what happened to Molly, and two other people were missing.... yes, he knew what they were thinking.

At least they knew he wasn't involved in John's death – that was clearly nothing to do with him. As far as the police were concerned, though, it could have just been a coincidence that John fell down a hole at the same time as three people went missing, and not throw them off the track of trying to persuade a jury that Norman, the lone wolf gardener misfit, was the guilty party.

When he had overheard them talking by the forest wall, they had said something about a Mr Hoggsmith not having been seen going into the woods, and that maybe he hadn't gone there after all. What did that mean? Was that the chap that the cops had been quizzing him about? They wouldn't say his name, but the police who arrested him were asking if he had seen a tall blond chap. That must be him then. So after all that, and getting arrested because he panicked and mixed his words up, the person they were quizzing him about wasn't even there?

That didn't improve his mood. He looked at his watch again, then back at the cellar door. No sign of activity. It was no good, he had to work to earn and eat. Brushing the earth off his hands, he grabbed his trug and set off back to the store room in a state of self-induced gloom.

It was twenty minutes before the small party emerged from the cellar and headed back to the flat. Jeremy's mind was in overdrive, churning through what he had learned about the vent, the tunnels, the shaft, and of course, that animal.

They had covered some ground just through incidental questions, but he needed to dig deeper, if that was not an inappropriate phrase. It was not his job to determine cause of death – that was Berriman's department – but to deal with this creature he needed to be sure that it really did attack and eat human beings. It sounded ludicrous even as he thought it.

But then the video showed what looked like an enormous rat, albeit with huge teeth, and rats fed on almost anything, including scraps of meat. So maybe if you took an ordinary rat and super-sized and evolved it, it would take advantage of its bulk to tackle larger prey. Underground though? And what did it feed on normally?

So far, all they had as evidence of carnivorous behaviour was a grainy video of a shape attacking a lump, and the Clarks' account of the incident. He needed more than that, and so would Berriman.

He felt a hand on his shoulder and turned to see Berriman indicating with his eyes that they should hold back. "You go on in," he called on to the others. "I just want a quick word with Jeremy first."

They moved up the path a little, out of earshot. Berriman kept his voice low.

"While we were down there I texted Piper to send two officers round to pick up the Clarks, and Norman Baston, and take them to the station in separate cars. We can meet them back there. I need to get forensics in to check that trapdoor entrance for evidence of Mr Firwell's fall or anyone else who might have fallen, if you catch my drift."

"I do. And you told the Clarks not to go in there again now."

"Better than that, I have the key. I was going to see if we can get a copy cut but I'm not sure how easy that is with something that size. In any case, we need to secure the scene. Should have done it before really, but, well, you know, given what happened...."

"Of course. Forensics, is that more than one person? My worry is if that thing runs along the tunnel while samples are being taken and makes that noise that you can hear on the video, then that's more people who know about this."

Berriman pulled his uniform jacket down with a sharp tug - it had been riding up to ease the pressure on his belly.

"Agreed. I'll use Buckley – he's reliable enough and very experienced. We'll tell him that the fact that there's no body is classified, and also not mention the animal. We'll just have to hope it doesn't put in an appearance. If it does, I'll give you a shout."

"Thanks. Ok, let's do that. I don't think we have any better options. I need to make some calls too, actually. There are a couple of scientists on the team and one of them has a zoology background – we wheel her out for stuff involving animals. But we can't just pitch her down that vent and tell her to get busy."

"Not unless you want another body."

"Exactly. I'll have a chat with her about what we have learned but before she comes down here I'll need to find a safe way for her to gain access to this thing."

"Do you have a plan?" Berriman looked doubtful.

"Not as such. But I have some contacts who can help me with that. I'll ring them now."

"Are you going to kill it?"

"The animal? I'd rather not. Trapping it would be a more productive approach. How we do that, given the size of it, and then still keep everything secret, is another thing."

Berriman paused for a few seconds, then cleared his throat and fixed Jeremy in the eye.

"Tell me, if we capture all the animals, assuming there's more than one of them, can everything come out into the open then, seeing as there would be no danger to the public any more?"

Jeremy held his gaze. "We generally don't do that. Who's to say these beasts aren't in other unknown tunnel systems too? People will think that, won't they? That could spread panic, especially if they start coming out at night, like it looks this one could have done. I mean, if this one has been down there for decades, or centuries even, why it is only venturing outside now? Perhaps others elsewhere will do the same. It's a difficult one, though. I'll need to discuss it with my boss once we know where we stand."

"Fair enough." Berriman clapped his hands together. "Right, let's get busy. I need to tell the Clarks to get ready to come to the station, and find Mr Baston. It's been quite a while since I did any interviews like this. Just like old times, eh?"

"Indeed so," said Jeremy out of politeness.

The two men exchanged simultaneous 'after you' hand gestures before Jeremy relented and led them both back into the apartment, worrying as he did that he may be faced with a task that had inglorious failure written all over it.

CHAPTER 47

Trey checked his watch. Eleven twenty three. He could hear a mumble of voices outside the interview room – probably the police chief and the Home Office guys discussing tactics for the grilling he was presumably now about to receive.

As long as he stuck to his story, and told them the same as he told those detectives Collins and Bartrum, and Lauren did the same, then everything should be ok. He would just have to be ultra careful, not rush his answers, and avoid scratching his ear or any other signal that could indicate deception served on a bed of mendacity.

He jumped slightly as the door was flung open and the two older men walked in.

"Hello again Mr Clark," said the chief superintendent brightly, "sorry to keep you waiting."

"Not a problem," replied Trey, although really everything was a problem at the moment.

They both brushed past him and took seats opposite.

"I've sent Jason on some errands, so it will just be the two of us," advised Jeremy, pushing his glasses up his nose as he sat down. "Saves us having to get another chair, too."

Trey smiled, as he felt would be expected from an innocent party. He was relieved though, that he would not have three pairs of eyes trained on him, looking for signs of guilt. Two pairs were more than enough. Did they suspect anything? Well, he was about to find out.

Berriman made a play of neatly arranging some sheaves of paper next to his notebook and pen, while he collected his thoughts.

"Now, Mr Clark," he eventually began, "I just wanted to make it clear that you are not under arrest at this stage. However, a man has died, and the death involved you, and another man has gone missing, which also involved you, and both were on the same day. I think you would agree that to an impartial observer that sounds.... er... peculiar."

Trey tried to swallow but found he couldn't. "Ok, yeah, it does, I suppose" he replied weakly.

Berriman assumed a frown. "So obviously we need to make sure we fully understand every detail, so that you can help us to establish the facts. For that reason, the session today will be recorded, ok? There are cameras above you."

Trey nodded. "Yes, fine." What else could he say?

Berriman reached out to the recording device on the table and flicked down a red switch.

"Good. For the benefit of the tape, this is Chief Superintendent Berriman, together with Home Office Deputy Director Jason Stanton-Davies, interviewing Mr Trey Clark, who has attended voluntarily, on Monday 15th September. Although not under arrest I must advise you, Mr Clark, that you are not obliged to answer any police questions, but that whatever you do say will be recorded and may be used against you as evidence in a court of law. You do not have to say anything, but it may harm your defence if you do not mention when questioned something which you later rely on in court. Anything you do say may be given in evidence. Is that clear?"

Trey's mouth was beginning to feel dry. Those words, heard so often in police crime dramas on TV, were generally aimed at low-life criminals squirming to avoid being handcuffed by three burly officers. Hearing them directed at him had taken him by surprise.

He nodded again, more slowly this time.

"Do I need a lawyer?" he asked, still basing his knowledge on TV shows.

Berriman turned it back on him.

"Do you want one? It's entirely up to you."

Trey scrunched up his face a little. Did he need one? Surely you are as good as admitting that you are in some way guilty of something if you say yes, when all they want to do is have a chat. But then supposing they tried to trap him into saying something, where a lawyer could have stepped in to defend their client. Then again, the only lawyer he knew was the one they had just used to buy their house, and he doubted that they would want to get involved in this. He'd have to pay them, too, no doubt.

"No, I'll be fine," he replied, immediately worrying that maybe he wouldn't be.

"Good!" said Berriman a little too eagerly. "Let's begin then. This morning you showed us the vent down which Mr Firwell fell, but before revisiting that I would just like to dig a little deeper into the disappearance of your friend, Darren Hoggsmith, or Hoggo, as I believe he was known, on the same day."

"Of course," replied Trey. That had taken him a bit off guard, but maybe that was deliberate. Remember the story, remember the story…….

"How long have you known Mr Hoggsmith?"

Trey almost smiled at the thought of his friend being called Mr Hoggsmith. It just sounded so wrong. But then the reminder that he would never see Hoggo again brought him back to reality. "Since school. We were old mates."

"*Were?*"

Damn. Tripped up already. He was going to struggle not to let slip a few past tenses; he had to concentrate. First, though, retrieve the situation. "Yeah, we were old mates back at school. And we've been mates since school too."

Berriman arched an eyebrow and wrote something down.

"And he lives in Matlock."

"Yes, quite close by car."

Berriman fell silent and studied the notes in front of him. Trey assumed this was a tactic to make him feel uncomfortable. If so, it was working. A stubby hand slid a sheet of paper to one side, then another, before the chief superintendent's forefinger traced a line half way across the next page.

"On Saturday just past, at around eleven o'clock, Mr Hoggsmith arrived at Ridley Manor. What was the reason for his visit?"

"He'd come to collect his ladder."

"And why did you have his ladder?"

"Because he'd brought it round last Wednesday to see if it would fit in the hole in the cellar. It didn't, so he said he'd come back on the Saturday to pick it up."

"And why didn't he just take it back with him on the Wednesday?"

How had they agreed to explain this? Ah yes…..

"Mainly so we could think about maybe a way we could use it but also, he said he'd got to go off to a job where he might need to use the roof rack for something else."

He watched as Berriman made another note, and realised with rising alarm that there was every chance that this would be followed up. They would find Hoggo's office, go through his records, and see if he did have an appointment and whether it would be likely to need a roof rack. Perhaps even visit the client. Oh shit, why hadn't they thought of all this? It had all seemed strangely straightforward when he and Lauren had created their protective web of deception, but now that one strand had already been pulled at, he realised that it being easy might have been a clue that they had not given it enough thought.

All he could do was hope that Hoggo didn't keep records. He didn't even know if he was still a one-man band or now had people working with him who could answer these questions.

He hoped his new levels of anxiety were not visible, especially as the Home Office chap was staring at him much more intently than was comfortable.

Berriman finished writing and looked up.

"Let's stay on Saturday, when Mr Hoggsmith returned to collect his ladder. Perhaps you could just outline what happened from the point at which your friend arrived. He rang the doorbell, then what happened?"

Trey felt a dull pressure growing behind his forehead. This was so hard, and they had barely started. He took a breath. Ok, here goes....

"I went to let him in, we said hello and walked across the atrium and into our apartment. We were just chatting about general stuff, you know football, TV, that kind of stuff. Lauren had gone to work so it was just us two. We made a cup of tea, and sat down to drink it. Then after a while Hoggo says 'mate, I'm feeling a bit queasy for some reason. Ok if I get some fresh air?', and of course I said yeah, fine, go ahead. I had some work to be getting on with anyway. I thought he meant he just wanted to go and stand in the garden for a bit, so I let him out of the French windows, but then he turned round and said that he might just go for a wander in the woods, seeing as he hadn't been in them before, so he could clear his head. So I said fine, and off he went. That was it really."

Jeremy, silent until now, leaned forward.

"What time was it at this point?"

"Just after half eleven, I suppose."

"And is Mr Hoggsmith the kind of person who likes to go for walks? What sort of chap is he?"

The present tense again. It sounded so wrong, knowing that Hoggo was dead. Have to keep up the pretence, though……

"He's larger than life, you know? An extrovert, big guy too so usually the centre of attention, and that's how he liked it. And still does. I don't know how much he likes walking, it's never really come up before. We've done sporty stuff together before, like golf and – well, I suppose that's a kind of walking isn't it? But I don't live with him so I don't really know.

Anyway, he wasn't doing it for the exercise, it was just because he felt a bit ill."

Berriman took over again.

"And when did you start to get worried that he hadn't returned?"

"To be honest, I went back to my work and got absorbed with that. Then I started to get a pain in my stomach."

"My, my, must have been something in the tea, eh? Both of you falling ill one after the other?" The tone was engineered to sound sympathetic but the words were disbelieving and they both knew it.

"Yeah, I know, it sounds weird, but that's just how it was. The pain was really bad, too, so I phoned Lauren and asked her what I should do. She told me to stay there and she would come back home."

"Really? Could you not phone a doctor or something?"

"Well, she's a nurse, isn't she? So we knew it would save me bothering the NHS if she could deal with it."

Even as he was saying it, Trey realised how feeble this seemed. But it was too late to step back now. Judging by their expressions, his interrogators seemed unimpressed.

"In that case couldn't your wife have just advised you over the phone?" asked Jeremy, looking genuinely puzzled.

"Probably. But she was worried. She's like that. She likes to look after people, especially me." That much was true, at least.

Berriman took over again. "And when did she get home?"

"About forty minutes later, but before that John came round."

"You were having a busy morning! And what was Mr Firwell after?"

"He was asking about the cellar. He had seen Hoggo taking the ladder in there on Wednesday and put two and two together about the trapdoor and what was under it."

"He already knew about the trapdoor?"

"Yes, he had helped me try and open it previously, but we couldn't. That's why I first called Hoggo in, and he came round on..... on....... I think it was Tuesday? Yes, it must have been. That's when we opened it, saw the hole, and realised we'd need a ladder. So he came back with one on Wednesday, but as I said it was too big to fit in."

"So why did Mr Firwell wait another three days before enquiring about the trapdoor?"

"No idea. Maybe he felt a bit uneasy cos he'd told me to count him out of helping to open the door after the last time."

"So he asked you about what was under the trapdoor, then what?"

"I told him about the vent, and if course he wanted to see it, but just then the doorbell rang. Again."

Berriman exchanged glances with Jeremy. "The words Piccadilly and Circus come to mind. And who was it this time, Uncle Tom Cobley?"

"No it was you guys. Cops."

"Ah yes, Rakowska and Davis. I was wondering when they would make an appearance. That was at.... let me see...... ten past twelve, is that right?"

"It would have been about then, yes."

"And you were still in pain at this point?"

Trey caught himself before replying. Berriman would check with the two officers, who would report that Trey showed no signs whatsoever of being in great discomfort.

"Not so much. It had already started to get better."

"That was fortunate. Although a bit of a wasted journey home for your wife then."

"Yes, it did turn out to be, in the end."

"And you didn't ring her to tell her not to worry coming back?"

"No, she would have already left by then."

"She could have turned round and gone back."

"She wouldn't have done, though. She'd want to check for herself."

Berriman's silence as he returned to his notes made it clear that this ruse about the mysterious stomach pain was stretching his credulity. But he couldn't prove anything to the contrary, could he? He could hardly launch an investigation into an historic case of trapped wind.

As Berriman moved bits of paper around, Trey once again felt obliged observe the top of the bowed head opposite him. It glistened slightly, and he became absorbed by the faint outline of shaved hair around the edges, wondering what Berriman would look like if he grew it out, and long, like a mad professor.

Then suddenly he was looking at Berriman's eyes instead as the chief superintendent flicked his head up.

"The officers were asking you about Anita Rackman, yes?"

"Yes."

"When did you last see her?"

"It was when she came round to the flat last Sunday, to ask about me doing a book cover for her."

"Ah yes, you are an illustrator by trade then?"

"Yes."

"And you always work from home?"

"Mostly, yes."

Berriman made a note; Trey wasn't sure why.

"Now, you told our officers that Ms Rackman had spoken to you for about fifteen minutes, then left."

Trey's stomach sunk again. That was indeed what they had said at the time, he remembered now. But that wasn't what he and Lauren had agreed as part of their manufactured account of events. They had decided to admit that Anita had been taken down for a quick look at the cellar, so that they could account for the evidence that Norman would give, now that they knew he had seen Anita go into the cellar with Trey on Sunday. But why would Trey have failed to mention that potentially important fact to Rakowska and Davis? At least detectives Collins and Bartrum hadn't followed up on that – their focus had been on John's death, the animal, and Hogg's disappearance.

"Yes," he said, unable to think quickly enough to weigh up what to do. All he could do now was hope that Lauren didn't contradict him. But then, if pressed further, he could just say that part of the time that Anita spoke to him, she was in the cellar, but that wasn't really important because at that point the coal was still there so neither of them knew about the vent. So it didn't really matter where she was and was therefore not worth mentioning to the two officers. Perhaps this was ok after all, then.

"And after that, neither you nor your wife saw Ms Rackman again."

Trey steadied his voice. "No."

"And at this point there was still no sign of your friend, so you mentioned this to my officers."

"Yes."

"Presumably you were quite worried by now? After all, it was now.... er... about forty minutes since he had walked off?"

"Not so much worried as..... kind of puzzled, I suppose."

"So what happened next?"

"Your officers left to go and look for him. Then, once John had gone....."

Jeremy, who had been sitting very still, cross-legged, observing Trey, put his hand up.

"Hang on.... Did you not take John down to see the vent?"

Remember the story, remember the story.....

"No, I told him to come back in the afternoon as Lauren would be back in a minute, and obviously I still had a bit of pain in my stomach, so I didn't want him standing there while we talked about that."

"Well of course," replied Jeremy, in a way that implied the opposite. "Carry on."

He doesn't believe me, but he can't prove anything. Keep going.

"So once he'd left I checked to see if Hoggo's van was still there, and it was. Then Lauren got back."

"Did you not go and look for him? He could have had a brain haemorrhage or something and been lying on the forest floor."

"Well there was no point really, because the cops... I mean... you guys, you know, the two officers, said they would have a scout round. Then about twenty minutes later we saw them coming out of the woods with Norman in handcuffs. That was a shock."

"And what did you think at that point?"

"That maybe Norman had done something to Hoggo in the woods."

"So you rushed out to see if your friend was ok?"

"No, but....."

"But what?"

Trey knew almost as he said it that it was a mistake, but the words came spilling out. "We knew the police would be handling it, so I rang his mobile instead," he said.

It was what they had agreed to say, but now he felt a sudden movement in his stomach as, sitting in a police station, he was reminded that probably police could access phone records, and check whether or not he had rung Hoggo when he said he had. Or could they? He'd seen them do it in films, but that was fiction. Yes, but the type of fiction that is based on reality, and then there are those cases on the news where they reveal that a lorry driver was on his phone just before he crashed into the back of car. Oh shit. This wasn't good. Supposing he said he'd misdialled the number? No, he had Hoggo as a contact, that wouldn't wash. He could delete him though, after this interview. But do phone companies keep track of activity like that? Oh, this was such a mess.

He tried to keep his face emotionless, masking the turmoil inside, but was he looking suspiciously insouciant? Should he look more upset, less calm, when talking about Hoggo? He was over-thinking this, and that wasn't helping.

Berriman was nodding, as though expecting his answer. "I wondered when you would. There was no answer, I take it."

"No."

"So then you presumably had lunch. What time was it when you finished?"

"Hard to remember exactly but probably around half past one, maybe quarter to two."

"By that time your friend had been clearing his head for, what, about an hour and three quarters, possibly two hours? That's a long time to be wandering around in a small wood."

"He might have gone into town," replied Trey, sounding even to himself like a small child coming up with an implausible excuse as to why he had chocolate on his mouth. It was the contingency answer he and Lauren had invented, but spoken out loud it breached the far side of unlikely.

Berriman put his pen down on the table and leaned back in his chair, steepling his fingers, as though deep in thought. He let Trey's answer hang in the air for a while, to drift around the room and amplify itself in everyone's thoughts, before replying.

"Do you not think he would have rung you to let you know what he was doing?"

"You would have thought so, yes. But he didn't. Although he's not great at that type of thing."

Berriman sighed deliberately, and pulled his fingers apart to turn over a sheaf of paper. "So what happened next?"

"At two o'clock John came round like I'd told him to, so he could have a look at the vent."

"So all three of you went into the cellar and, well, perhaps you could repeat, for the benefit of the tape, what you told us earlier this morning when we were at the house."

"Sure. Ok, so I went in first and John and Lauren followed behind me. She closed the door and I walked across the centre of the cellar towards the vent, sort of leading him towards it, I suppose. He walked around the other side of it though, I guess so he could get a better look down without me in the way."

Jeremy held his finger up.

"Can I just ask..... surely there would have been room for both of you to look down from the same side, the closer side? After all, that's what we all did this morning."

"Well, yeah, I guess. But he didn't do that. I don't know why. So anyway, he walked round that side, and knelt down so he could peer in and see the bottom a bit better, I suppose. Then we talked about the shaft for a bit. Just about the construction, how long it must have taken, how deep it was – that kind of thing. Then he tried to get up again."

"Not to speak ill of the dead, but wouldn't you say that a man of his age, clambering to his feet next to a very deep hole, would be extremely careful to do so safely?" asked Jeremy. "After all, I speak from experience this morning when saying that even if you are approaching a shaft like that you are extraordinarily careful to watch your footing. He was right next to it."

He's trying to bait you, thought Trey, but in this case, he's barking up the wrong tree. The bit about John getting to his feet and falling forwards was true. He kept his voice level.

"Everyone's different I suppose. He came across a quite a confident man, perhaps he didn't...... well, I don't know. All I can say is he wasn't careful enough this time, obviously."

"Indeed," said Jeremy, giving nothing away. "Please continue."

Trey cleared his throat. "Right, well, his right leg sort of gave way – I have no idea why. But it meant he stumbled forward and started to fall, like I showed you this morning, straight into the hole. I could see it happening like it was in slow motion. His chest hit the side next to me and as he went down he flung his arms up and grabbed my right foot and the edge of the vent with his other hand. Having my left foot yanked like that meant I fell backwards, but my other leg was now pushed into the ground trying to shove me back as I slid forward. Then I felt Lauren grab my hand and she anchored herself to the workbench with her other hand, or at least that's what she told me afterwards."

Berriman shook his head slightly at the thought of it. "Horrific experience. So at that stage you could hold him there?"

"Yes. He was too heavy to pull up, though, so me and Lauren were screaming at him to let go otherwise he would kill all of us. But then Lauren couldn't hold on any longer and had to let go of the vice on the workbench. My right leg on its own couldn't hold John's weight so I slid over the edge and followed John down. All I remember is starting to fall, then nothing. We hit the bottom, obviously but I don't remember that bit, just waking up and lying there, slowly realising what just happened."

"And you had landed on top of Mr Firwell?"

"Yes. I was still lying on him too, which was gross. Still makes me gag just thinking about it. But my leg really hurt so it was hard to move. And it was dark, so I couldn't see a lot until my eyes adjusted."

"Was Mr Firwell already dead at this point?"

"It looked like it. Lauren was looking down from above and she told me how to check his pulse, but there was nothing. Couldn't detect any breathing either. Also his head was messed up."

"What do you mean?"

"Covered in blood and cuts and grazes. Must be where he scraped it down the side as he fell."

Jeremy winced. "Poor chap."

Berriman, well used to dealing with cases of bodily harm and death, was less empathetic.

"If the fall didn't kill him then having another man landing on top of him probably did."

Jeremy leaned forward and smiled. "Not that he's blaming you for that, of course!"

"I should hope not," said Trey, returning a forced smile. The blame to be apportioned happened at the top of the vent, not the bottom.

"So," said Berriman, bringing the conversation back, "you were now down the bottom of a deep hole with a dead body for company. What did you do?"

"We had a brief chat about what my options were, but then I heard the noise."

"The animal."

"Yes, and of course that changed everything. I had to get away."

"Indeed, as you recounted this morning. Perhaps you could just go over that again."

The word 'perhaps' was not an invitation to refuse, so Trey once again described what had happened to him when he encountered the gigarat and shone the torch in its eyes. At least that section was all true, so he felt considerably more comfortable in his account than he had done previously. It became slightly trickier though, as he began to describe how Lauren and Mel had planned to rescue him.

".... so they decided to use the garden hose to pull me out."

"And why was a call to the fire brigade not the easier and quicker option, do you think?"

Trey remembered what Lauren had told him. They couldn't make this bit up, as Mel would be giving evidence too. So this was all about the explanation for her decisions.

"People do unexpected things in stressful situations, and she said she thought it would be quicker to find a rope or hose than to call the fire brigade. Also she didn't want them turning up and having to wait around for me to come back down that tunnel. I mean, I might not have come back at all."

"Actually," said Jeremy, shifting in his chair, "that turned out to be a good call. If a fire brigade crew had got to find out about that animal my job would have been a lot harder. Probably impossible, actually."

Trey took that as a vindication of Lauren's reasoning even though that was not actually what Jeremy had said.

"She was trying to do the right thing," he said. "And she got me out, didn't she? So she was right."

"Just in time too, it seems."

"Yeah. Well, you saw that second video. That was taken about a minute after I got out."

Berriman clicked his teeth. "A close call. Talking of calls, the phone call that came through to us in the end was from Mr Wilson, not your wife. Why was that?"

"We were too busy hugging each other, to be honest. Also, Tony volunteered to do it, so why not?"

Berriman looked across to Jeremy. "Anything you'd like to add?"

Jeremy gave a slight nod. "Thank you, yes. I'm sure you are aware, Mr Clark, that for the sake of public safety and piece of mind we must keep this business under wraps for now. You must say nothing to anyone about the creature you saw, or your adventure in the tunnel."

"Yes, we were told that by detective Collins."

"Good. I can tell you that there are incentives for you to do so, and penalties if you don't."

"Like what?"

"Let's just say that I have a lot of influence in government circles and leave it at that for now. I hope you understand me?"

Given his situation Trey felt it best not to push any further – he had got the message.

"Sure," he said. "What about Mel and Tony? They already know."

"Jason is seeing to that as we speak, amongst other things. They will be under the same strictures. You are quite sure that no one else knows?"

"Yes. Well, no, actually. I did tell Norman, the gardener, about the hole in our cellar. But I didn't mention the giga.... the animal."

Jeremy's initial look of alarm subsided.

"Right, ok, well that is manageable then. We still need to speak to Mr Baston, don't we?" He looked across at Berriman, who nodded.

"No sign of him at the moment, but hopefully your man Crisp will notify us of his return from wherever he is."

"He's probably working," suggested Trey, before realising that this was a fairly obvious thing to say and unlikely to have come as a surprise to the gentlemen opposite.

"Indeed," replied Jeremy.

Berriman shuffled his papers and chopped them into shape as a newsreader would do when signing off.

"Right, I think that should do for now. Thank you, Mr Clark, you are free to go. Although you will no doubt wish to wait for your wife, who we will see now, after we've had a little chat."

Trey rose hesitantly to his feet as Berriman turned off the recording device. "Oh, right, thank you. You don't want me to send her in?"

"Not yet, thank you. Good day, Mr Clark."

It was as though he was no longer important – he'd served his purpose, now he could get lost. It would sound strange replying with 'good day', especially as it wasn't any such thing, so he just mumbled a goodbye and left the interview room. If Lauren was still in the waiting area at least he could give her a smile or a few words to convey that he had not put his foot in it.

But she wasn't there. Thy must have put her in another room somewhere to avoid collusion. A shame, but not a surprise, on reflection. He sat down on a blue plastic chair and wondered if when Lauren emerged from her interview, an officer would be walking over to arrest him.

The Chief Superintendent waited for a few moments after Trey had closed the door behind him, taking the opportunity to get up and stretch his legs.

"Well?" he said after walking to the door and back again. "Convinced?"

Jeremy also rose to his feet, smoothed back his hair, and went to look out of the window. A herd of assorted police cars grazed in a back yard, the concrete space ringed by a tired wood panelled fence wearing a skirt of weeds. It wasn't much of a view.

"I think some of that was true and some of it was not. None of the tale about his friend going for a walk in the woods made a lot of sense to me. There were too many inconsistencies in his account, in my opinion. You?"

"Agreed. Ironically, I was far more easily swayed by the bit about the bear-sized rat."

"Yes, but did you notice how much more naturally he recounted that? Until that point he was being very careful and precise with what he said, but as soon as he got into the account of falling down the hole and his experience in the tunnels, his narrative flowed a lot more easily. I'd say that up to that point, he had something to hide."

"Bodies, perhaps," mused Berriman. "Although what would his motive be? We'll do some digging on his background, and his wife too. See what we've got on them in the system. He seems a decent young man on the surface, so if there is anything going on there, he's keeping it well hidden."

Jeremy completed his survey of the car park and turned round. "Everything is hidden until someone finds it."

Berriman chuckled. "That's either very profound or a statement of the bleedin' obvious."

"Or both. Oh, don't forget I need to get back to the house by two o'clock."

"Yes, to meet your specialists that you spoke to earlier. That's fine. We can give you a lift. What about Baston? You'll want to be in the interview with him, won't you?"

"Ideally, yes. But if necessary I'll send Jason to that. As long as we cover it all between us. I definitely have to speak to these experts myself."

"And now for Mrs Clark. Let's see if her account stacks up under scrutiny. You ready?"

Jeremy made his way back to his seat. "Go for it."

Berriman walked stiffly to the door, as though his uniform was preventing him from moving properly (which to some degree it probably was), and opened the door. "Sergeant Piper, go and fetch Mrs Clark, would you?"

CHAPTER 48

"Not sure why I'm here, to be honest. I was just told to drop everything and meet some Home Office chap at this address. Bloody cheek if you ask me, I've got loads on at the minute. Still, it's a day out, innit?"

Tommy Medina rocked from one foot to the other, gently crunching the gravel beneath his feet, and cast an expectant eye at the lady standing opposite him.

She was about his height, but then he wasn't a tall man – something that had proved useful in his chosen line of work, crawling about in tunnels. You don't see many seven foot men potholing, but then you don't see many seven foot men. Five foot eight was plenty for that kind of work.

She looked about fifty but Tommy was no great judge of age. After all, he was forty seven himself but looked ten years older. His wispy brown hair had not only thinned from where it was needed, but also turned grey at an alarming rate in the last few years, and his face had collected wrinkles and folds faster than most. He was lucky he'd got married when he did, but before she died his poor wife was probably yearning after the handsome young buck that she thought she had partnered with, and who had quickly turned into Gollum's father.

Mind you, she'd been no bed of roses herself when she left this world, it had to be said. If you start smoking at 14, it's not just your lungs that get ravaged. But to go at forty three, that was ridiculous. She didn't deserve that. Nor did he, widowed so young. But two years had passed, and his urges hadn't. He missed being with a woman.

And here was a very useful one standing next to him. Polly Midhurst, if he'd remembered her name properly, and no sign of a wedding ring. She was a handsome creature, with a strong mouth and rather large eyes, deliberately accentuated by mascara and kohl. Quite striking, actually. He cast his mind back to the days when he could make a suggestive remark to a woman he didn't know and usually get away with it. Those days were long gone, so now the heavy lifting had to be done by his sunny disposition and gale force personality. Not that this always worked, and he suspected that this Polly girl was going to prove that.

She had more hair than he had ever had even in his student days; black tresses sweeping down to her shoulders, blowing and flicking about in the gusty breeze. Smart grey trouser suit, shapely…. steady, Tommy, no sense in getting ideas. Despite everything, this was a job, and if he was going to be working with this lady he wanted to get off on the right foot.

"So you're a biologist, then?"

Polly had been gazing past the house, trying to find something interesting to divert her. She turned round.

"Sorry? Oh, yes, that's right. Mostly, anyway."

"What does that actually mean? What kind of things…."

"… do I do? I can't really say, I'm afraid. Mostly research – I can tell you that much."

Tommy nodded sagely. "Research, eh? I do some of that too. I don't just crawl about in holes, you know."

A hand went up to move a stray strand of hair that had caught in her eye. "I didn't imagine that you did. Shouldn't he be here by now?"

Tommy checked his watch. Five past two. He'd misjudged the journey and rocked up at just before one thirty, standing around like a lemon until Miss Perfect next to him had arrived two minutes before two o'clock.

"Yep, he's late. Hold up, is this him?"

The sound of displacing gravel under car tyres drew their attention to a marked police car now trundling its way towards them along the entrance drive. It eased to a halt and a silver-haired man with glasses got out, reaching back in to pull out a dog-eared briefcase and say thank you to the police officer driver who was starting to get out of the other door.

Jeremy faced his two new recruits and smiled.

"Hello Polly, nice to see you again. Now, Tommy, isn't it? We haven't met." He stretched out a hand. "Jeremy Stanton-Davies. Pleased to meet you. You've come highly recommended. Is Jason not here? I'd assumed he would have met you. Hang on, I'll text him."

He punched a few words into his mobile. "Right, now Polly, we spoke earlier so you know the basics. Tommy, you were nominated by my contact, so welcome to the team. For this particular task you are now officially part of DUST, with all that this entails."

Tommy scratched his ear. "I am? Dust? What's dust when it's at home? Apart from being stuff you 'oover up."

"It's the name of our division. Declared Unexplainable Specialist Team, DUST. I'll need you to sign some forms before I say any more. Ah, here's Jason."

The front door of the house had opened and Jason Crisp was trotting towards them, looking apologetic.

"Sorry all, I got tied up. Some interesting leads, Jeremy."

"Excellent. Those are the best type. Let's discuss them where we have a bit more privacy. I'm going to suggest the cellar, seeing as that is where the action is. Rob gave me the key."

He reached inside his jacket pocket and flourished it at Jason before turning to the new recruits.

"This is Polly and Tommy, by the way."

Nods and hellos were exchanged.

"Looks like I'm outnumbered then," said Jason.

"In what way?" asked Polly.

"All your names end in 'y', mine doesn't."

Jeremy smiled at the new arrivals. "Sharp as a tack this lad. Nothing gets past him. Now, if you'll bear with me a second."

He turned back to the police car, where the officer was reaching into the boot for some police barrier tape.

"Once you've cordoned off the woods, when Mr Baston comes back you'll text me, yes? On the number I gave you earlier? If I don't reply feel free to come and find me."

The officer nodded. "No problem."

With a turn of his heel and a "follow me" Jeremy was on his way around the side of the house, his DUST accomplices close behind. Jason jogged to position himself at Jeremy's side.

"You were right," he whispered, "it *was* a security camera."

Jeremy smiled. "I thought it was. 1st floor, yes? Whose flat was it in?"

"A nice old couple called Tony and Suzanne Wilson. Both retired."

"What area does the camera cover?"

"It's quite wide-angle, so it gets in most of the parking area and front of the house, looking towards where the drive comes in. You can't see the front door but you'd see anyone walking up to it."

"Is their footage backed up?"

"Yes, it's all stored to a home hub every time it records an incident. If it detects movement it records about a fifteen second clip. Suzanne said they have it because her husband is paranoid about his car getting broken into, after it happened to him once before he retired. She can't see the point, but at least it could help us."

"Have you got the files?"

"Yes, I downloaded everything from the last two weeks onto a pen drive. That's what had diverted me. I'll go over them tonight."

"Who needs TV for entertainment, eh? I'm not convinced it's going to help, but you never know. At least we'll see this Hoggsmith fellow coming and going, if nothing else. Then we can hand the clips to Berriman. I have to say I'm a little surprised that his people hadn't got there before us."

They reached the steps down to the cellar door. Jeremy stopped to turn to his accomplice.

"The Clarks should be back from the station any minute now. Go and see if they're here yet, and if not put a note under their door, would you, letting them know they might hear noises in their cellar? Don't want them thinking that animal is in there."

"A talking rat?"

"You know what I mean. Other noises."

"Of course. Right, back soon."

As Jason went back round to the front, Jeremy led his two guests down into the cellar.

"I'm sure I don't need to tell you to be careful," he said over his shoulder as he walked in, "there's a very deep hole in here. I should also tell you that a forensics chap should be here later this afternoon, and so to avoid effectively trampling over a potential crime scene, I need you to stay back on this side of the cellar, and don't step towards it. You can see it from a distance for now and take my word for it that it is approximately twenty feet deep."

A shaft in a cellar was certainly a new one on Tommy.

Twenty nine years now he'd been in the tunnelling business, starting as an apprentice for a building contractor who assigned him to a couple of road bypass schemes that involved tunnels. Then he was moved to a tunnelling project at Heathrow Airport as a skilled engineer, and within three years, partly thanks to his overbearing confidence and ability to motivate his crew, he'd worked his way up to Foreman.

A new road tunnel in Staffordshire gave him the opportunity to start a project from scratch, working with the Project Manager whose job he eventually took over, when the incumbent was suddenly dismissed for gross misconduct. The nature of the misconduct was never officially revealed, but all the men knew it involved Sally from Accounts and an illicit encounter or two, the resultant dismissal probably not helped by the lady in question being married to a board director.

So he'd stepped up and surprised everyone by doing a half-decent job. But there was too much stress and responsibility – it crushed his ebullience and he couldn't be himself. He gave it a couple of years but that was enough. He decided to move into consultancy and began specialising in mines, advising on new technologies for building them and techniques for maintaining them.

As so often with consultants, he learned as much from his clients as they did from him, despite them paying him lots of money and him paying them nothing. He'd since become one of the foremost experts in the country when it came to exploring and mapping holes in the ground. Not bad for a council estate lad from Leytonstone.

And now here he was looking at a shaft in a cellar but not entirely sure what he was here for.

"What's with that massive trapdoor? That's thick enough to stop a cruise missile."

"Yes, it seems entirely out of proportion, and we don't know why. It was also buried under a coal store for decades, which is why no one knew about it until now."

"It's almost as though someone knew what was down there," said Polly.

"I know." Jeremy walked over to the workbench and laid his briefcase on it, clipping open the rust-spotted gold metal catches. "It all adds to the mystery."

"So when can I have a look down it then?" asked Tommy.

"Hopefully tomorrow. For today, I've agreed with Rob that we will be ok if we stay within this corridor of about three feet in width, so my apologies for the inconvenience. I have some documents here you need to read and sign, Tommy, then I need to explain in more detail why you are here and the unusual aspects to this work. Polly, you'll know some of this already."

Polly smiled wisely and Tommy felt somewhat belittled. Just because these two went to some posh university and hobnobbed with the great and the good, didn't mean he was any less of a person than they were. He needed to know what they knew, so he took the papers, skim read through various parts about secrecy and confidentiality, and signed them.

He'd go over them in more detail later, but there was nothing in there about sacrificing his children or pledging allegiance to the devil, and after all, if it was good enough for Polly Two-Shoes then it must be good enough for him.

"There you go," he said, handing the duplicates back.

"You're a quick reader," observed Jeremy.

"Yeah, well, I don't muck around, you know? So what's this all about then?"

"Down there," said Jeremy, pointing at the hole with one hand and returning the signed papers to his case with the other, "are a series of tunnels and shafts – presumably an old mine."

"Ok..." said Tommy slowly. Unusual, but so far not really worthy of a cloak and dagger operation.

"In one direction the tunnel leads to a large and very deep shaft that originally surfaced in what is now the lawn outside and appears to have further tunnels leading off it as you go down. In the other direction, there are caverns and more tunnels. And in those tunnels is at least one very large animal."

Aha, now it got interesting.

"It appears to be carnivorous, and could be connected to the disappearance of four people in this vicinity. We understand that there's a cavern down there with bones in, for a start. I hope you can see why we are endeavouring to keep this from the public. If news got out it could cause pandemonium."

Tommy's mouth had opened slightly as he listened. "When you say very large, how large?"

"From the one witness we have, about the size of a bear."

"Panda? Teddy?"

"Grizzly."

"Stone me. But....... how?"

"Exactly. That's why Polly is here. It's her job to classify it, work out how it got there and how it lives, and advise on how best to capture it."

Polly grimaced. "A little easier said than done."

"Indeed. This is not a scenario that any of us are familiar with."

Tommy scratched his ear. "So why...... what do you want me to do then? I'm not going down there if that's what you're....."

"No, don't worry," interrupted Jeremy, "we need to keep you alive." He smiled to make it clear that this important clarification had a humorous element. "Your job will be initially advisory, but once the brigadier arrives you will be working with him on a plan of action."

"The brigadier?"

"Yes, Charles Shaw. He should be with us any minute; he's running about fifteen minutes late. Said he'd text me when he got here."

He checked his phone. "Aw, crap, no signal. Jason, can you run round the front and keep and eye out for him please?"

"Sure." Jason, having only just joined them again, disappeared once more.

"Who's the witness then?" asked Tommy. "The one who saw the animal."

"Trey Clark. He and his wife own the flat above here, and this cellar. He's been down there, and encountered that thing. He escaped by shining a light in its eyes."

"I was mulling over that, after you told me this morning," said Polly. "The fact that it still has eyes, even though it seems to live in almost perpetual darkness, would indicate that it wasn't always underground, and may only have been down there for a short evolutionary time period. If it was a species that had been down there for tens of thousands of years, or longer, you would expect the eyes to close over and become non-functional, like a mole. But you also said that four people had gone missing, and I don't suppose they all fell down this hole. So if this animal is responsible, it sounds like it is coming out to the surface somewhere, presumably at night, and could use its eyes in low level light to help find and grab its prey."

Jeremy raised an eyebrow. "Spot on Polly. That is exactly what we are thinking. The first person to go missing was a homeless lady called Molly Baines who was living in the woods, so it's possible that this animal was more used to truffling out other animals in the middle of the night, and hadn't previously encountered any humans. But then it found Molly, got a taste for human flesh, and wanted more."

Tommy wiped his brow with his sleeve. This was something else. "You serious with all this?" he asked. "I mean…. guys, come on. A man-eating bear living in a mine in the middle of Derbyshire? Going out at night eating people? You're havin' a laugh, ain't yer?"

"I didn't say it was a bear," Jeremy pointed out. "I said it was the size of one. It looks more like a rat or a mole. But yes, I'm serious, and I hope you can see why I asked you to sign those papers. I should mention, though, that one chap went missing during the day, which doesn't fit our theorem, and another one actually died falling down this hole. Although to be fair he was dragged off by the animal so he does count as an indirect victim of it too."

Tommy was beginning to wish he hadn't signed those papers quite so readily. "Are we getting danger money for this? I'm not being funny, but this ain't what I expected, you know?"

Jeremy smiled. "I would have been surprised if it was. If the operation goes well, and you keep your silence, you will be well rewarded, yes. If you don't, there will be consequences. Just so you know."

"Consequences?"

"Absolutely. We don't go to all this effort to keep things under wraps for nothing. I'll elucidate later, though – I can hear voices."

The noises outside grew louder, and the cellar door opened. Jason led in a tall, wiry man dressed in army fatigues. His hair was short, light brown, and side parted. His ears looked as though they had been taken from a much larger man, but they were appropriate bookends to an imposing Roman nose that cast quite a shadow over his mouth. Tommy sensed a whiff of aggressive aftershave.

The brigadier's eyes swept the room. "Morning everyone," he said with a brief but professional smile.

After a mumble of responses Jeremy took charge of introductions and, having encouraged him to sign the secrecy forms, gave Brigadier Shaw a brief resume of where they had got to, before sending the yo-yoing Jason back up to wait with the officer in the car, so he could come and tell Jeremy when Norman had returned. Then he got out his phone.

"I was saving this until you were all here. We have two videos of this creature, taken by Lauren Clark. One is a bit grainy, the other much clearer. But it shows you what we are up against. Both were taken looking down the vent next to us. Right, who's first? Polly, as you're nearest....."

One by one the three newcomers peered at the images and one by one their mouths dropped and their eyes widened.

Tommy was second in the queue. "Oh my good god," he exclaimed when the full face view of the animal came up on the screen. "That is one evil looking bugger isn't he? Look at those teeth. Why is it making that weird noise? I'd shoot the thing, personally, not muck about trying to catch him."

"It might be a she," pointed out Polly, "and no, we'd rather capture it than kill it. Humans have killed off far too many animals on this planet already. Taking it alive could tell us a lot, scientifically."

Tommy sniffed. "Yeah, and it could kill us too. Better we take it out first if you ask me."

"Well it's a good job no one did ask you, then. We'll only kill it if we have no choice, although I would hope it won't come to that."

Brigadier Shaw, now watching the second video, gave a slow whistle and turned to Polly. "I'm not sure a tranquiliser dart will stop an animal like that charging at you in a tunnel. I wouldn't want to put any of my men in that kind of danger."

Polly shook her head. "No, no, I was thinking of a trap of some kind. Lure it into a net or something."

"A big piece of cheese?" suggested Tommy, not entirely seriously.

Polly frowned at him. "It's not a mouse."

"What is it then?"

Polly glanced at Jeremy. "Am I free to talk about this?"

"Absolutely," confirmed Jeremy, "every discussion between us must never be disclosed to anyone else without my authority. We've all signed the papers agreeing to that."

Polly wandered over to the work bench, turned, and leant back on it.

"Alright. Well, I did some internal research before I set off this morning. Went through some classified records for our department, and stumbled across something that could give us some clues. Back in the 1950s and 60s, there was a government building in Clayper, about six miles from here. Officially it was just a cold storage facility but there were actually a small suite of underground laboratories doing animal research. It's not there any more, by the way."

"Government cuts, no doubt," muttered the brigadier with what sounded like some bitterness.

"Indeed," agreed Polly. "Although it sounds like they were not the most professional outfit known to man, so that might have had something to do with it, if their continued funding was dependent on results. Went a bit rogue in some of the things they tried. From what I could see, though, they were doing a number of experiments based on the concept of genetically modifying animals for potentially increased meat production."

"Did they have the technology back then?" asked Jeremy.

Polly laughed. "No! Well, obviously to nothing like the degree we have now. But of course you don't know what you don't know yet, and what you will know in the future has to come from what you do in the present."

"Good job I'm sober or I wouldn't have understood that," said Tommy under his breath.

"So the scientists back then were experimenting, trying the things that would lead us to where we are today. One of their areas of research was focused around...." - she paused for effect – "the pituitary gland."

"Growth hormones?" asked Jeremy.

"Exactly. They seem to have been charged with finding ways in which livestock could be made to grow bigger, in order to increase the meat yield, as it were. So they were targeting the pituitary gland and trying to replicate what happens to humans when it produces too much growth hormone, which can lead to acromegaly and gigantism."

"Like Robert Wadlow?" The brigadier chipped in.

"Who?"

"World's tallest ever man, nearly nine feet tall, huge feet and hands. I stood next to an actual-size representation of him in a museum of some kind when I was young, and never forgot it. Not a great advantage in the trenches being that size, of course."

"Or tunnels," said Tommy.

"Or submarines," added the brigadier.

Jeremy held up his hand. "Perhaps Polly should continue."

"Thank you. As I was saying, they were trying to simulate this growth function through the application of what I would call primitive methods, but back in those days were cutting edge technologies. From what I could see they had a collection of small animals that they were working on, including rats and voles."

"They always use rats in science, don't they?" mused Tommy. "Is that because there's so many of them all around us? If you need a fresh one, grab a net and stand by a drainpipe. Bosh, job done."

He grinned expectantly, but all he earned from Polly was a look that could not have been interpreted as admiration.

"Not quite. Rats are used because almost all disease-linked human genes have counterparts in the rat. We also have less emotional attachment to rats than other animals like kittens and puppies. But yes, there are lots of them, as you imply - they're not exactly an endangered species."

Jeremy interrupted. "You said the scientists went rogue? How?"

"Well that was my reading of it. There were notes about crossbreeding, and I found some letters reprimanding the chief scientist there for widening the scope without authorisation; using different animals for example."

"Not just rats then?"

"Not just rats. But that's all I know. The letter just talked about irregularities in animal species selection that had come to the minister's attention, that kind of thing, but no detail. If they did succeed in creating a cross-bred animal, that could explain things like the strange noise it makes. Rats don't sound like that at all. What I do know is that they were trying to create synthetic tumours in the brains of these animals to spur growth hormone production. The trouble they had is that we know now that most pituitary tumours don't lead to any symptoms. So to get positive results they would have been relying on a fair bit of luck."

"And did they have any?" asked Jeremy.

"I don't know."

"Redacted?"

"Yes, highly classified, which in itself is interesting. There are more files, but I don't have clearance. I was thinking maybe you could...."

"Yes, of course. I'll make some calls when we have finished here. Very interesting, thank you Polly."

Tommy felt obliged to state the obvious.

"So you reckon that must have something to do with the animal in the tunnels? That would be a helluva coincidence if it wasn't."

Jeremy smiled. "Indeed it would. That could also explain why we haven't seen creatures like this already somewhere else in the country. Hopefully this is a one-off."

"Hang on though," said the brigadier, "that was all back in the 1950s. How could this thing have stayed out of sight for 60-odd years? And how could it have lived that long? How long does a rat live for?"

Polly acknowledged the point. "In the wild, no more than two years generally. Pet rats can reach seven years in extreme cases. But there are other ground dwelling animals they may have used that live a lot longer. Naked mole rats live for thirty years, for example."

"Still not sixty, though, is it?" said Tommy. "But if this lab did actually create these monsters, and more than one of them escaped, they could have bred, so the one in those videos could be like a grandchild or something. Well, not a child, obviously. Dunno what else to call it."

"Descendent would do," said Polly, rather too sharply for Tommy's liking. He was going to have to work hard to win her respect.

The brigadier shivered slightly. "Good lord, there could be hundreds of the buggers down there. How big is this mine?"

Jeremy looked pointedly at Tommy. "That's part of the reason you are here, my friend. We need you to find out the history of this mine and how big it might be. I have to say that I did a quick scout around some websites yesterday but could find no mention of it, although of course I was probably looking in the wrong places. We need to know as much as possible about it, not least the possible access points. If this animal is getting out at night, there must be a fairly large but well hidden hole in the ground somewhere not too far from here, where no one tends to go. Charles, I was thinking maybe you could get together with Chief Superintendent Berriman, who is our police representative on this mission, and organise a search of the areas he thinks could be candidates. Obviously only tell the searchers what they are looking for, not why."

"Of course," nodded the brigadier.

"And don't go searching at night, of course. Not that you would."

"No."

"Ah, and here's something I've just remembered. Polly, this might interest you too. Rob was talking earlier about the fact that when Molly Baines went missing the trail of broken undergrowth led towards the river. They sent divers out into the river but couldn't find a body. So to focus this search it would be worth finding out what inaccessible or hardly-used areas of land may lie next to the river for a mile or two either side of this spot, eh Charles? There could be a hole there. And Polly, from that you could deduce that our animal can probably swim."

"That doesn't really narrow it down much, I'm afraid," Polly pointed out. "Rats are very good swimmers but then all the animals that were being tested at Clayper would be able to swim too."

Tommy had been thinking. "You do realise that this tunnel system might be completely unmapped? There's mines dug back in the Roman times we probably don't know about, and even copper mines from the Bronze Age. It's mostly lead mines around here, though – there were thousands of them in Derbyshire over the centuries. I'll have a look though the records though, see what we've got."

"Thanks," said Jeremy. "Now, unless there are any more questions I'd suggest we head our separate ways for ninety minutes to do what research we can in our own specialist fields, so we can make a plan based on a surfeit of information over speculation. Charles – let's make the most of this time to get you hooked up with Rob the chief superintendent, and organise some searches for tunnel entrances. I'll give you his number. If you find any clues in your records, Tommy, please let Charles know. Polly – I'll make that call first, to get you access to those classified documents. I'm assuming you've all got the internet on your phones; the signal isn't too bad upstairs, but if you need any help just shout. I'll see if I can borrow a wifi-code from one of the residents too to speed up your connections. I appreciate I'm hurrying things along but you will appreciate why. Can we meet back here at four o'clock? Actually no, make it three forty-five. That should be enough time. Ok with everyone?"

He was met with a uniform set of affirmative grunts so waved the embryonic team out through the cellar door, casting a quick look back as he did so, at the hole in the floor that held so many secrets.

CHAPTER 49

"I can hear voices but nothing distinct. Just mumbling. At least that means they can't hear us either."

Trey got awkwardly to his feet. Pressing his ear to the carpet like that had required quite an uncomfortable position.

"We should have put a bug down there," said Lauren. "They're probably talking about us. Shall I sneak out to the cellar door and see if I can hear them from there?"

"Nah, not worth it. Suppose you coughed or sneezed, or someone came out and saw you running off? Or someone came round the corner and saw you eavesdropping? Talk about suspicious."

Lauren sighed. "Good point."

She paced back and forth in front of the window.

"I still reckon they'll have caught us out. Something I said won't match exactly with what you said."

Trey tried to sound positive. "I don't know. It seems that we said the same things, and you weren't here when Hoggo went for his 'walk in the woods' either, so they can't really trip you up there."

"I know. But then we didn't ask if the police had found him, did we? I reckon they didn't believe our excuse on that one."

"Yeah, I think that's the worry for me too. Although... how can they disprove our story about Hoggo? They have to present evidence conclusive enough for a jury to be certain that we are guilty. And anyway, we didn't kill Hoggo, did we? That animal did."

"No, but we were guilty of lying about it." Lauren stopped pacing and turned to face Trey. "It's probably academic anyway, if they work out what happened to John and Anita."

"But how can they?"

"Oh, I don't know. They have ways. And they've brought the top brass in now, haven't they? Those two interviewing us were clever people, you could tell."

"Especially that Home Office guy who's right beneath our feet now. The way he looked at me, all the way through, like he was looking at a burglar who'd left his fingerprints all over the house. It was like he knew when I was lying."

"Maybe that's what he wanted you to think. I just tried not to look at him except when he asked a question. I know what you mean though. Do you think we need a solicitor?"

"What? Oh, erm, maybe. I don't know. We didn't request one for our interviews, but I suppose if they haul us in again then maybe we should."

"I think if they do call us in again, then they'll do it for a reason, and that will be to get us to confess to something, or because they've found some evidence. That's why I was thinking we should be prepared this time."

"Yeah, you're right. I'll find out who the local ones are. You said evidence, though? What could they find?"

Lauren thought for a minute. "Fingerprints? No, that wouldn't help them. Good job we haven't got CCTV here, otherwise they might be able to prove that Hoggo never walked over to the woods. Anything forensic in the cellar they might stumble across? Can't think of anything."

"Me neither. So it's all circumstantial. There's Norman of course but I think we've covered off what he said he saw. As long as we stick to what we agreed and they don't trip us up, we might be ok."

Lauren ran her hands through her hair and sighed. "God I hope so. I don't know how much more of this I can take. I'm not even sure I can go back to work again now, I'm so stressed."

"Don't if you don't want to. Just tell them you've got chickenpox or something."

"I've already had it."

"Rabies?"

Lauren couldn't help smiling. "Yeah, caught it off my dog of a husband after a love bite. They'd believe that."

"Pneumonia then. Or shingles. Something like that."

"I'll think about it. Maybe see how I feel tomorrow."

"That police car still there out the front?"

"How would I know?"

"I was kindly giving you something to do." He edged backwards towards his desk. "I've got work to be getting on with."

Lauren put her hands on her hips and gave him a stare that had no effect. "Ok, I'll have a look. Not sure why I need to though – we can still hear them downstairs."

"I was thinking there might be other police cars, or more people. Including that latecomer army chap we saw, that's three more people now who've turned up. They're obviously bringing the experts in to work out how they deal with the gigarat."

Lauren strode past him and paused at the door. "If I see a tank rolling up the drive we'll know it's got serious."

She disappeared towards the front bedroom. Trey called after her.

"It's the rocket launchers we should be worried about."

***

Jeremy closed the cellar door behind Polly, who was the last to return to the DUST team's new temporary underground bunker headquarters.

He turned and brought his hands slowly together, in what would have been a clap were he to have moved faster and been a more ostentatiously dynamic leader.

"Right. Here we are again, a little later than planned but with good reason. Thank you everyone; I hope you had a productive ninety minutes. Just so that you know, Jason has gone back to the police station after Mr Baston the gardener returned, as we need to interview him. Mr Baston, that is, not Jason. Polly, sorry it took a little while to get you that clearance. As you know I left you alone after that so that you could concentrate, so I think it is best to hear what you have to say first."

Polly had a look of suppressed excitement, as though she was about to announce a lottery win to an office syndicate.

"Ok," she said, "strap in everyone, you may be as surprised as I was. I can see now why it was classified to the highest level. Here's what I discovered actually happened at Clayper. It turns out that it wasn't set up to engineer greater meat yields – there was a catalyst. A large one. Originally it was a standard lab tacked on to a cold storage facility and used for secret government research on things like viruses and medicines. Then, in 1956, they found something two miles down the river from here, washed up in some reeds. A huge dead animal, unknown to science - one which sounds very much like our friend below. The description pretty much mirrors what we saw in those videos."

"My God," muttered Jeremy. "That means these animals have been down there for decades, perhaps centuries. And there's definitely more than one of them."

"Exactly," agreed Polly. "Anyway, they loaded this dead one onto an army truck and, as luck would have it, Clayper was relatively close. So they rushed it to the cold store, and then quickly repurposed the labs, so they could do the analysis. You can kind of see why this took priority. They targeted a group of biologists with finding out what this rat-like animal was and why it grew so large."

"All sworn to secrecy, no doubt," noted Jeremy.

"Of course. What they discovered was that it had a seriously enlarged and overactive pituitary gland which had ballooned this animal to giant proportions. That's where a high ranking Home Office mandarin stepped in with the idea of trying to replicate that in other domestic animals to help the post-war food effort. All this was top secret too, of course."

"They'd probably have had the same concerns about potential panic in the general population over a giant rat as we have now," suggested the brigadier.

Polly agreed. "Very likely, and as far as we know, back then it hadn't attacked and eaten any humans yet. Now, here's what they found about the animal itself. They reckon it was fundamentally a rat, but different in some respects, not just its size. In humans, excessive growth hormones can lead to a form of gigantism known as acromegaly. This causes some parts of the body to accelerate in growth faster than others. So the jaw, the brow, the feet and hands, for example, can all enlarge to a proportion even greater than the general growth of the individual. The Clayper scientists proposed that this could explain the rat's larger teeth and any other unusual traits, like its clawed feet. Personally, though, I'm not entirely convinced by that when it comes to the claws – I think some kind of evolutionary development could have had something to do with it too. I mean, I've already mentioned its eyes. It takes more than one generation for adaptations like that."

Tommy's mind was in overdrive. "Hang on. If this animal has been around for centuries, how come no one saw one before? A thing that size, surely there'd be sightings all over the place?"

"You'd think so," conceded Polly. "But if you think about it, rats generally don't let themselves be seen if they can help it, and an enormous rat like that running about outside and in daylight would find it impossible to hide. And maybe it knew that although it would be quite a predator it would also find itself hunted by humans. So I guess it realised that if it could find some caves or tunnels and only come out at night, its chances of survival were greatly enhanced."

"So that's why it ended up in the abandoned mines," said Tommy. "But how come I've never come across one before? Rats breed like rabbits, don't they? These things should have spread through old mines all over the country."

"How would they get there, though? A normal sized rat can scurry through undergrowth with no one noticing. Something that size – not so easy. They must have occupied this particular tunnel system and decided to stay put, which could well have forced them to adapt their breeding strategy."

"They could do that?"

"It's amazing what animals can do to adapt to their surroundings. If there is a limited food supply, the last thing they want to do is pump out hundreds of new huge competitors that hoover up all the food. It doesn't take them long to realise this."

Jeremy turned back to Polly. "What puzzles me though is not just how the first rat got so big, but then also how it managed to produce offspring the same size. Pituitary enlargement isn't hereditary, is it?"

"Yeah, and how did it, you know, do the deed?" Tommy felt he had to ask. "That first huge rat trying to have it off with a tiny rat, or a tiny rat trying to... well, you get my drift. That ain't gonna to work, is it?"

Polly smiled. "That's actually a good question."

That was either a compliment or an insult, thought Tommy, but he let it go.

"I haven't had a long time to think about this but my first answer would be that perhaps the rat with the pituitary issue was a female, and they can breed when they are only eight weeks old. So she may have been large but not too large at that point, if the growth continued past the normal expected growth period. If she then passed that trait on genetically to her offspring, you would immediately have a litter of potentially enormous rats, anything between eight and eighteen of them."

"So it could be passed on genetically, then?" asked Jeremy.

Polly gave a little wince. "Well, perhaps not the enlarged pituitary gland itself – although I'm not ruling that out - as much as whatever caused it to enlarge and pump out those growth hormones. And from my initial analysis I'm not sure the scientists had an answer for that."

"That first litter, though, would all be siblings. Could they mate?"

"In rat world, incest is not considered a barrier to mating."

"So Mummy and Daddy rat could be brother and sister," observed Tommy.

"Yep."

"To be honest, that doesn't surprise me. I wouldn't put anything past those little buggers. Bloody nuisance they are."

"You must see a lot of them in your line of work," said the brigadier.

"You're not wrong. Tunnels can be full of them, getting under your feet, springing out at you when you least expect it and giving you a fright. I'm not keen on them at the best of times, so supersize them and I'm even less of a fan."

The brigadier snorted a laugh. "Especially if they are trying to eat you! Seriously though, if there were dozens of these enormous rats down there, what did they eat? Did they find out what was in its stomach?"

Polly nodded. "They did. They didn't have the technology in those days to be as certain as we can be today, but the report detailed traces of all kinds of stuff. A lot of it appeared to be rat."

Jeremy blinked. "What, cannibalism, you mean?"

"Yes, and that could explain why there aren't that many of them. If rats can't easily find food, they will eat each other. A huge rat kills another huge rat and that's a lot of food. It's possible that they breed partly to generate a food source."

"You mean they have litters just so they can eat them?"

"I know that is counter to what I said earlier about them not pumping out huge litters, but it's possible. It can't be discounted. There might only be two alpha rats down there, eating all the others. That's unlikely though, I expect there is a small colony. They'd also have all the smaller normal rats that they could no doubt swallow up if they caught one, and it's clear that they did venture out of the tunnels at night. There was a bit of vegetation matter in the stomach of the dead one, as well as some traces of wool, so it looks like they were catching sheep."

"Strange it's the only one that's been found," said the brigadier.

"Not really. A dead rat that size is a good meal, isn't it? Normally it would probably have been dragged back into the tunnels."

"How are they getting out though? How extensive are these tunnels?"

All eyes turned to Tommy, who cleared his throat in a way that often precedes bad news.

"I'm afraid, guys, I drew a complete blank. There's no record of a mine in this exact location. Nothing. It's undiscovered. And that means I don't know how large it is or where it goes to."

There was a short deflated silence and a few 'ah's'.

"I suppose it isn't entirely surprising," he continued. "They reckon that a quarter of the population live above an abandoned mine, and new ones pop up quite often when a sink hole appears, or maybe someone finds an old entrance shaft in their garden. I'd be straight down there to start mapping it out if it wasn't for you-know-what."

Jeremy tapped his foot, thinking. "Yes, of course. And this is where you come in, Charles. We need to construct a trap, and I'm not talking rat poison."

Brigadier Shaw scratched his ear. "I'm not being awkward or anything, but how would you get them out? We know they won't fit up this vent, and we don't know where they are getting out at night. You could trap them, but then what?"

"I have two answers to that. Firstly, there may be younger ones down there that haven't yet grown too big to be hauled out of the vent here. That's not a very workable strategy though, and to be honest they probably would have come up here by now if they could. My second answer is that we find the main entrance, which Mr Clark advised us originally came up somewhere in the garden. That appeared to be a large shaft, big enough for the giant rat to move through. It's capped off now."

"Do we know where exactly this shaft is?"

"No, I suspect we will need Mr Clark's help with that, unless you have some aerial reconnaissance technology that can detect what is under the ground."

The brigadier thought for a second. "I'll see if I can organise a drone to take some aerial photos and see if there are any outlines in the grass, but it might be quicker just to ask Mr Clark."

"Yes, we can get a rough idea from him, then maybe drill a few holes into the lawn until we hit a hard surface."

The brigadier, recognising that poking a stick into the grass would be less onerous than sourcing a specialist drone, nodded quickly. "Good plan. Sounds the better option."

Tommy had raised his hand. "I just wanted to know, there's other residents in this building, yeah? Have they all signed this secrecy document? If they see us digging a hole in the lawn then dragging up a huge rat, they'd have to be pretty dumb not to realise something's up."

"Yes, and something would definitely be up, literally. It's a good question. Jason's been catching up this morning with the two households already in the know, but that leaves two others, if you include Mr Baston the gardener, who knows about the tunnel, I think, but not what's in it. Clearly we want to keep this whole operation watertight so the fewer people know the better. But these people live here so….. right, ok, I'll have a think about that and talk to Rob. We don't want them to be in any type of danger, either. Meantime, we need to put our plan together. Anyone got any final questions or comments before we do that?"

"What happened to Clayper?" asked the brigadier. "Why did it close?"

Jeremy gave a little start. "Ah! Yes, thank you, I forgot to ask that. Particularly since DUST has no record of this, which we should do, and we certainly don't have the carcass or skeleton of a huge rat in our vault, so what happened to it?"

"There was a fire," said Polly, simply.

"In a cold store facility?"

"Yes. It started in the labs. There was accelerant involved, and the whole place was destroyed, taking whatever was left of the rat with it."

"Arson, then."

"Yes, and they couldn't prove who did it, although the Chief Scientist had just been given a final warning over the irregularities I mentioned earlier so my money would be on him, as a kind of revenge act or maybe to stop them finding anything else on him. They said all the staff had alibis, but he could easily have paid a break-in specialist, or given the keys to someone who could sneak in at night and torch the place. There wasn't any CCTV back then, though, and security would probably have just been a guard at the entrance asleep in a booth. There were no prosecutions, and of course the whole investigation stopped after the fire."

"What year was this fire?"

"1962."

"Ah, well that would explain it. DUST was formed in 1965. It never came to our attention. Shame. Do we know the names of the scientists? If we could talk to one of them and find out what they did first hand, that would really help."

"The report only mentioned a few by name – the more senior ones. I checked and they are all dead. Only the youngest of them might still be alive, and finding their names in some dusty old record, if it exists, wouldn't be easy."

"No, indeed. I'll speak to Alice in the Records Office, she'd be our only hope there I think. Right, thank you Polly. Anyone with anything else?"

There was a general shaking of heads.

"Ok, it's four fifteen. I suggest we take the weight off our feet and all return to the police station, commandeer a room, and work out how we are going to deal with our friend the rat. Mr Clark had christened it a gigarat; Polly, did Clayper come up with anything?"

Polly shook her head. "Not that I could see. They just called it a giant rat. They hadn't got round to classifying it."

"Ratus giganticus?" suggested Tommy.

"I wasn't thinking of getting into the Latin quite yet," said Jeremy, "but I'm happy to continue with gigarat if everyone else is. Just so we can distinguish it from an ordinary rat."

Polly and the brigadier looked at each other and shrugged. "No issues," they said in unison.

"Good! Ok, our friends down below will henceforth be known as gigarats. And now, to the police station. My car's still there, so could someone please give me a lift?"

CHAPTER 50

Norman knew this would happen. They still thought it was him, obviously. He was their prime suspect. And now they were going to trap him into saying something that they'd use in court. Why else would they bring him back to the station just two days after his first interview, when he was completely innocent?

He watched the chief superintendent shuffling papers opposite him, preparing to grill him. Next to him sat some posh lad in a suit – from the Home Office, he'd been told, Jason somebody. Observing. Well, he would observe him back, see how he liked it. He caught Jason's eye and watched him unblinkingly until Jason felt obliged to become diverted by his phone.

There, a small victory already.

Berriman finished arranging his papers and cleared his throat.

"Now, Mr Baston, thank you very much for agreeing to come here for this interview."

"Didn't think I had a choice," Norman mumbled through his beard.

"Well, yes, you did, although if you had refused….. you can see how that might look. But I need to be clear that you have not been arrested and are not under suspicion at this stage."

At this stage, thought Norman. Give them time…..

"This interview will be recorded, and you are of course welcome to have a criminal lawyer present, although normally that would be the case if you had been formally arrested, which you haven't. But I'm sure you will understand that with four people in a week either missing or dead in the vicinity of Ridley Manor, we need to leave no stone unturned."

Norman said nothing. He'd turn over a couple of dirty stones for them in a minute and give them something to think about. Then maybe they'd stop harassing him and leave him alone.

Berriman, having expected at least some form of response, cleared his throat again. "Right then, no lawyer asked for, let's begin."

It took a while for this more important policeman to go over all the stuff Norman had told the other officers on Saturday about what happened in the forest the night Molly disappeared. Why he had to repeat himself again, he did not understand. But he bided his time, waiting for the right questions. Then the first ones came.

"My officers then found you in the forest again, around Saturday lunchtime I believe. What were you doing there?"

"I went for a walk."

"Do you often go for walks in those woods?"

"Sometimes." He didn't, not during the day, anyway, but they weren't to know that. It was only a small white lie to stop them thinking he was running from the police.

"Were you aware that my officers were at Ridley Manor when you set off for your walk?"

"I saw them arrive. I was in the front garden."

Berriman gave a little sniff and wrote something down.

"You were asked if you had seen a young man with blond hair, were you not, when you were found in the woods?"

Here it comes. "Yeah, but how could I have seen him if he weren't there?"

"What do you mean?"

"He weren't there, was he? Those questions, they were wrong, trying to trap me into something, 'cos you knew all along that the bloke never went into those woods."

His heart was racing. He'd never stood up to anyone before in his life yet here he was having a go at a top policeman. But he was angry, he felt cornered, and he was fighting back.

Berriman gave him a five second stare. "What makes you think that my officers knew this?"

"I heard you! You and him" – he pointed at Jason – "and that other guy with the white hair. You said that Mr Whatsisname, Hoggsmith, who's the blond guy, isn't he, had not come that way, or something like that. You said that. But your people handcuffed me and dragged me to their car. That was false arrest."

That was possibly one of the longest speeches he had ever made, and now his head was hurting a bit. He squinted and blinked a few times. Had he gone too far? But why had Berriman broken into a smile, closely followed by the other young guy. It wasn't funny!

"What?" he almost shouted, anger rising. Now they were mocking him.

Berriman pulled with one finger at the inside of his collar, as though the act of smiling had tightened it. "I'm sorry Mr Baston, but your theory is somewhat flawed. When my officers questioned you they had no idea that Mr Hoggsmith might not actually have gone into the woods. They had just been told that he had, so were following up on that lead when they came across you. Naturally they asked if you had seen him. Your answers were confused, so they became suspicious. But how do you know what the three of us might have said?"

"Hiding in the garden while we were by that broken wall, I guess," suggested Jason.

"I wasn't hiding!"

"You were listening though."

"I overheard. Couldn't help that."

"Not that it matters," said Berriman. "These are all just theories at this stage, we don't know for certain whether he went into the woods or not. Perhaps we can move on?"

"You don't believe the Clarks though. They told you he went to the woods, didn't they?"

"I'll ask the questions if you don't mind, Mr Baston."

Norman felt a tinge of humiliation. Ok, then, play it like that if you want. See how you like this next little nugget.

"I'll tell you what else you need to know then. I saw a tall blond man go into the cellar with Trey and John on Saturday. About thirty minutes later, only two people came back out, and the blond guy wasn't one of them."

He sat back in his chair with a smug look on his face, his upper beard pushed almost horizontal by his faded shirt collar.

Berriman and Jason glanced at each other, the former trying to keep his composure for what could at last be a concrete lead.

"Are you sure?"

"Absolutely. And what about this. That Anita woman. I saw her go into that cellar last Tuesday, and she didn't come out again either. See, it's not me you should be after."

"What time was this on Tuesday?"

"Afternoon sometime. Around three, probably."

"Ok, so you definitely saw her go in and not come out."

"Yes. Well, I saw her go down those steps. I was in the garden."

"And she didn't come back up?"

"No."

"How long were you watching for?"

"On and off, about an hour."

"On and off means there was some 'off'. I take it you weren't staring at those steps for an hour."

"No, but...."

"So you might have been looking the other way when she came out again."

"I'd have heard her. She had footsteps."

"We all have footsteps. Are you saying that she had hard heeled shoes on?"

Norman toyed with his beard, somewhat frustrated that he was being challenged. "I don't know. I would've heard her though."

"Would you have noticed if Mr Hoggsmith had left the cellar before or after the other two gentlemen?"

"Not him, no. I was doing other things, like."

Then he remembered something important. "They said she didn't go in."

The two men opposite frowned.

"Who? Where?" asked Barrowman.

"Anita, in the cellar. She said... the woman, you know, Mrs Clark..., she said that Anita might have heard them arguing in the cellar, and not gone in."

Jason felt he had to say something. "But if that was the case she would have come straight back up again, within a minute probably. Wouldn't you have definitely seen her?"

"Yeah." He couldn't swear on it, but surely he would have noticed, even if out of the corner of his eye. And heard her, of course.

Berriman grunted. "So would you be prepared to state in court that you saw these two people go into that cellar and not come out, and that you would definitely have noticed if Anita Rackman had turned back and not gone in?"

Norman felt his throat go dry. All those people staring at him, a judge frowning under his wig, the jury assuming he was the killer and not the accused. He shook his head vigorously. "In court? No. No way."

Berriman's eyebrows rose like two kites. "Really? Why not?"

Norman realised his hands were now clasped together, kneading each other, and his legs felt restless, so he shifted in his seat. The mere thought of standing there in a court with all those eyes on him, judging him, was making him nervous.

"Too many people," he said after a while, without looking up.

Berriman appeared to realise that perhaps he would need to be careful with the way he conducted this interview. Norman Baston may not be the most mentally resilient of people, so if he was innocent, he didn't want any backlash inflamed by social media.

"Alright," he said, "but we can take a formal statement, though, yes? You wouldn't have any objection to that?"

That sounded better. Norman nodded. "No. No objection." He'd got nothing against the Clarks personally, and they seemed pleasant enough, but he'd got to look out for himself. If what he said put pressure on the Clarks, so be it. All he was doing was telling the truth and saying what he saw. He knew he'd done nothing wrong and it was up to them to defend themselves. And all that stuff going on the cellar looked fishy. Talking of which, there was another thing. In for a penny, in for a pound....

"What you done with John's body, then?"

It came out slightly more aggressively than he meant, so he qualified it.

"There was no ambulances, no forensics. If he fell down that hole in the cellar and you pulled him out on a rope or put a ladder down, where was all that stuff?"

Berriman had been caught by surprise and Norman could see that he was thinking furiously. How was he going to answer this one then, eh? Even that Jason chap was looking worried. What were they hiding?

"Again, Mr Baston, it is not your job to ask the questions in this interview."

"So you can't answer the question then." Norman was surprising himself at how confrontational he was being, but he was angry, and he wasn't often angry. If they were going to try and find ways to pin these deaths on him, he'd fight back. Why shouldn't he?

Berriman was looking rattled now. "I could answer the question if I wanted to, but I have no reason to. Now, I'd like to ask where you were...."

Norman pretended not to hear him. "I could go to the press, then, and you wouldn't mind. Alright then, that's what I'll do."

Berriman sat back in his chair and let out a long sigh, as though about to admonish his child.

"Mr Baston, that would not be wise. There are....." – he searched for the right words – "extenuating circumstances in this case, which, apart from anything else, is why you are being interviewed by me and not a detective, and why we have the Home Office involved. The less press intrusion the better, at this stage, and your co-operation in that would be appreciated."

Norman felt as though the power dynamic had swung in his favour a little. "So what's in it for me then? If I don't tell them."

Berriman shifted uneasily in his seat, which creaked in protest. He glanced at Jason, who appeared keen to say something but less keen to step on any toes. This was a police interview, after all. But Berriman's raised eyebrow was an invitation.

"There are incentives," said Jason, looking back at Berriman for confirmation. The chief superintendent gave a little nod. Norman didn't know about the gigarat, but he still knew too much.

"If you promise to say nothing about what you have seen in the cellar, or anything else about this case that you may overhear at Ridley Manor, you will find yourself financially rewarded. And by that I mean on a long term, weekly basis, including an enhanced pension. But, and I want to make this very clear, that will immediately stop, and the money paid taken back, if you break the agreement. Do you understand?"

Norman's head began to swim. What was going on here? Why were they offering him money? Well, it was better than being handcuffed and marched off to a cell, which is what he had expected. But he still didn't trust them.

"How much?"

"It will be based on a percentage of your earnings through PAYE up to a limit, which, to be honest, I don't think you are going to exceed. Jeremy has the forms – he can go through the detail and get you to sign them. Obviously, this is dependent on you not being involved in the disappearance of any of the three missing people or the death of Mr Firwell."

There they go again, implying he could have killed them. "I'm not!" A fleck of spit landed on Norman's beard and nestled there, distracting the two men opposite. Norman didn't notice.

"I'm sure that is the case," said Berriman, leaning forward again, "which is why there should be no issue in us just reviewing with you exactly where you were and what you were doing during the time that the four unfortunate people met their fate, whatever that fate might be."

"How do you know they're not still alive?" Norman asked, emboldened by the success of his previous tactics of answering back.

"It's possible, but highly unlikely. Molly Baines has been missing for what, just over a week now? And the chances are that whatever happened to her has happened to the other three too. Well, two, as we know what happened to John Firwell."

Do they, though, thought Norman. He fell down that hole, but they didn't bring his body up. The fact that they wouldn't answer his question proved it. Why wouldn't they? He resolved to throw caution to the wind and have another chat with the Clarks when he got home. They must know more than they had let on to him so far. Once he had signed this agreement to secrecy, they could tell him, couldn't they? He smiled to himself. He wasn't as stupid as everyone thought. In fact, he was proving that he could even outwit a senior police officer.

He settled in for the rest of the interview, happy to tell the truth because, unlike the two gentlemen opposite, he had nothing to hide.

CHAPTER 51 - TUESDAY

"That was quite a day yesterday," observed Jeremy. He debated whether or not to tackle the bedraggled fried tomato that he had inadvertently scooped up from the buffet along with some sausages, but concluded that an almost-cold fried tomato is for some reason a lot less appealing that an ordinary cold tomato, and there was a strong likelihood that bits of red tomato skin would lodge in his teeth and annoy him all day. He pushed it to one side and laid down his knife and fork.

Jason, looking as fresh, smart and young as Jeremy wished that he felt after the previous evening's whisky-fuelled analysis of events, took a last sip of coffee.

"Sure was. I'm enjoying it though. Beats sitting in a meeting for four hours discussing budget targets. Have you settled on the plan for today?"

Jeremy wiped his mouth with the napkin and crumpled it up on the table. They were the only ones in the dining room apart from a sales rep in an overworked suit on the other side of the room, who was slowly chewing his toast with the look of a man who wished he had made better life choices. It was safe to talk.

"I think so. But much will depend on the brigadier now. He's going to have had a busy evening."

"Rallying the troops, as it were."

Jeremy smiled. "You could say that. The plan we all put together yesterday depends very much on him. Assembling a crack team with so little notice, and all the machinery too, without being able to fully explain why he is doing it – not easy."

"And anyone he brings in could have to sign the secrecy papers too. It feels like too many people are going to be in the know about this animal. I was thinking actually, as I was trying to get to sleep last night - when we catch this thing, where will it go, might it be better after all, just to send it to a zoo? Then we wouldn't have to worry about the secrecy. It would all be out in the open."

"No, I'm not keen on that. It would need to go to Polly's lab first for analysis, and before you ask yes, she does have facilities for large animals like this one. But the only way we could lift the curtain of stealth after that, though, is if we could be absolutely certain we had rounded all of these things up. Imagine the panic if the general public knew there might be a man-eating rat in a zoo, but there could also be more of them under their feet, all over the country? No, a zoo is out of the question until we've mapped out these tunnels and confirmed there are no gigarats left down there or in any other abandoned mines."

Jason leaned forward. "Ok but supposing there are ten or fifteen of them? Or more? How much room has Polly got in her lab?"

Jeremy smiled grimly. "Who said anything about keeping all of them alive? These things are killers. If one of them escaped it would be like releasing a sabre-toothed tiger onto Guildford high street at night. Of course Polly wants to catch them all alive but she's got her biologist's hat on and hasn't really thought through the implications. She certainly hasn't got room to keep that many, in any case. My view is we try to catch one male and one female and..." he lowered his voice, "... shoot the rest. And unless there is very good reason, we keep the male and female apart. Why would we want to breed these things?"

Jason gave a little laugh. "I'm with you there. They should be caught for research purposes only. It's like if you caught a mosquito with a new more deadly variant of malaria you wouldn't want to start a breeding programme, you'd kill the bugger, wouldn't you?"

"I'd not put it quite like that when presenting my thesis, but yes, exactly. You'd keep risks to a minimum."

"Ok, so you'll tell Polly then?"

"I've already spoken to her, on the phone. Shame the others are in a different hotel – I'll ask if they can be transferred over here. It would make things easier. Anyway, at least our police colleagues are doing what they can to keep it under wraps. They're not doing any press conferences mentioning John Firwell or the two more recently missing persons. With Molly Baines they can just keep saying she's still missing, no progress. Hopefully the press won't dig too deep."

"So what do you think Berriman is going to do about the inconsistencies between the Clarks' story and what Norman Baston told us yesterday?"

"Yes, that shed a different light on things, didn't it? Although we did already have our suspicions. There's definitely something they are not telling us, and I don't know why. We need to get into those tunnels. If we find the remains of four bodies down there, then in theory three of them could have got there via their cellar, or possibly four if the Clarks were lying about when they opened that trapdoor."

"Yes but Norman Baston heard the gigarat take Molly, didn't he? Also, Rob can confirm that, though, with that guy who bought the coal and helped discover the trapdoor. If he confirms what Trey Clark told you, that would mean that the trapdoor was opened after Molly Baines disappeared, wouldn't it?"

Jeremy was always pleased when his young protégée showed the kind of promise and quick thinking that had led to his appointment. It confirmed that when he retired, DUST investigations would be in safe hands.

"Two good points! And so if her body is indeed down there, it must have entered the tunnels somewhere else. Which means that could have happened to two other victims too. That's not helping, is it? Oh Lord, who'd be a detective, eh? Talking of whom, I understand that Rob is getting on with that search along the uninhabited areas next to the river banks looking for tunnel entrances – he said he'd tasked an Inspector with organising it."

"That's good. Oh, I forwarded those security camera videos on to Rob like you told me."

"Thank you. Shame they didn't tell us much that we didn't already know, although I suppose it did at least confirm what Norman Baston told us about Anita Rackman – the fact that the camera recorded her going out of that front door and round to the back of the house on the Tuesday, when Norman said he saw her going into the cellar and the Clarks say she didn't."

"Yes, and also that she came back through the front door the first time she went into the cellar, but not the second time. So that's a bit odd."

"Yes, but that first time she would have just knocked on the Clark's internal door, wouldn't she, when she was talking to Trey about his book cover. The second time.... well, I don't know. What would have prompted her to head off around the back of the house? Did she see something out of her window, I wonder?"

"If she was heading for the cellar, she must have done. You wouldn't do that on the off-chance, would you?"

"But it might have been nothing to do with the cellar. She might have gone for a walk in the forest. One for Rob to puzzle over, I suppose. At least we got to see Darren Hoggsmith in the flesh, and we know he did turn up when the Clarks said he did. I have to say, though, it would have been a lot more helpful if they'd had another camera pointed at the woods."

"True." Jason sat back and folded his arms. "Do you know what, I could just about believe that this gigarat creature could drag off a small woman like Molly Haines, but a big unit like Hoggsmith? He could be Freddie Flintoff's double, looking at him. Must be all of seventeen stone. Yet a guy that size is just....taken down by a rat. How is that possible?"

Jeremy shrugged. "Well we still don't know for certain that is what has happened to him, but there's a lot we don't know about nature, my young friend. If I was up against a polar bear I know who would win. This mutated rat is colossal."

"Yeah, I suppose. Brought it home though, seeing those pictures of the guy."

"I know. This is what we are up against. No room for complacency, eh?"

He stood up. "Ready?"

Jason rose too. "Of course. Let's go."

***

"With the precautions we're putting in place, I think we should be safe enough opening it up," said Polly. "You were absolutely certain that it was your torch that frightened it off, weren't you?"

"Absolutely." Despite Jeremy and Jason's misgivings about his account, Trey had found himself temporarily invited into the team, pulled away from his laptop to demonstrate where the main shaft might emerge from the lawn. He watched as an army man with a direct push probe plunged it repeatedly into the lawn, searching for a hard surface beneath the soil. "Have you seen the second video too, where we shone our lights at it? Scarpered pretty quickly."

Polly nodded. "Yes, I saw. So if we open this shaft up to the light, I wouldn't expect to see any gigarats emerging."

Trey turned to look directly at the biologist. "You're calling it a gigarat too?"

"For now, yes. No reason to change it."

"Ok, right. Nice one." Trey felt a frisson of pride that he may now find a name that he coined turning up in biology lessons of the future. Then he remembered that if the Home Office had their way, that wouldn't be happening.

Polly had noticed Brigadier Shaw striding into view from around the front of the house where a number of army vehicles were now parked.

"Ah, sorry, I'll need to catch up with my colleagues. Nice to meet you."

And before Trey could agree how nice it was, she had taken her leave and joined the group twenty yards away comprising Jeremy, Jason, and Tommy Medina. The brigadier joined them.

"Right chaps!" he announced, "oh and chapesses, sorry Polly, no offence."

"None taken."

"I just briefed my men round the front. They're offloading some gear. Tommy, your digger should arrive soon?"

Tommy checked his watch. "Ten minutes, depending on traffic. Although to be fair the digger is probably what's holding the traffic up. I was lucky we've got a contractor not far from here. Had to pull some strings though, like you wouldn't believe."

"Good man. Right once we've located the shaft and removed the topsoil, we'll leave the cap, which should be wooden supports, yes?" – Tommy nodded – "... and assemble our support structure and nets. If the blighter does make a dash for freedom he'll be instantly trapped. The nets will be very securely anchored, believe you me."

"Supposing a whole herd of them come galloping up," said Tommy.

"They're not horses," pointed out Polly. "A horde or a mischief of rats. Or a plague. And they don't gallop."

Tommy sniffed. This Polly woman was clearly not warming to him, nor he to her now.

"How do you know, darlin'? You haven't seen one yet, have ya? It might surprise you. Anyway, my point is, what if more than one of the buggers come barrelling out at the same time?"

"It's a good question," said the brigadier. "In that event, I will have marksmen stationed there and... over there – not pointing towards the house of course. If more than one ends up the net, we take it out."

Jeremy had been watching with interest how easily the brigadier had slipped into 'commanding officer' mode, and to be honest he was quite comfortable that some leadership pressure had been taken off his own shoulders. "What have the marksmen been told about the reason that they're here?" he asked.

"No more than is necessary. Just that this is a military exercise and they are to train their rifles on the exit of the shaft and await orders. I'll be the one giving any instructions to fire."

Polly was looking worried. "Supposing there are two gigarats in the net and you give the orders to kill one of them, then each marksman could fire at a different animal, so you end up killing them both."

The brigadier gave a little frown. "Ah, yes, good point. I will just have to be very precise in my order."

"I'd imagine that the soldiers might find it hard to keep their composure," said Jeremy. "So let's hope it doesn't come to that. But at the end of the day, Polly, better a dead gigarat than an escaped one. And of course there could be more of them down there, ready for us to capture them."

Tommy laughed. "Yeah, holding their paws out waiting for the handcuffs."

There was a cry from the soldier on the lawn. "Sir! I've found something."

Brigadier Shaw broke off from the group and walked quickly across to the point of the discovery.

"Just here, sir, feel for yourself. I've tried two other places too within a foot of this spot, same result."

The brigadier took hold of the probe and jiggled it up and down a bit.

"Yes, that feels pretty solid, doesn't it? Mr Clark!"

Trey was already walking over. "Yes?"

"Does this location look about right to you?"

Trey looked back to the house and pictured the tunnel in his mind.

"Yes, that could be it."

"Thank you. Tommy, has that digger arrived yet?"

"I'll go and check."

As Tommy loped off around to the front of the manor house, the brigadier turned to Jeremy and Jason, who had followed him over. He rubbed his hands together.

"Time to get to work, I think!"

CHAPTER 52

The afternoon of Tuesday 17th September was one that the residents of Ridley Manor would not forget.

It was like something out of a film set, thought Jean as she looked down on the garden from her first floor apartment. Everything was being locked down – even out at the front a senior policeman with a shiny bald head had turned up in a van with four officers and stationed two of them at the entrance of the drive, controlling who went in and out - most of whom seemed to be in uniform.

A young man had come round again this morning and told her that there would be some important investigative work going on that involved digging in the garden, and it was related to the search for Molly Baines and Anita Rackman, and not to worry. But what was going on outside now seemed completely out of proportion.

Why was the army involved, with all those trucks out the front – she'd counted five of them. Then a digger turned up and trundled round on to the back lawn and scooped out a huge hole, ruining their nice lawn and leaving a huge pile of earth on it too. Norman wouldn't be happy about that.

And now a team of soldiers was erecting a huge structure across the top of the hole they'd just dug, over which they had draped thick netting which they were securing to long metal stakes that had been hammered deep into the ground. And the netting led into a large army van, back doors open, with a ramp down to the ground. What on earth was going on? There couldn't be any bodies buried there – no murderer would choose such an exposed spot, and leave no sign of disturbance. And why the nets? And the van? It made no sense.

She felt confused. The world today was so different from her day. Everything seemed more straightforward then. Nowadays she just didn't know what was going on or understand why. What was happening outside was actually probably no more bewildering than half of what life threw at her in her old age, from mobile phones to complicated televisions. It was all just too much.

She pottered back to her comfy recliner chair and lowered herself into its warm embrace. She'd leave them to it, whatever they were doing, and have her afternoon nap.

***

By half past three the rig was up, the net fully secured, a pulley mechanism created, and some careful brushing had revealed the damp wooden boards that lay over the shaft. Although blackened, pitted and wet to the touch, they still looked solid enough.

"We'll lever them up later," announced the brigadier, rather too confidently. "Ok everyone, thank you for your efforts. Those I have spoken to, that's McGuire and Peters, stay here, the rest, you are free to go. Sergeant, take the men back to base, but leave one truck out the front. And this one, of course."

He glanced at the khaki green slab sided truck, emptied of equipment, into which any emerging gigarat would hopefully be guided, enticed by a bucket of seeds, chicken and vegetables that would be brought in once all the men had gone. It had been quite a job finding a vehicle with metal sides – most army trucks were canvas.

The sergeant nodded. "Yes, sir." It was not in his job description to ask questions. He gathered the remaining men and they disappeared around the corner of the house, free now to chat and speculate about what it was they had just been working on and why the army had to be involved in it.

The brigadier turned to McGuire and Peters.

"You two, get practising on closing the doors of the truck as quickly as possible using those ropes attached to the doors, now that the netting is in the way. Make sure it works, and the doors lock shut, ok?"

The two men looked nervously at each other, still unsure as to what was going on.

"Sir....." ventured Peters, "can I ask...."

"No, you can't," interrupted Brigadier Shaw. "Not yet, anyway. Just do it, please. I need to talk to my civilian colleagues here."

Before Peters could respond he had turned on his heel and was striding over to the small group at the edge of the lawn comprising Jeremy, Jason, Rob Berriman, Polly and Tommy.

"All set?" asked Jeremy.

Shaw nodded. "Just about. Shame we couldn't come up with some kind of a trip wire to close the van doors automatically but time was not on our side. It's a bit Heath Robinson, I know, but it's the best we could do. So I'm giving the lads a bit of practice there, but then I think I've no option but to let them in on what we're doing before we get started."

Jeremy winced slightly. "There probably no other way, is there? Far too many people know already and our budget is going to be taking a hammering."

"How can they not know? They'll be the one dealing with the gigarat if it appears. If they don't know what's coming, they could panic. They're good lads too, I am told. I asked the sergeant for his two most trusted men and he immediately suggested those two."

Jeremy sighed. "Ok, we'll get them to sign the secrecy papers. Good job I got some more photocopies done of them last night."

"What if we kill all the rats?" said Tommy suddenly. "Then there's nothing for the public to worry about, is there? So would we still need to keep it secret?"

"That's up to us," said Jeremy, "and by us I mean the Home Office. Polly would have dead specimens to examine instead of live ones, so we then have to judge whether or not the revelation that rats could grow to this size and start eating humans would make joe public think that there could be more of them, or not believe us when we said they'll all been eliminated. You could still spread a degree of panic."

"Right, but if you do fess up, do we still get our money?"

Jeremy smiled. "I'm not sure you read that contract too closely, did you? All payments and future payments will cease as soon as the requirement for secrecy is lifted. That doubles as an added incentive for all involved to keep their mouth shut while asked to."

"Ah, crap. I guess we all need to keep at least one of these things alive then."

Jeremy waved his arm at the apparatus surrounding the shaft. "Hence the trap." He moved the subject on. "How long did you say that rope was that you sourced?"

"380 ft. Don't often use that one, to be honest; had to get a contact to do some overtime and search through an old storage unit for it. Then he had to get his son over to help him lift it into the van. Right old faff, he said. It's not that thick – it's more of a guide rope - but it still weighs a ton, as you saw."

"Yes, that wheelbarrow came in handy, didn't it? Likewise for the extension cable for the light. How long was that again? A hundred metres, I think? So that will limit us to, what, about 330 feet. So that will be our first task once the shaft is opened – send the light down on the rope, and measure the depth while we're at it. If we haven't reached the bottom we can detach the light and send the rope down the extra fifty feet with the depth gauge. You're quite sure we couldn't send a drone down there? Would have been a lot easier."

"Yeah, I know. Just too tricky though. Apart from anything else the level of light it would throw out might not be enough to deter that rat."

"And I suppose we know this thing is attracted by noise so a buzzing drone could be attacked."

"Yep, and on top of that, one false move if it brushes the edge as it descends, and that could be game over. At least you know where you are with ropes and searchlights. Old school, but safer."

"Agreed. This will do for now, and that light should keep any gigarats at bay I hope. Then we lure one up once it starts getting dark. Your tranquiliser dart gun here yet, Polly?"

Polly, dressed down now in jeans and a jumper, held up her hand and checked her phone. "Almost. Should be here any time now."

"And you are definitely authorised to use one of those things?"

"What, the phone?"

"The gun."

She grinned. "I was joking. Yes, I'm fully trained and licensed."

"Good. To recap then: if we can get it in the van, we have holes in the sides you can poke your gun through and then it's a case of hit and hope really. If it is still thrashing about inside after a few minutes, we try again. If it won't go in the van and you have a sighting through the netting, on my command fire."

Polly cocked her head slightly. "No offence, Jeremy, but I don't really need your command."

"Well, no, I suppose not. Just use your initiative then."

"I always do."

"Yes, of course." Jeremy cleared his throat, changing the subject. "Now, chief superintendent, I take it the entrance to the house is secure?"

The still resolutely uniformed Berriman nodded. "Absolutely. No one's coming in or out without my say so. Access through the woods is taped off as you know but I have an officer stationed there too just in case, and also as we've got another more analytical search going on at the scene of Molly Baines' disappearance. And of course I have someone on the front door of the manor to make sure no residents come out while the, er, operation, is pursuant."

Jeremy smiled internally at the strained police-speak language. "Excellent. And the residents..... Jason, I think I am right in saying that we have just the two households who are not familiar with what we are doing or the existence of the gigarat?"

"Correct. I've told them about the mine shaft but that's it. No mention of the gigarat. So the old lady Jean Edwards, and Norman Baston the gardener. The others all know and have signed the form."

Jeremy suddenly craned his head and scanned the gardens next to them, then lowered his voice to the group.

"Do we know where Mr Baston is? It's obvious he spends a lot of time lurking around in this garden, overhearing things. Maybe...."

"No, don't worry," said Berriman. "He went off to some jobs this morning, told my officer he wouldn't be back until around four thirty. We've put a trail on him too."

"Half four? That's not long from now. Once we know that he and Mrs Clark have returned from work perhaps we could seal up the gates somehow. Just in case. You know."

"In case what?" asked Tommy. "Are you saying this thing could escape?"

"We have to consider all eventualities, however unlikely," said Jeremy diplomatically, but having said this out loud now a little more worried than he had been before.

Polly shifted uneasily. "I have to say, I don't think some closed gates would stop it. Rats can climb up vertical walls for a start - look at that shaft. If it gets away then it will go where it wants, especially given its size."

"So it could climb up the walls of the house? Isn't that dangerous for the residents? Shouldn't we evacuate them?" asked Tommy.

Polly shook her head. "They should be safe. We'd have lights on by then and it would be trying to get away from the light, not trying to climb up a house that is lit up."

"It won't get away," exclaimed Brigadier Shaw with conviction. "If we can't tranquilise it, we'll shoot it. Peters and McGuire have their army issue rifles in the front of the van."

"Aren't they going to be busy trying to shut the van doors with those ropes?" Jason pointed out.

"Yes," replied the brigadier, "but only if the rat's in the van. If our bucket of food scraps doesn't attract it onto the van, and for some reason we can't tranquilise it, they'll give it both barrels, so to speak. A rat wouldn't survive a round of bullets, however big it is."

"Shall we get started, then?" said Jeremy, pointedly looking at his watch. "We've got that power cable extension lead ready, and our little bundle of gadgets to lower down, so…"

An oath rang across the lawn as Peters lost grip on his rope after pulling the door closed with it, and fell on his backside. This was followed by a bellow of laughter from McGuire and some carefully chosen words of ridicule.

"Your best men, eh, brigadier?" said Jeremy quietly, a glint in his eye.

"Years of training," sighed the brigadier.

"Still, before we open the hatch, as it were, I think the time has come to ask them to sign the forms and then tell them what they are here for. Ok if I interrupt their exercises?"

"Of course."

Fifteen minutes later, McGuire and Peters, notably less effervescent than they had been earlier in the day, wriggled under the nets and attached their safety harnesses to fixed length cables that ran to the back axle of the truck. They had already practised releasing their safety catches and slithering under the net as quickly as a ferret up a trouser leg. This had suddenly become serious.

They began nervously levering up the first of the heavy wooden beams. The earth had been dug away such that it sloped gently towards the beams, which were just a foot or so below the surface, so that the two men could afford themselves a firm foothold as they wielded their spades.

They worked quietly, now that they were fully aware of what lay beneath, starting with the middle beam. When that was finally wrestled free, they shone the floodlight through the gap.

"What can you see?" asked Jeremy.

Peters looked up. "A bloody great hole, sir."

Jeremy smiled. "Can you see the bottom?"

"No, sir. Looks like it goes down for ever."

"Thank you. Let's carry on then."

The two men withdrew the light and resumed their work on removing the planks, working their way outwards across to each edge. As the gaping hole grew larger, they became more cautious, choosing their foot placements like mountaineers on an ice slope, before leaning forward to lever away the next beam. Both would probably have downed tools and retreated if they had not been soldiers with a commanding officer watching their every move.

To one side of the shaft was a large round wooden disc about two inches thick, fashioned by the army crew earlier. It would re-cover the hole when they were finished. Some heavy weights in the form of large planters filled with earth would be laid across it, and even if this was not sufficient to stop a determined gigarat, the hope was that there would be no reason for the animal to try to batter its way out when, to all intents and purposes, from the inside the exit remained covered just as it always had been.

The blackened beams, clodded with earth, were laid to the other side, leaving the path from the shaft clear to the van. As soon as the last one had been lifted, the two men picked up each end of a lightweight wooden structure, like a long coffee table with a big hole in the middle of it. Not exactly Ikea, the brigadier had said, but the best we could cobble together in the time available. They carefully walked each side of the hole before lowering it down over the shaft and forcing the legs into the earth.

McGuire looked across at the assembled group, standing outside the net, Polly now armed with the dart gun at her side. Berriman was absent, having gone to check on how the search of woods was progressing, and perhaps relieved to have a reason not to risk being jumped on by a giant killer rat. This made it easier to temporarily retain Trey's services just to verify any initial gigarat noises they might hear. As a suspect, Berriman definitely would not want him involved, but Jeremy was looking at the bigger picture.

Polly stood a little to one side, dart gun pointed down but poised, just in case. McGuire picked up a small metal cage, about a foot square, which was attached to the rope and also a heavy reel of electric cable, and contained a powerful LED light, a camera, and a depth measurement device.

"Ok?" he asked.

"Go ahead!" instructed the brigadier. He held a tablet to which the camera would transmit over a dedicated wi-fi connection. Trey, Tommy and Jeremy prepared to peer over his shoulder.

McGuire clicked the light on, then placed the cage on the end of the table, pushing it with the spade towards the hole in the middle, no doubt reflecting as he did so that this was not the cutting edge technology the army recruitment process had promised him. It fell through and dangled underneath, centred and waiting, the rope and cable channelled through a deep groove in the wood. Then he began to lower it, Peters feeding out the cables from both reels but focusing more on the rope.

"Ten feet," said Jason, who was holding the depth gauge control unit.

"Look, there's the tunnel entrance," said Jeremy, craning to get a better view of the tablet screen. "And is that another one, further down?"

"Looks like it," agreed Tommy. "These LED flashlights are so strong these days, you can see right down the shaft. Looks like it's mostly limestone."

The brigadier adjusted the angle of the tablet. "Still can't see the bottom though," he observed.

"It's a deep one ok", agreed Tommy, "but that's not unexpected. See the walls, though? Much smoother than you'd think, but then they're covered in scratches, see that?"

Jeremy grunted. "Gigarat claws."

"Can they do that, though? Wear the walls down like that?"

"Depends how long they've been down there," said Polly from one side. "If they've been scrabbling up and down for decades, centuries even, then it's possible their feet and nails developed into claws which kept hardening as they scurried about on the rock, and over time the surfaces were smoothed down. Evolution can work surprisingly fast."

The picture on the screen drew level with the first tunnel.

"Hold it there!" hissed the brigadier at the two soldiers.

The cage's descent was abruptly stopped. It rocked slightly and swayed from side to side before coming to a halt.

"Right," said the brigadier, "let's try this." He pressed the up arrow on the screen and the view panned upwards until just the pitted grey and white shaft wall could be seen. Then he hit the left arrow and they watched as the blackness of the tunnel inched into view.

With the light shining down rather than sideways, they couldn't see very far inside it, but short of seeing a gigarat staring back at them, they were not anticipating any surprises.

"Is that your tunnel?" Jeremy asked Trey.

Trey squinted at the screen. "I think so. I mean, it has to be, doesn't it? But I guess they all look the same."

The brigadier re-adjusted the camera to look downwards again. "Ok! About another twenty feet, then stop."

The next tunnel down leading off the shaft revealed nothing surprising either. Both just disappeared into blackness, the walls damp and glistening.

The cage continued its downward journey, like a bathyscope descending to the depths of the ocean floor.

"Hundred and twenty feet now" said Jason.

"Still can't see an end to it," murmured Jeremy. "Quite incredible."

"Look, is that another tunnel entrance?" said the brigadier suddenly. "There, on the right."

Before he could tell McGuire to prepare to halt the descent again, the solider swivelled round to look worriedly at the group behind him. "I can hear something sir!"

"What does it sound like?"

"A sort of rumbling, but with a noise like someone's tap dancing. Seems to be coming from down there."

The five people on the other side of the net exchanged glances.

"What do we do?" said Tommy, tensing himself to run.

"We wait," said Jeremy.

"What? Why?"

"Because if we are right, that extremely bright light, let alone the daylight from the top of the shaft, will push it back again. If it got scared by a small torch, that searchlight will do the job for sure."

"Supposing it's coming out of one of the tunnels the light has already gone past, though?" whispered Jason urgently.

"Good point. Well, there's still plenty of daylight shining down, and we know they don't like that either otherwise they would have been spotted out and about before now. We should be ok. If it gets too close though, brigadier, call the men out and we'll assume positions to capture it. Ok?"

The brigadier nodded and relayed instructions to McGuire and Peters, who were both now putting two and two together and none too happy about the position they found themselves in.

The noise grew loud enough for everyone to hear, albeit very faintly.

Trey felt himself becoming slightly nauseous. "That's him alright," he muttered beneath his breath, still conditioned not to make any noise when that creature was approaching.

Yet the view on the tablet screen continued to show only the walls of the shaft, and a circle of mysterious blackness below.

Polly and Jason began to edge towards the base of the net, ready to lift it high enough for the two soldiers to slither under.

But then the noise stopped.

"Thank crikey for that," breathed Peters under his breath, using a far coarser word then crikey but still audible to all.

He spoke too soon though, for almost immediately the noise returned, if anything slightly louder. McGuire let go of the rope, unclipped his safety harness, and scrambled to get away from the shaft. The cage plunged downward, the slack of the cord slithering up onto the wooden table but halting suddenly – Peters had not let go at his end.

Seeing McGuire bolt past him, he lifted the bottom of the heavy pile of coiled rope up a couple of inches and quickly shoved the part he was holding underneath it, dropping the bulk of the rope back down on top of it to hold it fast. Then he released the catch on his safety harness and dived for the underneath of the net, following McGuire to safety.

The two men scrambled to their feet on the other side, ready to run to their positions at the end of the ropes connected to the van doors, while the others were stepping smartly back.

Jeremy held his hand up. "Wait!" he hissed.

Everyone froze. "It's stopped again."

They listened hard, ears straining. The breeze brushing through the trees, a far-off car horn, a dog bark, but nothing else.

Jeremy took a few steps back towards the net. "Maybe it saw the light and retreated."

"Bloody hope so," said Tommy, who'd managed to get himself furthest away from the netting. "Either that or it's sitting there plotting its next move."

"Sitting where?" asked Jason, "that's the question. Trey told us it came up the shaft to get into the tunnel he was in, so it could be anywhere down there."

Brigadier Shaw, used to dealing with enemies holed up in trenches and underground tunnels, found himself struggling to apply his experience in this instance.

"We could throw a smoke grenade down the bottom to disorientate it," he suggested, looking at Polly and drawing the words out such that it sounded as though he did not believe in his own idea. He was right to have reservations. Polly shook her head.

"If it doesn't use its eyes while it is down there, smoke won't stop it. And the smoke will fill up the shaft so our camera can't see anything. A bang could scare it off though, I suppose."

"Stun grenade, then?" said the brigadier, keen to bring some weaponry to bear.

"We're trying to catch it initially, though, remember?"

The brigadier scratched his ear. "Yes, of course. I was thinking more about if...... if that's not possible."

"I think it's gone back," said Jeremy, despite having no evidence to that effect. "Can we carry on with dropping the cage?" He turned to his assistant. "What depth is it at now?"

"Hundred and eighty four feet."

"That's more than Nelson's Column already. You got the screen there, Charles?"

The brigadier glanced at it. "Yes, same view as before and no sign of the bottom. What are we expecting, Tommy? Say again how deep could this thing be?"

The mine shaft expert edged slowly back towards the others as he spoke. "I'd love to give you a number but, hey, could be anything. There's coal mines up in Yorkshire that had shafts nearly 3,000 feet deep, and that's nothing compared to some of the gold mines in South Africa that are over 2 miles down. This one's not coal or gold so it won't be that deep, but I'm telling yer, there's lead mines with main shafts well over 600 feet deep. So what we've got here is nothing special so far. We don't know exactly when it was sunk, of course - if it's really old, it's less likely to go down as far. Also, they did sometimes just go down about a hundred feet, then move sideways a bit before sinking the next shaft from there."

The brigadier shook his head. "Still unbelievable what they managed to do with the tools they had back then."

"Yeah, but they were digging for lead, and if you take the 1700s as an example, back then it was like, number two after wool in terms of the UK economy. Big incentive. Even for things like windows, they needed the lead to hold the glass panes together. So there was money in it. That drove them to keep digging."

"Fair enough. Shall we recommence lowering the cage then?"

"Let's give it a few minutes, shall we?" suggested Jeremy, to the evident relief of McGuire and Peters, who were sitting on the grass looking as though they had just got back from a tense bomb disposal mission in Iraq. "If we hear no more noises from below, then we'll recommence. Mr Clark, thank you for confirming the noise, but as a civilian I think it's time now for you to head back into the building."

"You quite sure? I don't mind staying."

"Yes, I'm sure. There are protocols to follow, as I'm sure you'll appreciate."

Trey sighed. "Alright, I understand." Making himself as helpful as possible would not be helped by arguing over the judgement of the man in charge. He turned and headed reluctantly back to his apartment.

CHAPTER 53

Trey watched from the lounge window. Although initially annoyed, he'd realised that two encounters with that giant rat had told him that he didn't really need any more of them. Not only that, but apart from Lauren, no one knew about his horrific experience listening to Hoggo being killed by it, so he had more reason than anyone to be afraid. He just hoped they knew what they were doing out there, and what they were up against.

He wondered what the other residents would be making of it all. At least Mel and the Wilsons - Tony and Suzanne - would have been given the full story. Norman and Jean knew nothing about the animal.

The doorbell went, making him jump. Who the hell was…. ah, maybe it was Mel. He'd not wanted to go round to her flat because, not to put too fine a point on it, he'd recently helped kill her husband. Even if she didn't know that, he was sure that she would be able to see into his soul and work it out. So he had not intruded on her grief, what little she seemed to have of it. Perhaps she was in need of company, though, especially given what was going on outside, and Lauren wouldn't be back for a couple of hours yet.

Force of habit dictated a quick confirmatory glance in the hall mirror that his hair was presentable and there were no splashes of soup around his mouth, then he opened the door.

It wasn't Mel; it was the rather less pleasant sight of Norman, with a slightly wide-eyed look that did not signal serenity.

"Oh, hi Norman," began Trey, "have you seen…."

"We need to talk," interrupted Norman, "but not out here."

"You'd better come in then."

Trey could smell grass and a hint of body odour as Norman squeezed past. "Go on through to the lounge."

Norman headed straight for the French windows. "What are they doing? You know, don't you?"

Trey joined him at the window. "Didn't they tell you?"

"Said they were checking out an old mine shaft."

"That's right."

"Why's that woman got a gun then?"

Trey flinched. That was a great question. How was he supposed to answer that?

"Don't know. I guess you'd have to ask them."

"They said not to go out there. The copper said so. So I can't ask them. You know though, don't you, so I can ask you."

"You just did. Look, even if I did know I couldn't tell you. I had to sign an agreement."

Norman fixed him with a steely eye before glancing away, his sense of injustice shoving aside his normal reticence to engage in conversation. "So you do know then, like I said. You also know what happened to John."

"What do you mean? We all know what happened to John. I told you about that."

"You told me how he went down that hole, but you didn't tell me how he came back up."

"I'm sorry, but what are you talking about?"

"Why didn't they bring his body back up?"

"How do you know they didn't?"

"There were no ambulances, no emergency services, no people that do autopsies and take bodies away – all that stuff. No one. So his body is still down there, isn't it?"

Trey had been watching the two soldiers nervously slither back under the net, clip their safety ropes back on, and take up their positions lowering the cage down the shaft again. Without looking at the man standing next to him, he turned away from the window and paced to the other side of the room, giving himself time to think.

"Look, whatever I do know, I can't say. I just can't. I've signed...."

Norman turned round, angry. "I know! You've signed a bloody agreement. So what? So have I! Sworn to secrecy I was, as soon as I brought up the subject of John's body. So it makes no odds whether I know or not. You might as well tell me."

"If they wouldn't tell you, then I can't either. Sorry."

Norman turned back to the window. The soldiers were playing out the cable again, the rest of the group looking at devices in their hands apart from the woman with the gun, who kept her eyes on the mine shaft. When Norman spoke again his voice was calm and measured.

"I suppose you can't tell me about Molly either."

"Molly? You know perfectly well I don't know anything about what happened to Molly."

"Don't know or can't say?"

"Don't know. Look, she disappeared before I even knew there was a hole in the cellar."

"So you say."

"Yes, I do, because it's true. Ask the police, they're checking out my story with the guy who came to collect the coal."

Norman said nothing. He could see Trey in the reflection of the glass – he wasn't so stupid as to turn his back on him – and it was obvious that his neighbour was uneasy. He had also as good as admitted that he was hiding something, not just about the mine shaft, but also John. And all of this surely had to be connected to what happened to Molly.

"What was the noise I heard?" he said suddenly.

"What do you mean?"

"When Molly was attacked, there was this noise, like a machine. Tak-tak-tak, like that. What was that about? You know, don't you?"

He was staring at the reflection now, hoping Trey hadn't realised that he could see him. Trey was stretching his neck, trying to de-stress. He didn't reply immediately. That was a sign.

"Look, Norman, I don't know, and there's no point asking me all these questions. If the police wanted you to know stuff, they would have told you. And if you think they are trying to pin all these deaths on you, they're not. They know you had nothing to do with it."

Norman whirled round and faced Trey, eyes ablaze.

"Oh yeah? So why...... why do they keep dragging me in for interviews? Looking at me like I'm guilty? Just 'cos I'm the odd guy who lives in an attic, that's why. They need a scapegoat, and they found me. If they don't find anyone else, they'll cook up a case. I've seen it on TV."

"TV? Maybe back in the 70s there was some of that going on, but not now. Well, not in a case like this, anyway. They'd need evidence, and I'm guessing they haven't got any?"

"They'll make some up. Plant a murder weapon in my flat. I know what they're like."

"With respect, I don't think you do."

"I've had enough of this. Everyone's lying to me. Everyone."

And Norman opened the French windows and walked out onto the lawn.

"Hey," said Jason, jabbing his mentor in the ribs, "watch out. Look who's coming."

Jeremy turned to see the shaggy figure of Norman Baston marching towards them, a determined and not entirely convivial look on his face.

"Mr Baston, you are supposed to be inside. Can you please return to the house!"

Norman paid no attention but strode up to the group.

"Why's she got a gun?"

He stared aggressively at Polly, who had been trying to nonchalantly hide the gun behind her back. She brought it back into sight.

"What, this?" she questioned, as though Norman might have been referring to something else. "It's not a gun, it's just a tranquil......" she stopped herself, but it was too late. Norman had heard.

"Tranquiliser dart? That's for animals. What's goin' on? Why have you got a net? You telling me there's a tiger down that hole or something?"

McGuire and Peters had stopped feeding out the rope and were now stood up, watching. Jeremy looked at them, then at his little team. This was getting out of control; there were too many people involved. He wanted the daylight shining down the hole to ward off the gigarat until night-time, which is why he and the brigadier had not covered the whole structure in tarpaulins, and the net also allowed Polly to get a clear sight with the dart gun. But it did risk leaving their activities exposed to the gaze of the residents like Norman who did not know about the gigarat. In hindsight he should have evacuated all of them from the house, but there just hadn't been time to organise that.

There were just too many competing issues that he had to juggle, and now as a result he couldn't see any alternative but to let this oddball gardener in on the big secret too. At least he'd had already signed the agreement. The only problem was that he seemed like a bit of a loose cannon, led by his emotions. Could he be trusted? He let out a sigh.

"Alright, I think it's best you know. Charles, you carry on while I take Mr Baston to one side and explain the situation. Mr Baston, if you would be so kind as to walk this way...?"

He held out an arm to point to the other side of the lawn. Norman hesitated, slightly flummoxed by what appeared to be a sudden and rather unexpected victory. He frowned at Jeremy, considering whether or not he was being palmed off, but then, judging that he had nothing to lose, walked slowly along with him towards the flower beds.

Trey watched from his lounge windows. It looked like Norman was about to be given the full story, and that was probably a good thing – it might get him off his back. Once the gardener realised that it was almost certainly the gigarat that attacked Molly, he'd no longer suspect Trey of anything. That just left the police. But surely, the more that they knew about this creature, the more they'd come to the conclusion that he and Lauren were not involved in any killings, and the rat, and an accident with John, explained everything?

Then he remembered. There was one major problem – light. Neither Hoggo or Anita had gone missing at night time, and if the gigarat really did avoid daylight, as all the evidence would indicate, then even when the police found their remains in the tunnels below, their disappearance would still be suspicious. Unless..... he started to formulate a germ of a thought.

With a bemused and somewhat alarmed Norman escorted back into his flat, the team could recommence lowering the cage. They passed three more tunnels at intervals of about twenty feet, one of which appeared to be more of a storage chamber. But finally, at two hundred and ninety four feet, they spotted water below.

"It's a well!" exclaimed the brigadier.

"Don't think so," said Tommy, "not with all those side tunnels, and also the water table would be much higher. The water's draining away somewhere, possibly through a sough."

"A what?"

"A sough – drainage tunnel. Look, above the water to the edges, you can see the space opens up."

"For God's sake don't drop the cage in the water," said Jeremy, "we don't know how deep it is. Tell your men to slow it down, Charles."

"Very slowly now, men," barked the brigadier, his eyes still fixed to the screen, "slowly does it, on my command..... stop!"

The cage shuddered to a halt and swung gently, McGuire wrapping the cord around his wrist a few times to hold it steady. The brigadier used his device to redirect the camera lens up ninety degrees.

"Hey now, look at this. The light's not great but it looks like it's a cave of some kind."

"A chamber," said Tommy, stretching to get a better look at the screen. "Try switching to infra-red, you'll probably see more. Kill the light and.... Ah, sorry, forgot. The rat."

The brigadier looked up from the screen. "We'd still see it coming with the infra-red, right? Then if it does we just bang the light on again and see what happens. Could be a good test."

Jeremy thought for a second. "That makes sense actually. Ok, let's turn the light off. Ah, problem – the switch is on the light itself. We'll have to switch it off at the socket. Jason?"

The young apprentice sighed. "Who else. Ok, shout 'off' when you're ready, then when you want it switched on again......"

"Don't tell me. Shout 'on'?"

Jason grinned. "I was going to say 'elephant' but, no, you're probably right." He turned and followed the cable over to the external communal electrical socket just around the corner of the building. Seconds later his head appeared.

"Ready when you are!"

Jeremy glanced at the brigadier, who nodded.

"OFF!"

Jason's head disappeared and two seconds later the device's screen went briefly black before the infra-red kicked in.

"That's better," said Tommy. "Yeah, look, like I thought, it's a storage chamber – quite a large one. And hey, there, at the end, there's two tunnels leading off it. I can see....."

"I can hear something again!" McGuire was looking back at them now, urgency etched across his face. "It's coming back."

Jeremy immediately turned to Jason, standing at the corner of the house. "ON!" he shouted.

Jason nodded, but even before he had disappeared back round the corner, the brigadier was shouting "My God, what's that?" as a dark blur appeared out of one of the far tunnels and flew towards the camera.

McGuire's hand, wrapped around the rope, was yanked violently downwards, causing him to overbalance and crash down onto the makeshift table straddling the shaft. The table, made from thin planks of wood, could not hold his weight. Splitting down the middle, the two halves toppled into the shaft, followed, with a rapidly fading cry of shock, by McGuire.

His safety harness rope snapped straight and there was a scream of pain that echoed up the shaft.

Peters instinctively grabbed hold of the slithering rope and cable attached to the cage, but couldn't hold them. "Someone help me!" he cried.

The three men on the other side of the netting dropped their devices and rushed to slide under the netting. Polly dropped her dart gun and followed suit.

"Get McGuire up first!" shouted the brigadier. "Peters, leave the rope for now. Over here! Right, all grab a bit of the safety harness cable and when I say heave, pull hard. Ready? HEAVE!!"

The five of them, trying to get purchase on the safety rope, dug their feet into the ground and pulled hard.

"That's it! Good. HEAVE.... and again!"

McGuire came up sideways and lifeless, and as his body flopped over the lip of the shaft and was hauled up the short slope and onto the grass, they could see why. His right hand was in ribbons, skin and flesh shredded from the wrist down as the rope sheared through it.

"Oh my God." Tommy suddenly felt sick and turned away, while Polly gave out a little shriek.

"Good God," muttered Jeremy, horrified. "He must have fainted from the shock."

The war-hardened brigadier had seen far worse. "Right, Peters, Tommy - get McGuire round the front will you, and ensure he gets to some medics? Obviously don't say anything about how it happened – just say it's classified, ok? Jeremy, Polly, let's quickly try and save our equipment."

They stepped smartly over to where the rope and electric cable were still unravelling, as the gigarat way down below made off with the cage.

"We need to grab it together!" said the brigadier. "Leave the electric cable, just go for the rope."

They crouched down, Jeremy wishing he had knees that were thirty years younger.

"Right, all set? Three, two, one, NOW!"

They tried desperately to clutch the rope, but it was travelling too fast, unravelling from the reel like a metal chain dropping anchor. The minute a hand clasped hold of it, it was jerked forward so quickly they had to let go.

"It's no use," said Jeremy almost immediately. "It's way stronger than we are."

The brigadier stood up and jumped with both feet down onto the rope but was immediately upended and fell backwards. He quickly scrambled back to his feet and ran his hand over his shining forehead.

"Not sure why I did that. I don't want to lose that equipment, though. If we don't stop it, it's going to pull the whole thing down, reel and all."

Jeremy turned back to the house to see Jason arriving at the netting. "Maybe we can use the electric cable. Jason! Unplug the cable and tie the end to the van, quick as you can. Run like hell!"

The young apprentice raced back across the lawn to the socket, yanked out the plug and ran with it across to the van.

"Front axle! Front axle!" Jeremy called out. The cable reel was spinning furiously, almost emptied.

"Right!" said Jason, as he slid under the front of the van. He frantically wrapped the cable around the axle, securing it with a rudimentary reef knot, the only type he knew.

Almost immediately the cable was pulled out of his hands and twanged taut, stretching around the edge of the front tyre.

"Watch your legs!" called Jeremy as the cable leapt to one side and began biting into the netting supports. Thankfully Peters and Tommy had moved McGuire to one side and had been unclipping him from his harness while they wrapped his shredded hand in cloth ripped from his trouser leg. The cable, stretched tight, suddenly went slack, as did the rope, with just fifty feet of it remaining unravelled.

Jeremy looked at Polly. "Maybe we've broken its neck?"

Polly pulled a daisy out of her now-ruffled hair. "If it grabbed the cage with those teeth and ran off with the cables over its shoulder, then was suddenly yanked bank as it was pelting along, then yes, that could have given it a nasty injury."

"I hope so!" called Tommy, as he and Peters began to manoeuvre McGuire under the net, assisted now by Jason on the other side. "Look what it's done to this poor guy. Bastard rat."

Jeremy struggled to his feet and watched the three men carry McGuire round to the front of the house, where a police car would rush him to hospital. This was awful. Not only had his plan led to an innocent man being badly injured, but now the operation he was responsible for was falling apart. He was exhausted, not just physically, but mentally too.

This was unlike any other DUST mission he had been involved in. People getting physically hurt wasn't part of the deal. But was that his fault? The buck stopped with him, and he was the one who told Jason to turn off the light. With hindsight, that was obviously foolish, but how was he to know what would happen next? The gigarat must have broken the light when it grabbed the cage, so turning it back on had had no effect.

Mulling over what-ifs wasn't going to help, though. He could sense Polly and the brigadier watching him, and he knew what they were thinking: what next? It was a good question.

CHAPTER 54

Trey watched with mounting horror as events unfolded outside. One minute it seemed like the little group outside had a plan, which, apart from the brief interruption caused by Norman, appeared to be plodding along nicely. The next minute, chaos.

One of the soldiers had been pulled violently towards the shaft and disappeared down it. Then the army chap could be seen pointing and barking out various commands as those outside the netting rushed to get inside it to help. They got the soldier pulled out, then that Jason Whatshisname could be seen rushing over to the van with the cable and tying it to the van. It pinged taught, then slackened, and then it was all over.

They'd hurried the injured soldier around the front and the woman and two remaining younger men had started to pull the cables back up now. Jeremy was standing outside the netting checking something on his phone.

Trey knew he'd been told to stay away, but what the hell – they looked like they could do with some help. He opened the French window doors and walked out.

"Oi! Back inside please, sir!"

It was Berriman, his nemesis, striding back along the path from the woods, looking all important, but unaware of what had just happened.

Trey stopped where he was, then decided to ignore him. He walked towards the shaft.

Berriman reacted as though he had just been slapped in the face by an escaping criminal. With an expression of surprised fury, he hitched up his trousers and trotted magisterially onto the grass, ready to apprehend the miscreant and administer justice.

But Jeremy, hearing the shout, had turned round and seen the two men coming. "Don't worry," he called, "it's fine. It might be helpful to talk to Mr Clark, actually."

Berriman clearly didn't think that was fine at all, and his expression barely changed.

"What's being going on here, then?" he puffed, reaching the netting.

Despite everything Jeremy smiled to himself at the chief superintendent inadvertently reciting another classic British police-speak trope. All that was missing was the "hello, hello, hello" at the beginning.

"We've had an incident. You guys ok to continue?" he asked the brigadier, Jason, and Polly, who were still pulling on the rope and cable.

"Of course," replied Polly between yanks, having by now recovered her professional composure. "It's what I signed up for." She smiled sweetly at him.

"Thanks," said Jeremy, not rising to the bait. He turned to Berriman and Trey.

"Alright, an update for you" he said, "as Mr Clark here may have seen from his flat, we lowered the cage into the shaft, and were getting good pictures back. We even reached the bottom. It's just under 300 feet."

Trey whistled. "No wonder Hogg….." he stopped himself just in time. He had been going to say 'no wonder Hoggo couldn't hear his stone hit the bottom'. What an idiot – why did he say that? Now Jeremy was looking at him like a cat eying a cornered mouse.

"No wonder Hogg what?" he asked. "By Hogg do you mean Hoggo?"

"No, no, don't worry, it was nothing!"

He smiled, in the vain hope that a sunny disposition would dispel the clouds of suspicion.

Jeremy exchanged glances with Berriman, who looked as though he wouldn't mind giving some handcuffs a bit of exercise at this juncture. But they were in a uncommon situation. They had a potential murder suspect in front of them, or at least someone who was clearly not telling them the whole story, yet he was the only person who probably knew more about the gigarat than they did, and had actually been in the tunnels. He could still be useful.

Until Berriman actually found some evidence, or had enough reason to charge him, Trey Clark remained innocent.

Berriman could not stay silent though.

"Is there something else you would like to tell us, Mr Clark? We know you are hiding something, and we will find out what that is, don't you worry about that. The sooner you tell us, the easier it will be."

Trey doubted that very much. Easier for Berriman, perhaps, but not for him. A way out of this self-induced mess suddenly burst into his thinking like a St Bernard rescue dog bounding up to an avalanche survivor.

"Ok," he said, "It was just something that Hoggo said, and I'm sorry I didn't mention it before. It was when he first saw the vent in the cellar, he told me that these tunnels and shafts can go on for miles and be hundreds of feet deep. So that was why I was about to say no wonder Hoggo told me that, even though I didn't believe him at the time."

There was a silence as Berriman and Jeremy looked at each other impassively, neither indicating any damascene willingness to swallow what they had just been told.

"How would he know about tunnels and shafts?" asked Jeremy, now wondering whether this scrap merchant fellow may have found a tunnel in the woods and been tempted to go into it because of his expertise. But that made no sense – a knowledgeable person wouldn't take such a risk.

"Don't know, really," said Trey, now wishing he had stayed inside. "So what happened when you got down to 300 feet? Did the rat grab your rope?"

Jeremy recognised the change-the-subject tactic but answered anyway. "Pretty much, yes. And McGuire got pulled in."

Berriman's eyes opened wide. "What? Really? Is he dead?"

"No, thankfully the safety rope held and we hauled him back out. His hand is in shreds though, as he was holding onto the rope with it, twisted round his wrist."

"Oeugh! Nasty. Poor chap. Could have been worse, though, I suppose."

"Exactly. But now we are a man down, and I'll have to rethink the plan."

Trey sensed an opportunity to get into the good books of the men trying to make him admit to murder. "What needs doing? Anything I can help with?"

"No," said Berriman firmly before Jeremy could open his mouth. "It wouldn't be appropriate." He gave Jeremy a look that brooked no challenge.

"I think the answer is no, then Mr Clark," said Jeremy, "but thank you for your offer. I would just like you to look at the footage we got of the gigarat, though, just to confirm it is the same creature that you saw."

"Of course."

"We'll just wait for the brigadier to become free then he can play the video back on his device. Charles, do you need a hand?"

The brigadier, who with Polly was standing a good ten feet back from the shaft as they pulled on the rope and cable, looked up.

"Have to say the old arms are getting a bit sore. Too much time at my desk, not enough in the field these days. Must be about a hundred feet of rope left to pull. There's definitely something still attached to it though, you can feel the weight."

"Not the rat, I trust?"

"Ha, no, not unless Polly here is superhuman."

Polly stood up straight, careful not to let go. "I tend not to boast about it," she said, her heavy breathing perhaps betraying her. "Having said that, this is hard work. Anyone fancy taking over?"

Tommy had left Peters with McGuire and returned to the group, and he stepped forward. "If someone can help me, sure."

"I don't mind," said Trey.

Jeremy looked at Berriman. "It's either him or you, Rob."

The Chief Superintendent tightened his jaw. He knew a trap when he saw one.

"Alright, just this once, we'll allow Mr Clark to assist," he conceded. "I need to go and.... er ...... check with the.... speak to my officers round the front."

He tugged his jacket down, turned, and marched off round the side of the building.

Jeremy and Trey exchanged a glance of concealed amusement, both judging it best not to say anything. Trey followed Tommy under the netting, taking the rope and cable from Polly and the brigadier.

Five minutes later, what remained of the injured cage, buckled and crushed in one corner, was on the lawn. Although the camera and depth sensor, securely taped to the bottom of the cage, had fortuitously survived, the light had been shaken loose and smashed.

The brigadier, crouched down next to it with Polly as she looked for traces of saliva to get a DNA sample, shook his head slowly.

"Were you expecting it to be this aggressive?"

"We think it attacks people and eats them. So yes. Weren't you?"

The brigadier got to his feet. "Not to this extent, to an inanimate object. Surely it didn't think that this contraption was something worth eating, did it?"

"Probably not, but it was invading its territory and had to be dealt with."

"I'm a bit surprised that cable didn't snap," ventured Trey. The more that he could integrate himself with this little team, the more it might throw them off the scent or, at worst, help his defence should he end up in court. "I've seen how fast that thing moves, and from the size of it, it must weigh about half a ton."

"It's the metal wires inside it that did the job," said Tommy. "That's a good chunky electric cable by the looks of it, at least 4mm. Although we were still a bit lucky it didn't snap. Now the rope, that's designed to take a lot of strain. It's used in life or death situations. But whichever one we'd used I guess it might depend how much grip that thing had on the cage too."

Jeremy looked at the brigadier. "Can you show Mr Clark here the footage? It would be useful to know if the animal looks the same as the one he encountered in the cavern."

The brigadier nodded and started fiddling with his tablet until he had retrieved the short passage in the video where the gigarat shot out of the darkness and launched itself at the cage.

"It's moving so fast it's hard to be sure," said Trey. "Also, how big is that tunnel, to get some scale? All I can say is, it's not a completely different animal or anything. It could be the same one, but it might not. Sorry I can't......"

"That's ok," said Jeremy, "I was just thinking maybe if it had some distinguishing feature you hadn't seen on the other one, but obviously that was a long shot. Thank you for your assistance, Mr Clark, can I ask that you return to your flat now while we consider our next moves."

It felt a bit like a footballer who'd been brought on as a substitute, played ten minutes, and was now being hauled off again, but Trey understood that he was in no position to argue.

"Sure," he said. "Just shout if you need me."

"Ok, thanks."

Jeremy watched Trey trudge back across the grass. Was he a candidate to replace McGuire in their operation? It would be one less person to add to the mounting list of people he needed to keep the secret. But Berriman would have other ideas.

This all felt too rushed. He made a snap decision.

"Charles, Polly, Tommy – I'm going to halt any further activity for tonight. We need to take stock and gives ourselves more time to plan. Let's get this hole covered up. It's, er, twenty past three. You've got until

5pm to catch up on emails and do whatever research you need to, and we'll meet up at the police station. I'll go and inform Rob. See you in an hour and forty."

On the top floor, peering from the sloping window in his kitchen which gave him just about enough of an angle to see some of the lawn, Norman Baston watched as the brigadier organised the round wooden disc to be slid across the shaft. He observed the group heaving the earth-filled planters onto the wooden cover.

What were they doing? Why had they given up? At least he now knew how Molly had died. They said they weren't sure but it was obvious. That noise he heard in the forest – it was the gigarat, it had to be.

Ok, so the cops probably wouldn't be chasing him any more, trying to accuse him of things he hadn't done, but Molly's death had to be avenged. That rat needed a taste of its own medicine. The Home Office chap had mentioned capturing it, but that wasn't enough. It had to die. If they weren't going to do it, then Norman would. For Molly.

CHAPTER 55

"Can we start without Rob?" asked Polly.

Jeremy glanced at his watch. Ten past five.

They were all crammed into the same interview room that some of them had been in yesterday. Not ideal, but Rob had advised that it was the most sound insulated space in the station, and where they were least likely to be disturbed.

The brigadier, Polly, Tommy and Jason were squashed round the interview table, each looking uncomfortable at the lack of personal space. Two more chairs had been secured for Jeremy and Rob.

"Let's give him two more minutes. He said he would be here....."

He trailed off as the door suddenly burst open and a slightly flustered chief superintendent stumbled in.

"Sorry I'm late, but I was getting a useful update from our search party."

He closed the door firmly behind him and glanced at Jeremy. "Shall I expand on that or do you have a running order?"

Jeremy smoothed back his hair, something he had begun to realise was turning into a bit of a habit. "I have a list of points to address, but now that you have got our pulses racing, you may as well kick things off. Over to you."

Berriman nodded, not sure as to whether he was being gently mocked or not.

"Right then. As you know, with the kind assistance of the brigadier here, we have had teams of men scouring the fields and riverbanks for a distance of approximately two miles in either direction from the forest. Their brief was to look for tunnel entrances, but also bodies in the river, and question the owners of the land – obviously we had to first inform them of our presence and request their co-operation."

"Did any refuse?" asked Tommy.

"All were sensible enough to realise that it would be unwise to do so. I'll cut a long story short – we didn't find any bodies in the river, and we didn't find any large holes in the ground from which a gigarat could have emerged."

There was a collective deflation of breath within the room.

"Yes, I know. But it was not a completely wasted exercise. Two of the landowners are farmers, and both have reported missing sheep; one of them also breeds cows and has had calves go missing."

"How many of each?" asked Jeremy.

Berriman consulted the scrap of paper he had brought in with him.

"Eight sheep and three calves over the last three years. The farmers assumed it was theft and beefed up their security – new locks on their gates, that kind of thing."

"Security cameras?"

"I was coming to that. Mr Johnson, one of the farmers, put hidden wireless cameras up pointing at all the entrances to his fields, but of course what we know and he doesn't is that the farm animals were not being stolen by humans via the entrances, they were being dragged into a tunnel somewhere by a gigarat."

Jason held up his hand. "So if those cameras haven't picked up any gigarat movements – and I'm guessing they have a reasonably wide field of view - presumably that narrows down where this tunnel entrance could be. After all, there's only so far that they are going to drag.... hang on - the river! Yes, that's it, the tunnel entrance must be underwater. It has to be!"

He looked round at everyone, eyebrows raised. "Do you not think?"

All eyes looked at each other, then back to Jeremy, who nodded.

"It seems logical. Would you agree Rob?"

Berriman thought for a second. "Well, that was going to be our next angle, once we had exhausted the possibilities on land."

"It was?" asked the brigadier.

"Yes, well, those were my thoughts, anyway. Jason is quite right, it is entirely feasible that the tunnel is........ although, wouldn't that flood the tunnels?"

"Not necessarily," said Tommy, sitting himself up straight on his uncomfortable chair. "You know how beavers build dams? They engineer in u-bends, so the water doesn't rise above the water table. So in this case, the tunnel could start underwater, then rise a bit once in the ground, before falling again. That way the water wouldn't get in."

His explanation was accompanied by explanatory arm movements that the brigadier, sitting next to him, was fortunate to avoid.

"I'm assuming," said Jeremy, "that there would only be any point looking at the side of the river that Ridley Manor is on, for the tunnel entrance?"

"Not necessarily," said Tommy. "Depends how extensive the tunnel system is. But more likely, yes."

"Well, there we go then, Rob. A new task for tomorrow! How many divers can you get hold of?"

"I had four of them last week when we were first looking for Molly Baines. That should be enough to work their way up the river."

"Excellent! Not sure it makes our jobs any easier, but if we can find it, then we will know how these creatures are getting out, and hopefully contain them underground. Once we've found that entrance, I guess we should block it up, to stop them getting out. All agreed?"

There was a general nodding of heads, although the brigadier voiced what Berriman was also thinking.

"That doesn't sound that easy. To do a proper job to stop that thing, you'd need underwater machinery capable of heavy lifting. But even if you push a few heavy stones into the hole, that animal will just burrow out again. We wouldn't stop it."

Polly sat forward. "Why don't you just rig up a motion-sensitive underwater floodlight? As soon as it sticks its head out, woosh, on comes the light. That should frighten the living daylights out of it and send it back where it came from."

"Good thinking, Polly," said Jeremy. "Although you'd have to position it carefully otherwise it would be going off every time a fish or a bit of weed went past. Not my area of expertise though. Rob?"

The chief superintendent shook his head. "No, me neither. Charles?"

"I can ask and see what equipment we might have. Leave it with me."

"Thank you. Anything else Rob, on the search?"

"No, that was it. Although I would point out that if the intention is to block that hole rather than use it to explore the tunnel system, I would suggest that that will not assist me in my investigations, so should fall directly under your remit?"

Jeremy smiled. "It's a fair point. We may need to borrow your divers though. Charles, one for us to discuss later this evening."

The brigadier nodded. "Of course."

"Ok, moving on, let's review were we are with regard to the gigarat operation. I appreciate that there is a significant parallel investigation underway to establish the cause of death, or reasons for the disappearance of, all the unfortunate souls who have gone missing in the last couple of weeks. Although we think that the gigarat is likely to be responsible for most of them, we cannot rule anything in or out at this stage. The jurisdiction of the team in this room extends only to assisting the police in this aspect, not to directing them in any way. That is Rob's domain."

Berriman nodded gravely, then added "we all need to bear in mind, though, that as things stand we are only reasonably certain that one of the four missing persons – Molly Baines – was attacked by the gigarat. We are led to believe that John Firwell fell down the vent in the cellar of his own accord, although his body disappeared and you can draw your own conclusions from that. Both Anita Rackman and Darren Hoggsmith were last seen during daylight hours, so we have, as yet, no evidence that a gigarat was involved in their deaths. Hence why, until we know otherwise, we still have to retain the possibility that they were murdered."

"Any suspects?" asked Tommy, not standing on ceremony.

Berriman sniffed. "I'm not at liberty to divulge any details, but we do have some suspicions. Obviously, if you see or hear anything in the course of your work that doesn't seem right, let me know immediately."

Jeremy steered the conversation back to his own domain. "So while Rob is working all that out, our sole focus as a DUST team will be on capturing the animal or animals, and containing the situation. Now, firstly, our thoughts this evening should be with McGuire. The latest update I have is that he is conscious and stable. He's had a skin graft operation but no bones were broken. He should make a full recovery, albeit with some lifelong scars. Could have been a lot worse. So that's good news."

"Absolutely," said the brigadier with an unexpected thump of his fist on the table. "A fine soldier, can't afford to lose men like that."

A general murmur of agreement simmered around the room, although Jeremy did wonder at such a personal endorsement, given that the brigadier had only met McGuire for the first time that morning.

He resumed. "I called a halt to proceedings tonight after what happened to McGuire, but also because I appreciate that we have, through no fault of our own, had to rush things a little, given the seriousness of the situation. So I wanted us now all to take stock and re-assess what we are doing. For example, I was not happy that, were we to have gone ahead with our plan to trap the gigarat this evening, some of the residents of Ridley Manor who had not signed the confidentiality papers may have seen what was happening out of their windows. Telling them not to look would almost certainly just have piqued their interest, especially if they heard that thing squealing or making that rumbling noise. Before we go any further, I think we should move them out. Jason, could you organise this please?"

Jason scratched his ear. "Yes, I suppose I could. You've told Norman Baston now haven't you, so doesn't that just leave Jean Edwards?"

"Ah, yes, so it does. Just her then."

"How long shall I tell her that it is for?"

"Well, that is the question, isn't it? I think use the phrase 'just a few days' and make it clear that she arrange to return to her flat during daylight hours if she needs to collect anything under supervision. Rob, will you be able to station a 24 hour guard at the entrance to Ridley Manor?"

Berriman nodded. "Already in effect. If Ridley Manor does prove to be a murder scene, I don't want tradesmen trampling over the evidence, so I've got officers briefed at the gate, working shifts. We're not exactly overflowing with resources, but needs must. We're talking a likely 4 deaths already so we'll just have to manage the manpower and prioritise."

"Thank you. So Jason, can you tlk to Jean Edwards this evening? A personal visit would be best I think, not a phone call. Then she can move tomorrow morning. Get her a nice hotel if you can. Four star, that kind of thing. Don't want her running to the press, although at her age I doubt she would do that. Although you could be clear too that she must keep this whole thing under her hat, and if she does we will compensate her for her troubles. And if she doesn't, well, you know."

He frowned at the room, silently reminding the assembled team that what he had just said applied to them as well.

Jason was tapping notes into his phone's to-do list. "Ok, will do. Seems a bit mean, though, to threaten a dear old lady, Jeremy. Didn't know you were that type of chap." He smiled innocently.

Jeremy sighed. "I'm not rising to the bait, Mr Crisp, but your comment has been noted and I will get you back later. Right. Rob, Charles – I believe you two have been planning the underwater sweep of the river. What have you got?"

Berriman nodded at the brigadier, who cleared his throat.

"Right! Yes, well, we agreed this would be best as an army operation, so I spoke to our Senior Diving Officer earlier, and secured a team of experienced divers to start tomorrow. Pretty handy having this level of authority, I must say, as some of them were on other missions and had to be re-assigned. Obviously none of them will know the reason for this operation, just that they need to find a tunnel entrance and rig up some lighting."

"Excellent," said Jeremy, "thank you. Now, as far as capturing the gigarat is concerned, we do now at least know a bit more about that shaft in terms of its depth and what leads off it. But I'm wondering if we have underestimated this animal. My concern is that if we do manage to coax it out of the shaft, the speed at which it moves, and the strength it has demonstrated to date, could put us all in danger. After all, the buckets of food we are putting in the van might be less attractive to it than the smell of a few meaty humans on the other side of a net."

"How good is its sense of smell?" asked Jason.

All eyes turned to Polly.

"Well, actually pretty good. Rats can register not only scents, but also chemicals that denote a change in atmosphere and emotion. However…. that doesn't tie up with what Trey Clark told us. He said he was hiding in a tunnel in the dark with the gigarat sniffing around in the cavern but unable to detect him. He would have been giving off all kinds of smells and emotional chemicals, I would imagine – it should have detected him instantly. So I'm wondering whether for some reason this super-sized rat has lost its acute sense of smell."

Tommy, wedged in between the wall and the brigadier, tried to shift his seat a little. "S'pose it was just a really old rat, losing its senses, like an old fella might lose his hearing? If there's a group of them down there the others might be younger and … well, you know."

"It's possible," agreed Polly.

"So it's a risk then," summarised Jeremy. "The gigarat might come haring up out of the shaft, sense some humans standing close by, and make a beeline for them. I'm not sure I would stake my life on that net holding it back."

The brigadier made a valiant defence of his net. "Yes, but even if the rat uproots the stakes holding the net down, it could still get itself tangled up," he pointed out. "That would seriously impede its progress and give us a chance to fire at it."

He caught a frosty look from Polly.

"Fire tranquillisers, is what I meant."

Jeremy was unconvinced. "But by that time it could have knocked down and seriously injured any of us standing anywhere near, including the owner of the dart gun."

He looked at Polly, who said in a small voice "anyone want to take over firing the tranquilliser?"

The brigadier realised he was beaten.

"Alright, we'll need to beef up the containment apparatus. I'm convinced the net will hold, so the answer might be to bring in another truck and secure the netting, nice and taught, between the two vehicles. Even a gigarat won't be able to pull two trucks along behind it. Then its only option would be back down the hole, or into the back of the truck with the food in it."

"That sounds better," agreed Jeremy. "I'm wondering also if we can rig up a better closing mechanism for the truck doors – maybe put some heavy duty self-closing hinges on there, like they have on fire doors, you know? Then rig it so a tripwire inside the truck activates them, or they can be remotely operated. I'm not happy with this idea of the ropes attached to the doors, especially with McGuire out of the picture now. Can you look at that, and get it all set up tomorrow, ready for the evening?"

"I'll do my best. Can I ask, though, assuming we catch this thing and drive it off to Polly's lab, what then? If there are more of the things down there in those tunnels, do we catch another one or go down there and…. er…. extinguish them?"

"I want at least two of them," said Polly. "Male and female."

Tommy chipped in. "Has your lab got cages strong enough to hold them?"

"We've got two that can house an elephant if necessary. So yes."

Jeremy attempted to answer the brigadier's question. "If we are successful with the first capture, we can try again so that Polly has two. But there could be any number of those things down there, so….."

"I don't think there are, though," interrupted Jason. "If you think about it, eleven farm animals have gone missing in three years. That's not a lot if there was a big colony, given the size of those things. Perhaps Polly was right about them feeding on each other, and maybe that is how they survived for centuries, trapped in the tunnels. But then three years ago something changed. Maybe that's when they dug through to the river and created an exit to the outside world. By that time their eyes couldn't handle bright light, so they just came out occasionally at night to grab a badger or something, then came across sheep and cows. But up to that point they would not have had enough food to sustain a large group."

Polly turned to face Jason. "That doesn't account for how they found the body of a gigarat in the river in 1956, though."

Jason's face fell. "Ah, yes, good point. I'd forgotten about that." He thought for a second. "Maybe it got out by digging the first exit, then couldn't find its way back in again. Not sure why it died though. I still have a gut feel that there aren't too many of them down there, though."

"We don't know what we don't know," said Jeremy, "so all we can do is work with what we do know. And that being the case, let's put all our focus for now in capturing at least one of the things rather than worrying about how many of them there are. In the meantime, Charles and Tommy, can you put your heads together to consider what machinery could be brought to bear to carry out some remote investigation down there, so there is no risk to humans. This time we keep the lights on, of course."

The two men nodded.

"Unless anyone has anything else to raise, I suggest we all get ourselves a good night's sleep ready for tomorrow. And can I remind you that there must be no conversations in public spaces – over dinner, for example. The slightest titbit overheard could end up in the papers and then our job becomes significantly harder. Reporters snooping around as we are trying to work will jeopardise the whole operation. Is that understood?"

It was a rhetorical question, but a reminder of just how careful they all had to be. They were not to know that their task was about to become even more challenging.

CHAPTER 56

Norman felt the edge of his garden scythe. He didn't use it much so the blade was still nice and sharp. Good, that would do. He had an axe, too, and a couple of sturdy wooden planting stakes about four feet long, sharpened to a point, assembled on the floor in the middle of the shed. A spade completed the armoury.

He checked his watch. 8:20pm. It was fully dark outside now. Time to avenge Molly.

One by one he took the garden weaponry components out through the door and leant them against the outside wall. Closing the door quietly behind him, he scooped them up in his arms and crept round into the garden.

There was half a moon up above, waxing a pale grey light across the lawn. Three of the windows in the house were lit, but dimmed by curtains. No one would be looking out of their windows now.

Ahead of him, the army truck sat still and silent, very much out of place in the garden of a stately home. Behind it, like the bulbous back end of an ant, a net was draped over a frame, secured to the ground with stays.

He could see his breath in the air, and felt the temperature drop slightly as he walked away from the house. It didn't help that his heart was racing – he was all too aware that what he was about to do would entail considerable risk. But Molly was the only friend he had ever known and he had to do this, for her. No one else would.

He looked round nervously before quietly laying the tools on the ground, then sliding them one by one under the net. Scrambling under himself, he stood up and surveyed the covered shaft in front of him. He'd need to remove the planters, but he was used to moving sacks of peat and earth around; lifting heavy things was not a deterrent. But first....

He picked up the spade, stepped back towards the truck and began digging two holes. Into each one he pushed a wooden stake, angled at about 45 degrees and pointing towards the shaft. The earth was packed back tightly and some rocks placed at their base to keep them steady. Next, he laid all the tools behind his makeshift barricade.

That done, he stood up and looked around him. Everything was quiet and still apart from his breathing, misting the air. An owl hooted from the forest.

Carefully he stepped down onto the wooden disc covering the shaft. The two planters were heavy, heavier than he thought, and awkward for one man to lift up and out onto the grass. He glanced round and noticed the spade on the ground behind the stakes.

A few minutes later, and with fresh piles of earth next to the netting, he was able to lift the half-empty planters out and place them to one side.

He checked his watch. Ten to nine. There were four windows now lit up at the back of the manor house, curtains still drawn. People were about, but no one was looking at him; no one suspected anyone would be out here. Satisfied, he turned his attention to the wooden disc. This is where he had to be really careful. One false move, one slip, and his life was over.

Crouched down on his haunches, he levered the spade under the wood and raised it up enough to be able to reach slowly forward and grab an edge. Holding it up with that hand, he pulled the spade out and then used both hands to waddle backwards, pulling the disc across the hole and up onto the lawn.

The deep maw of the shaft revealed itself, looking even more sinister in the darkness. Norman could feel his heart rate racing, but he had to do this. He wasn't going to chicken out now.

Jeremy Stanton-Davies had told him about the food scraps in the van they were going to use to entice the gigarat, so next he climbed the ramp, onto the hard plastic floor of the truck. It wasn't hard to tell there was food there – it reeked. Right at the back, covered by a blanket, was a row of buckets filled with God knows what, giving off a pungent stench that reminded him of the bins at the back of a supermarket.

He peeled back the blanket and picked up one of the buckets, carrying it gingerly back out and down the ramp. He could make out some cabbage leaves and carrots, and lumps of what looked like cheese. Placing it next to the shaft, he carried the spade back behind the wooden stakes to be reunited with the scythe and the axe.

Right, everything was in place. His defences were ready. The murderous gigarat would come hurtling out of the shaft and with a bit of luck impale itself on the wooden stakes. Even if it didn't, Norman would catch it by surprise with one swift flash of the scythe, and that would be the end of the animal. The axe was his backup and the spade, though less effective, was contingency, although how he would use it to batter a giant rat he wasn't entirely sure.

He grunted to himself. Yes, he was ready. Time for action. He picked up the bucket and hurled it into the middle of the shaft. Surely he'd hear the bucket when it hit the bottom, and so should the rat. That would bring it running. It would find the food, then hopefully feel the draught and realise the shaft was open. Would that be enough to entice it up? He'd soon find out.

He waited, ears straining. After about five or six seconds he thought he heard a very distant clang echoing a little way up the shaft. Or had he imagined it? No matter. The gigarat should have heard it.

He scurried back behind his makeshift defences and clutched his scythe. All he could do now was wait.

***

Jason stood outside the door of Jean Edward's flat and composed himself. It was gone half past eight and he was starving.

It took a few progressively harder knocks on the door before he heard noises and imagined her peering through her security peephole and trying to work out who the spoon-faced man was. Clearly she couldn't, as he then heard 'who is it?' in a wavering voice coming from behind the door.

"Jason Crisp, from the Home Office. I came and saw you briefly yesterday."

There was a pause, then a key was turned, a chain slid off, and the door opened. Jean peered up at him.

"I do remember you now. Hello, come in."

"Sorry to disturb you at such a late hour. It's been a busy day."

"Oh that's fine, I wasn't doing anything useful anyway. I rarely do these days."

She gave a little laugh, then led him through into the lounge, where the dirty pink walls were losing a battle to be seen from behind furniture and shelves weighed down by cluttered ornaments and photographs.

"Is that your husband?" asked Jason, focusing on a large photograph that took pride of place in the centre of the mantelpiece.

"Yes, that's Roy," she said, smiling. "Still watching over me. Have a seat."

Jason lowered himself onto a yellow throw that had a hidden armchair beneath it, and sunk into it rather further than he had hoped. Jean took the chair opposite him.

"I won't take up too much of your time," he said, hoping to hurry things along.

"Oh don't worry about that," replied Jean, "take as long as you like. It's so nice to have someone to talk to, you know."

She smiled, the effect of which was to make him feel worse, not better, as he now felt partially obliged to engage in at least a modicum of small talk, if only to do his bit for the community and keep an old lady company for a while.

And so he asked how long she had lived there, how long she had been married, how she got on with the neighbours, and a small assortment of associated questions, all of which she answered with an enthusiasm that told him it had been a long time since anyone had last shown any interest in her.

But he had to move things on and tell her the bad news that she would have to temporarily move out.

"Mrs Edwards, there is a reason for my visit."

"Well, I suppose there had to be, didn't there? You wouldn't have come round just to have a chat."

He raised an eyebrow. "I admit, I probably wouldn't. But it's to do with all the activity out on the lawn. Have you seen what's going on out there?"

"Well, yes. Lots of soldiers, making things and rigging up that net next to a truck. But heaven knows what they are doing it for. Did you tell me yesterday? My memory is not what it was. And is that a hole in the ground? It is quite hard to see from here. It's funny you know, that truck reminds me of one we used in Clayper once, when I worked there. It took me back. That would be all of sixty years ago now. Doesn't time......"

But Jason interrupted. "I'm sorry, but did you say Clayper? Where did you work?"

Jean blinked at him, slightly irritated at having her flow broken. "It was in a lab. I can't tell you much, it was all very hush-hush. I was a scientist for ten years, you know, before I married Roy."

"This is too good to be true," said Jason under his breath. "Are you telling me you worked at the Clayper government scientific laboratory in the 1950s?"

"I'm not sure I'm supposed to tell you any details. We all signed papers that swore us to secrecy. I've probably said too much already, young man." She shook her head, admonishing herself.

"Absolutely not," Jason reassured her. "In fact, what you have just said could be extremely important. Let me just ask – were you doing animal research? On things like pituitary glands?"

Jean looked up as though her chair had just given her an electric shock.

"How did you know that?"

Jason pumped his fist. "Yes! Mrs Edwards, the project we are working on in the garden here is directly connected to what happened in Clayper in 1956. You mentioned the truck. Does it look like the one they used back then to carry.... an animal?"

"An animal, yes. A big one."

"A rat?"

Jean sat back in her chair and took a deep breath before looking directly at Jason.

"I don't know what to do. Am I supposed to tell you? Those papers I signed were very clear. I was to tell no one. Financially, I could be in trouble if I do. I need the money to live here. Do you understand?"

"Completely. And don't worry, you won't be in trouble. Jeremy and I report to a man who in turn reports directly to the Home Secretary. We have clearance, and the authority, to make sure that...." he paused. "Wait, what's that noise?"

"I can't hear anything."

"I can. A sort of ticking, but loud. Can you hear that now? What is it? I can't make out where it's coming from."

Jean held her head still. "Oh yes. I can hear it now. Oh, it's stopped."

"I wonder what that was."

They both sat, listening.

"No, it's definitely stopped. Now, where were we? Oh, wait, there it is again. You don't think it could be.... Hey, now that was a scream. Something's happening outside. Oh Lord, and another one! What the hell's going on out there?"

Jason leapt out of his chair and bounded over to the window overlooking the garden, yanking back the curtains.

"I can't see anything. Could you turn off the light please?"

"I'm sorry?"

"The light – could you......?"

"Oh, right, yes, of course. Hold on a minute."

As Jean struggled up and made her way to the door where the light switch was, Jason pulled up the sash window and tried to adjust his eyes to the darkness outside. The noises had stopped, and at first glance everything looked as it had done when they left the shaft earlier that afternoon. The truck was still there, the netting intact. As soon as Jean switched off the light, though, he could see that the shaft had been opened, and the planters were on their sides, pushed into the netting. Something had happened, but he wasn't sure what. He needed to get down there, but first, he had to let Jeremy know.

He closed the window and stabbed at the contacts list on his phone, tapping on Jeremy's number.

"Hi Jason."

"Jeremy, something's happened. There's been some activity at the shaft, and the lid's off. I heard some screaming. I think you'd better get over here. Maybe bring Charles and Rob. I'm in Jean's flat, so just going down now. Oh, and I've got other news, but I'll tell you afterwards. See you later."

"Ok, I'm on my way."

Jason ended the call. Jean had switched the light back on, so he made his way over to where she was at the front door.

"Mrs Edwards, please stay here for now. I'll probably need to bring Jeremy back up here with my once we've established what's happened outside. Is that ok?"

"Well, I usually go to bed at 10:00pm."

"Right, ok, we'll try to be back by then. If we're not back by 10:30pm, we'll leave it until tomorrow. We have a lot to talk about with you!"

That in itself was enough to bring a little flutter into Jean's heart. She was going to be the centre of attention, and that hadn't happened since Roy died.

"Of course!" she said, as Jason stepped past her. "I'll look forward to it." She closed the door, feeling invigorated but also slightly fearful. Her memory of recent events might be failing her, but what had happened at Clayper was something she knew she would never forget, and as she thought about what had just happened out on the lawn, her mind starting racing with possibilities, none of them pleasant.

CHAPTER 57

Norman heard a distant, very faint noise. Although very far away, he recognised it as the same noise he had heard when he was in the forest, the night that Molly disappeared. He felt a chill, a dark prod in his chest, reminding him of that night.

He gritted his teeth and clutched the scythe more firmly. Ok, rat, prepare to pay for what you've done. Come on then, run up that shaft and show yourself!

But the noise stopped. Had it found the bucket and the scattered food? It was probably snouting around eating it all. He waited.

After what felt like fifteen minutes but was unlikely to have been more than five, he heard the noise again. It started to get steadily louder. It was coming; it had fallen for his trap! Time for the showdown.

Taka-taka-taka, closer and closer. Norman felt some sweat on his forehead. Then, just as it sounded as though the rat was about to emerge, the noise abruptly stopped. There was a prolonged, penetrating silence. Norman's heart rate was by now so accelerated that he felt sure the rat could hear it. Where was it?

His eyes focused intently on the opening and he gripped the scythe as though his life depended on it, which, in this situation, it did. As soon as the rat appeared he would leap up from behind his barricade. The rat would charge towards him, impale itself, and simultaneously have its head lopped off by the flashing blade of the gardening hero. Norman was ready.

What he wasn't ready for was the rat emerging on the other side of the hole. There was a sudden sheen of shiny brown fur as the huge creature propelled itself up and over the edge, turning sideways to reveal four dirty brown fangs beneath a twitching nose, and a couple of tiny jet black eyes. Its head darted left and right, sensing what was around it.

Norman was shocked at how ugly it was, and suddenly frightened too. This thing was huge, just like Trey had said. And now it was coming slowly towards him around the edge of the shaft, and starting that noise again. He slowly rose to his full height and drew the scythe back behind him, ready to attack.

But he was not ready enough. Despite its size the gigarat, having presumably detected its prey, bolted forward. It neatly avoided the sharpened wooden posts, rounding them so quickly that Norman had only just started his downward swing as the front claws of the rat slapped into his chest and ripped down his front as he fell. He screamed out in pain as the scythe flew back out of his hands and the vast bulk of the rat fell on top of him.

The last thing he saw was a vision of hell. Sharp brown teeth descended; the last smell was sharp and rancid; his last breath was a final scream.

The gigarat took hold of Norman's throat with its teeth, shook back and forth to ensure its prey had no life left, then dragged him over the wooden stakes, scattering them asunder. It threw Norman's body into the shaft and slithered headfirst after it, back from whence it had come.

Just fifteen seconds after it had emerged, it was gone. And so, now, was Norman, a troubled and misunderstood soul whose bravery, however misguided and foolhardy it might have been, was unlikely ever to be publicly recognised.

CHAPTER 58

As Jason hurried out of the front door of the house he saw one of the policeman stationed at the front gates walking swiftly towards him, holding up his hand.

"Sir, you need to go back. Back in the house please."

This was all Jason needed. The police sentries had strict instructions not to leave their posts, but must have heard faint screams and decided that one of them should investigate. He couldn't be allowed to, though. Jason fumbled in his pocket and brought out his ID card.

"Jason Crisp, Home Office. Listen, I'm working closely with Chief Superintendent Berriman on this, and you'll need to clearance to go any further. I'll call you if I need you, ok?"

The officer checked the card, sensed the urgency and authority in Jason's voice, and nodded.

"Alright. But if I hear another scream..."

"Of course, thank you."

He left the policeman backing slowly up the drive. Rounding the back of the house at some speed, he stumbled as he saw two dark figures huddled on the path next to the lawn.

One held his head in his hands, the other was looking round frantically. It was Trey and Tony, who had evidently rushed out when they heard the noise and were now in two minds as to what to do.

"Gents!" hissed Jason as he loped towards them. "Back in the house, please!"

"Someone's hurt though," cried Trey, "did you hear the screams? We need to help! We're just worried about the rat."

"Exactly!" said Jason as he joined them. "It could be loose. Get inside!"

"He's right," said Tony. "Look, there's no one lying on the ground, so there's no one to help. Let's leave this to these guys, eh? Come on."

He patted Trey on the back, then marched off back round to the front of the manor house.

Trey looked at Jason. He wasn't going anywhere. The gigarat had killed his friend and if it had now attacked someone else he needed to know. "I'm staying. We need to check the hole, make sure it's closed."

"It's not, it's been opened."

"Oh shit. Has the rat forced its way out? It has to be too big to have squeezed under the netting, doesn't it? Suppose it's gone back down to get reinforcements, and a whole load of them come out?"

"That wouldn't be good," agreed Jason. "Not at this precise moment, anyway. So you heard the screams too?"

"Yep, two of them. Came straight out but as Tony said we couldn't see a body or anything from this distance."

Jason sighed. "I really hope we haven't got another death on our hands. That would be five, for God's sake."

"Who would be out here in the dark though? It doesn't make sense. Look, we need to get that shaft covered again. Have you got anyone coming to help?"

"I've called Jeremy."

"I'm not being funny, but he's not going to be much help."

"No, but he'll bring Charles and Rob."

"How long will that take?"

"Maybe ten, fifteen minutes."

"That might be too late. Look, two of us can cover that hole again. You coming?"

Jason realised he had no choice.

"Yep, ok. Come on. Let's do this."

The two of them crept across the lawn, looking all around them, praying that a charging gigarat wouldn't suddenly emerge from a bush. As they drew closer they could see that there were some objects scattered round the shaft.

"There's a spade, look," said Trey softly, pointing. "Over there."

"I see it. Some bits of wood too. And is that an axe? What the hell is going on?"

Trey had started to form a thought but he really hoped he was wrong.

"Those bits of wood are stakes, used to tie saplings to. And the axe and the spade – they're garden tools. It's Norman, I reckon."

"Was he trying to commit suicide or something?"

"God knows. He wouldn't use an axe for that. And look! There's a scythe right over there. Doesn't matter now though. Let's slide under and put that cover back on."

The grass was damp now, so they crouched like crabs to slide under the netting. Although they were no longer safe from whatever might come hurtling out of the hole in front of them, the dark abyss of the shaft was silent, and that was good.

"Right!" whispered Jason, feeling that he should really take the initiative, "let's grab one side each and slide it over. You ready?"

Trey nodded, and between them they got hold of the wooden cover and carried it over to the shaft before lowering it gently, hearts in mouths. The planters were then placed back on top and the earth shovelled back in using the spade.

"You seen this?" said Trey, pointing at one of the wooden stakes. "Looks like blood on the end of it."

"Ok, let's bring everything that shouldn't be here with us."

"Don't you want to leave the stakes and the axe for forensics? Fingerprints and stuff?"

"Good point. Leave them there, then. Let's go."

The two men scrambled back under the net and hurried round to the front of the house to await Jason's colleagues. A long evening was about to turn into a long night.

CHAPTER 59 - WEDNESDAY

It was a tired and frustrated group who assembled at 9:00am the next morning in the police interview room at Hixton Police Station.

Berriman looked particularly morose, with the first signs of dishevelment creeping into his attire – his tie was noticeably askew.

"The first thing to say is that all the indications are that last night's incident was centred around Norman Baston," he announced, kicking things off. "He is not in his apartment, no one else accessed the tool store yesterday, and our witnesses, including Jason here, confirmed that the screams they heard sounded as though they came from a male. It appears as though, for some reason known only to himself, he went armed with an axe, a scythe, a spade, and some wooden stakes, and tried to entice the gigarat out. One of the buckets of food is missing so we assume he must have thrown it down the shaft."

"Did he maybe want to act the hero?" suggested Tommy. "You know, show the cops he was a good guy and save the day?"

"It's possible. As you know, if he had killed the rat he wouldn't have been helping anyway. It was just..... an incredibly foolish thing to do. And now I have another death on my watch, again with no body. Five deaths, probably, and no bodies. It's ridiculous. I have to tell you, this is also becoming increasingly difficult to keep under wraps, especially as I can't mention to most of my colleagues anything that might give the game away. Just so you know, I've brought Collins, Bartram, Rakowska and Davis together to form a sub-team to assist me, as they had all already signed the confidentiality papers. But of course the other officers are talking, and rumours are flying all over the place. I'm not sure how much longer I can keep the press off my backs either. They know that Anita Rackman and Darren Hoggsmith are missing, and that we haven't solved who murdered Molly Baines. With Mrs Firwell's agreement we've not released details of John Firwell's death, as we don't want them sniffing round the house, and how do we explain the disappearance of his body? It's a mess. Telling the press that we'll let them know when we have anything to say, and then saying nothing, is just making us look incompetent."

Jeremy, arms folded and chin down as he listened to Berriman's update, raised his head.

"We all appreciate the predicament you are in, Rob. Out of all of us, you probably have the most pressure on your shoulders. We're here to help you, so anything we can do, please shout. Meanwhile, we need every bit of luck we can get right now. Talking of which, the blood samples from last night. Could be rat or human – any news from your labs, Polly?"

"Yes, they're going to work on it all day today, top priority. Should have some results back late this afternoon."

"Can your guys be any quicker than that, Rob?"

Berriman shook his head. "No, we're more likely to be tomorrow."

"Well, if it's human blood that should confirm it was Baston, but if it's the gigarat that might give you something to work with, Polly?"

"I hope so. I wanted to ask – can I speak to Jean Edwards after this meeting?"

"Yes, of course. I think you all know now that we discovered just before last night's incident that she used to work at Clayper. I suppose that when it comes to that good luck I was talking about just now, that's the only bit we've had. We didn't get a chance to follow up on that, so this morning I was proposing that you and I, Polly, go and talk to her. I've already told Jason that there is no point moving her to a hotel now, as she probably knows more than we do! Charles, you'll be monitoring the diving team's progress today, yes?"

"Absolutely."

"And although I am loathe to say it, we need to get our camera back down the shaft during daylight hours to see if there is anything at the bottom, not least Norman Baston. Can we still use the cage?"

The brigadier gave a little wince. "We can fix the light, but obviously McGuire smashed the wooden frame we were lowering it through, so we'll just have to scrape it down the side of the shaft. Not ideal, but it should work. Also, an update for you. It occurred to me last night that when the light went off, the camera should have switched automatically to infra-red mode, so at the hotel last night I went through the recordings."

All eyes in the room looked expectantly at the brigadier.

"No luck, I'm afraid. Just lots of jagged movement and darkness as the rat was running with the cage, then when it jerked back the camera ended up pointing back the way it had come, so if the rat was still there, it didn't see it. Really frustrating."

Jeremy sighed. "That's a blow. For all we know, there could be a dead gigarat lying there, and the one that took Baston was another one. And I guess it's too far along the tunnel to see from the bottom of the shaft."

"I'm one step ahead of you there'" said the brigadier. "I've been trying to source a remotely controlled bomb disposal robot. They run on caterpillar tracks. If we drop it down the shaft – not literally of course – then it could crawl along the tunnel and send pictures back. The only problem is connectivity with something that far underground."

"Ah," said Tommy. "We've both had the same idea. Last night I was seeing how quickly I could get hold of one of our cave exploration robots. Similar principle, but probably more agile as the one I'm thinking of has grippy wheels. Mind you, shouldn't need to go up any steep slopes down there so agility probably doesn't matter. Also, it's got good connectivity with the wif-fi – at least 400 metres. We work with universities to build them as prototypes."

"Sounds like yours might be the better option," said Jeremy. "I guess they are easier to manoeuvre and control than a drone, and a lot less noisy?"

Tommy shrugged. "They still make a noise. Not as much, but there's a motor in them. Thing is though, if you've got a dirty great LED light array strapped to the top of it, that's like kryptonite to the rat, ain't it?"

"You're right, that should protect it. Good. At some point, though, the wifi range is going to run out though, isn't it?"

Jason sat forward. "How about if we lower a range extender down there, to hang just above the bottom of the shaft? That should give you an extra 300 ft or so."

"Good thinking. Can you look into that, Tommy?"

"Sure."

"Thanks. The question is now: can we do some exploration today, then be ready to try and capture the gigarat tonight?"

Berriman cleared his throat. "Whatever your plan is, it needs doing fast. As I said, I've now got five victims almost certainly associated with this animal, the last thing I need is another one. The sooner you guys can nullify it, the better."

Jeremy smiled grimly. "Tell me about it. That's the dilemma we face, knowing the longer we leave it the more damage could be done. Especially now this thing has got a taste for humans, and knows there is another way out if it can bash open that lid. But we've already seen what happens when we rush a solution in."

"I don't think we had much choice," observed the brigadier. "This isn't the kind of job where you spend a week putting a project plan together. We had to act first and think as we were going along, and we are still in that situation today."

"That's true. Right, anyone with anything else?"

Polly raised a finger. "That seemingly counter-productive rumbling and ticking noise the gigarat makes – I'm looking into the possibility that it might be some kind of echo location device, like bats use with their clicks. They might have developed that as a way of getting around quickly in the dark and locating prey."

Tommy shook his head. "I'll never understand evolution. Not to that level, anyway."

Polly shrugged at him. "I know, it sounds incredible, but nature does things like that. There is still so much we don't understand. But I can't think of a better reason as to why they wouldn't want to sneak around silently. Can you?"

All Tommy could think of to say was "no".

Jeremy brought things to a close. "Ok, thank you Polly, that's an interesting thought, worth progressing. Time is of the essence so let's wrap up. You all know what you need to do. Let's reconvene at 4pm at Ridley Manor and see if we're in a position to attempt to catch the gigarat tonight. Good luck everyone. Oh, and you're all on the WhatsApp group I set up, so any information you think is worth us all knowing, post it on there. Let's go!"

Chairs were scraped back and everyone funnelled through the door in silence. Another challenging day lay ahead.

CHAPTER 60

Jeremy took a sip of Earl Grey tea. The cup was bone china, which somehow made the tea taste classier. It seemed slightly incongruous to be enjoying a small luxury like this when people where dying like flies just yards from where they sat. He placed the cup back on its mat.

"Mrs Edwards, how clear are your recollections of your time working at Clayper?"

Jean smiled. "It's strange but things from a long time ago I can remember. But ask me what happened yesterday, or last week and, well, it's all a blank, you know? Getting old is no fun, I can assure you."

Jeremy reflected that Polly probably thought of him as old already. He looked across at her, inferring that she should take over. This was her domain, after all.

She nodded and turned to Jean.

"Mrs Edwards, when did you start working at the Clayper Research Lab? Roughly, that is."

"When? Ooh let me see." She did some maths in her head. "That would be about 1955, I think. I was brought in as a junior scientist. Cheap labour I suppose! We were doing government research projects at first, and yes, some of it was on animals. Things were different back then, it wasn't such an issue, although to be fair hardly anyone knew what we were doing. We were hidden away, you see. It was mostly mice and rats and voles, and in those days, well, you just got on with it, didn't you? It was for the betterment of humanity, that's what we were told, and we did what we were told. Well, most of us, anyway. Sorry, I'm rambling. What was your question?"

"No, that's fine," Polly re-assured her. "You were there on the day that the truck with the gigarat turned up then?"

"Gigarat?"

"Oh, sorry, yes, that is what we are calling the animal. Did you have a name for it back then?"

Jean raised her eyes up to the ceiling and squinted. "Do you know what, that's one thing I can't remember. Just 'giant rat' I think, or 'big rat'. But yes, I was working on the day that the truck arrived. There were only about ten of us biologists, and we all came up to have a look. We were in the basement but luckily for them there were cold storage units on the ground floor. They'd used a squadron of men to get a tarpaulin under it and lift it, well, slide it, into the truck from the river, and so they did the same in reverse to get it out, and hauled it into our largest cold store. What a day that was. We were all so excited, I can't tell you."

"I'll bet," said Polly. "So what kind of tests did you do on it?"

"Well, obviously, all our attention was diverted onto this creature. We had to move quickly as even in a chiller the body will start to decompose after a few weeks. So our main task was to establish was kind of animal it was, and how it got so big."

"And did you?"

"Did I what?"

"Establish.... what you said."

"Oh, sorry, well, yes, mostly. It was a mutated rat of some kind, that was clear, although with some very peculiar features."

"Such as?"

"Claw-like feet, small eyes, and huge yellow incisors. An ugly great bugger, he was. Pardon my French."

Polly glanced at Jeremy. "Same, then."

"Looks like it," agreed Jeremy. "Anything else?"

Jean thought hard. "Yes, yes, it's coming back to me now. Isn't it funny how it can? Did I tell you I can't remember things, normally? Not recent things anyway. What was I saying?"

"The rat's peculiar features."

"Oh yes. It had a very hard, scaly underbelly – much tougher than a normal rat."

"Interesting," said Polly, making a note. "Could be from all that scrabbling around in tunnels. With such a huge body its belly must scrape on the floor."

"You've found another one, then, have you?" Jean was leaning slightly forward, suddenly a scientist again.

Jeremy nodded. "At least one, yes."

"Is that why you're digging in the garden? Is that where it lives? There'd be more than one, presumably."

"Yes on both counts," said Polly. "Although we have no idea how many of them there are down there. One on its own wouldn't have lived down there for sixty years or so, unless its mutation somehow affected lifespan as well. It's an old mine system below us, all sealed up."

"It could be the last one, of course," pointed out Jeremy. "If the others have died off."

"That's true, yes. We don't know, either way."

Jean was nodding slowly. "That's one thing that baffled us – where it came from. We wondered if it was just living in the river, but then someone would have seen it. It was an unanswered question. We didn't know there was a mine here."

"No one did, it seems. It may have closed centuries ago and faded into oblivion, until now. One thing I do need to know, Mrs Edwards, is what kind of testing you did on the animal and what you found out."

"Ah well," – she made a play of arranging her skirt over her knees – "that's the thing isn't it? The answer is: not as much as we would be able to do today; you have so many clever techniques and machines now. We had mainly lab benches and test tubes by comparison. We studied the pituitary gland of course, and as expected it had an adenoma – a tumorous growth. But it wasn't like any adenoma we had seen before. It was integrated into the gland in a way that would indicate that it had been there from birth, not grown as an aberration later on. So the stimulation to produce growth hormone was pretty much constant, to a certain point. That's what got us thinking about seeing if we could reproduce that in other animals to improve food yields. Our Chief Scientist mentioned that to the minister and was given the green light to experiment. Imagine a half ton pheasant, and the amount of food that would provide. Or chicken eggs the size of footballs. That is what we were thinking, to begin with. Obviously it would have to be very tightly controlled, but in those days that was easier."

"How do you mean?"

"There was more respect for authority." She smiled. "And respecting your elders and betters. Not that I was either of those things back then."

"Ah, but you are now!" flattered Jeremy, realising as he said it that this was only half a compliment.

Jean looked at the floor. "Oh, I don't know about that. Older, yes, but...."

Polly moved the conversation on. "Am I right that you were trying to create synthetic tumours in the brains of these animals to spur growth hormone production?"

"Well, yes, we did look at that. We didn't have much success though."

"Ok, so the fire," prompted Polly. "That was six years after you found the gigarat. Can you tell us what happened? And what had happened to the carcass in that time?"

"We'd obviously dissected it pretty thoroughly and pickled or frozen all the key parts, so everything that was left was in jars and bags. All of it was lost in the fire though."

"What do you know about it? The records imply it was probably started deliberately…."

"Well, yes, it might have been."

Jeremy noticed how Jean looked at Polly then averted her eyes.

"Do you know more than you should about this, Mrs Edwards?" he asked.

Jean gave a nervous little laugh and shook her head. "It's not my place to say."

"I wouldn't worry about that – everything you say here is confidential to this operation and will go no further, you have my word on that."

Jean thought for a few seconds.

"I suppose I have nothing to lose now," she said quietly. She took a deep breath.

"There were three of us. Betty and Roger are dead now, as far as I know, so no point trying to talk to them. We…. we……."

She looked up at Jeremy for a final re-assurance. He nodded his head gently.

"We did it. We destroyed the facility. We had to. It had become….. well, we were playing with nature. Trying to create monsters. The managers and the politicians, it was all about 'yields' and money to them, but where would it end? They were so focused on the short term. If we had succeeded in being able to breed giant animals, and that technology got into the wrong hands, well, it didn't bear thinking about. Before you know it, rogue countries would be releasing thirty foot long tigers at their enemies, or breeding locusts the size of cars to decimate the crops of their neighbours, that kind of thing. And we'd all be living in fear."

"We'd be living in a real world Jurassic Park," mused Polly.

"A park?"

"Sorry, yes, it was a film, about dinosaurs."

"Dinosaurs, yes, exactly. Imagine the size of a genetically modified elephant or giraffe. And think of what a naturally aggressive animal like the Tasmanian Devil could do if it was the size of a rhino. It doesn't bear thinking about. It could have turned into Armageddon. And our bosses were too wrapped up in their short term targets to understand this."

Polly smiled. "A GM elephant. And we've been worrying about GM crops."

"Indeed." Now she had unbottled her secret, Jean couldn't stop. "So we had made quite some progress in those six years, but there was just too much that we still didn't know. We'd managed to isolate some of the growth hormone from the giant rat and produced larger than normal rodents, although without the adenoma on the pituitary gland. We'd tried some cross-breeding too, to see if two larger animals of different species could produce a mutation where the adenoma was there from birth. And that was the catalyst really."

"What do you mean?"

"We had moved onto sheep and goats. It was too soon, but the managers wanted results. I don't think the politicians knew what we were doing. Our Chief Scientist, oh, what was his name now? Professor.... Professor Booth, that was it. He was a maverick – a bit mad really. He made us breed an animal that was a cross between a sheep and a goat, both of which had been given the rat's growth hormone. Those two, the parents if you like, were larger than average but not excessively so. But the offspring, it was grotesque. It grew like crazy, but especially the head. After four weeks it was nearly 40kg – that's well over three times what it should have been. And its head...... well, it was misshapen, and so large and heavy that the poor creature couldn't hold it up, so ended up just resting it on the floor. We couldn't tell if it had the adenoma until we killed it, but we were seeing how large it would grow. Professor Booth was delighted. He didn't care about its discomfort. The head could be held up in a pen, he said, while it grew. Then it would be slaughtered once it had reached maturity, whenever that was. Then we could move onto cows. But what we had done was just so cruel."

Jeremy intervened. "But you were already testing on animals – that's cruel in itself isn't it?"

Jean sighed. "I know, I know, in theory, yes. But rats and mice are very different from lambs, you know? Those big eyes staring despairingly at you, and the bleats were sometimes like the cry of a child. It wasn't the same. I'd had enough, and so had Roger, who worked with me, and Betty, who had only been there a few months and hadn't realised what she had got herself into. The bosses wouldn't back down, so we decided to do something about it."

"What did you do?"

"We hatched a plan. We were so scared, but…. we just had to do it, you know? It wasn't going to stop otherwise. We had to make it look like it wasn't us, that was the challenge. In the end, we just went back to basics. There was a basement store room on one side of the building, where we kept chemicals and other things. We knew some of them were highly flammable or reactive when exposed to heat. The room had one of those small, high-up windows that was below ground level but got daylight in through a grill above, like those big posh houses in London with basement suites. We made sure it was unlatched before we went home. Then both Betty and I each concealed a small bottle of diethyl ether in our bags on our way out. That way if one of us was stopped, the other might still get through. But to be honest once the security chap knew you, he generally didn't bother searching your handbag every time. So we both sailed past him, waving goodbye as though nothing was amiss."

"I'll bet your heart was in your mouth," observed Polly.

"Oh my goodness yes. I'd never done anything like that before, ever. I was a good girl! So this was terrifying."

"What was the diethyl ether for?" asked Jeremy.

"We used it sometimes for anaesthesia, but the thing is, it is highly flammable."

"Ahh, I see. Say no more."

"Anyway, a few hours later, after dark, the three of us met up at a pre-arranged spot, I can't remember where. Roger had brought a bottle with petrol in it so between the three of us we thought we had enough accelerant."

"Why didn't you just use the petrol?"

The petrol was the back up, in case the diethyl ether wasn't enough, or the bottles didn't break or something. We thought that if we could avoid using the petrol it might more easily be explained as an accident. An electrical fault or something."

"You'd thought of everything," said Jeremy with a wry smile, "quite the criminal mastermind!"

Jean shuddered. "Oh, don't! It still makes me nervous even talking about it now. To be honest, I rather wish my memory about those days was as bad as it is about everything else. It's something I wish I could forget, I really do."

"So what happened?" asked Polly, now very much tied up with the story.

"Well, there was virtually no security other than walls and gates. I think they thought that if they put up barbed wire fences and had patrolling security guards it would only attract attention. So every night the security guard would do his rounds, then lock it all up at 8pm and go home. All Roger had to do was scale the wall at the back, and luckily he was pretty athletic so that wasn't a problem. Once he was over, he helped Betty over too. I was the lookout. I handed them the bag with all the liquids in it, together with a hoe and a piece of drainpipe."

Polly sat back. "A hoe and a drainpipe?"

Jean grinned mischievously. "Don't worry, I'm not senile quite yet. Well, not completely, anyway. Yes, they had to poke the hoe down through the grill and hook the window open all the way up, so they could push the drainpipe down through the window, wedging it open. Then they withdrew the hoe, and let the bottles of diethyl ether drop down the drainpipe onto the floor of the store room."

"Clever."

"There was only one problem though."

"They didn't smash?"

"Exactly. They'd taken the lids off just in case, but that wasn't going to release as much of the liquid as if the bottles smashed, but all they heard was the bottles bouncing all over the floor. The glass was stronger than we thought. So obviously there would have been some spillage, but perhaps not enough, so they had no option but to throw the petrol down there too. That was a bigger bottle, but not designed for chemicals, and I heard that smash from where I was behind the wall. Then between them they lit a petrol soaked rag, released it down the pipe, and whoof! It went up in flames instantly. Poor old Roger and Betty ran like rabbits to the wall, hurled everything to me and then scrambled over as quick as they could."

"Wow," breathed Polly, enthralled. "Were there any houses nearby, who might see you running away?"

"There were a few at the end of the road, so once we'd reached them we slowed to a walk and split up, so as not to attract attention, and so if one of us was caught, the other two could say they had nothing to do with it. Roger went one way, and Betty and I the other, walking on opposite sides of the road, at about a fifty yard interval. It was very quiet though. It was a Sunday evening, so there was no one about. We knew there would be soon though, as we could hear little pops going off as some of the bottles of chemicals exploded. We walked quickly, let me tell you! I've never felt so scared in my life."

"And you got away with it?"

"Yes, when we arrived for work the next morning the whole place was just a charred ruin, smoke everywhere and firemen still hosing it down. We were told to go home, then the next day the police came and interviewed everyone, but of course we just denied all knowledge and provided alibis for each other. They couldn't prove anything. Thank goodness they didn't have those cameras we have these days."

"CCTV, you mean?"

Jean nodded.

"Or forensic DNA profiling," said Jeremy. "That's quite a story."

"Strangely, I think you did the right thing," said Polly. "We weren't ready back then to be tinkering with things like that. I know now we are experimenting using bovine growth hormone to stimulate cow's milk yields, but we know much more about what we are doing, and, believe it or not, the authorities are very strict about what is allowed with anything to do with growth hormones, knowing the potential consequences. Back then, it was wild west, effectively."

"I'm glad you said that," said Jean. "I still feel guilty about the animals in there that died, including the deformed lamb. It still haunts me when I think about it. But we had to think about how many we saved as well. I hope that outweighed it."

"I'm sure it did. There is one more thing that we both need to ask you, related to the situation we are in now. From all those years studying the dead gigarat, did you come across anything that might help us deal with it? Anything we could use to flush them out of the mine, for example?"

Jean clasped her hands together and brought them to her chin. "Well, now you are asking. I'll need to think about that."

Jeremy got to his feet and wandered over to the window. Out on the lawn Jason and Tommy were lowering the cage, with its newly restored lighting, down into the shaft. The brigadier stood clutching his tablet device, studying the picture on it as the cage descended. One of Berriman's in-the-know detectives was there too, although PC Rakowska's only real function, should the camera reveal a body, was limited to reporting back to Berriman. Would they see Norman down there, or just an empty bucket and some rotting vegetable remains?

He turned back to Jean.

"Any thoughts?"

Jean looked up at him. "Not really, I'm afraid. We were hampered really, by the rat being dead. If it had been alive, who knows what else we would have discovered."

"Exactly!" said Polly, with some feeling. "This is why I want to capture gigarats, not kill them all." She saw Jeremy smile. "Although you know that already."

"Yes Polly, your views are indeed known, and I understand them. But if we can't catch at least one of them tonight, we might just have to consider our options, if only to stop more people dying."

"But Norman Baston effectively killed himself! We can't base important scientific decisions, ones that could have profound benefits to humanity, on one person making a stupid decision, however tragic the consequences."

Jeremy gave a little shrug and walked back to his chair to pick up his briefcase. "Let's see what happens tonight first, shall we?"

"Oh, there was one thing!" Jean had sat up straight and was looking rather pleased with herself. "I just remembered!"

Jeremy hovered over his chair and then sat back down as he spoke. "Go on...."

"In the weeks prior to us finding the rat in the river, quite a few local people reported hearing a strange noise at night, a sort of loud ticking, they said."

Jeremy and Polly glanced at each other.

"Then once the dead rat was found, the locals didn't hear anything. So we wondered if there was a connection. Rats don't make noises like this normally, so had this huge rat developed a different method of communication – that's what we thought. So we did a lot of work looking at its vocal chords and ears."

Polly was getting excited that her theories might be verified, but didn't want to put words into Jean's mouth.

"Did you come to any conclusions?"

"Not conclusions so much as theories. We knew that humans affected by abnormal growth usually have much deeper voices, so we did some analysis on the vocal chords of the rat and discovered the same thing had happened to it, but also that the sounds heard by those local people could very easily have been made by this creature. Then we thought, why would it do that? Given that its eyes were so much less effective than a normal rat, this got us into thinking about....."

"Echolocation?" Polly couldn't contain herself any longer.

Jean looked a little startled. "Yes! How did you know?"

"Just a theory I had."

"Well, great minds, as they say. We all knew about the work done by a couple of scientists called...... what were they called now..... they both began with the same letter. Ah yes, Griffin was one and, er, Gal-somebody was the other. Galambos!"

She chuckled. "I'm surprising myself, now. Anyway, those two, and a few others over the previous two decades, had been researching how bats use echolocation, so this was a bit of a hot topic still. We compared the biology of the rat with the bats, and although we couldn't prove it, our findings were that it was entirely feasible that this rat was using a basic form of echolocation, albeit at a much lower frequency - one that humans can hear."

"Fascinating," said Polly softly.

"That being the case," mused Jeremy, "is there any way we can use that knowledge in our favour? Can they be disorientated if we somehow jammed their signal or something? I know this isn't radio frequencies but you know what I mean."

Polly looked at Jean, who smiled.

"It's possible, yes," she said. "I did quite a lot of study into it back then, as you might expect. One thing you might be able to make use of is that a creature that uses echolocation can become confused if you play back its own sonar to it. It causes the animal to make mistakes and become disorientated. So if you have a recording of it....."

"We do indeed," confirmed Jeremy, "although we might need to enhance it. But that is really useful, Mrs Edwards, thank you. And thank you for your time; what you have told us has been fascinating. And if you do think of anything else that might help us, please contact any one of my team immediately, won't you?"

Jean nodded. "Of course. And good luck."

Jeremy gave her a little wave after ushering Polly through the door ahead of him. "Thank you. We're going to need it."

CHAPTER 61

"Anything happening?"

"Not really. Still lowering that cage."

Lauren turned back from the window, ambled over to the sofa and flopped herself down. She checked the time on her phone: still thirty minutes before she had to head off for work.

"When is this going to end? The stress is killing me. Why can't they just pump some gas down there or something, kill the rat, find all the human remains, figure out the rat ate everyone, and tell us we are in the clear? Simple as that."

Trey emerged from the bedroom, screwdriver in hand, the loose handle on the wardrobe now fixed.

"I wish it was." He glanced out of the window, then sat down next to his wife, putting his arm around her. "But instead it's ridiculously complicated, 'cause they want to catch the thing alive. And meanwhile that police chief still suspects me. Can't blame him really."

Lauren sighed. "It would be quite hard to, seeing as he's kinda right. Babes, I'm so sorry. I started all this when I pushed Anita, but now you're the one in their sights as much as me, thanks to what happened with John. Why did that stupid woman have to barge into our cellar?"

Trey gave her shoulder a squeeze. "Exactly. She only had herself to blame, in a way. If she'd kept her nose out, she'd be alive, and so would John, probably."

"I don't think that's how a jury would look at it, though."

"No. No, they wouldn't."

They sat and stared at the dark, silent TV screen opposite. It looked almost like a horizontal hole in the wall, black and featureless. A least a rat wouldn't jump out of it, thought Trey.

He manoeuvred himself free and got up to look out of the window.

"I suppose it takes quite a while to lower something three hundred feet – they're still at it."

He turned to face his wife.

"But look on the bright side. As soon as they do find those bones, the chances are they will just have to conclude that somehow Anita and

Hoggo ended up in those tunnels, and were maybe dragged in by the rat through some other entrance."

"A rat that doesn't like daylight and only appears at night so wouldn't have snatched them during the day."

"Well, yes, I know. But.... I've been thinking about that. And the more I think about it the more I think I might have an idea."

His eyes shining with hope, he hurried over and crouched down in front of Lauren.

"As you said, the biggest issue with our accounts of what happened is Hoggo and Anita going missing during the day, yes?"

"Yes."

"So to disprove our argument that the rat must have dragged them into the tunnels and it was nothing to do with us, they have to prove it couldn't come out in daylight. For all they know it just squinted a bit to keep most of the light out, or closed its eyes and navigated by radar or something."

"Maybe that's what all those clicks and noises were about?"

"Yes! Yes! Like bats. Echo location. Brilliant! So the only way they could confirm that the gigarat didn't come out during daylight hours and grab Hoggo and Anita from the woods, would be if they can catch one alive and test its sight and what it does in daylight. So, you see where I'm going with this?"

"No."

"We make sure none of those rats, assuming there is more than one, comes out alive. I mean they can probably check the echo location thing on a dead one but not so easily. But how would they know how well it could really tolerate light if it was ravenously hungry? Maybe its food sources dried up down there and it had come out to find a badger or something but stumbled across Molly Baines and realised humans made good meals too. It couldn't find any more at night so decided to risk coming out during the day, and bingo, there in the woods were Anita and then Hoggo. It could make sense!"

Lauren stared at her husband, processing his logic.

"Well, ok, that's all well and good, but there's just one tiny problem."

"Yes, I know, we'd have to kill the rats before the DUST team capture them. Let me think about that."

Lauren's eyes widened. "Oh. No, babes, no. You're not going down there again. No way. I'd rather go to jail than that. Do you hear me?"

Trey winced slightly as he rose to his feet.

"Yeah, well, it's the last thing I want to do too. And I can't see an easy way I could do it anyway, now we can't get into the cellar. So maybe there's another way."

He returned to the window.

"Maybe the DUST team can help us."

"Why would they want to do that?"

"They wouldn't. So we engineer things a little bit. I've got some thoughts but I just need to mull them over, ok?"

"Fine, just promise me you won't go down there again."

Trey didn't answer. Nothing should be off the table. It was either that or both of them ended up in court for murder and manslaughter charges, and in his view, that was worse.

CHAPTER 62

"Right," announced Jeremy. "It's five thirty pm and as far as I'm aware we are on target for tonight's operation. Thanks to everyone for coming, as I appreciate we are all busy. Welcome also to our four police colleagues who are attending for the first time. This is definitely a case of all hands on deck now."

Davis, Rakowska, Collins and Bartram, out of police uniform in jeans and t-shirts, glanced nervously at each other.

"We're meeting in the cellar here because it would waste too much time to head back to the police station."

"For you, maybe," noted Berriman, tugging at his jacket, "that's where we've just come from". He hadn't dressed down, as his intention was very much to direct and observe, not get hands-on. A senior officer needed to retain some dignity and authority.

"Agreed," conceded Jeremy, "but I think we would also have struggled to all fit into that interview room."

Berriman looked at his feet, unable to disagree.

"So, let's crack on. Charles – thank you for organising that temporary cover for the vent behind us. I'd always felt uneasy about leaving that open and the trapdoor was just too heavy to be lifting up and down should we need to."

The brigadier nodded, despite knowing that Peters, standing behind him, had done all the work. Peters had now returned to the team after being detailed to watch over McGuire in hospital, in case the wounded soldier started to say anything he shouldn't have done.

"First things first, so that everyone is up to date. Charles, can you please advise the group on what your initial cage drop exercise this morning revealed."

The brigadier cleared his throat. "Yes, when the camera reached the bottom of the shaft, there was no sign of a body unfortunately. However, one of our metal buckets was there, and also a lump of material on the tunnel floor which we subsequently identified as being a scarf. Investigations by our police colleagues here, talking to the residents, confirmed it to be one often worn when gardening by Norman Baston."

"It looks pretty conclusive then," observed Jeremy.

Berriman chipped in. "All the evidence to date would lead us to conclude that Mr Baston has become another victim of the gigarat, and that in this particular case at least, we are not pursuing a murder inquiry."

"Not for Molly Baines either?"

"Almost certainly not. For the other three, we cannot rule anything in or out yet."

The frustration in his voice was clear. He was under pressure to solve multiple mysteries, yet to a great extent his hands were tied. If the DUST team were not successful in their mission, there was every chance he would fail too. He needed them to get those rats out of the mine.

Jeremy turned to Polly. "Any luck with the blood samples, Polly?"

Polly held up her mobile phone. "Yes, preliminary results came through just fifteen minutes ago. The blood was human. The lab analysed the in vitro quality, including aggregation, deformability, osmotic fragility, microvesiculation, phosphatidyl......."

"Polly," interrupted Jeremy, "none of us has any idea what you are talking about."

"No, right, sorry. Basically, the tests were pretty conclusive that this is from a person, not a rat."

"Have you got a match with Baston?"

"So far, not conclusively, but it is looking likely. We're doing further tests now and getting hold of his medical records."

Jeremy looked at Berriman. "Sounds like that will be the absolute proof you need when the results come through. Thank you Polly. Tommy, you managed to source your exploration robot."

Tommy nodded. "Yep, it arrived around lunchtime. We call it Charlie, don't know why really. Anyway, so we sent Charlie down on the rope around half past one, together with the wifi range extender on a separate rope. We also sourced more cables and connected them to the old ones at the surface. That way we could get Charlie as far as the wifi signal would allow us to see pictures."

"And what did you see?"

"Tunnels. That was it. No sign of any rat."

"So we reckon its neck wasn't broken when it had the cage in its mouth?"

"Not unless it can run around with a broken neck. We've just pulled Charlie back up."

"Right. Ok." Jeremy ran his hand through his hair. "This rat seems to be not only indestructible, but always one step ahead of us, too. Charles, you have some better news though."

"Yes, our divers in the river have found what must be the entrance to the tunnels, underwater. About three hundred yards west of here, the river passes a bit of a rocky outcrop, and about fifteen feet down, they found a hole about six feet wide, heading back up into the rock. Obviously they were briefed not to venture in to confirm where it went. But it looks like we've found where our friend the rat was emerging from the mine."

"Excellent. Progress at last! So they're rigging up the lights now……"

"Yes. Running cable to a generator. They'll switch the whole thing on as soon as the sun sets. It's a powerful LED floodlight, secured to the rock and pointed directly at whatever decides to try coming out."

"That should stop it in its tracks, if our theory is correct. And the cover story?"

"The men have been told that it's a scientific study of unique cave dwelling river otters and one was spotted here. We've rigged up an underwater camera too, to back that up, which could come in handy."

"Why would that need the army though?"

"More of a training exercise, we told them."

"For which they had to be dragged off other jobs at short notice?"

"All part of the training. See how responsive we can be."

"Clever."

The brigadier smiled. "I thought so too."

"And the additional truck has arrived?"

"Yes, I've had some lads getting that into position and tying the netting directly to each truck as well as leaving some stakes on the ground. It's ready. If the rat is thrashing around in there, it won't get out."

"Thank you; let's hope you're right. Great work everyone. Now, tonight. I have the plan."

He held up a piece of paper covered in scribbled action points, some of which had been crossed out.

"Everyone needs to be crystal clear as to what they are doing, and where they should be. We can't afford to have any accidents or incidents like yesterday."

Peters could be heard mumbling a quiet 'hear hear'.

"So, this time we have the advantage of not having to worry about there being anyone inside the netting. We will all be outside, most of us well away from the danger area."

He directed his gaze directly at Polly.

"Your last chance, Polly, to change your mind?"

She shook her head firmly. "Absolutely not. I want to be the one firing the tranquiliser. I know what I'm doing."

"Alright. Thank you. In that case, you will be stationed around twenty feet back from the netting, ready to fire as soon as the gigarat emerges."

"'Scuse me!" Tommy raised a hand. "How long will it take? The tranquiliser, you know, to take effect? When will we be safe?"

"It's a good question," replied Polly. "I've not sedated a giant rat before. But given its size I'm estimating three to five minutes before it's completely safe to approach based on the dosage. Don't hold me to that though."

"So it could still be charging around in our truck, or even the net, for five minutes before it calms down?" The brigadier was looking worried.

"It would be getting gradually more woozy though."

"Just put loads of fermented apples in those buckets as well, that should knock it out," suggested Tommy. "Make it happier too."

"Not a bad idea actually. But we've no time for that now I'm afraid."

"Talking of the truck," said Jeremy to the brigadier, "did you manage to rig up a slicker way of closing those doors? I saw some army mechanics with power drills doing something to them earlier."

"Ah, yes, they were putting self-closing mechanisms on them. We've rigged up a little trip wire – just a bit of string really – which will activate the doors and they will swing shut, hopefully trapping the rat inside. We've tested it and it works."

"Great, thank you. Now, back to people. Polly I've mentioned already. Private Peters, you'll station yourself adjacent to Polly, ready to shoot and kill the gigarat if anything goes wrong. That command will come either from Polly, the brigadier here, or myself. Do not fire without authority. Understood?"

Peters nodded.

"As backup, we have Detective Sergeant Collins, who I understand is an AFO – an authorised firearms officer, that is - and the brigadier. You two will position yourself on the other side of the grass, but all of you facing away from the house. No one is to stand on the other side of the netting, for obvious reasons, with one brief exception, as I will now explain. Some of you will have seen that we've now got a handle screwed into in the cover for the shaft, and a rope attached to it on both sides stretching out underneath the netting. I need two volunteers to crawl under the net at around eight o'clock, and remove the planters from the cover, then come back out on the far side, and pull the cover off at my command. That done, you'll need to quickly run back round to our side and get ready to pull the cover back over the shaft if the gigarat comes out, so it can't get back down. I'm thinking the younger, fitter members of our team may be best placed. Anyone?"

Jason raised his hand, and, seeing that, Detective Constable Bartrum felt he should too.

"Thank you gentlemen. In the situation I described, once the cover is back on you are effectively spare hands to help out wherever is needed. You are my contingency, in that sense. Tommy, you're in charge of the floodlight – the one we used on the cage. It's a last resort as we don't want to frighten the rat, but if all else fails and things are getting out of hand, switch it on. It will also give us a clearer sight if we need to shoot it. We've got an interim switch this time so you won't have to stand round the corner of the house like Jason did."

"Righto."

Jeremy surveyed the room. "So, that leaves Rob, and constables Rakowska and Davis. I'll need one of you please to assist in filming everything, so that we have backup footage if we need it. I say assist because we have a video camera on a tripod upstairs at an open landing window, which Jason set up earlier. After this meeting he will go up and start it recording. But it would be sensible to have someone else filming down here at ground level from the back of the house, using the camera on their phone."

All there looked at each other. Rakowska was the first to slowly raise a hand. "I'll do it. My phone is good in low light."

"Thank you. So Rob and Constable Davis, could you guys please keep the residents informed and under control and make double sure that none of them switch on their lights at the back of the house or attempt to come out into the garden."

The two men murmured their agreement, neither of them too disappointed not to be out on the lawn at the mercy of a potentially escaped gigarat.

"Thank you. To be clear then. Once it is dark, at around 8pm, we haul off the cover, then, with the tree lopper we found in the garage, I'll push our pre-positioned bucket of fresh rotten food – bit of an oxymoron, that – into the shaft. We think that's what Norman Baston did and it seemed to work. Then we stand back and wait. The rat should remember it got a human meal last time and it might be looking for another, but the smell of food in the truck – it really reeks, doesn't it - should lure it straight in there. The doors close behind it, and bingo, we've caught our gigarat. There's a hole in the side for Polly to point the dart gun, if she hasn't already fired it of course. Ok Polly?"

"Yes."

Polly looked understandably nervous. She would probably get closer to this violent, man-eating rodent than anyone. But it was worth it. To capture and work on a creature like this could be a career-changing opportunity.

"Good. Then Peters, once you and Charles here have unhooked the net from the truck, you both jump in the front with Polly, and she'll direct you to her lab. She'll have a team at the other end ready to unload the cargo. Are we all clear?"

There were grunts and assorted nods of agreement.

"Excellent. Now, let's all proceed with our preparations and assemble at our positions no later than a quarter to eight. Melanie Firwell on the ground floor has very kindly offered to do us sandwiches, despite having only just lost her husband. We'll get those distributed to you all later. So, let's get to it and catch a gigarat!"

CHAPTER 63

Trey had watched the army men finish up their tasks and troop back round the house, chatting and joking. Must be nice to have so few worries that they can do that. He hadn't properly laughed at all since Anita fell down the vent, he reflected. When your heart and soul is crushed, the medicine of laughter is on too high a shelf to reach.

All the people he recognised, including the police officers who had first questioned them, had continued to mill around out there doing this and that, until suddenly at half past five they all disappeared, and he could hear the mumbling of voices beneath his feet. They must be in the cellar, having an update meeting. This was his chance.

Lauren was now at work so he had no one to vet his actions or hold him back. He stepped out through the French windows and glanced at the cellar door. Firmly shut. Good.

He walked quickly over to the truck containing the buckets of by now quite pungent rat enticing matter – ratnip, if you like – and made his way round to the other side, where he could look back and see the house. He was looking for faces at windows, but there were none.

He dropped to the ground and slid under the back axle of the truck. The ties for the net had been very tightly secured to the shafts either side of the differential, using knots and plastic cable ties. Trey had watched Peters working on this earlier, the binoculars he got for Christmas coming in handy.

He reached into his pocket and pulled out some wire cutters. To be fair Peters had done a good job. There were about thirty or forty ties, all securely cable-tied and tightened. This wouldn't be easy. He levered the cutters under the first cable tie, wiggling to get it in as far as possible before squeezing hard and snapping off the first thick plastic strap and putting it in his pocket. The next three were a little easier, once he had honed his technique.

Once he'd clipped off all of them, if they caught a gigarat in that net, chances are it would pretty soon start pulling the stays out and squirm out of the net. By the time they realised what had happened there would be no time for a tranquiliser dart to take effect - they would have to shoot it. Result: a dead gigarat, less able to disprove his theory about it coming out in daylight. It wasn't a foolproof plan by any means, and he could be wrong on what they could test on a dead animal, but it was all he had got.

But then, as he angled the cutters under the next tie, he paused. He needed to think about this; perhaps it wasn't such a good idea after all. Suppose the gigarat injured or even killed someone? That would be terrible, and worse even than what happened with John; he would never forgive himself. He was relying on them shooting the animal, but what if a gun jammed, or the gigarat was too quick for them? He'd seen the video of it taking down the cage with the camera in it, and it came out of nowhere. It was seriously fast.

He lay there, panicking, his mind swirling. He had to decide, and quickly. They could all come out of that cellar any minute and then he would have no escape route.

No, he couldn't do it. This was wrong, it was too risky, and putting more lives in potential danger. He quickly backed himself out from under the truck and got to his feet, brushing the grass off his clothes. There were four loose net stays now but hopefully the others would be enough to still hold the net firm. He checked: yes, all the snipped off bits of plastic were in his pocket – mustn't leave any evidence. Unless someone from the DUST team got back under the truck again, they would be none the wiser.

He checked the windows of the house; still no sign of anyone. He ran back across the grass and into his apartment, his heart rate far higher than was good for him.

He had only been back in his lounge for three or four minutes when he heard the cellar door open and voices emerging into the garden. That was a quick meeting - close shave or what? If he had stayed out there and carried on sabotaging their rat trap, that could have been curtains for him. He had made the right decision, from all perspectives.

He turned on the six o'clock news to try and calm himself down, but the newsreader may as well have been reading out nursery rhymes as nothing she said registered with him. His brain was still pre-occupied by what he had planned to do, what he actually did, and what he didn't do. On this occasion, it was what he didn't do that gave him the greatest reason to be thankful.

CHAPTER 64

"Rob, could you be so good as to check with your men stationed on the gate that no one is in the house or grounds who shouldn't be?"

Berriman sniffed. "No need, my friend. I spoke to them ten minutes ago. They know their instructions. The woods are taped off too, of course, and I have an officer stationed discretely at the entrance from the road. Don't want to attract attention."

"Indeed. Thank you."

Jeremy checked his watch.

"Right, it's five to eight. I think everyone is in their positions. Except you perhaps! Time to head inside and help Davis keep tabs on the residents?"

Berriman suddenly felt somewhat excluded from the action, but then remembered that inside was safer than outside, so nodded.

"Yes, I'll head off. I'll keep an eye on what's going on in case you need me. Good luck."

Jeremy watched the rear end of the Chief Superintendent disappearing round the corner, then turned to look at the assembled team who were standing nervously in their positions, waiting for his signal.

The sun had dropped and star-speckled blackness was fast spreading across to sky to crush down the sinking hues of blue and gold. There was a thickening chill in the air.

He walked across to where the brigadier and DS Collins were standing, clutching their weapons, legs slightly apart.

"You look ready," he said.

"We are," said the brigadier, patting his army issue Glock 17. "Although I have to say, if I don't hear your command and that animal is putting anyone in danger, I'm firing anyway. Just so you know."

"That's fair enough. Last resort though, yes? Ok, DS Collins?"

She nodded, her jaw set firm.

"Good. I'll be just behind you, keeping an eye on what everyone is doing."

He moved across to where Polly was standing, finger hooked on the trigger of her dart gun, 16mm feathered dart loaded. Private Peters, next to her, held a Heckler and Koch SA80 assault weapon. No rat was going to survive a burst from that.

"You both ready?"

"As we'll ever be," said Polly. Peters just said "sir", with a growl that made it clear he was focused on what lay ahead.

"Thank you. Stand by."

Jeremy walked slowly back to the centre of the lawn, thinking. Had he forgotten anything? Had they covered all eventualities? Probably not, but you can't foresee the unforeseen.

Jason had set the video camera running up on the landing and was now on the far side of the netting with Bartrum, both of them holding the rope and waiting for the signal.

Jeremy took one last look all around him, then, like a Roman Emperor, gradually raised his thumb. "Ok, go!" he cried.

The two men pulled at the rope and the heavy wooden cover slid and bumped its way onto the grass, revealing the gaping hole beneath. Jeremy stepped forward to the net and grabbed the end of the pre-positioned lopping shears. A series of small thrusts, aimed at the bucket of vegetable matter, tipped it over, tumbling it and most of its contents into the shaft to begin its long descent.

"That'll do!" he grunted, getting hastily to his feet and retreating behind the brigadier and Collins. "Now we wait."

It was no more than ninety seconds before they heard something. That familiar rumbling, tak-a-tak noise, in the far, far distance. The nervous joking and laughing stopped. They tensed, heartbeats rising as one. The gigarat was down there. It was coming.

The faint noise stopped. Jeremy could imagine the massive rat snuffling around at the bottom of the shaft, hoovering up the vegetable matter so kindly offered up by the equally tasty humans above. He glanced at Polly. She had her dart gun raised, trained on the entrance to the hole. Three hundred feet would be a lengthy climb for a human, but the phrase 'rat up a drainpipe' was associated with speed, and despite its size, they knew the gigarat moved quickly.

He checked his phone. He had an audio recording of the gigarat, the volume turned up to maximum. As soon as it was in sight and started making its noise, he would press play.

Then the distant clicking started up again, and got louder. And louder. Any second now...

Just as it sounded as though it was upon them, it stopped. Silence. Polly threw a worried glance to Peters, standing next to her, whose eyes did not stray from the target.

Then it was there. A huge shiny-furred, yellow-toothed head, rising menacingly up from the depths, over-sized whiskers twitching as it sniffed the fresh night air, claws pressed against the sides of the shaft.

This was the first time they had seen it in the flesh, and there were a couple of suppressed gasps. The rat twisted its head left and right. Had it heard them? Could it see them standing there? It looked as though it could, the way its head turned. Suddenly the net felt like no protection at all.

Polly trained her sights on the animal but she couldn't shoot it in the face – she had to wait.

Without warning the rat moved. Despite its size it was up and out of the shaft in a split second. Polly fired but the body she was aiming at had gone by the time the dart arrived, and it flew harmlessly into the dark night behind.

The gigarat shot straight up the ramp and into the truck. The doors slammed shut behind it, to the accompaniment of a "YES!" from Tommy and a fist pump from Bartram.

Jeremy and the brigadier glanced at each other, eyes wide. What? Had it been that easy?

As Jason and Bartrum started to pull the cover back over the shaft, everything changed. A second gigarat scrabbled out of the shaft.

Polly had been loading a second dart into her gun from the pouch on her waist, but had only got as far as getting the dart out when the movement caught her eye, and she looked up.

"Shoot it, Polly!" she could hear Jeremy cry, but she wasn't ready. With the truck door closed this gigarat had only one food source to hone in on, and as luck would have it there was a variety of human meals awaiting it on the other side of the net.

Its clicks and growls might have helped it identify potential food, but it had obviously not previously encountered a net and its echolocation was not that refined. It ploughed headfirst into it.

"Don't kill it yet!" called Jeremy as all of them stepped back sharply. "Polly, fire when you're ready!"

Given more time Polly would have looked up at Jeremy and given him a "really?" look, but suddenly her fingers were made of jelly, and as she tried to push the dart into the gun's loading chamber, she dropped it.

"Shit!" she exclaimed, bending down.

Jeremy quickly fumbled with his phone, pressed 'play' and held it out in front of him. Two sets of clicking met each other.

The gigarat, now loudly firing out its taka-taka signals, backed away from the net and shot across to the other side at such speed that it again careered straight into the netting, stretching and pulling it but this time getting one of its teeth caught.

It thrashed and squirmed, bucking its head up with such force that the four loosened net stays flew free and, unseen by the DUST team on the other side, a small gap appeared between the bottom of the net and the ground.

"Now, sir?" called Peters, finger poised on the trigger, eyes unblinking.

Jeremy flashed a look at Polly. She had the dart now, and was slotting it into the gun.

"No!" he shouted. "Polly, quickly!"

Polly didn't need telling, but as she raised her rifle, the gigarat, now with some leverage at the base of the net, flung its head up and ripped up a whole row of net stays in the grass. Before anyone could react, it was squeezing out, heading behind the truck.

"Fire!" ordered Jeremy, now talking to Charles, Collins and Peters. "Kill it!"

All three fired once but the gigarat was too quick, and had already disappeared from sight.

"Tommy, the light! Guys, run back!"

As the others headed for the house, Tommy, extension lead socket in one hand and the plug from the light in the other, froze. Like Polly, fright got the better of him, and he fumbled to connect them, the 3 pin plug managing to get half way in before jamming.

"Bugger," he muttered, looking up to see a blur of yellow teeth and fur heading towards him at breakneck speed.

As he felt impact and the rat's claws sliced into his torso, a burst of gunfire rang out as Peters was the first to turn and shoot. A hail of bullets thudded into the hindquarters of the gigarat, which let out a curdling scream, let go of Tommy, and turned to address the source of what had just injured it.

It started to run at Peters, but found that one of its back legs no longer worked. Dragging it and clicking furiously, it tried to charge at the soldier, whose response was to stand his ground and keep his finger on the trigger, screaming a testosterone roar as bullet after bullet slammed and spattered into the face of the slowing animal.

Just ten feet from Peters it finally stopped and collapsed, blood pouring from a forest of facial puncture wounds, and the clicking ceased. The tail twitched, its stomach heaved one last time, and then it was still.

Peters pumped one last three-shot burst into its body and let the assault rifle drop to his side. His aggression sated, he started to breathe heavily, compensating for his lack of oxygen intake while dealing with the gigarat.

"Help!"

Tommy was lying in a twisted heap on the grass, groaning. Collins and the brigadier, both first aid trained, rushed over to him, before Collins sprinted off to the police car to get a first aid kit.

Jeremy noticed Polly was on the ground too, and hastened over to her. "Are you ok? What happened?"

"I tripped over as I ran away. Maybe that saved me as it brushed right past me and headed for Tommy. Is he badly injured?" She rose unsteadily to her feet.

"Probably, I would imagine. I guess he presented a bigger target than you, standing up. Oh, hang on...." He looked back over his shoulder. "Jason! Can you and Bartrum get that cover back over the hole ASAP and stick the planters back? We don't want a third one appearing."

The two men, already edging slowly back, nodded and got to work.

"Right, the first rat, we need to sedate it. That truck is taking a bit of a hammering and I don't want those doors giving way. Got your dart gun ready now?"

Polly had been loading while Jeremy spoke. "Yes. Right, here goes."

She strode over to the shaking truck and looked through the 3 inch wide hole that had been drilled in the side of it. All she could see were blurs of darkness, some slightly shiny, constantly moving as the rat bolted around the inside of the van trying to escape. She rested the barrel of the rifle on the lip of the hole but it was jolted every time the animal banged into the sides of the truck.

"We need to calm it down," she cried at Jeremy above the noise of the banging. "I can't see what I'm firing at."

"Hang on." Jeremy got his phone out again and opened the sound app. He pressed play and held the speaker end of his phone close to the hole as it fired out a barrage of gigarat clicking.

Almost immediately the rat stopped moving.

Polly took a shot.

"Got it! I think so, anyway. Let's give it ten minutes. If nothing happens I'll try another one."

Jeremy turned his phone app off. "Thanks to Jean for that. It worked. Now, let's check the others."

He hurried over to DC Collins, now crouching next to the wounded Tommy and applying bandages. "We need an ambulance! He's bleeding heavily."

Jeremy cursed internally. The last thing he needed was an ambulance crew on site with the dead gigarat just yards away. He strode over to see for himself, remembering that his concern for poor Tommy couldn't override the mission, which was now to get both these rats offsite as quickly as possible before anyone else saw them.

Tommy's thick black jacket was shredded at the front, and damp with blood oozing through each tear. His jeans had some minor rips too, from which blood was seeping through. Thank goodness it was not a warm summer's evening, thought Jeremy, otherwise his clothes might have provided no protection at all.

"Can we carry him round the front of the house?" he asked.

The brigadier looked up. "Could be risky. He might have internal injuries, or broken ribs."

"No," grunted Tommy, his face contorted in pain, "I'm ok. Just a flesh wound."

He tried to grin but it turned into a grimace. "No bones broken. You can lift me. I won't scream the whole time. Just most of it."

Jeremy smiled. Still the cheeky chappy despite his injuries. "Charles, once Jason and DC Bartrum have got the planters back on the cover, let's get them over here and the four of you can carry Tommy round to the front. Maybe take him to hospital in a police car if he is up to it."

DS Collins stood up. "Not sure the super would be too keen on our seats getting covered in blood, though. Oh, talk of the devil."

She had spotted the destined-to-be-rotund figure of Berriman hastening around the corner of the house, arms swinging as though on a military parade in order to hurry himself along without the effort of running. He marched up to the group.

"I came down as soon as I saw what had happened. How's Tommy?"

"In need of medical attention," said Jeremy. "Can we use one of your police cars to get him to hospital? And is there any chance you could go with him?"

"Why me?"

"Because with injuries like that the doctors are going to think there has been a knife crime, and want the police involved. Either that or they'll think Wolverine is on the loose. You can nip it in the bud by telling them the case is confidential, not to spread fear in the community, and you have it under control. They may not be so inclined to believe a lower ranking officer." He glanced at Collins. "No offence."

Collins shrugged. "Not much taken."

Berriman sighed. "Alright. Erica, can you get a blanket out of the boot and lay it across the back seat. Once we've dropped him off at the hospital though, we're coming back."

"Good, thank you. Oh, and are the residents ok? Did they see anything?"

"Davis was with the Wilsons, I was with Jean Edwards, and we kept them away from the windows. Don't want an old lady having a heart attack seeing what happened."

"To be honest I don't think she was the one who needed protecting. What about Melanie Firwell and the Clarks?"

"Only Trey Clark is home but yes, we told them, but I'd be surprised if they didn't look, especially when they heard the noise. And they'll all see that rat on the lawn now."

"Yes, well, at least that proves we weren't making it up. You'll check their phone for photos and videos, won't you?"

"Of course." Berriman hadn't thought of that and so made a mental note to instruct Davis to command that the residents wipe any photos they may have attempted to take.

Jason and DC Bartrum had worked quickly to get the planters back on the shaft cover and were now ready to assist carrying Tommy to the police car, so they and the brigadier and DS Collins carefully lifted him up and made their slow way round to the front of the house. All of them would be washing blood out of their clothes the next day.

Jeremy turned to Polly.

"How are we doing with our friend in the truck?"

"Less agitated now, but that could just be because she's getting tired. I'll give it another 5 minutes. Don't want to over-dose her on sedatives."

"No. How do you know it's a 'she'?"

"Because the one on the lawn is a 'he'. I checked. So I'm assuming it was a mating pair. Could be wrong of course."

"So what are we going to do with the dead one? I suppose you want to get it to your labs too?"

"Definitely, especially if they are different sexes. Just a shame we won't be able to breed them."

"A shame? I'd say it's a blessing. Anyway, good job we have a 2nd truck. The problem is going to be getting it in there. We'll need a strong sheet like a tarpaulin, then a big effort from all of us to get it up the ramp and into the back of the truck."

Polly looked sceptical. "But that thing must weigh at least 300 kilos."

"Well, that's true, yes. When Charles re-appears I might just have a little job for him."

CHAPTER 65

In the dark of the apartment it was easy for Trey to observe what was going on outside without being noticed. There was no way he was missing this – Berriman could say what he wanted, Trey wasn't listening.

But he had watched in horror as events unfolded. Had those four cable ties he had removed allowed that second gigarat to escape? Ok, this had led to it being killed, and that is what he wanted, but his worst fear had come true too when the rat torpedoed into Tommy like a train hitting a car stranded on a level crossing. Was that down to him? Would the rat have escaped anyway?

His stomach was churning. Not only had he hastened the death of an innocent man to save himself, but now his actions might have led to the severe wounding of a guy who probably had a wife and kids, and from what he had seen, had been badly mauled. Supposing he didn't survive either?

He punched the sofa, hurting his hand. Why did he start cutting those ties? Why did he ever think that encouraging a gigarat to run wild with people close by was a good idea?

It was just over a week ago now that Lauren had inadvertently pushed Anita down that vent, which had set off this terrible chain of events. So much awfulness in such a short space of time. Before that, his life was normal, happy, unremarkable. Now..... the definition of a nightmare. He'd become a person that he would despise if confronted with himself.

Was there any point carrying on? Should he and Lauren consider a suicide pact? No, no. Why should she end her own life? She's done nothing wrong. But he had.

He went to the kitchen and opened the cutlery drawer. A selection of knives stared back at him. He slammed it shut again. Too soon, Trey, too soon. See if the man survives his wounds first.

But, the other big problem – the DUST team have caught a live gigarat. They can test its vision, expose it to different levels of daylight. See how likely it might be that it would come out during the day. If they conclude that it never would have done, it's back to Trey Clark to explain the disappearances of Anita and Hoggo. The spotlight would be intense. More interviews, more opportunities to trip up.

But what's the answer, and is there anything he can do while the live gigarat is still out there in a truck on the grass? He went back to the window and scanned the lawn.

There was Mr Stanton-Davies with the female scientist and Private Peters, and he could see that PC Davis was joining them now. Doing some verbal post-mortems, perhaps. Their operation had only been partially successful and the dual failures of the dead gigarat and the tunnel expert's injuries meant that whooping and back-slaps were out of the question. He wondered if they would check how some of the net stays had come loose and realise that the plastic cable ties had gone - they'd be going in a council rubbish bin in town tomorrow before anyone searched his flat.

The brigadier, DS Collins and DC Bartrum appeared to his right, walking glumly and silently back across the lawn.

Should he go out and join them, see if they need some help? Anything he could overhear might give him an opportunity to...... he didn't know what. Short of wrenching the assault rifle off Peters, running across to the truck and pumping a round of bullets into the surviving gigarat, he was all out of options. And he'd never used a gun in his life, let alone a type of machine gun, or whatever that was. Also, by doing that he might as well put his hands up and plead guilty there and then. It was hopeless.

In any case, if he did walk across to them, Stanton-Davies would pretty soon tell him to go back in. He stayed where he was, his brain thrashing about in a foggy maze, trying to find a way out.

"I don't understand," said the brigadier. "The net gave way like we'd not secured it. Private Peters, have you anything to say?"

Peters, still buzzing from his Rambo-style heroics in saving the day, and envisaging being awarded at least a commendation and possibly a gallantry medal, was brought suddenly back down to earth.

"Me, sir?"

"Yes. You secured the net stays, didn't you?"

"Yes, sir. Very securely sir. I don't understand how that animal could have done that."

"No, nor can I."

The brigadier walked a few feet over the where the edge of the net lay.

"Looking at all these net stays, there are a few at the end here with no ties on them. Did you miss these?"

Peters joined him and examined the stays.

"That doesn't make any sense sir. I tied them all with a double reef knot as we agreed, every single one, with a cable tie threaded through and tightened as far as it would go. Hundred per cent I didn't miss any of them sir. It's impossible."

The brigadier glanced across at Jeremy. "Something odd here."

Jeremy nodded. But sabotage?? That didn't make sense. Why would anyone want one of these animals rampaging around outside?

"Ok let's park that for now. Now we are all back our focus should be on getting both gigarats out of here. Charles, before you and Peters head off with Polly in the truck, how do you suggest we get this dead one into the other truck? Have you got a tarpaulin we can slide it onto?"

The brigadier gave a little snort. "Ha! As luck would have it – yes. In the back of the other truck. I made sure it came with some emergency kit, just in case. Can everyone help now in taking down this net so we can free up the truck? Then we'll move the ramp over. And let's get that light switched on so we can see what we're doing."

Trey watched as the lawn was suddenly illuminated by the LED floodlight that Tommy had struggled to connect. The seven figures busied themselves around the truck like a team of ants dismembering a cockroach, and soon the net was down and the back of the second truck open, ramp laid ready.

The tarpaulin was tucked under one side of the dead gigarat, then the other side pulled over the top of it such that it was wrapped in green. Looks like they were going to try and roll it over, then drag it into the truck. That wouldn't be easy. Maybe he could help.

Jeremy didn't see Trey approaching until he was right next to him.
"Need a hand?"
"That's kind of you to offer, but..."
"More hands the better!" called out the brigadier.
Jeremy relented.
"Alright, thank you."

Trey nodded at Polly, who he had spoken to earlier, and took his place next to her.

All eight of them crouched down, and pushed their hands under the still warm, fleshy, furry body of the rat. If it had been a dog everyone would have been fine with it, but knowing it was a rat caused some of the group to feel distinctly queasy.

"Three... two... one... lift!"

On the brigadier's command they all heaved, and like a strongman lifting a giant tyre, the rat was slowly rolled over.

With the body now upside down on the tarpaulin, exposing its hard, scaly belly, they all took hold of the ropes attached to the ringlets on one side, and pulled and hauled, inching it up the ramp. Davis and the brigadier, being the largest in body weight, took station at the rear to push and also make sure the rat didn't slip.

When the doors were finally closed on the truck there were some fist pumps and hand slaps accompanied by exclamations of relief.

With the live gigarat now sedated and silent in the back of the other truck, it was decided that Peters should drive it with Polly directing, and the brigadier would follow in convoy in the other truck. The lab, the location of which should be restricted to as few people as possible, would be waiting for them with their fittest scientists, to remove both animals from the trucks using the tarpaulins.

Given that it was now a quarter to nine, Jeremy thanked the police officers and bid them goodnight, reminding them once more of their responsibilities to say nothing to anyone, even to their families, of what had happened or why they might have blood on their clothes.

That left the two Home Office men and Trey, who was still doing his best to demonstrate what a fine fellow he was.

"Right, we'd better head back to the hotel," said Jeremy. "Thank you for your help, Mr Clark."

"Not a problem. Can I ask you something?"

"It depends what you ask me."

"Do you think there are more of them down there?"

Jeremy scratched the back of his neck. "Hard to say. I hope not. Tomorrow I'm going to suggest we drop some more food down the shaft, followed by our camera, and see if any gigarats turn up to eat it. If they don't, that's a promising sign. But I'm not sending any men down there until we are convinced there are no more. We've had enough tragedy already, and I'm not looking forward to explaining tonight's events to my boss."

"It wasn't all bad, though," said Jason, "the primary mission was achieved."

"True, but it didn't go perfectly, and that annoys me. I don't suppose, Mr Clark, you saw anyone skulking around the truck while we were in our meeting?"

Trey assumed a face that was almost too innocent. "No, no. No one. Although I wasn't looking out of the window the whole time, of course. Why?"

"Just wondered. Well, thanks for your help, we'll head ba...."

"Oh, there's just one more thing," said Trey, sounding like detective Columbo. His heart rate rose; this last-minute realisation could be his final throw of the dice. "I just thought I'd make sure you knew that if your chief inspector friend...."

"Superintendent."

"Yeah him, if he does start trying to put me or Lauren on trial for any of these deaths, even though we had nothing to do with them, then I think that is going to really make your life difficult, as well as ours."

"And why would that be?"

"There'd be a trial, with a jury, and press, and what do you think Lauren and I are going to say? We'd be sworn to tell the truth, and that means we'd have no choice but to spill the beans on the gigarat, signed contract or not, and the whole existence of the DUST team and what they do, and have been doing here. It will be all over the papers. Everything you have done to keep this hushed up will have been in vain. The whole country will panic about what giant creatures could be under their feet, and you will have failed. I'm sorry, but if it comes to a choice of us being banged up in jail for most of our lives for something we didn't do, or telling the truth and not getting the financial incentives you offered us, we'll have no choice. There's only one outcome."

Jeremy winced inside. It was a fair point. His department had considerable influence and he could pull a lot of strings, but he couldn't overrule a court of law and silence witnesses. That in itself was a criminal offence.

If Berriman went ahead and charged the Clarks with anything, a whole world of pain awaited. Why hadn't he thought of this before? With everything else going on it wasn't an outcome that had occurred to him, nor Jason, evidently, although it seemed pretty obvious now. None of his previous DUST projects had involved murder and courts of law, so all his experience told him that as long as the confidentiality document was signed, all was well. But the law was the law. He could sense his trainee's brain was whirring too – the two of them needed to talk.

"Thank you for bringing that possibility to my attention, Mr Clark. You will understand that we cannot stand in the way of the due process of the law, but at the same time there are other factors at play. Jason and I will have a think and let you know our conclusions. We'll be in touch if we need to be."

Trey watched them trudge away, beginning to talk earnestly once they were out of earshot and rounding the corner of the house. Well, that hadn't gone too badly. Perhaps he had found a way out of this after all. Lauren was back at ten – he'd see what she thought. But for the first time in a long time he felt an ember of hope.

CHAPTER 66 - THURSDAY

"This is ridiculous!"

Chief Superintendent Berriman got up and walked over to the window, as though this would help. He turned back to face Jeremy and Jason, who were sitting at the interview table.

"You cannot ask me to pervert the course of justice and not charge the Clarks, if I find enough evidence to suspect that they were responsible for the deaths of up to three people, or had some role in them. That's just not on. If they have killed people, they need to go before a judge and jury. That's how the system works. You can't make exceptions."

Jeremy looked down at the table, then looked up again.

"I'm not asking you to pervert the course of justice, Rob. All I did was explain the situation we are in, so that you are aware of the consequences, and the seniority of government and police figures who would then be put into very difficult positions, and may not wish for this to happen. That's all."

"That's all? I'm not daft you know. I can see what you are doing. But the fact remains, we cannot let murderers off scot-free just because you say so."

Jeremy tried another tack. "What is the evidence you will need, Rob? You've already admitted that you don't have any proof that the Clarks' account of the death of John Firwell was not, as he claims, an accident. How are you going to convince a jury that they killed Anita Rackman, or John Firwell, or Darren Hoggsmith, or all of them? Correct me if I'm wrong, but I believe all you have at the moment are some slightly inconsistent accounts from the two suspects. No motives, no forensics that could prove anything, and a man-eating rat around the place being, on the surface, a far more likely explanation. And your only key witness, Norman Baston, is dead. So what will you need to persuade the CPS to prosecute?"

Berriman leant back against the wall. "Alright, I agree we have a weak case at the moment. We don't even have the bodies. That, for me, is the crucial part. If we can get some DNA samples, and get our pathologists to do the autopsies, we can see if that tallies with what the Clarks were saying."

Jeremy sighed. "You do realise that it is highly likely that the gigarats have taken their bodies and eaten them? The chances of you getting any useful data from a pile of bones and remaining scraps of flesh will, I would suggest, be virtually zero. Would you agree?"

"Well..... yes, that could be true. When will you be sending teams down to find their remains then?"

"Once we know there are no more gigarats down there. I spoke to Polly last night and she said it was quite possible that the two we caught were the last pair left, and the reason they had surfaced over the last couple of years is because they had run out of food. Perhaps the dominant female had become sterile and they'd eaten all the youngsters. She's going to be checking that – don't ask me how. So if we can be sure there are no more, we'll send people down to explore those mines, get them mapped, and hopefully find some human remains. Well I say hopefully, but you know what I mean. I don't think there is any chance at all of finding any of them alive."

"Agreed. So, what you are saying is, if we can DNA match the bones to the three missing people, and I just can't get any concrete evidence implicating the Clarks, we leave it at that, and... and say what to the public and the press? I can't even say that they were eaten by a giant rat. You expect me to stand up at a press conference and just shrug my shoulders and say I've no idea how they died?"

Jeremy was tempted to say 'yes' just to see Berriman's reaction, but stopped himself just in time.

"Alright, let's run through them chronologically. Molly Baines – assumed drowned in the river, perhaps drank too much and stumbled into it. Tripped over and hit her head on a root, knocked unconscious, body washed out to sea. Anita Rackman was walking across the lawn when the mineshaft cover collapsed and down she went. Hoggsmith was four days later, wasn't he? Maybe he went to look at the hole and......"

"No, no, no," interrupted Berriman, "the other residents would have seen the hole in the lawn. We didn't open it up until a week after Anita Rackman disappeared. That theory wouldn't hold water."

Jason chipped in. "What about the vent in the Clark's cellar? That was open before the main shaft. We already know that John Firwell fell down it, why not the others too?"

"Perhaps the extreme unlikelihood that they all got through a locked door and wandered blindly over to an obvious hole in the floor and fell down it?"

Jason winced. "This isn't easy, is it? Ok, we know Hoggsmith went missing on the same day as John Firwell. How about they and Trey Clark went down the vent to explore and got caught in a tunnel collapse? Only Clark escaped."

The two other men looked at each other.

"That's got legs," murmured Berriman. "I'll have a think. That still leaves Anita Rackman though. Can't imagine she'd have joined the tunnel exploration team."

"Probably not," agreed Jason.

"I'm sure you'll think of something, Rob" said Jeremy, wrapping the unwanted task in flattery before handing it over to the chief superintendent. "Oh, I keep forgetting to ask - did your forensics pick anything useful up from analysis of the entrance to the vent?"

"Just some skin cells which matched those found on John's Firwell's clothes in his flat. Nothing else."

"Ok. So that backs up the Clarks' version of events. Whatever you say to the press about Firwell just ask his wife to back up whatever story you come up with. From what I hear she should be very accommodating and of course she knows the situation and has signed the papers."

"I suppose we could just log them all as missing persons," said Berriman. "Loads of people go missing every year. It's far more common than people realise. Most years it is over 300,000."

"What? Really? Three hundred thousand people in the UK just vanish?"

"At least, probably more. Most of them are found within 24 hrs, but that still leaves a lot who are never seen again. Although how plausible is it that five people, four of them from the same residence, all separately decide to disappear within a week of each other."

"It would be a remarkable coincidence."

"There might be a good explanation for Norman Baston" said Jason. "We could bring the main shaft on the lawn into play. We can suggest that it looks as though he must have got curious, and for some reason gone out one evening and removed the cover to have a look at the hole, then slipped and fell down it. What do you think?"

Berriman shook his head like a chess player contemplating his likely defeat. "I don't like all this subterfuge, but yes, that sounds better.

Especially as he did actually fall down the shaft. Alright, I'll have a think about all that. As I say I don't like it, but I'll go with all this for now. But…. if we do find their remains, and we find the Clarks DNA on them or anything like that…."

He left the words hanging.

Jeremy and Jason glanced at each other. They both knew that wouldn't happen.

CHAPTER 67

"Here's your Christmas present: keys to the office," said Jeremy, handing Jason the treasured metal objects. "The penultimate part of the handover. You happy?"

Jason looked around his new office, rich with wood panelling and paintings. "I think so. As I said, my apologies for not catching up with you before today – the day job has been manic. To summarise then, all DUST cases closed for the moment, except one that is closing. So, before you head off onto the golf course and swap your shoes for slippers let's go over the Ridley Manor situation one last time and make sure we cover every detail. I'd rather pester you now than when you're in the middle of watching Homes Under The Hammer."

Jeremy leaned back in his reclinable office chair, putting his hands behind his head for possibly the last time in a business setting.

"Very amusing. Reading War And Peace more like. Yes, Ridley Manor. So, as you know Polly's gigarat died two weeks after she started studying it in the lab, most likely from the pieces of clothing that she found stuck in its gut that was stopping it eating enough. Seems Norman Baston's old gardening jacket was made of stern stuff."

"Probably reinforced by years of sweat and grime."

"Very likely, yes. Nice. Anyway, the rat's death was not good for Polly and her science, but good for us."

"No risk of another escaped gigarat."

"Yes, and no time for them to start trying to breed anything with it, although it turns out that that wouldn't have been possible anyway."

"Why not?"

"When she did an autopsy on it she found that it had cysts on its ovaries, so it couldn't reproduce any more. There wouldn't have been any point doing any artificial insemination, which to my mind is a good thing. Tinkering with nature. I don't like that."

"No. Me neither. And we know one hundred per cent there are no more gigarats down there that she could replace it with?"

"Yes, looks like Polly's theory was right. They were the last two. I wouldn't have liked to be in that first search team, though, even though we waited until a month of no sightings and no bait taken. SA80 rifles and flashlights were very much to the fore!"

"I'm not surprised," said Jason. "How far did Polly get through the eyesight tests?"

"Not far enough. She couldn't be conclusive that there was no way it would have come out in daylight and found food if it was desperate. So that could after all explain Anita Rackman and Darren Hoggsmith. Not that I think it does."

"Lets the Clarks off the hook, though."

"Indeed. I never quite understood that. They seemed like a really nice couple, wouldn't say boo to a goose, salt of the earth, yet they were definitely hiding something. Still, that's not our department, and not for us to worry about now."

"And Polly's still analysing the pituitary glands of both gigarats."

"Yes, and all the other parts obviously. Nice touch, wasn't it, to invite Jean Edwards over so the two of them could go though the findings together and do comparisons. Given the old dear a new lease of life, I hear."

"She was a sweet old lady. Talking of sweet, when was the last time you spoke to Rob Berriman?"

Jeremy smiled. "Just a couple of days ago, actually. He says the press interest has eased a little, now there haven't been any more deaths for nearly three months. And of course he has no evidence that would allow him to take any murder cases to the CPS."

"No, funny that, wasn't it, that we found nothing that might have helped him. Mind you, did our search teams find anything at all that might have been of use? Off the record, of course."

"To be honest, not really. We could identify the bodies through dental records but it would have been impossible to determine any stab wounds or strangulation marks or anything like that. There just wasn't enough left."

"Have all the bones been removed now?"

"Yes, removed, catalogued, cleaned and stored for future reference - the animal bones, that is. They were mostly sheep, calves and small mammals. And of course the human victims – all five of them were in the tunnels, including Anita Rackman and Darren Hoggsmith."

"Do we know yet how those two ended up down there?"

Jeremy shrugged. "No idea. Maybe the Clarks were telling the truth after all, and the gigarat was out in the forest during the day and dragged both victims into the river and into the tunnels from there. I'm really not convinced, but as I said before it is not my job, or yours now, to worry about that."

"Good job too. How did Berriman explain their deaths, then, in the end, to the families and the press?"

"We had a dilemma with that. The fact that all that was left of them were bones made it even harder than we thought. He couldn't just say they'd fallen down a shaft and then give the families a pile of bones. How do you explain that to them and also the media? So for two of them, those with the fewest relatives, we said they had somehow entered the river and must have been swept out to sea. That's Molly Baines and Anita Rackman."

"Both of them?"

"Molly slipped, knocked herself unconscious and fell in – that's the premise. Anita, we don't know what happened but we say some of her clothes were washed up further down the river. Still officially a missing person case but highly likely she drowned."

"And John Firwell? We know he fell down the vent in the cellar."

"Yes, and we know Norman Baston went down the shaft in the garden, but that wouldn't explain the state in which we handed over their remains. So for those two plus Darren Hoggsmith, we maintained the story that they had all gone missing, but that what remained of their bodies had not been discovered until November, miles away, by which time there was almost nothing left of them, as their bodies were mostly consumed by rats and maggots by the time we got to them."

Jason shook his head.

"This is all stretching credulity a bit, isn't it?"

"Yes."

"Not found in the same place, I take it?"

"No. One in a reservoir, one in a different forest, one in a local quarry. How or why they ended up there we said we didn't yet know but were working on it."

"Did the press buy that?"

"They had no choice. Neither Rob or I enjoyed the subterfuge though, lying through our teeth like that. But it had to be done, for the greater good. That's what I kept telling him, anyway."

"I'll bet he wasn't happy. How come there wasn't much coverage on it though? I didn't see anything on the news."

"We requested that. We made out that publicity could jeopardise the case in terms of working out the finer details of what happened to the three victims, given that they may have been murdered. So far the media has been good enough to comply, and the hope is that it will be old news soon and they'll move on to other things and not try to resurrect the story."

"Good luck with that!"

"I won't need it, I hope. As of the end of today, I'm retired now, remember."

"Nicely timed. I don't think the press are just going to slope off and never mention the Ridley Manor deaths again, though. Poor old Berriman, left to fend them off."

Jeremy smiled. "Expect your phone to ring now and then, is all I can say. He might need some guidance and support."

"Ah, right. Not what I wanted to hear. That monkey on your back is suddenly on mine."

"I couldn't do a full handover without offloading my monkey."

"Not a phrase I thought I'd hear you say. I can see a succession of bridges ahead of me that I'll have to cross when I come to them. What's the latest on Tommy Medina?"

"Fully recovered, pretty much, thank God. They stitched him up and he says he's got scars everywhere still but plans to make up some story about him fighting a tiger or something, to impress the ladies."

"Nice one. Typical Tommy! Is he back at work then?"

"Yes, since about two weeks ago. Easing back in, directing the exploration."

"So he's mapping all the tunnels. What has he found so far?"

"A surprisingly large tunnel system. He reckons it could be from Roman times, enlarged in the middle ages, then sealed and abandoned. Seems pretty stable though, despite those gigarat claws smoothing down the sides of the shafts and tunnels over the years. They don't reckon there's any danger to Ridley Manor. I looked into that, you know. It was built by a young industrialist, Herbert Ridley, back in the 1890s. You have to wonder why he chose to build it there, right on top of a mining ventilation shaft."

Jason shook his head. "Well that doesn't make sense either. I guess we'll never know."

"He had no descendents either, so no family stories about it got passed down."

"So what about the policy decision on eventually releasing the details, letting the public know about the gigarats? What's the latest on that?"

Jeremy, blood draining out of his arms, brought his hands back down onto the desk. "I've had a long chat on the phone with our esteemed boss."

"Mr Webber."

"The very same. We went through the pros and cons of making the existence of giant man-eating rats under our feet in the 21st century – and if it happened here it could happen anywhere - a known thing. The cons outweighed the pros."

"Some would argue that is censorship. Two old blokes – if you'll forgive me – deciding on behalf of everyone else."

"That's how government works most of the time, as you well know, young Jason. Democracy is only democratic up to a point. You can't have the public voting on every decision a minister makes. Anyway, the PM agreed with our decision."

"Dozens of referendums every day, wouldn't that be fun for everyone. It's a fair answer, I'll give you that. Practicality can tread on the toes of ideology sometimes."

"Exactly. I think that pretty much covers it as far as the Ridley Manor case is concerned. Was there anything else?"

"Yes, are you sure you won't mind me contacting you for advice if I need it?"

"Just so long as you use my mobile and not the landline. If Mrs Stanton-Davies answers the phone you are likely to receive some choice words along the lines of 'don't you know he's retired' or 'I hope he's getting paid for this'. So just be careful."

"I will."

Jeremy stood up and pushed his chair back, taking one last look round at his office.

"Well, it's been an adventure. I just hope you never have to deal with anything like Ridley Manor again. Quite a note to end my DUST career on."

Jason got to his feet and followed Jeremy to the door. "At least it wasn't a bum note. You should be proud of what you did. You held it all together. I learned a lot from that."

"Good, good. I'm pleased. It wasn't text book, but then there wasn't a text book for that, was there? So it could have been worse, I suppose. Right! Farewell, office."

The two men walked through the door, Jason escorting his mentor down the stairs and out of the building, as civil service regulations dictated.

CHAPTER 68

"Happy Christmas!"

Lauren pushed a brightly wrapped box at her husband, who brought it up to his ear and gave it a gentle shake.

"Hey, careful, it could be fragile!"

Trey grinned. "But it's not though, is it?"

"Well, no. Open it, then!"

Trey made a play of being unable to get a fingernail under any of the edges of the wrapping paper. As usual Lauren had sellotaped it to within an inch of its life.

"I can't. Never mind."

He put the box down. "Now, what about your present?"

Lauren reached over and took the gift. "Not so fast. Here you go."

She inserted one of her manicured nails into the one small area that had not been overlapped with tape and tore away some paper.

"Back to you."

Trey laughed and finished the job, wrenching away the paper with great drama.

"Hey, a new shaver. That's great! My old one – well, you know."

"Yes, it's filthy, and it's noisy, and you must have had it for about twenty years."

"I wasn't shaving when I was seven. I know what you mean though. This looks wicked. It's got a digital battery gauge and everything."

"It's not the best present though, is it?"

"What do you mean?"

"The best present we ever got, either of us, was that 'insufficient evidence' decision."

Trey raised his eyes to the ceiling.

"Oh my God yes, what a week that was. I'll bet the chief superintendent was livid. I still think my little chat with the two Home Office guys did the trick, though. That and when Jean told us that the gigarat they captured had died so they couldn't finish doing all their tests on its eyesight."

"To be honest, I don't care too much about the details. It's just the relief, after all that stress. Although I still think about that Anita moment almost every day. That's my punishment, I suppose, the way that haunts me."

Trey nodded, serious now. "Yeah, me too. What I did to John...." He shivered. "It's horrible. Part of me feels I should go to jail and serve my time for what I did. Pay the price. But then I'd lose you, and that's what I was fighting against all the way through."

Lauren stared into his eyes. "Firstly, as I keep telling you, what you did to John, kicking him like that, was completely understandable - you were trying to save your own life. Also, he could have dragged all three of us down there, and then we'd all be dead. It was self-preservation. Secondly, you're not a threat to society, are you? Are you? What use would you, or me even, have been in jail? We're not going to re-offend. Wasting time and resources holding us there when we could be contributing to society instead – it doesn't help anyone. You have to think of it like that, don't you?"

He put his arm round Lauren and gave her a squeeze. "Yeah. That's one way of looking at it, I guess. And like you said, we're punished mentally every day, thinking about Anita and John and Hoggo. Especially Hoggo. Him dying like that, right in front of me, was.... hell. Just a nightmare. It was all a nightmare, the whole thing. First thing after Christmas, the flat goes up for sale, yeah? Are we agreed?"

"Definitely. A new start. A new home. No reminders. And one thing in particular."

"What's that?"

"No cellars with trapdoors in them."

AUTHOR'S NOTE

Thank you for reading my book. I am very grateful.

It you liked it, it would be great if you could share your thoughts about this book with friends, family, and random strangers. All social media exposure welcome as long as it is good!

It would also be really helpful if you could post a nice review on whichever site you bought or read this book from. Your feedback and support is so important – you would not believe how much encouragement one good review can provide.

I can be contacted on angus.silvie@outlook.com *for any queries or feedback.*

OTHER BOOKS BY ANGUS SILVIE

The Mysterious Fall
(Book 1 of the Mysterious Series)

Marlo Campbell's life was going nowhere. Dull job, a meek personality, depressing looks, and no relationships. Something had to change, and it did: he came across a Victorian diary of a young lady and soon his life was set on an incredible path through time that would change everything.

This multi-genre book whisks the reader into new worlds and new experiences where a Victorian serial murderer must be caught and punished by a 21st century average guy, helped by one of his victims. If you think this doesn't make sense, read the book and prepare to give your mind a workout.

The Slightly Mysterious Death
(Book 2 of the Mysterious Series)

Lillian Jones used to be a Victorian girl living in 1886. Now she suddenly finds herself in 21st century London, brought back from the dead by Marlo Campbell, an ordinary office worker who has inadvertently stumbled into a time traveling adventure bigger than anyone could have imagined.

Yet she now feels she has to go back in time again and bring someone else back from the dead too. To do this both of them must risk their lives, and take the very real chance that, if they cannot track down a killer and get justice for the victim, they will never come back.

Printed in Great Britain
by Amazon